THE
FLOUR CONVOY

CHAITRAM SINGH

THE
FLOUR CONVOY

iUniverse, Inc.
Bloomington

The Flour Convoy

iUniverse books may be ordered through booksellers or by contacting:

iUniverse
1663 Liberty Drive
Bloomington, IN 47403
www.iuniverse.com
1-800-Authors (1-800-288-4677)

ISBN: 978-1-4620-6199-0 (sc)
ISBN: 978-1-4620-6200-3 (ebk)

Library of Congress Control Number: 2011918941

Printed in the United States of America

iUniverse rev. date: 10/27/2011

For Andrew and Candy

Special thanks to:

Berry College

Zab (Dyal) Panday

Maureen Morgan

PART ONE

ONE

"**A** LAN," LIEUTENANT BEHARRY WHISPERED by the bar, "the Chief of Staff wants us in his office at 09:00 tomorrow."

"He's been here?" Captain Moore asked, feeling his stomach tighten. "At the Mess?"

Lieutenant Beharry nodded. "He left not too long ago, they say. But he came up to the base to see me."

"Awright," Moore said, "we'll go down after we give our report to the Base Commander in the morning. Try to be there at 08:00 sharp." Moore stood there looking into Beharry's face but thinking of the Chief of Staff and dreading another confrontation with him.

"Captain, your turn," Lieutenant Mentore called out.

"Okay," Moore said, turning away from Lieutenant Beharry and stepping up to the throwing line. "Just watch the bull's eye."

"Captain Moore!" the Mess attendant called out. "Telephone."

"Christ!" Moore uttered as he watched the dart strike the upper perimeter of the dart board. "Look, tell them I'm coming. Awright?"

"Captain, is the airport. They got a big, big problem."

Moore glanced over at the agitated look on the Mess attendant's face and, without another word, followed her out to the telephone resting on a chair.

"Captain Moore, here," he said.

"Are you the Duty Officer?" asked the voice at the other end.

"Yes. Who are you?"

"Captain, this is Constable Monroe at the airport. We got a bomb threat."

"How did you find out?"

"One of the people in the tower got a call about a bomb in the luggage."

"When?"

"About ten minutes ago."

"Well, comrade, what y'all been doing?"

"We called Police Headquarters at Brickdam, and they trying to get a bomb squad together."

"Comrade, it's Sunday! It will take them hours to do that and to get up here."

"Yes, Captain, so they wanted to know if the army got anyone here on the base. They asked about the Recon Squadron."

"The Recon Squadron is on exercises at the firing range today. I'll check to see if any of the officers are on the base. What's the situation with the passengers?"

"They are off the plane. But is pandemonium here. And we need to off-load the baggage."

"Awright, I'll be over in a few minutes." Moore hung up. Lieutenant Beharry had walked up and was standing next to him. They lingered briefly by the phone.

"Ramesh, they got a bomb threat at the airport. We need to get a squad from the Standby Platoon up there and cordon off the plane."

"Yes, Captain."

"Get McCurchin. He's in the kitchen. We're going to the base." Lieutenant Beharry ran to the kitchen. Moore heard him order McCurchin to stand by the jeep. Moore telephoned the Recon Squadron's barracks and then the Officers' Quarters. No luck. He called the Guard Room at the base. Corporal Liverpool answered.

"Corporal Liverpool, this is Captain Moore. Call out the Standby Platoon."

"Captain, I think most of them are up in the base mess hall."

"Get them out! We have a situation at the airport. And ask the signaler to stand by. I'm coming over."

"Yes, Captain."

Moore and Beharry went up to the bar, retrieved their cartridge belts and revolvers, and headed out of the Officers' Mess. McCurchin was waiting for them with the jeep. They both entered, Moore in front and Beharry in the rear.

"Base compound, McCurchin," Moore said.

Corporal Liverpool had opened the main gate in anticipation of Moore's arrival, so McCurchin drove in and stopped in front of the Guard Room. Corporal Liverpool saluted. "Morning, Captain. Morning Lieutenant." The officers returned the salute. "I have the signaler here, Captain."

"Awright, hold on." Moore noticed that the Standby Platoon was assembling by the flag pole. "Lieutenant Beharry," he said, "pick a squad and get them on the truck. Tell the radio operator to get into my jeep. Dismiss the rest. Let them go and eat. We might need them later."

"Yes, Captain." Beharry saluted and left.

Moore turned to the base signaler. "Let me have the pad." He wrote: "Bomb threat against Hudson Airways. Assembling bomb detection team. Police HQ notified. Please notify Chief of Staff." Handing the pad back to the signaler, he said, "Send this to the Duty Officer, Camp Ayanganna."

"Yes, Captain," the signaler said.

Moore strode over to the drill square. A squad from the Standby Platoon was climbing onto the truck, their squad leader trying to hurry them up. Moore paused to observe the last two soldiers climb up, then signaled to Lieutenant Beharry to follow in the truck. The two-vehicle convoy sped to the airport building and pulled up to the gate at the side entrance where Constable Monroe was waiting for them. He let them in and closed the gate.

The jeep pulled up to about forty feet of the Hudson Airways plane and stopped. Moore ordered the radio operator out. "Try to get the CO of Recon Squadron. His call sign is 'Para One.'" Moore left the radio operator on the tarmac and walked back to the truck that had pulled up behind him. Lieutenant Beharry was out, watching his soldiers disembark. The radio operator rushed up to Moore to report that Recon Squadron did not have their radio turned on. Moore thought for a moment, then turned to Lieutenant Beharry.

"Look, Ramesh, I'll supervise the men here. Take the jeep and go out to the firing range. Ask Captain Mitchell if he can assemble a bomb detection squad. We'll still try to get them by radio, but hurry!"

"Alan, you know he's out with a British training mission."

"Yes. Just tell him the situation."

"What if any of the British officers want to come?"

"We'll take one, no more. We don't want people thinking we don't know what we're doing, that we're still relying on white people to do things for we."

Lieutenant Beharry saluted and left with the jeep for the firing range. Captain Moore walked over to the squad of soldiers from the Standby Platoon.

"Corporal," he said to the squad leader, "place four soldiers around the plane, one at each corner. Have the rest of the men stand at ease."

"Yes, Captain."

The pilot and co-pilot of the Hudson Airlines plane were standing with two tower officials about thirty feet to the front left of the plane. Moore asked for a briefing on the situation. The pilot explained that he was notified by the tower that they had received a bomb threat from someone claiming that there was a bomb in the luggage. The pilot had asked the passengers and the stewardesses to deplane, and they were now in the waiting room of the airport building.

"What do you intend to do?" the pilot asked.

"I've sent for a bomb detection team," Moore replied.

"When will they get here?" the pilot asked.

"Another 15 or so minutes. They are at the firing range about six miles away. In the meantime we should off-load the luggage." Turning to the police constable, Moore said, "Monroe, ask the Hudson Airlines people inside to send out the baggage handlers and the trucks."

The viewing deck at the terminal building was crammed with people, and Moore could hear loud speculations about the situation. People in the bar on the first floor were peering through the glass windows. Along the north and south sides of the building, people were clutching the fences for better monitoring positions. The sun was almost directly overhead, and the heat was making Moore perspire. He suggested to the pilot and co-pilot that they go into the terminal building, but they preferred to stay close to the plane.

A few minutes later, two baggage trucks with four baggage handlers came out to where the group was standing. Moore spoke very loudly.

"Look, we need to get the luggage off this plane as quickly as possible. Drop them off about one hundred paces behind the plane." Turning to the army corporal, Moore said, "Corporal, have four of your men help them."

"Captain," the pilot called out. "Don't forget the overhead compartments. They are full of luggage as well."

"Thank you," said Moore, "I didn't think about that. Corporal, pull those soldiers away from guarding the plane. I don't think we need that. Have all the soldiers stack their weapons and assign one man to guard them."

The corporal yelled out to each soldier on the perimeter of the plane to come in. In a few minutes, the weapons of nine soldiers were stacked with one soldier standing guard. Moore came up to the group.

"Awright, you four men help the baggage handlers. Corporal, I want you to go one hundred paces to the rear of the plane and direct the off-loading of the baggage. Let them place the baggage on both sides of the runway."

The four soldiers and the corporal left to carry out their instructions. Moore told one soldier to stay by the guard in case he was needed; then, turning to the other four, he said "You men, listen to me. I want you to come into the plane with me and take out the luggage from the overhead bins and from under the seats. Awright? Let's go!"

Moore led the soldiers to the center of the plane and then gave them further instructions. "So you don't get in each other's way, you two use the front exit and you two the rear exit. It should go faster. Move!"

Moore watched briefly as the soldiers began opening the bins and taking down the luggage, then he exited through the front of the plane. He stood by awkwardly as the off-loading began. Lieutenant Beharry should be at the firing range by now, he estimated. Another seven minutes more, maybe ten. Until then, there was nothing much else he could do. He was not a demolitions expert, a deficiency he now lamented. Yet he sensed that his presence and that of the Standby squad had a calming effect on the onlookers. He walked over to the cargo side of the plane. From there he could see the corporal directing the soldiers who were off-loading luggage from the cargo hold. Arms akimbo, Moore paced back and forth, trying to appear engaged but all the while wondering how long it would take Beharry to get back and who the hell would want to put a bomb on the only foreign airline still flying into the country. He thought of the sugar workers currently on strike but ruled them out. More than half of the passengers on these weekly outbound flights were Indians from the sugar and rice areas. Why would they want to hurt their own people? That left just Black people, but he couldn't see them doing this either. Sure, many were disenchanted with the government that claimed to be representing them, but they were also leaving the country in droves. Maybe it was just a prankster. God, I hope so, Moore thought to himself.

The off-loading seemed slow, even though the men worked continuously and their utterances conveyed every sense of urgency. The repetitive lifting under the unfriendly glare of the overhead sun made the men perspire profusely. The first baggage truck, now full, moved to the rear of the plane. The baggage handlers began to dump the luggage on one side of the runway, continuing the row already started by the pairs of soldiers working inside the plane.

"Oi, oi," the corporal called out. "Let the baggage down easy; don't throw it! Is a bomb we looking for, you know. You want to blow us up?"

The fourth load of baggage was being off-loaded on the runway when the jeep returned to the side entrance. Constable Monroe ran over and opened the gate. Lieutenant Beharry had brought back Recon Squadron's Commanding Officer, Captain Charlie Mitchell, and a British Army Captain, whom Captain Mitchell introduced as Captain John Featherstone.

"What's the situation?" Captain Mitchell asked.

"We are unloading the baggage," Moore replied. "We're about half finished in the cargo hold and about one-third in the inside."

"What system are you using to clear the inside?" Mitchell asked.

"Well, we got two two-man teams working from the center of the aircraft and using the front and rear exits. The problem is that the aisle is narrow, and they can only bring out the luggage two pieces at a time."

"Well, let's give them a few minutes more, then we'll start at the center of the aircraft, and the British officer and I will check the inside of the plane."

Moore and the pilot agreed. Moore called the army corporal over to where the weapons were stacked and instructed him to keep watch so that the two soldiers standing there could join the others inside the plane to quicken the pace of the off-loading.

Mitchell and the British officer entered the aircraft and began inspecting, Mitchell from the center to the front, the British officer in the other direction. When the cargo hold was finally cleared, the baggage handlers formed a chain at the front and rear exits, and this accelerated the emptying of the luggage from the inside. After about ten minutes, Captain Mitchell and the British officer emerged from inside the plane and signaled to Moore and the others that they had found nothing. They descended the plane and went with Moore and Beharry to the cargo hold, which, following a brief check, they declared to be bomb-free.

"Well, let's get the passengers out to pick up their luggage and open them for inspection," Captain Mitchell said.

"How about if we ask the pilot to move the plane further up the tarmac, to be on the safe side?" Moore asked.

"Good idea," Mitchell replied.

Five minutes later, the plane began moving slowly towards the far end of the runway, leaving a long trail of luggage behind it. Moore instructed Constable Monroe to get four tables out so that they could set up inspection stations. The soldiers were detailed to help. Moore walked into the passenger waiting room and instructed the passengers to follow him onto the tarmac, pick up their luggage, and then report to an inspection table.

Four inspection tables were set up on the eastern side of the runway. The inspection lines would be perpendicular to the runway. On the recommendation of Captain Mitchell, Moore and Beharry would monitor the two inside tables while Mitchell and the British officer would be at the outside tables and could render assistance to either of them if it became necessary.

The tarmac became a weave of black and brown figures seeking their luggage. A sweater or heavier winter garment in hand differentiated the returning passengers from the first-time travelers, for whom mid-January weather in America was probably another something to be imagined. Most of the passengers were grouped in families of varying sizes, but about a third seemed to be pursuing their luggage alone.

The two rows of luggage made it easy for the passengers to identify their own. Still, they walked up and down to gather up all of their luggage before drifting over to the inspection tables. Moore could see that this was going to be a slow process. People were joining the inspection lines as soon as they picked up a sizable piece or two of luggage, which they deposited to mark their place before returning to the runway to retrieve the other pieces. The process was punishing on the old men and women, traveling alone. They had evidently had help with their large grips when they arrived to check in their luggage. Now, without able-bodied relatives to assist them, they were hauling one piece at a time to the inspection lines. They stopped frequently to rest and to wipe perspiration from their faces. Indeed, passengers of all ages, already in the lines, were wiping or fanning themselves. Occasionally, there was a most welcome breeze, but most of the time, the heat from the overhead sun and from the concrete runway combined to bake them all.

Four uniformed Customs officers approached the inspection tables and positioned themselves one to each table. The British officer looked over to Captain Moore, as did Lieutenant Beharry.

"What's going on here?" Moore asked the Customs officer next to him. "We're looking for a bomb, you know?"

"Look for your bomb," replied the Customs officer. "We want to see what else they taking out of the country."

"You're joking!" Moore exclaimed. "Why didn't you inspect the bags before they got on the plane?"

"Look, Captain, you do your job and leh we do we own. Is a lot of things leaving the country illegally, you know."

"And now, of all times, is when you want to search for them?" Moore asked.

"We're not going to interfere," the Customs man said calmly. "We just want to make sure everything is in order."

"You want to make sure everything in order?" Moore asked. "Are you a demolitions expert?"

"Captain, we're just doing like we were told," the Customs man replied, holding his ground.

Moore knew he had lost the argument and that the Customs people would be part of the inspection team. He refocused on the inspection lines, where the mutterings of the passengers conveyed fear and frustration. He instructed passengers to remain with their luggage at all times. They were to place their bags one piece at a time on the table, open each piece, and lift such items as the inspecting officer directed. Once searched, the luggage would be placed to the side for reloading, and the passengers would return to the waiting area for eventual reboarding.

Passengers came up to the inspection tables fetching some of their luggage and moving other pieces forward with their feet. Faces were bathed in perspiration. Colored dresses and dashikis, shirtjacs and blouses clung to the wearers' bodies. Moore's glasses were smudged by streaking sweat; his fatigues were soaked.

Occasionally looking up from the table, Moore scanned the crowded airport lounge and viewing area. Along the perimeter fence, taxi drivers, airport employees, out-of-uniform soldiers and others moved about for better viewing of the inspection. He could hear a babel of voices from the different sections of the crowd, apparently commenting on every aspect of the search. Female passengers were especially embarrassed when occasionally an undergarment or more flew off the inspection table and had to be chased across the tarmac. The laughter from the fences and from the viewing deck was loud and boisterous, punctuating what was an otherwise tense and expectant situation.

The contents of the bags examined by Captain Moore typified what the other officers were seeing. Apart from the items of clothing and toiletries, people had containers of various sizes, but no incendiary devices. What the containers had were pickled peppers, mango chutney, tamarind chutney, bhoonjal chicken, bhoonjal hassar, fried banga-mary, bottles of casareep.

One element of the search had bothered Moore from the moment the Customs men positioned themselves at the inspection tables. Each Customs man was armed with pen and paper. They seemed too calm for the type of exercise being conducted. They seemed not the least bit concerned about the possibility of a bomb being out there, and they always halted the search whenever jewelry or foreign currency showed up. They would take the names of the passengers and ask them to stand aside with the luggage.

When the search was finally over, Moore felt relieved, but bleached and thirsty. He had no doubt everyone on the tarmac shared his feelings, though he sensed frustration from the passengers. No bomb was found. All but ten passengers had returned to the waiting area. The Customs officers left with the ten and their luggage for the terminal building.

Moore looked at his watch: almost 14:00 hours. Turning to Lieutenant Beharry, he said, "Ramesh, why you don't send the Standby squad back to the base. I'm going in to the waiting room to let the pilot know we didn't find anything."

"Right, Captain," Beharry replied and walked over to the soldiers standing by the truck.

"Alan, can you drop us off at the Sergeants' Mess?" Captain Mitchell asked.

"You're not coming to lunch with us?" Moore asked.

"Well, Captain Featherstone and I promised the NCOs to join them for a drink. That was before this thing came up."

"Okay," Moore replied, "no problem. I'll be right back."

In the waiting room, Moore spoke to the pilot and co-pilot and confirmed what they had already heard from the passengers and may have suspected themselves: the officers had not found a bomb in anyone's luggage. The pilot thanked Moore, and Moore walked out of the waiting room to find that McCurchin had pulled the jeep up to the door. Lieutenant Beharry was sitting in the back of the jeep with Captain Mitchell and the British officer. Moore climbed in beside McCurchin and, in less than a minute, the vehicle passed through the side entrance and was making its way out of the airport compound.

The British officer spoke first. "I say, Mitchell, that was damned funny, the behavior of your Customs people?"

"Yes, like they knew there was no bomb," Beharry added.

"Well, it was a fair assumption," Mitchell replied. "Why would any of the passengers put a bomb in their luggage?"

Moore sensed the defensiveness in Captain Mitchell's tone. He was sure the British officer was not going to be put off. He seemed to want confirmation of a hypothesis that Moore felt certain they all quietly shared, namely, that what had just transpired was an official search, under the cover of a bomb scare.

"Still, bomb threats should be taken seriously!" the British officer insisted. "Your Customs people seemed too keen on searching pockets."

"I felt like we were interfering with their search," Beharry interjected. Moore suspected Mitchell did not like Beharry confirming what the British officer suspected.

"What were they looking for anyway?" the British officer asked.

"Probably gold," Mitchell replied, "foreign currency too."

"What's the limit?" the British officer asked.

"Well, you are allowed to take out no more than fifteen dollars, U.S., except if you are a visitor and you brought in more." Moore knew that Captain Mitchell would have preferred not to answer questions like this. They were embarrassing—they gave others a window into just how miserable things were. He was relieved he was not the one responding. Right then, he was too angry to provide this type of information.

"I see," the British officer said. "How about jewelry? One woman in my line was pulled aside because of the jewelry in her suitcase."

"I don't know," Mitchell replied. "I know they are trying to stop people from taking out gold, especially raw gold."

"What will happen to those people?" the British officer asked.

"I hear that the Customs officers would offer people with excess jewelry or foreign currency the choice of leaving it behind or facing prosecution," Captain Mitchell replied.

"Are you saying this is routine?" the British officer asked.

"No, no," Mitchell said, adding after a slight stutter, "You know I am not sure what they really do out there."

Moore listened in silence, teeth clenched. Why would they call in a bomb threat to check people's bags? Why didn't they check the shagging bags before they put them on the plane in the first place?

The jeep came out of the airport down the hill and continued straight into the army barracks area. It pulled up to the front stairway of the Sergeants' Mess. Captain Mitchell and the British officer got out.

"Thanks, Alan," Mitchell said.

"You're welcome, and thank you both for helping us out. By the way, when is the exercise ending?" Moore asked.

"Oh, it ended just before Beharry came to get us. The British team's leaving tomorrow. You sure you two don't want to come up for a drink?"

"No thanks," Moore said. His stomach growled.

"Get this man some food!" Mitchell said. The others chuckled. Moore signaled to McCurchin to drive, then waved to the two officers ascending the stairs of the Sergeants' Mess. The jeep drove past the WAC barracks and crossed the Airport road into the diagonal driveway to the Officers' Mess. McCurchin brought the vehicle to a stop by the front stairs, and Moore and Beharry got out.

"McCurchin," Moore said to his driver, "Why you don't park the vehicle and come 'round the kitchen. I'll see if they can't fix you up with some lunch."

Neither Moore nor Beharry spoke as they ascended the stairs. They went into the lounge and turned over their cartridge belts and revolvers to the bar attendant. The lounge was alive—loud music, officers and civilian guests. Neither officer wanted to linger there. Besides, they were very hungry, so off to the dining room they went. It was empty. The food from the buffet table had been cleared away. Moore sat down at the center of the table facing the kitchen, while Beharry walked up to the kitchen door.

"I'll give them a shout in the kitchen," Beharry said, opening the kitchen door and sticking his head in. "Private Bell!" he called out.

"Yes, Lieutenant Beharry?"

"We got a couple of officers here for lunch."

"I'm coming, Lieutenant."

Beharry took a seat next to Moore. Bell soon emerged from the kitchen.

"Awright, Bell," Moore said, "we're hungry."

"Is curry chicken and rice we got, Captain Moore. We got mauby too."

Moore signaled with his hand for her to bring it on. When Bell reemerged from the kitchen, she was carrying two plates, each half filled with rice and draped with a couple pieces of lettuce. She set one in front of Moore and the other in front of Beharry then returned to the kitchen.

"I couldn't believe the Customs people, butting in like that," Beharry said. "You can't tell me they didn't know what was going on. I nervous like hell and them boys cool like cucumber!"

Moore had his chin resting on the arch of his clasped hands and his thumbs.

"You think that was what the drill was about?" Beharry asked.

"What?" Moore asked.

"To search people's luggage?"

"I don't know what to think," Moore replied.

"Boy, we're really getting desperate in this country."

"Is not we, is they," Moore said, sensing that Beharry was probably afraid to make the reference to the government.

"But why? Why not do it quietly before loading the luggage?" Beharry asked. "I have never heard of this before."

"You've never heard the old creole saying: 'A word to Beniba does make Quashiba take notice?'"

"So you think they want people to know they're searching bags at the airport?"

"Of course! Now all the spectators will spread the word."

Private Bell came out with two bowls of curried chicken.

"How about a knife and fork?" Beharry asked.

"How about the mauby?" Moore asked. "I'm still sweating from the blasted heat."

Private Bell hurried back into the kitchen and came back with silverware for the officers then returned to fetch the mauby.

"What you think they're going to do to those people with the excess jewelry and foreign currency?" Beharry asked.

"It wasn't much, you know," Moore said. "It's just that people seemed to be hiding what little they had. This one lady had her wedding jewelry in a dress pocket. But it wasn't much!"

"One chap had three hundred U.S. dollars," Beharry added.

"Well, they're going to confiscate it. They're going to threaten to prosecute them, and you know none of them wants to stay back. So they will leave the money and the jewelry."

"They fleeing," Beharry observed.

"Of course! And you can't blame them, the way things are. The worse part of it is that much of what they leave behind will be stolen by the Customs people. It's a racket!" Private Bell came out with two large glasses of mauby and set one down next to each officer. Moore gulped his down in Bell's presence. She smiled and picked up the glass and left to refill it.

"Did you see the kind of stuff people were taking out?" Beharry asked, grinning.

"You mean the fried banga-mary and so on?" Moore was smiling too.

"Yeh! Is like they expect to find a famine in America!"

TWO

*I*T HAD SEEMED LIKE the usual Sunday morning at Timehri. Moore remembered stepping onto the damp concrete base of the shower stall that morning, turning the knob and sucking his teeth when the shower sputtered before going silent. The zinc bucket he had filled the previous evening sat in the same corner where he had left it, the pint-sized tin cup still floating on its side. He dipped his finger into the bucket. The water didn't feel very cold, but he shuddered anyway at the thought of it colliding with his warm body. He moved the bucket to the center of the shower stall, made a silent count before submerging the cup and, in a continuous motion, brought it over his head, repeating the fluid motion of cup-to-bucket-to-head for three rounds before lathering up with the withered bar of Zex soap resting on the back ledge.

Before Jeanene hung up the phone the previous evening, she had said how tired she was of contending with calabash and bucket at home. Not a conversation ended these days without her telling him how much she wanted them to leave this socialist paradise! Last night, it was the water problem. At least she didn't mention the toilet. She said that it wasn't as if she sat around dreaming of those "fair lands afar," it was just that she was concerned about the children's future. With all the shortages, she wasn't sure what she would give them to eat before sending them off to school, and all they seemed to be learning there were slogans that they didn't understand, such as "The Party is the Vanguard of the Proletariat."

Moore too was worried about the children but didn't know of anything he could do right away. He thought of Jeanene's reference to the first stanza of the pledge, the words fresh in his mind as they must have been in hers. He sang:

> *Oh, I care not that others rave over fair lands afar,*
> *Where silvern lakes and placid streams mirror the evening star;*
> *I care not though their wealth be great, their scenery be grand,*
> *For none so fair as can compare with my own native land.*

The words became garbled when water got into his mouth, and he paused occasionally to spigot the water out but continued tracking the words and carrying the tune.

Stepping out of the shower stall, Moore used the threadbare towel draped over the door to dry himself in the ablution area before walking down the hall with the towel wrapped around his waist. Before the wall mirror in his room, he pulled the steel comb through his hair several times, teased the front with a pick, then began to dress. He put on the same uniform he had worn the day before, but left the cartridge belt and revolver in the cupboard, choosing instead to strap on his stable belt. Boots and puttees on, he walked over to the small dresser to pick up his beret where he had left it covering the *Weekly Church Bulletin,* an advance copy Jeanene had brought him Saturday afternoon. He lifted the beret, folded it, and pushed it, badge facing forward, under his left epaulette, all the while looking down at the *Bulletin,* which had been the source of restlessness last night. Dated Sunday, January 16, this was the second issue of the year.

Thinking how best to respond to remarks officers might make, Moore turned the page past the Bishop's weekly message to his uncle's editorial. *"The episode at the Timehri Airport last Thursday is another sign that this "land of the palm tree, the croton and fern" is being transformed into an East European-style police state,"* Moore read.

> *Reported only in the Opposition's Red Star, the dragging of a university lecturer out of her seat on Carib Air just before departure was a carefully calculated humiliation of a minor critic of the Party, whose only offense seems to be that she joined a handful of her colleagues in calling for free and fair elections. All of the Party's mouthpieces—and they have many, don't we know?—all of them trumpet the strides the Party has made towards socialism, the nationalization of the commanding heights of the economy foremost among them. In this grand scheme, elections are viewed by the Party as a distraction, and reminders that they should be held and be free and fair are simply discordant voices of reactionaries, which must be silenced. No more talk of consultative democracy, or of cassava bread and milk, only of dialectical materialism and the inexorable march of history. But whose history?*
>
> *We are descendants of slaves brought out of Africa and indentured laborers from India. We fought for our independence from Britain, and now after two decades of rule by the Party, what have we got to show? The*

treasury has been pillaged; yes, under the guise of socialism. The main pillars of our economy—sugar, bauxite, and rice—lie in ruins. Alien phrases from an alien ideology chart a progress we do not see and mask every deprivation we do see. But we are privileged, so the mouthpieces tell us, to have a Supreme Leader or, pardon me, a Comrade President, as they prefer to say. "Comrade?" Not in the sense of your friend and mine, but "Comrade" as in Stalin, Idi Amin, and Bokassa, demanding adulating subservience or silence.

    Is who say "Massa day done?"
    Rev. Lennox Moore, Editor

Moore shook his head and walked over to the window, *Bulletin* in hand. There wasn't any traffic on the Airport road, but it was only 06:30. It won't be long before swarms of reveling civilians descend on the base for the one Sunday flight out. These days people seemed happiest when they were leaving, but could you really blame them? It's been a decade since the Arab oil embargo, and things seemed to be going from worse to really miserable.

This was Alan Moore's seventh year in the army and the third month at Timehri in the current deployment. He had set up the company command post here at Camp Stevenson when his platoons were posted to hinterland locations last November. He made fortnightly visits to the interior to check on those deployments, but otherwise ran the company from the post here at Camp Stevenson. He could also go home every evening, except on weekends like this one when he was the Duty Officer.

Moore liked Timehri, especially its remoteness from the main army base in Georgetown and its proximity to his home in Eccles. Located in the hilly sand and clay belt, Timehri was blistering hot in the daytime and cool at night. Not a town or a village but a large clearing in the bush, it had just enough room for an airport and an army base. The airport itself was the termination point of the thirty-mile stretch of road running from Georgetown along the east bank of the Demerara River, and sat on the top of a hill, at the foot of which was Camp Stevenson, positioned like a sphinx guarding the main exit out of the country. The East-bank road skirted around the edge of Camp Stevenson proper, the base, as it was called, with its twelve-foot fence and guard house, all of which remained hidden from roadside view by trees and the elevation of the terrain. The rest of the army buildings, outside the main base, formed two rows, one on each side of the East-bank road and ending about a quarter of a mile from the airport compound entrance. This stretch of the East-bank road, passing by Camp Stevenson, was called the Airport road, but like the East-bank road, there was no sign declaring it so.

This was Moore's last weekend here; it was time for redeployment. He had spent the week overseeing the extraction of his platoons from the interior. The soldiers had weekend passes, but the officers had remained at Camp Stevenson. Lieutenant Beharry was the base Orderly Officer for the weekend, and Lieutenants Persico and Mentore were evidently making forays into Georgetown from their temporary billets in the Annex behind the Officers' Mess. Moore wondered how Mentore and Persico were making out in adjacent rooms in the Annex; they had been like two fowl-cocks pecking at each other on the flight from the interior last Friday.

Out here, Uncle Lenny's editorials hadn't been much of a problem, Moore thought, but if he had to operate out of Camp Ayanganna in Georgetown for the next three months, there would be no end to the barbs he would encounter. During his last posting there, Party officials who came to the Officers' Mess said his uncle was being used. They said that it was Black people like him who would bring down this government. Even the Comrade President once referred to Moore at an army function as Rasputin's nephew and later tried to pass it off as a joke. Anyway, there was no point worrying about this now, he told himself; he didn't yet know where along the coast the company was to be deployed. He knew though that anywhere along the coast would be welcomed by the officers and men—it was, after all, where most of them lived.

Moore stepped over to the dresser, slid the *Bulletin* into the top drawer, and walked out of the room, through the corridor and down the outside stairs onto the concrete strip separating the Officers' Quarters from the Officers' Mess. The sun was already above the horizon, casting sharp rays through the spaces between the mora trees on the left. The sand on both sides of the concrete strip was a bright white with no evidence of last night's heavy rains, and ahead, just past the Officers' Mess, the Motor Transport compound presented its sprawling litter of Bedford trucks and Land Rovers on jacks and concrete blocks, awaiting tires and other spare parts.

*   *   *

"Cap . . . tain!" Lieutenant Persico called out when Moore entered the dining area. Lieutenants Mentore and Khan, who were backing the Mess entrance, turned around and almost in unison said, "Morning, Alan." They seemed to have finished eating; Mentore was leafing through the *Cayman News,* and Khan was sipping a cup of coffee. Moore sat down at the center of the horseshoe configuration which opened towards the kitchen, Persico on his left and the other two officers on his right.

Moore looked over at Lieutenant Persico. "George, you up early?" he asked. "And you ain't even on duty?"

"Habit, you know, Alan," Persico replied, smiling and nodding his head.

"Habit my foot," Lieutenant Mentore chimed in, without looking up. "He couldn't sleep because of what was going on in Nizam Khan's room!"

"Don't worry with Mentore," Khan said, face flushed.

"So what you doing up here on a weekend, Nizam?" Moore asked.

"I got a flight to the interior this morning."

"Where to?"

"Madhia, Tumatumari, and Matthews Ridge."

"Alan, you should have seen what came out of the man's room this morning," Mentore said.

Khan was smiling and shaking his head, "Don't worry with him, Alan. He just joshing you."

"The man's covering his tracks," Mentore said.

"So what's in the news, Derryck?" Moore asked.

"Oh nothing new. The sugar strike's still on."

The conversation was interrupted when Private Bell came out of the kitchen to take Moore's order.

"Morning, Captain Moore. How you want your eggs?"

"Fried. Put some onions and some pepper in it. You got any cheese?"

"No, Captain, we ain't got no bread neither."

"Well, what you got?"

"We got some rice-flour bakes and guava jelly."

"Rice-flour, huh? Well, let me try it, and bring out another kettle of hot water." Moore reached for the jar of Nescafe and measured out two teaspoons into his cup. He added a spoonful of sugar and some milk from the decanter. He used his spoon as a pestle and worked the contents in his cup to a light brown consistency, then poured in the hot water that Bell had set before him, and stirred. He sipped with satisfaction. It was weak coffee, but it had a good flavor. This is going to be a long day, he thought. Maybe he'd go up to the airport and look around. That's where the action usually is on Sundays. Besides, he'd be performing his duties and still be within reach of the main base.

Private Bell emerged from the kitchen with a plate in one hand and a jar of guava jelly in the other. She laid them in front of him. On the plate were the fried eggs he had asked for and two rice-flour bakes. He examined the bakes disapprovingly and wondered whether he could eat them both. He started with the eggs. Lieutenant Khan rose and asked to be excused.

"Wait, wait, wait," Mentore said, his eyes fixed on the newspaper. "Listen to this. This woman is writing to Jackie Semple: 'My husband is in the U.S. I have been waiting for my papers to join him. I recently had an affair with a man I met in the line outside the U.S. Embassy, but I have broken it off. The problem, Jackie, is that I found out I am pregnant. I don't know what to do. Should I tell my husband?' She signed it 'Worried.'"

"She got a problem," Khan said. "Look like she gon lose both the iguana and the cutlass, as they say." They all laughed.

"I think all this immigration is destroying the damn country," Persico declared.

"It's not immigration, George," Mentore replied. "The country is destroying itself. People are just running away."

"When are you going?" Persico asked.

"When I damn well please," Mentore replied, "and you can report that, George."

"Awright, awright, let's hold it down, eh," Moore said. "Derryck, what are they saying in the paper 'bout the sugar strike?"

"Nothing much, except that it still on and, oh, they're saying it is a political strike," Mentore replied, refocusing on the advice column.

"Derryck, why you don't finish your coffee and let's go under the benab," Khan suggested, "you can read Jackie Semple out there." Then, looking over at Persico, he asked, "You coming, George?"

"Don't invite that crab!" Mentore said.

"You know, Derryck, I ignore malcontents like you," Persico said.

"I am not a malcontent, George," Mentore protested. "I like to tell my story straight. I just don't trust people with Party contacts."

"Better save some of that energy for the cane fields," Moore interjected, as he finished his fried eggs. "You might be going out there next week."

"You know, that's another thing," Mentore declared. "I didn't join the army to become a cane cutter."

"The Cuban army cuts sugar cane," Persico interjected.

"This ain't Cuba, comrade," Mentore asserted.

"The Comrade President said this is a people's army," Persico retorted.

"Look, George, I am just an army officer. I ain't no damn politician. Is people like you tying up this army with the Party. And the rest of us suffocating, man!"

"All I have to say is that officers will have to carry out their orders in an emergency," Persico said, as though reciting a section from a manual.

"Listen to this one! All-yuh listen to this one!" Mentore stood up and was pointing both outstretched arms in Persico's direction. "He talking like the President! What emergency, George? The people striking for food. Last month, it was the bauxite workers. Now is the sugar workers. Things bad, man! Things really bad! This government has even banned flour!"

It became very quiet around the table. Moore tore one of the rice-flour bakes in two and was applying some guava jelly to it, when Mentore began again.

"You see the bake the Captain getting ready to eat? You see it, George? Look at his face when he bites into it. I just ate one. The thing tastes like rice husk!" This brought on loud laughter. "And the rice they serve for lunch every day? That is what we does call duck rice back home. It's broken rice that they can't export!" Moore postponed his first bite as he rocked with laughter. Mentore turned to Persico. "You laughing, George? You laughing!"

"Yeh, I like your style," Persico replied. "You're a good rapman."

"Captain, how do you like the bake?" Mentore asked Moore.

"Is awright," Moore replied, smiling at the obvious tease, "I making do, comrade."

"See the man's face changing color," Mentore said. "I bet you didn't get rice bakes at West Point, eh Captain?"

"No, I felt really deprived," Moore replied. Then, turning to Lieutenant Persico, he asked, "So, George, why we having all these shortages?"

"Well, the government is trying to get we to grow we own food."

"George, have you ever grown anything in you life?" Mentore asked. "You're a city boy. Your father was policeman!"

"That's the point!" Persico said. "Attitudes have to change, comrade."

"You need to change your attitude. I for that!" Mentore laughed.

"Don't worry with you," Persico responded. "The problem is that we are spoiled, all of we."

"How is that, George?" Mentore asked.

"Look, we are a coastal people. We live on a ten-mile strip of land along the Atlantic. The entire interior of the country is undeveloped. We have vast potential to exploit."

"Good speech, George, and I don't disagree with you, but what that got to do with what's happening in the country?" Mentore asked. "By the way, I've just come back from three months in the interior."

"I did too, but that's the point—we only go in there to prevent the Venezuelans from occupying our territory a piece at a time. We need to develop the entire region. That is almost two-thirds of the entire country! Think of what it could do for we."

It became quiet for a moment. Moore retired his plate with an uneaten bake on it, sipped his coffee, and looked over his junior colleagues. It was Mentore who broke the silence again.

"Look, I'm from Windsor Forest on the west coast of the Demerara River. My father is a farmer. How about the rest of you?"

"So what you saying, Derryck?" Persico asked. "Because I didn't grow up planting baagie, I can't support this idea of growing we own food in this country?" Persico seemed to be gaining the upper hand. He continued, "I know things bad, but you got to understand that we going through a period of adjustment."

"Listen to the man—a period of adjustment! George, you talking like the IMF!" Everyone laughed. Even Persico was smiling. "People starving, and you talking about a period of adjustment? I thought the Comrade President said we were in a period of socialist transformation! Maybe that's the problem; we seem to be moving backwards. I say it's time to change course."

"The Comrade President said that it is easier to stop tomorrow than it is to stop socialism," Persico said, shaking his finger in the air.

"Well, he's succeeded in stopping tomorrow for a lot of people," Mentore declared. "That is why you see people leaving by the plane load."

"You better watch your mouth," Persico cautioned.

"Boy, this talk too heavy for me," Nizam Khan interjected, "I'm going out to the benab. I'd like to see who's going up to the airport."

"Get the dominoes," Mentore said.

"The bar area's not open yet."

"Ask Bell to get them for you," Mentore suggested.

Khan went to the kitchen door in pursuit of Bell.

"Alan, you want to slap some dominoes with the master?" Mentore asked.

"Yeh, I know, you invented the game."

"You damm straight." They both laughed.

"Awright, I'll try a hand just to put you in your place," Moore said.

Mentore rose from his chair. "Awright, George," he said, looking over at Persico, "you can come too."

"Lemme borrow the newspaper," Persico said.

"Give it to the man," Moore said. "I bet is the comic strip he looking for!"

* * *

Moore and Mentore sat next to each other on one of the two semicircular seats in the benab, its thatched, sloping roof only partially blocking out the morning sun. Persico seated himself on the other semicircular seat, a clear indication that he did not intend to play the first round. On arrival with the box of dominoes, Nizam Khan placed a card table in front of Moore and Mentore and sat in a chair across from them. Using both hands, Khan shuffled the dominoes face downward on the table before inviting the others to make their selection.

The game began with Moore placing the double-six on the table.

"So, when's the wedding, Derryck?" he asked Mentore.

"Christmas Eve. She's returning from New York a few days before. I talked to her last night."

"Boy, you were on that phone a long time," Khan said. "I put down three Bass Ales and came out to use the bathroom. The man was still on the phone. I can see where your money going," Khan said.

"Nah. It ain't cost nothing," Mentore replied. "I know one of the operators at Telecoms."

"All-yuh gon break this government down," Persico remarked from across the benab. "Is every night somebody here calling New York or Toronto and not paying. I telling you, y'all gon bankrupt the government."

"It already bankrupt, George, and is not my phone calls that did it," Mentore replied, slapping the double-four down to form a T with five-four on the table. "Is them big boys up there who're responsible. A lot of army people getting rich too. You know that!" He looked over at Persico. "We're just picking up some of the morsels falling off the table," he added, smiling.

"That kind of talk gon land you in trouble," Persico cautioned.

"Yes, because people like you does carry it back," Mentore retorted.

"Don't worry with you." Persico sucked his teeth loudly and resumed reading the newspaper.

"Your play," Khan reminded Mentore.

"I know. Awright, here's another four to you, Captain," Mentore said to Moore as he laid down the four-three next to the double-three at the far end of the row. "Rap your hand; you ain't got no fours."

"Rap," said Moore.

"That's it, game one," Mentore declared, holding up his last ticket.

"Wait," said Khan, contemplating his hand.

"You can't cover both ends, squaddie, and you got two tickets in your hand. Here's the winning ticket!" Mentore raised both arms in the air in a triumphant gesture.

Khan tossed the two dominoes down and began flipping the others over for the new shuffle.

"I telling y'all. Yuh playing with the master. I invented this game, you know." Mentore laughed out loud.

"Is that so?" Moore asked. "You know what they say? 'Mouth-tar and guitar is two different kind of tar!'"

"We gon see," Mentore replied. "Shuffle them, Nizam! I gon work the two of you today!"

Khan won the second game. Game three was well underway when Persico got up to move away from the sun. Mentore was slapping the dominoes down in rapid succession.

"I telling you, man, I invented this game. Rap your hands, both of you! Game two."

"Look like you getting love, Captain," Persico said, laughing with the others at Moore's losing streak.

"George, you know the old saying—'Never the day canoe bore punt?'"

"Yeh, but it looks like them boys mashing you up though."

"I know. Is real eye-pass!" conceded Moore.

"I see the Orderly Officer heading for breakfast," Persico said. "I think he needs the nourishment. The man look bruk up." They all laughed and looked over at Lieutenant Ramesh Beharry walking up the diagonal road towards the Officers' Mess.

"What you expect!' asked Mentore. "Imagine walking to every guard post several times during the night. The ammo dump alone is three miles away from the base compound. I remember having to do that."

"Did you actually do it?" Moore asked.

"First time, yes. Then I got smart."

"That's the problem," Moore said. "No one actually making the visits. Orderly officers phone the posts to inquire if everything is okay. They don't make the actual inspections anymore."

"You can't blame them," Mentore said. "There are no serviceable vehicles, except one 3-ton truck for the Standby Platoon and one 1/4-ton jeep."

"And then you have to conserve gas," Persico added.

"Yeh. It's called no foreign currency," Mentore said. "No foreign currency, no spare parts, no gas . . . I don't know what this place coming to."

"Oi man, just keep your eyes on the table," Moore said to Mentore, sensing victory; then to Khan, "How many tickets you got, Nizam?" Khan laid his three dominoes face down on the table. "How about you, Derryck?"

"Same."

"Well, keep them right there." Moore placed a five-two to present Khan and Mentore with fives at each end, then a double-five, a five-four, and it was over. "You see? Strategy—that's the key!"

"Captain, I think you're needed," Persico said, motioning to Lieutenant Beharry, who had changed direction and was now walking at a brisk pace through the woods towards the benab. Everyone looked over again to the approaching Orderly Officer. Beharry saluted at the entrance of the benab. "Morning, Captain."

Moore braced up in his seat to acknowledge the salute. "What's up, Ramesh?"

"The Chief of Staff's aide just called. The Chief wants you to provide the 1/4-ton jeep to meet him at the airport at 10:00 hours."

"What for?" Moore asked.

"Well, Captain, the ADC said that the Chief was coming up to meet the Hudson Air flight. He got some stuff he wants to take back to Georgetown."

"The Chief is off duty. He has his private vehicle. Why does he need an army jeep?"

"I don't know, Captain. He's probably bringing in a lot of stuff."

"Lieutenant Beharry, how many serviceable 1/4-ton jeeps we got?"

"Just the one, Captain—"

"Right, and how is this vehicle to be employed as per the contingency plan for the defense of the base?"

"Well, Captain, the contingency plan calls for the availability of one serviceable 1/4-ton jeep for the purpose of hauling anti-aircraft weapons to the airport."

"Please tell the Chief's ADC that."

"But, Alan, the Chief already knows that. The ADC was very insistent."

"Look, Ramesh. These are Standing Orders. Violations could result in a court-martial for both of us. Tell the ADC that. Tell him he can call me. I am the Duty Officer."

"Yes, Captain." Beharry saluted and walked off to the Officers' Mess.

Moore got up and began pacing about the benab, teeth clenched. The other three officers looked from him to each other. He knew they understood his predicament. Finally, Khan broke the uncomfortable silence. "Boy, I just glad is not me."

"And George, you complaining 'bout my phone calls?" Mentore said. "Watch the big boys in action."

A few minutes later, Lieutenant Beharry was back. "Captain, the Chief expects the 1/4-ton at the airport at 10:00 hours. What do you want me to do?"

"Nothing," Moore replied. "The Chief's request is in violation of Base Standing Orders." Turning to the other officers in the benab, Moore asked, "Is what kind of example the Chief of Staff setting? He expecting me to violate Standing Orders so he can use a military vehicle to transport his perks back to Georgetown. And everybody knows, he gon turn around and sell them. We have a Chief of Staff behaving like a common huckster!"

"Careful, Alan," Mentore cautioned. "These things could get back to the man."

"I don't care. Is true. Everyone knows what's going on. Every time he goes overseas he ships back stuff that he turns around and sells to the army or somebody. I didn't join the army for this." Moore turned to Lieutenant Beharry. "Ramesh, why you don't go and have your breakfast?"

Beharry turned to go but stopped and waited. Private Bell had stepped out onto the landing of the Mess and was shouting, "Captain Moore, phone! Is the Chief of Staff!"

Moore sucked his teeth loudly, walking back toward the Mess with Beharry. "Why is that shagging private hollering at me?"

When the two officers reached the landing, Moore turned to Private Bell. "Bell, don't holler out officers' names like that. If you have a message, walk up and deliver it, awright?"

"Sorry, Captain, but is the Chief of Staff, and he sound really vex."

"It doesn't matter. Just don't holler out like that."

"Awright, Captain."

Moore entered the Mess and turned left towards the lounge. The phone was off the hook on a chair in the open area leading into the lavatory. He picked it up.

"Captain Moore," he said.

"Moore!" The Chief of Staff's voice boomed. "Is what the skunt you think you doing? I asked for a 1/4-ton jeep—"

"General, I understand. But you know we only have one jeep and the contingency plan—"

"Don't give that rass, you hear?" the Chief shouted. "Don't tell me 'bout no contingency plan! I drew up the damn contingency plan!"

"That's the point, General—" But before he could finish, Moore heard the phone slammed down at the other end. He retraced his steps to the Mess door, then saw Beharry in the dining area and walked over.

"What we gon do, Captain?" Beharry asked, looking up.

"Nothing," Moore said, pulling out a chair and sitting. He poured some hot water from the kettle on the table into an empty cup, added some instant coffee, sugar, and evaporated milk. "The contingency plan for the defense of the base requires the availability of a serviceable 1/4-ton jeep. We only have one. It is what I am using to get around to do my duties. The Chief should not be requesting it for any reason, much less for personal use!"

"I agree with you, Alan, but what's the probability that the airport will come under attack?"

"That's not the point, Ramesh! Violation of Standing Orders is a court-martial offense."

"Why would the Chief of Staff court-martial you if the violation occurs on his orders?"

"What's the matter with you, Ramesh? Are you trying to tell me to give him the only jeep on the base so he can transport his personal goods? Where would it stop? What if another officer wants the jeep for his personal use?"

"I wasn't suggesting anything, Captain. I just trying to figure out where we stand."

"Well," said Moore, finishing up his coffee, "I gon get the vehicle and do an inspection. You can rest up."

"Does that mean we not sending the jeep to the airport?"

"Oh skunt, Beharry! Is what wrong with you too?"

"Sorry, Captain, sorry. I with you."

THREE

*T*HE STAFF CAR WAS pulling into the airport compound when the Chief of Staff heard the engines of the Hudson Airlines jet somewhere above. Scheduled to arrive at 10:00 hours, the plane was now ten minutes late. The Chief of Staff was relieved. He liked to arrive at Timehri ahead of the plane to chat up the Customs boys before the off-loading of the luggage. He would have arrived earlier this Sunday but for the delay in securing a second vehicle. The Motor Transport officer at Camp Ayanganna could not be reached, and the corporal on duty was not sure which vehicle was serviceable. Finally, the Chief had decided to take any 3/4-ton Land Rover that could be started, and with his ADC riding in it, had sped to Timehri.

The staff car turned by the south end of the terminal building and slowed. The Chief of Staff lowered his window. The airport was crowded. Departing passengers were checking in as part of two long lines that snaked out to the curb. With only two airline attendants on duty, it was slow going. The Chief had difficulty separating passengers from relatives who were also in the lines, helping with luggage. Nevertheless, the scene appeared quite typical of the Sunday flights. Passengers were presenting their tickets and passports and having their luggage weighed. Payment was then worked out for overweight, and seats assignments validated. The Chief smiled as he listened to one passenger trying to talk her way out of paying for what she said was just a few extra pounds.

The car cruised slowly along the eastern side of the building. Checked-in passengers were proceeding to the row of portable, waist-high, metal barricades for immigration check. Farewells had to be said here, and the Chief could see lots of final embraces. Relatives stayed behind the barricades to observe, though some appeared to be relocating after the passengers moved beyond the immigration checkpoint.

Processing at each of the two immigration stations, manned by uniformed police officers, was very slow. Passengers advanced on cue and surrendered their passports to the immigration officer, who took the passports into a side office. The Chief was aware of the controversy surrounding these procedures. The *Red Star* and the *Weekly Church Bulletin* were constantly commenting on these checks and the body searches in the waiting area. But this was the way the government wanted it, and in any case, it was a police matter.

The north end of the building, where the staff car stopped, was far more hectic. Two rows of portable barricades had been set up to create a walkway for arriving passengers after they cleared Customs. Relatives and friends had crowded on the outsides of the barricades to greet their arriving passengers, and taxi drivers had positioned themselves at the curb end of the barricades to compete with one another for the expensive fares to town.

The green metal pendant emblazoned with a silver star on the bonnet of the staff car drew immediate attention from the people huddled around the barricades. Through the open window, the Chief heard someone say, "Must be a big one!" And when his driver, a uniformed corporal, opened the door for the Chief, the taxi drivers quickly cleared a path to let him pass. People seemed to recognize the Chief of Staff even though he was in mufti, a cream-colored dashiki with an intricate design embroidered around the neckline and sleeves. The Chief strode up the pathway between the barricades, his ADC and the drivers of the two vehicles slightly behind. He heard whispers of recognition from this spectator gauntlet as he made his way toward the baggage area, and he nodded to the multiple faces on both sides. Once in the baggage area, he sought out the senior Customs officer.

Responding to the Chief's inquiry, one of the two Customs officers on duty pointed to their supervisor, Mr. Seaforth, who was having a cigarette with an airport employee by the off-loading platform. The Chief walked up beside Seaforth and placed his arm across Seaforth's shoulder. "Hear nuh, comrade," the Chief said, "I got some stuff coming in on this flight and I need to get back to town in a hurry. You think you can help me out?"

"Yeh, is awright, just bring it over here," Seaforth said, pointing to one of the two Customs stations. "We gon sort it out. No problem."

"Thank you," said the Chief, removing his arm from Seaforth's shoulder but remaining close to him. "Look like the plane came in a little late today?"

"Yeh," Seaforth replied, "but nine out of ten, that does be the case, you know." Tossing his head backward in the direction of the two

Customs stations as he stomped out the cigarette butt he had dropped on the platform, Seaforth added, "Well, we got to set up here before the passengers get out. Just bring yuh stuff when you ready."

The Chief thanked him again and looked around the baggage area. Located at the southwestern corner of the terminal building, the baggage area was completely open on the western and southern sides, and the Chief could see the plane parked about two hundred feet away. He could also see the rest of the southwestern end of the runway, as well as the trees beyond the runway. The floor on which he stood was more like a platform that ended at a diagonal, and the second level hung from above like a huge verandah, sheltering this area from the elements. There was no conveyor belt. The baggage trucks would go out to the plane to be loaded, return and cruise along the diagonal platform for a suitable spot to dump the luggage, then pull out and return to the plane again.

Passengers had completely disembarked from the plane and were starting to fill the baggage area. When the first truck pulled alongside the diagonal platform, passengers crowded the area where the luggage was to be offloaded. Earlier positioning enabled the Chief of Staff to quickly identify two large suitcases and three boxes, which his ADC directed the drivers to put in a corner. The second truck brought nothing, but the third brought in four more boxes, two of them about six feet long, and two small suitcases. The drivers pulled the boxes and suitcases aside, and the ADC looked to the Chief for confirmation that they had secured all of his goods.

"We got some more, Ulric," the Chief said.

The large accumulation of baggage was attracting the attention of passengers, jostling with their luggage to the two inspection tables. Waiting for the next truck, the Chief could hear the voices of the Customs officers repeating the same question, "Anything to declare?" The responses varied within a limited range of items that were barred from importation—"three cans of sardines," "some apples," "a few pounds of flour," "four cans of condensed milk." Some haggling ensued. Sometimes, the Customs officer gave in with an "Awright, awright, go 'long yuh way."

The baggage area was not as crowded as it had been a couple of luggage trucks earlier, but there were still many people there waiting for their luggage. Most of the other passengers were now in the two lines formed by the Customs officers, standing at the head of six-foot inspection tables. The space between the two tables formed the passageway for one line of passengers, and the table and the wall formed the other passageway. Passengers could pass through comfortably, after they laid their suitcases on one of the tables.

Waiting on the next baggage truck, the Chief of Staff kept looking over his shoulder to keep track of Seaforth. Finally, the truck arrived. The Chief identified two large duffle bags to his ADC and signaled to Seaforth that he was ready. Seaforth eyed the pile of luggage suspiciously, and, for a moment, the Chief thought Seaforth would change his mind.

"You can bring them through here," Seaforth said, pointing to the station nearest the Chief. Turning to the inspecting officer and the line of passengers, Seaforth said, "Let them through." His instruction temporarily aborted the inspection at this station. The two drivers began hauling the Chief's loot out under the supervision of the ADC and the watchful eye of the Chief himself. Passengers were pressed against the table as the army drivers passed behind them and the adjoining inspection table, fetching the large boxes and duffle bags in repeated trips. The low murmurs turned into loud complaints about how some people don't have to declare what they got while the small man was being stepped on.

"I want to know what is in those boxes," one man declared.

"Why you don't ask him?" the Customs officer replied.

Processing continued after the drivers passed through each time, but their to-and-fro hauling ignited more passenger grumbling. On the final trip, the Chief followed the drivers out, thanking Seaforth as he passed him. His steps quickened to elude the voices of complaint that followed him out. He heard one man say, "Y'all giving people a hard time for one or two apples and the big fish swimming by easily. Is so we building socialism?" The speaker then sucked his teeth loudly. Others in the lines joined the chorus of complaints.

"I just got two small bags and y'all checking it. That man just passed in with half the plane and nobody checking he. Is what really going on here?"

"Awright, awright, go 'long!" the Customs officer said to the complainer, waving him through, and also the others behind him. The Chief was relieved when he emerged among the waiting throng of relatives and friends of the passengers on this flight. The lively chatter from this throng drowned out the noise behind him.

The duffle bags, the large suitcases, and most of the boxes had been placed in the jeep. The smaller suitcases and remaining boxes were placed in the trunk of the staff car. The Chief told the ADC the itinerary and got in the rear of the staff car. With the ADC riding in the jeep's cab, the two-vehicle convoy left the airport compound for the army's Air Wing, next door. The sentry saluted sharply before opening the gate for the vehicles. The Chief of Staff got out by the small two-storied Admin Building where Colonel LaFleur was waiting for him. They walked away from the building toward the Islander sitting on the runway. Safely out of hearing of the off-duty soldiers under the Admin Building, the Chief stopped.

"How many pork-knockers going in on this flight?" the Chief asked.

"Four," Colonel LaFleur replied.

"Well, don't let them pay Lieutenant Khan," he said, looking at Khan, who was in conversation with the civilian mechanic by the plane. "You collect the money yourself."

Colonel LaFleur nodded.

"You taking in supplies?" the Chief asked.

"Oh yes. Fresh meat and rum for all three locations, and diesel for Tumatumari and Matthews Ridge," LaFleur replied, the glints from his front gold teeth harmonizing with the movement of his lips.

The Chief of Staff resisted a smirk. "Make sure the pork-knockers understand we saving them a lot of time and money. They would have had to come out to Georgetown and then haul this stuff in by trail. We want a good price. Gold! Nothing else!"

LaFleur nodded. "And the gold we buying from them," the Chief continued, "drive down the price! You know the drill." LaFleur nodded. "And remind them of all the services we providing, including protection."

"Yes, Chief," LaFleur said.

"Awright then," the Chief said, "let me not keep you. I got to sort something out at the Officers' Mess."

FOUR

DOWN THE HILL FROM the airport, the staff car turned left. Through the meshed screens on the outside of the two one-storied barrack buildings on the right, the Chief could see soldiers moving about. From the Sergeants' Mess next door came loud music and laughter. By the WAC barracks, the car turned right onto the East—bank road and about twenty yards later turned left into the driveway of the Officers' Mess and stopped by the main stairway. The jeep pulled up close behind.

Corporal Kyte got out and opened the door for the Chief of Staff, who stepped out and waited on his ADC. He looked over the four cars parked along the semi-circular driveway but did not recognize any of them. The two Austin 1100 did have a duty-free look about them that suggested they belonged to senior civil servants. The Chief mounted the stairs holding on to the right handrail, his ADC walking on the left. The Chief could hear the Sparrow calypso, "Mr. Walker," playing in the lounge. At the top of the stairs, his ADC held the door open for him. The Chief entered the Mess and was immediately greeted by the concierge, who seemed to have expected him, no doubt from conversations she might have overheard that morning.

"Good morning, General."

"Morning, Maxine. How you do?"

"I deh half-and-half."

"Look like the feting start early," the Chief observed, tossing his head in the direction of the lounge.

"Is some government people. You know how they like hanging 'round officers. One of them is a big one though."

The Chief raised his eyebrows but was determined not to be sidetracked from his main purpose for stopping in. "Captain Moore here?" he asked.

"No. He was here for breakfast. I think he out on inspection."

"How about the Orderly Officer?"

"Lieutenant Beharry? He gone back to the base compound." Observing the Chief of Staff looking at his watch, she asked, "You not staying for lunch?"

"No thanks, Maxine," he said, "I got to head back to town. By the way, who's at the bar?"

"Is a new boy, Private Jones."

The Chief nodded, moved to the lounge entrance, and peered in.

Private Jones was behind the bar arranging records in the order he was going to play them on the phonograph sitting on the wide shelf, below the drinks. Glancing over to his right and seeing the Chief of Staff, he immediately braced to attention and said out loud, "Morning, General."

The Chief smiled and replied, "Morning, Jones," adding with a wave of his hand, "carry on, Jones, carry on."

The exchange had attracted the attention of the guests in the lounge, and one of the men sitting in a twin-sofa backing the Chief turned around.

"Clive!" he called out to the Chief and rose quickly out of the sofa. "Is what going on, man?" The Chief was surprised to see Lionel Cummings, the Assistant Permanent Secretary of the Ministry of Home Affairs, and before he could respond, Cummings said, "Come and take a drink with we."

"Is what bring you up here, Lionel?" the Chief of Staff asked, assuming the role of host.

"I been up to the airport," Cummings said, stretching his hand out to take the Chief's.

"I just come from the airport myself," the Chief said, his brows furrowed.

"Well, I went up a lil early. You know they got a flight out later this morning? I just wanted to see how the immigration procedures working out."

"Oh," the Chief said. He thought he detected something in Cummings' tone and momentary discomfort that suggested something different was going on at the airport.

"And I said," Cummings continued, "while I up here, I gon stop in at the Officers' Mess and have a drink. I brought some friends. Lemme introduce you."

"Is awright, Lionel," the Chief said, remonstrating in a muted tone. "Look, I got to go by the base and then I heading back to town."

Cummings drew closer and spoke softly. "Come, man," he insisted. "Look, you see the girl sitting in the chair by she-self. She free, man. Come join we."

The Chief looked over at the group sitting in a U configuration with the young woman Cummings mentioned sitting in a morris chair facing the bar, and two older women next to each other in a twin-sofa across from the one Cummings had just left.

"I can't today, Lionel," the Chief insisted, "I got to head back to town. Another time."

"Well, at least take a drink with we. I got a bottle behind the bar."

"Awright, a quick one." Turning to Jones at the bar, the Chief said, "Rum and Coke, Jones." The presence of his ADC reminded him of his original purpose for stopping in at the Mess. "Ulric," the Chief said to his ADC, "see if you can get Captain Moore on the phone."

"Yes, General."

The ADC left, and the Chief turned his attention back to Lionel Cummings. "Lionel, who is that chap with you? He looks familiar, you know."

"He is the chief accountant at the Electricity Corporation. He in the newspaper a lot these days, what with all the black-outs and things. Two of the girls working with he. Come, lemme introduce you."

The Chief walked over with Cummings, aware that the women were staring intently at him. The accountant stood up.

"General, this is Compton Owen," Cummings said. "He is the chief accountant at the Electricity Corporation. Compton, you recognize the Chief of Staff, General Agrippa?"

"Oh yes," Owen replied, shaking the Chief's outstretched hand. "I am very pleased to meet you in person, General."

The Chief nodded and made a half-turn to the right for Cummings to introduce him to the women. "Girls, this is the Chief of Staff of the Army, General Clive Aubrey Agrippa. He out of uniform at the moment, so you can't see his medals, but this is the Comrade President's right hand man." Agrippa was surprised by this assessment of his standing, but the women seemed very impressed, so he didn't pursue it. The two middle-aged women sitting together stood up and stretched out their hands to Agrippa and were introduced as Mavis and Daphne. He shook their hands and welcomed them to the Officers' Mess. They giggled but said nothing comprehensible. Agrippa then turned to the young woman in the single chair, who had now stood up. Cummings said, "General, this is Brenda. She is a friend of these two charming ladies."

Taking Brenda's outstretched hand, Agrippa asked, "First time here at the Mess?"

"Yes, but I passed by it many times."

Agrippa was about to speak again when Jones appeared beside him with the rum and Coke.

"Leh we sit down," Cummings suggested.

Private Jones had anticipated this and rushed over to get a chair for Agrippa to sit across from Brenda, completing the rectangle. Agrippa sipped the drink, his eyes riveted on Brenda, who blushed repeatedly. Agrippa estimated her to be in her early twenties. She had an olive complexion, a shade or so lighter than his own. She was slender and almost as tall as he. Her hair was combed tightly back and secured with a hair clip. She had a slim, sharply chiseled face, a small mouth, and a thin pointed nose, suggesting that she was probably mixed. She wore a shirt stamped with brown and yellow flowers and a skin-tight pair of pants that profiled a narrow waist, wide hips, and a pronouncedly arched rear, which Agrippa had noticed when she stood up to be introduced. He continued to sip his drink as Cummings spoke, nodding his head not out of agreement with what was being said, but out of his own silent appreciation for the beauty of the woman before him. Sensing the presence of someone behind him, he set his half-consumed drink on the cocktail table in front of him and rose.

"Clive, you not leaving?" Cummings protested.

"No, but I got this officer waiting on me. I better send him on." To the entire group, he added, "Y'all excuse, eh?"

Agrippa walked back to the entrance of the lounge where his ADC was chatting with the concierge. Anticipating the Chief's question, the ADC said, "General, Captain Moore has not returned from his inspection tour. I spoke with Corporal Liverpool at the Guard House. He said Lieutenant Beharry is on the base. He sent a soldier to get him."

"Is awright; don't worry with that. I gon stop by the base. Look, Ulric, why don't you go on back to town with the jeep. Drop them things off by the house. Vera will show you where to put them. She doesn't have to be at work til 14:00 hours." The ADC cupped his hands, braced to attention, then left.

Agrippa turned to make his way back to the group when the concierge asked again, "General, you want me to prepare some lunch for you and yuh guests?"

"No, Maxine. I just having a drink with Comrade Cummings. But if you could arrange some snacks. Some fried chicken gon work."

Turning to go, the concierge said, "I gon tell the cook in the kitchen."

Agrippa nodded and rejoined the company in the lounge.

"Everything awright, Clive?" Cummings asked.

"Oh yes, I just sent on my ADC."

"What's an ADC?" one of the middle-aged women asked.

Cummings did not allow the Chief to respond.

"Is a French term. It means 'Aide-de-Camp.' Is an officer who does look after the welfare of a commanding general. The General here has important duties to attend to. He needs somebody to keep his schedule and make the necessary arrangements and so on. Is not everyone can get an ADC. The Comrade President is the only other person with an ADC. That is because he is the Commander-in-Chief." The women were impressed. They glanced from Cummings to Agrippa and nodded as Cummings spoke. Agrippa was pleased. It was a longer explanation than he would have given, but the fact that someone else had given it magnified the impact. Brenda seemed especially impressed. She looked at him and smiled throughout, and he took special note of this. He emptied his glass, and it didn't take much persuasion to get him to settle in for another drink.

"Jonesie," Cummings called out like a regular, "leh we have another round."

The women whispered to one another, excused themselves, and headed out of the lounge. When they were out of view, Cummings leaned over to Agrippa.

"Clive, you see how the girl looking at you? Stick around, man; you bound to catch thing!"

Agrippa smiled. "Not this time, Lionel. I got to go after this drink."

"Join we, man!" Cummings was insistent, but his speech was getting slurred. "We going up to the Co-op College. Compton's brother is a lecturer there. He got a cabin. You know the lecturers live up there. They all got cabins. Well, Compton's brother got a cabin but he on a course in Tanzania. He left Compton to look after the place. Is very private up there. Leh we go up there and sport."

Private Jones served the round of drinks when the women returned. Cummings and the accountant engaged them in small talk and Agrippa listened, laughing out loud with the group at various points. Occasionally he interjected a comment, but he remained pensive and withdrawn. He wondered why Cummings had really come to the Mess. Was the rumor true that he was likely to become the new Permanent Secretary of Defense after the old PS retired? They said he was rising fast within the Party. Agrippa also studied Brenda and, with each sip of his rum and Coke, found Cumming's idea of sporting more and more exciting. But his last experience at it was a humiliating one and, as he sat there passively listening to the cross chatter, the vividness of the vigil his wife staged on that occasion outside the den of iniquity gushed back into his consciousness.

It had occurred back in mid-December, but Agrippa remembered it as if it had happened yesterday. He had come up to Timehri to witness 1st Battalion's annual fitness run and to conduct an inspection of the Officers' Quarters. All officers at the base were required to ready their rooms for inspection. He had brought his staff officer, his ADC, and his new Personal Assistant, whom he had just made a second lieutenant. She had a few 'O' levels and was a good typist. She was also very attractive; mixed—Black, Portuguese, and something else; maybe Amerindian, he wasn't sure. Vera called her a Santantone, because of the mixture, but everyone else, it seemed, focused on her other physical attributes.

He remembered that he came up in the staff car; his PA rode with him, and the ADC and the staff officer followed in a jeep. He had spent the entire day at Camp Stevenson and had decided to have dinner at the Officers' Club before returning to Georgetown. After dinner, they had some more drinks with the senior officers in the lounge. Agrippa had arranged with his PA for them to retire to a room in the Officers' Quarters before heading back to town, but one drink led to another, and it wasn't until dark when they finally slipped over to the Officers' Quarters.

At about 02:00 the next morning, he heard the banging on the door and the blast of Vera's voice, loud and hysterical. "Clive, open this door! Open the blasted door or I gon bruk it down." He froze in place. He realized he had overslept. His PA was lying naked beside him in the cot, her legs intertwined with his, and his wife was outside the room. Oh, God! Is trouble here today! His chest was thumping. He wanted to disentangle his legs and to readjust his position, if only to allow himself to think better, but any movement, any sound, would not only confirm his presence, but worse, his PA's presence, in the room. Better lie still. His PA, now awake and frightened, clung more tightly to him, precisely when he wanted to push her away.

"Clive, open this door! I know you in there. You and that Santantone whore!" The pounding on the door seemed relentless. He was sure everyone in the building was awake now. Nothing to do but be still. Oh God! By 08:00, every soldier at every base would know about this. Oh Lord! How could I have overslept? Oh, all the rum, oh Lord!

"Clive, I gon break down this door and I gon kill that bitch! You say you coming up here to do inspection. Is this the inspection you doing?"

There was laughter from the other wings of the building. Agrippa felt trapped and humiliated.

"You hear them officers laughing at you, Clive. You hear them? You ain't got no shame? You like sweetness, nuh? Well, lemme tell you something—what does sweeten goat mouth does be bitter in he backside. And I gon make yuh backside burn before I done with you."

The laughter from the other wings of the building was raucous.

"You hear them officers laughing at you, Clive? You ain't shame? You disgracing yuh-self and you disgracing me. I put up with all the rum drinking, but this is real eye-pass. I used to hear how you does go off with this WAC and the other, but now I catch you red-handed. You in there! I know you in there. I ain't going til you open this door. I telling you, Clive, open the damn door." She pounded the door with her fists.

The laughter from the other rooms was loud. Agrippa knew that the WACs too had been awakened by the pounding and the screaming and were now an active audience to this unfolding spectacle. Judging from the proximity of their laughter, they must have come out of their building and taken up positions closer to the Airport road for better viewing.

"This gone beyond eye-pass, Clive. This is real rass-pass. Open the door, I say! Open the blasted door!" Then Vera started sobbing. The silence on both sides of the road was probably out of sympathy for Vera and probably a reaction to the pathetic nature of the spectacle. There was a lull. Then it began again. This time, Vera had secured a rock and was banging the door with it. Violence seemed imminent. Agrippa got out of bed and quickly put on his clothes. He looked out of the window facing the road. Yes, the WACs were up. Many were standing outside as he had thought. Others were peering through open windows. Officers were up too and talking among themselves. Then came Vera's voice in the loud and now familiar refrain.

"Open the door, Clive, or I gon break it down. I gon kill that red-skin bitch. Is what you see in she though? She just using you. I asked you why you make she an officer. You said it come with the position. Is this the position you talking 'bout?" The laughter within the building and from the WACs across the road roared back and forth as in a Roman amphitheater. Agrippa stood still. His PA, now half dressed, sat on the bed. They looked at each other but dared not speak.

"I put up with the rum drinking all these years. I ain't putting up with no more whoring. I leaving you. You disgracing yuh-self and you disgracing me." Her voice had become hoarse and raspy.

The drama had repeated itself over and over again for what seemed to Agrippa like hours. Then, probably from total exhaustion, Vera had begun to move away, her sobbing and muttering becoming fainter and fainter, as were the retreating voices of the officers and WACs. A strange silence had enshrouded the entire complex, posing a new dilemma to Agrippa—how to get away with his PA without alerting the erstwhile spectators.

Vera hardly spoke to him afterwards. At first, neither of his children, residing in Canada, wanted anything to do with him, but they needed money, and he had found ways of generating additional sums. Now he was hearing that Vera was friendly with some Cuban doctor at the Georgetown Public Hospital. People were talking. Even the colonels said he ought to put a stop to it.

"Clive! Clive!" Cummings called out. "Like you in a trance, man?"

"No, I just thinking; I need to swing by the base."

"How about another drink?"

"Thank you, Lionel, but I gon finish this one and go."

"You got to take one for the road, man. What you say?"

"Yes, man," the accountant urged. The two middle-aged women agreed.

"Just one more," Brenda pleaded.

The Chief smiled, "Awright, one for the road."

Other visitors were entering the lounge. Several walked over to greet Agrippa, who in turn, introduced them to his friends. Soon they were all on their feet and the introductions and small talk allowed for freer mixing. The Chief took advantage of this convivial confusion to step over beside

Brenda to chat her up. He asked her if she had seen the game room, which he was sure she hadn't, and then volunteered to show it to her.

They entered through the door at the rear of the lounge. It was a simple room, surrounded on three sides by screens. A ping pong table occupied the western third, and three square tables with chairs around them were evenly positioned through the rest of the room. The Chief explained that the tables were used as card tables or for dominoes. The door at the back of the room led out, down a set of outside stairs. The Chief invited Brenda to sit beside him at one of the square tables near to a window screen.

"So you work at the Electricity Corporation?" he asked.

"No," she said. "Mavis and Daphne work there. I work at the Ministry of Labor on Camp Street."

"Oh, I see. You know, the Officers' Club in town is even nicer than this one. You must come and have a drink with me there."

"You not going with we to the Co-op College?" Brenda asked.

"Well, I have to go to the base out here. Army business, you know."

"You could come afterwards." The soft but firm invitation sounded too promising for the Chief to pass up.

"Sure," Agrippa said. "I gon just swing by the base first though. Shouldn't take long. I gon see you up the highway."

The Chief walked Brenda back into the lounge. Cummings had settled the accounts and was waiting by the bar with the rest of his company. Brenda rejoined the women and, together with the accountant, they walked out of the lounge. Cummings had lingered behind to speak to the Chief of Staff.

"You coming, Clive?"

"I got to swing by the base," Agrippa replied, "I gon meet you at the Co-op College. Where you gon be?"

"Cabin number 9. When you turn into the Co-op College, ask the watchman at the gate for Lawrence Owen's cabin. Lawrence is Compton's brother. He in Tanzania for a course."

"Yeh, you told me so."

"It settled then?"

"Yeh."

"Good, man," Cummings said, shaking hands with Agrippa, "I sure you gon catch thing."

General Agrippa exited the Officers' Club through the main entrance and walked up to the green Austin 1600. Lance Corporal Kyte was not around.

"Kyte?" Agrippa called out but got no answer. "Is what the skunt going on here?" He went back into the Mess and sought out the concierge. "Look, anyone see me driver?"

"Yes, General. He having a little lunch in the kitchen. I think he finish. He talking with Private Bell."

"Send him down, please. Tell him I'm ready."

"Awright, I gon send he down."

Agrippa went out to the car again, and Kyte came running down the stairs outside the kitchen. He opened the rear door for Agrippa, then started the car.

"Swing by the base, Kyte."

"Yes, Chief of Staff."

The car pulled out of the diagonal driveway, crossed the Airport road, and headed out to the base.

"Just pull up to the gate, Kyte," Agrippa instructed his driver, "We not driving in."

Kyte stopped outside the main gate, stepped out, and opened the rear door for Agrippa. Corporal Liverpool had come out from the Guard Room and was about to swing the main gate open.

"Don't bother, Liverpool," said the Chief, pushing open the smaller side entrance and stepping through it. Corporal Liverpool saluted, as did the guard at the entrance.

"The Duty Officer here?"

"No, sir. He out on inspection. The Orderly Officer upstairs."

"Get him."

General Agrippa walked into the compound and looked around while he waited on Liverpool and the Orderly Officer. About two minutes later, he saw them coming down the outside stairs above the Guard Room. Lieutenant Beharry saluted, "Morning, General."

"Lieutenant Beharry," General Agrippa said very sternly as he acknowledged the salute, "I want to see you and Captain Moore in my office at 09:00 hours tomorrow."

"Yes, General."

General Agrippa waited for Beharry to salute before walking off to his car. The car skirted the fence around the compound, down the hill, and turned right onto the East-bank road to Georgetown. At the entrance to Soesdyke, Agrippa instructed Kyte to take a right turn onto the Linden highway, and they headed for the Co-op College some seven miles up the road.

The watchman at the Co-op compound was very obliging. Cummings had already alerted him about the visit of the army Chief of Staff and had given him instructions. The watchman felt honored to direct the Chief to Cabin 9. Once there, Agrippa did not wait for Kyte to get his door. Anticipation propelled him out of the car. He told Kyte to remain with the car and he walked up to the entrance of the A-frame structure. There was no need to knock. Cummings was already at the door and with him a blast of the Trade Winds' "Six Pence," spinning on the phonograph.

"I glad you could make it, Clive. This gon be a good sport."

Once inside the cabin, Agrippa scanned the room for Brenda, while giving the appearance that he was the checking out the cabin. The cabin was small and simply laid out on a north-south axis. At the south end was a small kitchen with a counter separating it from the rest of the space. Two bedrooms fronted a single bathroom across a narrow hallway at the north end. The rest of the cabin was open. A sofa and three smaller chairs around a coffee table were the only furniture in the open space. The only other table was in the kitchen area behind the counter.

Brenda, who evidently just finished dancing, was sitting with the other women on the sofa, fanning herself with her hand. The accountant was changing the music from records to a reel-to-reel tape deck, requiring less attention. He promised that the new music would really get them wining in no time. Cummings was playing bar-keep behind the kitchen counter.

"You got any beer here?" Agrippa asked.

"No, how about a Bass Ale?"

"That gon work," Agrippa replied.

Cummings reached into the refrigerator and handed Agrippa a Bass Ale, which Agrippa opened and took outside to the car. Handing it to Corporal Kyte, he said, "I gon be a few minutes, Kyte. Just hold on, awright."

"Thank you, General," Kyte said, taking the bottle.

Agrippa went back into the cabin, feeling more relaxed and frisky now that he had bought himself some time. Rejoining Cummings at the kitchen counter, he asked, "What the girls drinking?"

"They had shandies at the Mess, but they taking the hard stuff here," Cummings replied. They both laughed.

"Well, leh me have a quick one with you," Agrippa said, leaning against the counter with his eyes on Brenda. He thought he would make his move after the first drink.

Cummings must have read his thoughts. "We got everything you need here, you know. Just make yuh play!"

Agrippa and Cummings fired off a quick drink, and Cummings added some more rum and Coke to the glasses. The music was now coming from the tape deck, the Pioneer speakers blaring "*You only like me when you want Punanee.*" The accountant was on the floor synchronizing his hips to the melody and producing an exaggerated wiggle that caused the women to laugh and break out in applause. He continued to dance alone, the contortions of his hips evoking roars from the women, which encouraged him to produce even more pronounced gyrations.

Cummings tried to get the women involved. "Come on, ladies, y'all can't let the man dance alone; eh eh!"

The women seemed eager, but the exhortation was evidently not enough. Cummings turned to Agrippa. "Come on, Clive, show we some army moves."

"Yes! Yes!" were the cries from the women. Agrippa took a gulp from his rum and Coke, and with his head swimming from the accelerated infusion of alcohol, stepped out into the open space across from the accountant. He had both arms up out in front above his head, drink in the right hand, imitating but also trying to outdo the hip motions of the accountant. The intense hip competition caused laughing shrieks from the women, who were now themselves standing up. Cummings again encouraged the women to join in as he moved closer, and Agrippa beckoned the women in with his left hand. Success at last—the women were swaying where they stood and gradually moving to the center of the space where the men were. At first, they were just two clusters dancing to the same music, but by the time the next tune came on, the women were paired with the men, Agrippa across from Brenda. The dancing was continuous for several follow-on calypsos before one of the women suggested a breather.

Agrippa took the opportunity to check on his driver outside and to purchase Corporal Kyte's patience with another Bass Ale. When he returned inside, he observed Cummings at the counter fixing drinks and talking up Mavis, or Daphne, Agrippa wasn't sure which, nor did he much care. The accountant was dancing with the other woman to the tunes of Marvin Gaye's *"Let's Get It On,"* and Brenda was off to the side swaying by herself. Agrippa gingerly stepped around the dancing duo and stood behind Brenda. He placed his hands on her hips and began to sway synchronously. Brenda acknowledged his presence, placing her hands over his and tilting her head back until her hair had buried his face in the clearest suggestion of sensuous surrender. Emboldened by this gesture, Agrippa began to guide her toward the back bedroom, their movements flowing with the beat of Marvin Gaye. As they drifted down the hallway, Agrippa slipped his hands down her hips and began to massage her cheeks like a crystal ball whose mysteries he was determined to divine. A few inches through the bedroom door and Agrippa had undone the side zipper and was slipping his hands down the waistband of her skin-tight pants. But pants and panties seemed fused together and both slid downward under the pressure of his hands until his open palms rested on the smooth skin of her very firm cheeks. He unburied his face from her hair to look where his hands received such a great sensation and was exhilarated by the flawlessness of her light brown backside. He knelt down behind her as if to pay homage and buried his face against her cheeks, breathing more quickly and uttering guttural "oohs," as he nibbled here and there. Then the pace of his passion picked up. It must have been the beat of the new calypso, *"How You Could Knock So?,"* that he could hear in the background. With his face against her cheeks, he thrust both hands up between her legs and began to caress her vulva. Then he knelt upright, his chin against her lower back, and reaching forward in front of her, he placed his hands under the cups of her bra and with a quick tug released her breasts from their cotton encumbrance. Rising to a standing position, he rotated her around and, with his hands firmly grasping her breasts, lowered his head to her erect nipples.

FIVE

*A*GRIPPA AWOKE TO A sneezing sensation from Brenda's hair against his face. Lying behind her on his right side, he seemed fused to her, perspiration running down his body and accumulating at every area of contact with hers. He removed his left hand from her backside to check his watch: almost 15:00 hours. Extricating his right arm from under her neck, he lay on his back, looking up at the ceiling. His movements caused Brenda to stir. She repositioned herself facing him but did not open her eyes.

Exhaling short breaths through his mouth, Agrippa pondered his next move. He usually spent Sunday afternoons at the Officers' Mess at Camp Ayanganna. Vera used to go with him, even after the Timehri incident last December, but these past several weeks, she had been making excuses. First came the complaints that he was drinking too much. He promised he wouldn't, but he just enjoyed being with officers and couldn't well pass on the toasts they offered to him. He did get home earlier, though, but Vera would always start fussing after the Padre and Corporal Kyte helped him in from the car. Recently, she had been spending her free time with friends, so she said, but having had her tailed, he knew better. She wouldn't be home when he came back from the Mess, and she would lock herself in the other room after she did get in. He didn't see her again until Monday afternoon. Padre had her tracked a couple of times to the Starlite Drive-In Theater in the company of a Cuban doctor stationed at the Georgetown Public Hospital where she worked. Agrippa's jaws tightened. Imagine, eh, my car! This eye-pass has to stop.

No point going home first, he thought, might as well head for the Mess. Saddle Cadogan should be there by now. And Padre, after he finishes up with church service. What would I do without Padre? But God only knows why he is a preacher though; just like me, the man likes his fun too much. Praise the Lord and pass the bottle!

Padre had said that Vera was causing him to lose respect among the officers, that he should put a stop to what she was doing. He had asked Vera to leave, to go and stay with the children in Canada. But no, she wants to stay around that kiss-me-ass Cuban doctor, Agrippa thought. Well, he'd better watch himself, if he thinks he can come over here and give me blow.

Brenda awoke. She smiled at Agrippa before resting her head on his right shoulder, and he now wondered what he was going to do with her. He definitely wanted to see her again, but he had to set it up right. He could arrange to see her and then leave her with the others; that way he wouldn't be seen in public with her. But contacting her afterwards might be a problem. She probably didn't have a telephone at home, and he wouldn't want to call her at work or have her call him at all. It might be better to just detach her from the others and take her home. That way he could arrange things as they drove back, and he would see where she lived. It was Sunday after all, and there wouldn't be much traffic on the East-bank road or in town for that matter. Yes, that's what he'd do. He began to rise.

"You leaving?" she asked.

"Yes. I got to get back to town. You want me to drop you home?"

"Yes, but I should tell Mavis and Daphne that I going."

"Don't bother waking them up. They gon know you left with me when they don't see you." Brenda agreed. She got out of the bed and began gathering her clothes while Agrippa got dressed. He sat on the side of the bed tying his shoe laces. Over his shoulder, he said, "I'll go out and see what Corporal Kyte is up to. You can come out to the car when you ready."

"Oh-me-God!" she said. "That boy been waiting all this time?"

"Well, he accustomed to it. He probably sleeping in the car. But, don't worry. I gon give him a small piece. He gon be awright."

Agrippa sat in the back seat with Brenda beside him. Since there was no partition between the front seat and the back, Agrippa kept the conversation with Brenda to a minimum. But he looked at her constantly, and she blushed frequently. She was very attractive. There was no doubt in his mind about that. But she was also simple and straightforward.

The car had not been long on the East-bank road to Georgetown when, seemingly at a loss for something to say, Brenda blurted out, "I hope this is not the last time I see you."

No other utterance could have pleased Agrippa more.

"Oh no," he assured her, "no, no."

"Good."

"Yes," he said, recognizing the awkwardness between them and realizing that, but for the sexual encounter, they did not know each other. This was a great advantage to him, he thought. He surely did not want her to know anything more of him than she already did. It would be easier for him to compartmentalize this from the rest of his affairs. What he wanted was secure and unimpeded access to her, a sweet-woman on the side.

Agrippa learned that Brenda lived alone in Georgetown in a room she rented from an old Indian woman. As Brenda described it, the downstairs of the house was divided up into four rooms. Two Indian girls rented one each and two boys from out of town shared the fourth.

"Where is the house?" Agrippa asked.

"It's on Middle Street, between East Street and Cummings."

"Corporal Kyte," Agrippa called to his driver, "did you hear that address?"

"Yes, Chief of Staff."

Brenda worked at the Ministry of Labor and was concerned about layoffs in the Public Service because of the agreement the government had signed with the International Monetary Fund. Agrippa was aware of the layoffs that had already occurred and knew there were going to be a lot more, but he assured her she would not be affected, even though he had no basis for what he said. She seemed pleased, and right now, that was all that mattered to him.

Brenda did not ask any personal questions of Agrippa. She did not even ask about his wife. Maybe she was too intimidated.

"When do you get home from work?" he asked.

"Usually by 4:30."

"I see."

"You can come by."

"You don't go out?" Agrippa asked.

"No. There is too much crime at night. And prices so high for things, what can you do?"

"I see," said Agrippa.

"I used to go to the cinema once in a while with this friend, but he went to Venezuela to look for work. He didn't write or nothing, but I heard he took up with a Spanish lady."

Agrippa listened but wasn't sure whether to say he was sorry or to admit truthfully that he was pleased. He remained silent, hoping his facial expression would communicate sympathy.

The staff car made a right turn from East Street onto Middle Street, and Agrippa asked Brenda to point out the rooming house. It was in a cul-de-sac behind the house fronting Middle Street. The access was an alley wide enough for the car, so Agrippa instructed Kyte to drive in. They came to a stop in front of the aluminum gate. Corporal Kyte got out of the car and opened the back door for Brenda.

"You coming in?" Brenda asked. Agrippa nodded. He was curious about the living arrangement and wanted to know whether it would suffice for his purposes or whether he would have to take her elsewhere. They entered the front door facing the gate. There were two bedrooms on the right and two on the left with a narrow passage in between. Brenda's room was the last room on the right. There was no living room. What was formerly the living room had been compartmentalized and commercialized into four rooms with brown cardboard walls reaching up to about eight feet, leaving about two feet of open space to the ceiling. No one was about, but as the duo walked past the second room on the left, the grunting of lovemaking bombarded them. Brenda looked at Agrippa and giggled. She reached into her side pocket for her room key.

Aroused by the sounds, Agrippa reached forward and began massaging Brenda's behind. Brenda hurriedly opened the door and, preceding Agrippa into the room, turned around to face him. The door slammed, then the cardboard wall bowed and yielded to the intermittent butting from their bodies. The voices from the adjacent rooms rose beyond whispers but did not moderate Agrippa's pace or intensity. Finally, Agrippa stood there panting, his dashiki stuck to his back, and his glasses streaked by sweat. He pulled up his pants, telling Brenda, as he did so, that he was going to be back the next evening.

Agrippa was smiling as he strode triumphantly out, past the women from the two adjacent rooms who had come out for a glimpse of the intruder, to the front door. The car was still running. Corporal Kyte opened the back door for the Chief of Staff. The coolness in the car was so refreshing, Agrippa instructed Kyte to turn up the fan and he stretched out, his face still beaming with pleasure. He could see Kyte glancing back at him through the rearview mirror, and he was sure Kyte knew what had happened from the disheveled appearance he presented when he emerged out of the house, the trace scent of stale perfume sweated onto him. But this just added to the magnitude of his pleasure. He did not speak, except to direct Kyte to drive to the Officers' Mess at Camp Ayanganna.

The Mess was crowded, though the majority of the patrons were civilians. Agrippa knew that this was the club of choice for Party officials and senior civil servants, and he was aware of the grumblings from his officers about extending membership, but he had bowed to outside pressure.

Several officers were sitting on the stools at the bar, and there was a dart game in progress. Most of the tables in the lounge were taken, several of them grouped together to accommodate larger civilian parties. However, at the north end, looking out to the sea wall, was a large table where Padre sat alone. This was Agrippa's favorite table. It commanded the best view, and it was where he was headed.

Agrippa liked his entrances. Virtually everyone looked over at him and wanted to greet him. He walked over to the bar to chat briefly with the junior officers then began to make his way over to the table which the Padre was holding, but he knew it would take a while to get through this reveling gauntlet. Civilians from the first table invited him to have a drink with them. He shook hands with a few men, greeted a couple of others, and was introduced to the women, compliments to whom produced chirps of satisfaction. He repeated this at a couple of other tables before accepting an invitation from a group of Party officials to sit with them. He signaled the Padre to join him, and his host called over to the bar for Private Jarvis to bring a couple more glasses.

"Where is Saddle, boy?" Agrippa asked after the Padre took the seat next to him.

"Where he is every weekend," Padre replied, "the chicken farm."

Agrippa nodded. "He coming?" he asked.

"I believe so," the Padre said. "He should be here anytime now. I haven't seen Lo-lo LaFleur, though."

"You let the man hear you!" Agrippa warned, laughing out loud. "He flew in to Madhia this morning. He might be staying up at Timehri tonight."

The occupants of some of the chairs at their table changed from time to time, but the drinking, laughing, and music continued unabated. By the time Colonel Hartley "Saddle" Cadogan arrived with his sweet-woman, the Chief of Staff was in high spirits. His voice got louder and louder. He was vaguely aware of the steady stream of regular officers looking over as they made their way up to the dining area on the second floor or out of the Mess.

At about 19:00 hours, Colonel Cadogan suggested that they go upstairs for dinner, but Agrippa would have none of it. "Tell them to serve up some snacks down here." Looking over at the bar, he called out "Jarvis! Come, come, Jarvis!"

Jarvis hurried over to Agrippa, who was now standing. "Jarvis, look after your Chief nuh," Agrippa said, his arm around Jarvis' shoulder.

"I trying, Chief," Jarvis said smiling.

"Look, Jarvis, go up and tell the Mess corporal I want to see she."

"Yes, General," Jarvis replied.

"Wait, Jarvis," Padre said. "Chief, let me go up and talk to she. Is what you want?"

"Tell she to send down some snacks. I have guests, you know," Agrippa said, staggering backward and bumping against a chair behind him. Padre rushed over and tried to support him, but Agrippa pushed away his arm.

"I know y'all think I'm drunk, but is not so. I can drink all of you under this table, you know. I can aah—"

"I know," Padre said. "Have a seat, and let me go up and see the Mess corporal."

Agrippa's table was still going strong when Padre returned to join them. The Mess corporal was very quick with the snacks, much to the satisfaction of the civilians, who applauded the Chief on the way he looked after his guests. And Jarvis kept the music going. Some of the civilians from the other tables had left, but the officers were making musical requests of Jarvis while they chatted or played darts. Then the attrition of guests began at Agrippa's table. Each time someone announced he was leaving, Agrippa remonstrated, delaying the departure for a few minutes. By 20:00 hours, everyone at Agrippa's table had left except the three officers, and Colonel Cadogan's sweet-woman, who had gone up to the dining area.

Agrippa sat hunched over the table, staring intently at the glass he was clutching with his hands. He thought he heard Cadogan say something to him, or was it Padre? "Rass!" he uttered loudly, as he tried to straighten up only to fall back to a hunched position. Padre offered to take him home, but he batted his hand in the air. Finally, Padre leaned toward Agrippa, "Is what bothering you, Clive?" he asked.

"Is the damn woman!" Agrippa said. "She all over town with that Cuban fella."

"You should try and make up with Vera, if not—" Colonel Cadogan said.

"Make up? Where? I gon kill that rass! He ain't know who he messing with! I am the Chief of Staff. Who he think he is?" No one responded. Agrippa continued. "I don't care if the government bring he here. He think he gon give me blow? I gon mash he skunt up."

"No, Clive," Padre said, leaning even closer and stretching his arm around the Chief's shoulder, "why bark when you got dog, man?"

The Chief of Staff looked up from his glass at Padre and began nodding. "You're right, Padre. Why bark when you got dog?" The Chief drained his glass before slamming it on the table and wiped his mouth with the back of his hand. "Yes, why bark when you got dog?"

Cadogan's sweet-woman returned to the table but remained standing by the chair.

"Your friend," Agrippa said to Colonel Cadogan of his companion, "look like she checking the door a lot, like she expecting your wife!"

"No, no, no," Cadogan said. "Is just that I promised to take she home early. She got to work in the morning."

"All-yuh abandoning me," Agrippa complained.

"No, no, no, Clive," Saddle protested gently, placing his arm around Agrippa. "Leh we call it a night, nuh. I gon walk with you to the car."

Agrippa muttered a few words then tried standing up. Padre came over and helped him to his feet, supporting him as they walked towards the door. Cadogan and the sweet-woman followed behind.

The car was not outside. No one had sent for Corporal Kyte. Cadogan suspected Kyte was parked in the Motor Transport compound and volunteered to get him. Within a few minutes,

Kyte drove the green staff car up to the entrance of the Officers' Mess and stepped out to help Padre get the Chief of Staff into the car.

Once out of the compound of Camp Ayanganna, the vehicle turned left on Thomas Road for fifty yards or so and then left onto Vlissingen Road toward the seawall. This was the Chief's preferred route to his Bel Air house.

"Leh we get some fresh air," the Chief said, and Kyte lowered the left rear window nearest Agrippa.

Agrippa awoke to Corporal Kyte shaking his shoulder and telling him that they had arrived. He was comfortable where he was, but finally responded to Kyte's pleadings to step out. Once out, Agrippa could not support himself. Kyte slung the Chief's left arm across his shoulder, placed his own right arm around the Chief's waist, and began moving towards the front door. The gate was the first obstacle, but Kyte was able to support the Chief while he opened the gate. The Chief noticed his car was not under the house and began swearing at "that blasted woman." Through the door and up the inside stairway, the Chief continued the swearing, except louder. Upstairs, Kyte asked him whether he wanted to go to bed. Agrippa did not answer but pulled away towards the sofa in the living room, bumping against the coffee table and finally falling into the sofa. He sat himself up.

"You are a good boy, Kyte. Have a drink with me," Agrippa said.

"Thanks, General, but you should go to bed, you know."

"Have a beer man! And leh me have a rum."

Kyte brought the rum and Coke for Agrippa and went back to get a Bass Ale from the refrigerator. Agrippa had already downed the drink when Kyte returned.

"Leh me have another one," Agrippa said.

"General, I gon fix you one and then I got to go. I got to return the staff car to the MT compound, and then I got to go home."

"Awright," the Chief conceded.

Agrippa had slid into a lying position and was muttering when Kyte came back with the drink.

"You want me to set it down?" he asked.

"Yes, put it down," Agrippa replied. He closed his eyes but reopened them when Corporal Kyte said "Goodnight, General." Agrippa had heard Kyte's voice, but did not respond. All he could think about was the emptiness around him and his need to strike out. "Blasted woman! Rass! They ain't know who they messing with. I am the Chief of Staff!" He tried to get up but couldn't support himself. He fell back on the sofa. "I gon tend to them. I got soldiers. Kyte! Corporal Kyte! Ahh . . . Why bark . . ."

SIX

MOORE RETIRED TO BED at 22:15 hours, shortly after he ended his final inspection of the base. He stretched out on the cot facing upward and, almost by habit, clasped his hands and prayed. Then he tried to clear his mind of everything and relax. The cool breeze coming in through the open window helped, and he was tired enough. But he could not fall asleep. There was just too much noise around.Officers returning from Georgetown were opening and closing doors and talking about their weekend activities; nothing uncommon about that, just inconvenient. Finally, the noise subsided, and Moore adjusted his position for what he hoped was the last time. But the silence made things worse. Alone with his thoughts, he began to retrace the events of the day.

He had not called Jeanene that evening because he was afraid to tell her about the bomb threat and about what he thought motivated the hoax. He was sure the other officers on the scene thought the same thing. The British officer was no fool; neither was Captain Mitchell, for that matter, except he was embarrassed that the searching of passengers had occurred in front of a foreign officer. Beharry had figured it out too, but the episode would be relegated to the what-can-I-do-about-it column, Moore thought. He wished he could just push it aside but it was hard not to wonder about the type of desperation that would cause government people to call in a bomb threat and use it as a pretext to search the bags of passengers. What would happen next week when somebody else calls in a bomb threat? Christ! The irresponsibility of it all!

He recalled the Customs men saying they were following orders, but he felt certain they knew there was no bomb on that plane. The army officers were nervous during the search. Not the Customs men! They were organized, ready to take names. They could have searched the bags at the time of check-in, but they evidently wanted everyone at the airport to observe the entire spectacle, subjecting people to one final humiliation.

The faces made a lasting impression on Moore, not that he knew any of them. They seemed beaten and frustrated. Gone was the joy and the sense of celebration they had exuded earlier in the day when he had driven by the airport. And their clothes, so bright and colorful earlier, were soiled by sweat. They too had figured out the real purpose of the search and, with their resignation to the search, came stares of condemnation at their harassers, mutterings up and down the inspection lines against the falseness of the search, and symbolic acts of defiance. He thought of the Indian woman with a bottle of pepper sauce wrapped to prevent leakage on her clothes. She was taking it to a relative in New York. When asked by Captain Mitchell to unwrap the package, she complied. But as soon as he was through with her suitcase, she walked over and threw the bottle into the trash, as if the search had contaminated the contents.

Then there was the Chief of Staff and his illicit trading activities! Moore had heard the rumors; it was, after all, a small army. But this was the first time he had been confronted by one of the schemes. And in the course of official duties! Imagine the army Chief of Staff conducting himself like a common huckster!

The Chief had been uppermost in Moore's mind all morning, until lunchtime and the bomb threat. Now the prospect of a face-to-face confrontation was making him tense, but he was determined to stand his ground. With that, he rolled over on his side.

*   *   *

Moore jerked awake. Jesus, what was that? Must have been a door slam. Boots down the hallway. Running water. Flushing toilets. Voices. Must be time for PT. For the others anyway. He didn't have to go. Perhaps the only perk for being the Duty Officer. He could hear the talking in the ablution area. Much louder, all of a sudden, and laughter. Would be hard to go back to sleep now. He thought of his meeting with the Chief of Staff. That was enough to keep him awake. Then he heard the outside door slam and several pairs of boots down the stairs. The voices receded, and he dozed off.

Then came the locomotive. No, it couldn't be. There weren't any locomotives in the country, not anymore. Just several platoons shuffling down the main road. In front of the Officers' Quarters, they broke into a familiar chant:

Hey, auntie-man Jukka! Hey auntie-man, Jukka!
Hey, auntie-man Jukka, lemme lone, lemme lo-lo-lone.
Hey, auntie-man Jukka!

In a few minutes, they were down the hill in the direction of Georgetown, and he couldn't hear them. But there would be other contingents with other chants. Better get up and get started. Soon the other officers would be back, and there'd be lines for showers.

At 06:50, he was ready. Pressed fatigues with three pips inserted on each epaulette, lanyard, glasses, spit-shined boots, puttees, and stable belt. Beret secured under the left epaulette, he took one last look in the mirror and left the room for the Mess.

Moore entered the dining area to find other officers already at breakfast. Some had no doubt spent the weekend at Georgetown and only just returned to Timehri. Others might have attended the reveille formation and skipped PT. And then there was Colonel LaFleur, Llewelyn Ovid LaFleur, Lo-lo for short. The battalion commander was sitting like Buddha at the center of the horseshoe configuration.

"Morning, Colonel," Moore said briskly to the most senior rank present.

"Morning, Alan," replied Colonel LaFleur. "How you do, Alan? How you do?"

"Half and half, Colonel."

"Understand you had a lot of activity here yesterday?"

"Yes, Colonel, we had a bomb threat at the airport." Moore elected not to mention the incident with the Chief of Staff, but he was sure LaFleur already knew about it.

"You handled that very well, Alan."

"Thank you, Colonel," Moore replied, scanning the room. No one sat on either side of LaFleur. Lieutenant Beharry and two other junior officers sat on the eastern wing away from the Mess entrance. On the western wing, directly across from Beharry sat Captain Malcolm Felix, another company commander in Colonel LaFleur's battalion. Moore took the seat to the right of Captain Felix. From there, he was in full diagonal view of the Colonel.

He had hardly sat down when Captain Felix, in a loud, jocular tone, asked, "So, why you didn't give the man the jeep yesterday, Alan?"

Here it comes, Moore thought. He smiled and shrugged, electing not to commit himself yet. He looked over at Colonel LaFleur. A stocky, pitch-black man in his late forties, LaFleur smiled uncomfortably and seemed to be studying the newspaper as he chewed, but Moore was sure he would follow every word.

"I hear you've been summoned to Camp Ayanganna," Captain Felix continued in a loud stilted tone.

"Yes, as a matter of fact," Moore replied. Then, deciding he was standing on a principle, he boldly declared, "Imagine officers getting rebuked for carrying out Standing Orders."

"You'll be lucky if is only a rebuke you get," Captain Felix warned. "I hear the man vex bad."

"Is so?" Moore asked, not really expecting a response.

"Oh yes. It is all over Camp Ayanganna. Is going be high noon when you get there. But we with you."

"That's good to know. What would you have done, Malcolm?" Moore asked Captain Felix.

"Same as you. He off duty. He ain't entitled to no jeep to transport his stuff. Don't peel and crack while you're down there."

"I gon try not to," Moore replied.

Moore looked over at the Colonel again and then at the junior officers, who seemed to be listening with keen interest. Everyone seemed to be expecting a comment from LaFleur. But he did not speak, not on that subject. To support Moore would be to criticize the Chief of Staff. That he would not do, Moore was sure. Everyone there knew he was close to the Chief. On the other hand, there was no way he could approve of the Chief of Staff's actions in front of this group of officers. He changed the conversation.

"Alan, I will meet with the company commanders when you get back from Camp Ayanganna. After lunch?"

"Yes, Colonel," Moore replied, looking directly at the Colonel.

"We need to talk about the deployment. You know F-Company is going to Berbice County?"

"No, Colonel, I wasn't sure where along the coast we would be deployed," Moore said.

"Yes, F-Company will now be attached to the 2nd Battalion, so be sure to talk to Colonel Cadogan while you are at Camp Ayanganna."

"Yes, Colonel," Moore said almost mechanically, noting the uncontrollable gleam flickering from LaFleur's front gold teeth as he spoke. Like the intermittent beam from a lighthouse during a fog, it struck Moore as a flashing "Beware" sign.

Colonel LaFleur picked up his newspapers and left the dining area. Private Bell brought out a plate with two hard boiled eggs and a rice flour bake. Moore took a bit of the rice bake and set it aside. He tasted the sugar, but the rice flour was grainy and flat. The eggs should suffice, he thought.

"Imagine what the army coming to," Captain Felix said loudly. "We have to use soldiers to cut sugar cane." He was joined by a chorus of supporting protests from the lieutenants across the room, emboldened no doubt by the departure of Colonel LaFleur.

"Well, you know what they say, Comrade," Moore replied cynically, "'this time na stan like before time.'"

"You can say that again," one lieutenant exclaimed, and everyone laughed.

Lieutenant Beharry came over to tell Moore he would get the jeep and be outside the Officers' Mess in ten minutes. Moore finished the second egg and decided he had time for a second cup of coffee.

"Bear your chafe," Captain Felix counseled sympathetically.

"I gon try."

SEVEN

THE 1/4-TON WAS WAITING for Moore by the front stairway of the Mess, Lieutenant Beharry seated in the rear. Moore entered and motioned to McCurchin to drive. It was 07:45. The vehicle crossed the Airport road and headed toward the base HQ compound.

The main gate was open, and the vehicle entered and pulled up in front of the Guard Room on the ground floor of the Admin Building. The Base Commander's office was on the second floor, at the far end. Knowing that the Base Commander usually walked but would be there on time, the officers waited in the long breeze-way connecting the Admin Building with the enlisted ranks' canteen, leaning over the rail facing the flagpole, but in full view of the Base Commander's office.

"I, for one, am glad we going to Berbice," Beharry said. "Three months in the damn bush can drive a man crazy. Women, finally!"

"And sugar cane too, don't forget," Moore added, smiling.

Soldiers were sauntering across the main square, empty mess kits and cups in hand. The entire compound seemed to have an air about it that said "Not open for business." It's just amazing, Moore thought, how 08:00 hours will transform this compound. Come back at 08:01 hours and you will find a smartness in uniform, a briskness in walk, and an air of officiousness about everyone.

"Corporal Trim," the Base Commander's voice boomed.

"Sir!"

"Why are those soldiers loitering by the fence?"

"Major, I think they with Engineer Squadron."

"Corporal Trim, I don't care who they with. They shouldn't be by the fence whistling at women. Move them along!"

"Yes, sir!"

Moore and Beharry watched Major David MacAndrew ascend the outside stairs of the Admin Building. A few moments later, the slim six-footer was unlocking the door to his office. Moore gave him a couple minutes to settle in, then at 08:02 he knocked twice and entered.

Major MacAndrew was a mulatto man, proud of his British training, his Scottish father, no longer around, and ashamed of his black mother, visits from whom he discouraged. Such was the reputation he had. But the British were gone and blackness was in, so when "The Legend of Nigger Charlie" began playing at the local cinemas, he took to wearing "Nigger Charlie" tee-shirts off duty.

Moore saluted. He began his report by noting that the most significant incident had occurred at the Timehri airport. He described the bomb threat and the role played by the Customs officers. The Base Commander had evidently heard about the bomb threat, but this was the first time he was hearing the details.

"If they wanted to check people's bags, why didn't they do it before they loaded the damn plane?" the Base Commander asked and sucked his teeth.

Moore interpreted the question as rhetorical, since the Base Commander's upraised arms and eyebrows suggested exasperation. He told the Base Commander about the request for the 1/4-ton jeep on standby and his reason for declining the Chief of Staff its use; the Base Commander sat with clenched teeth during this part of the report. Moore concluded by letting him know that he and the weekend Orderly Officer had been summoned to Camp Ayanganna on this matter. MacAndrew shook his head this time but said nothing. Moore was disappointed—he had expected support for his action from the senior officer in charge of the base. Christ, he thought, everybody's thinking about their own survival. After a moment of awkward silence, the Base Commander asked about the redeployment of Moore's company to the coast and expressed the hope that the soldiers would not have to cut sugar cane. His report now over, Moore saluted and left the room.

Lieutenant Beharry then knocked and went in to render his report. In a few minutes, he was out and expressed to Moore his disappointment with the Base Commander's reluctance to criticize or support the actions of the two officers charged with ensuring the security of the base over the weekend. Moore listened as they hurried out to the jeep waiting for them by the flagpole. Without breaking his stride, he said to Beharry, "Look, Ramesh, we're on we own here. Don't bother with that rotten rope upstairs. He doesn't stand up for his own mother." He looked at his watch—it was now 08:15. He got in the jeep beside McCurchin and waited until Beharry had seated himself in the rear. "Awright, McCurchin."

Out of the gate, the jeep made a hard right, traveling along the compound fence then down the hill before taking a right onto the East-bank road to Georgetown. This was a regular commute for these officers, and Moore knew that on a good day you could cover the thirty miles to Georgetown in half of an hour. But at this time of day, they were likely to contend with school buses and rush hour traffic into Georgetown. Glancing over his shoulder, Moore could see the anxious expression on Lieutenant Beharry's face. He himself was not in a mood to speak. Besides, there wasn't anything to talk about. For him, the trip amounted to counting off the seventeen or so villages between Timehri and Georgetown, and that was all the thinking he planned to do.

Driving on the left-hand side of the two-lane road put the jeep within a few feet of the river's edge at several points on the way. Most of the rest of the time Moore could see the water between clumps of bamboo trees. The breeze coming through the open window was a soothing moderation of the sun's warmth, but Moore was certain Lieutenant Beharry would soon be sweating at the back of the jeep.

In less than five minutes, the jeep entered Soesdyke and, as they passed through the center of the village, Moore could hear the random voices of children coming from the primary school, a drab, weather-worn, two-storied structure tucked away behind the last row of houses on the right side of the road. The houses in Soesdyke were just a little less faded. What wonders a good coat of paint would work! But paint, like everything else these days, was scarce and expensive.

Soesdyke ended just past the junction for the perpendicular highway rolling out for some thirty miles to the mining town of Linden, but at the edge of its ill-defined border was the welcome sign of the Kiskadee Club on the left, a night club known for its importation of exotic dancers. Moore had never been there, but his two junior colleagues, Beharry and Mentore, had gone to see Madame Suki perform. The stories they told when F-Company was last posted to the interior savannahs may have been embellished and repetitive, but they held the interest of the soldiers and shored up morale when it seemed to be flagging.

From Soesdyke, the jeep sped through the B-line, as the soldiers called the next set of villages—small shacks alternating with large areas of bush. Then a wooden sign read "Garden of Eden." Here the army's Farm Corps maintained a huge farm, mostly between the road and the river. Soldiers were at work in the vegetable garden, and Moore could see the long rows of chicken coops, behind which construction was going on for pig pens.

At the next bend of the river was the village of Craig. No school or post office, but a very compact village with houses visible through the mango and genip trees in the front yards. From here, most of the villages were larger, less isolated and more urban, as though preparing travelers for Georgetown. This was the case with Grove, with its road-front cinema, its cake shops, beer gardens, and empty-shelved grocery stores. But Grove ended abruptly, and the road entered a solitary stretch that regurgitated the country's ugly history of slavery and indenture. This stretch of road marked the beginning of Diamond, the former British sugar plantation, now under state control. On the right side of the road, across from the drainage canal, sugar cane as far as the eye could see. On the left side, a more limited sugar cane field, but carved out of the field was a narrow strip of land parallel to the road set aside for a neat row of logies—slave quarters on stilts—each exactly the same as the other, a charcoal shingled rectangular box with one visible, wooden window and one external stairway. Passed from slaves to indentured servants and now lived in by their descendants, this row of slave quarters always gave Moore a sinking feeling as he passed by. Imagine this in a socialist system, he thought. And they say the goal is to make the small man a real man. Not in Diamond!

Just past the row of logies, the road rose to meet the bridge by the Diamond sugar factory and rum distillery. From the top of the bridge, Moore surveyed the sea of bungalows to his left front. Huge and brightly painted amidst large shade trees in fenced compounds with manicured lawns, these now housed the black and brown socialist successors of the European planters. To Moore, the new owners appeared to be just as indifferent to the plight of the downtrodden as were their white predecessors. What did George Orwell say about when the animals looked from man to pig and pig to man.?

Out of Diamond and its satellite villages and into Providence. I wonder how many slaves made it, Moore asked himself. Not many, judging from Providence's most visible and well-known landmark, the large creamish-yellow police station on the right, surrounded on three sides by sugar cane. Sugar cane and the law: old allies from the 1600s!

Now into Peters Hall, the traffic in both directions had picked up. The opposing traffic was probably heading to the Timehri airport for the eleven o'clock flight. The traffic ahead of the jeep was part of the rush hour traffic into Georgetown. The jeep came to a stop behind a tandem bus which was picking up passengers, several of them school children. How dangerous, Moore thought, to have one bloody bus towing another bus, and both taking on passengers.

"McCurchin, see if you can get around the buses," Moore said.

"Too much traffic the other way, Captain."

"Christ!" Moore uttered, looking at the rear end of the drab, gray Tata bus being towed.

"My uncle used to be a private bus owner," Beharry said. "It was a silver and blue bus that made short stops along the West Demerara Coast."

"Well," said Moore glancing over his right shoulder, "now we have tandem buses!"

He too remembered the large colored buses that plied the coast only a few years ago. They were beautiful buses with diamond-shaped luggage compartments on top. The red buses made the longer runs along the coast, from the mouth of one river to the next; the green and the two-toned buses ran to some point mid-way or along the river banks. Like race horses, they had names—*Duke of York, June Flower, Zorina, Her Highness, Debonair*—dignified names, Moore thought, and loyal fans. Older villagers timed their activities by the passage of particular buses on the road. It was said that housewives in Bengal, Tarlogie, and neighboring villages along the Corentyne Coast began cooking supper when *Blue Bird*, a large red bus, passed on its final run from Skeldon to New Amsterdam. Now all that color was gone—drab, gray, nameless Tata buses had replaced *June Flower, Her Highness,* and *Blue Bird*. The replacements had no luggage compartments above, and the drivers and conductors were government men, who called each other and everyone else "comrade." With very little money available for spare parts, the buses were becoming laid up, and the survivors limped along like the tandem bus now blocking Moore's way.

The last of the passengers had climbed aboard, and the buses moved forward.

"Try to get around this bus!" Moore ordered.

"Yes, Captain."

McCurchin tried several times to peer over the center line, but oncoming traffic made him pull the jeep back behind the buses. It was not until the buses entered Agricola that McCurchin was able to accelerate around them. Then it was around one short-drop hire car after another. Stop. Accelerate around. Stop.

"Christ!" Moore said, exasperated. He knew that this was going to be the pattern all the way to Georgetown. It was the same in Eccles. As they passed the street to his home, he wondered if Jeanene had already taken Candy to school. It was now 08:50. There was now no question in his mind that they were going to be late for the appointment with the Chief of Staff.

The traffic was worse in Houston. Now only a few miles from the southwestern entrance to Georgetown, the buses were bunching up. There were trucks and horse-drawn dray carts, bicyclists and pedestrians, and peddlers of all types. Beharry had moved closer to the front and was trying to calm Moore down.

"Alan, the Chief of Staff knows what the traffic into town is like."

"I don't want to give the man any cause."

"Well, Alan, I don't think we can help it. We're going to be late."

"Christ!"

McCurchin kept moving the jeep to the center of the road for a peek at the oncoming traffic but pulled back each time. It was just slow going. Finally, they entered South Ruimveldt, the industrial section of Georgetown. The pedestrian traffic was much heavier. People were walking to or from Georgetown. School children were crossing the road at various points, dodging between vehicles. Radios were blaring calypsos from the Morning Show. Car horns tooted, incessantly it seemed. Caught in this traffic, the jeep drifted towards the Independence Arch. Once inside, Moore directed McCurchin to take a right turn onto Carifesta Avenue and bypass the city. Even then, he knew it would take at least seven minutes before they would turn onto Thomas Road.

EIGHT

AT 09:23 HOURS, THE jeep pulled up to the main gate at Camp Ayanganna behind a car with civilian occupants. The corporal at the gate was pointing out buildings on the base to them. Already late for his meeting, Moore wished they would hurry it up so that his jeep could be logged in. A loud cackle of voices came from the benab outside of the fence just to the right of the main gate. The benab was almost half-full, mostly women, doubtless here to seek child support payments from soldiers or to present domestic problems to the officers in charge of their men. The handful of men in the benab were probably looking for work.

The car moved off, and the jeep inched forward. The corporal saluted Captain Moore and waved him on. In front of the Guard Room, the jeep turned left and pulled up in front of the army headquarters building, a white, two-storied bungalow with a wide porch running the length of the building on both levels. Except for waist-high siding, the porches opened out to the drill square facing Thomas Road. The rest of the building was sectioned off into offices, whose doors opened into the porch. At each end of the building was an internal stairway. Moore and Beharry went up the eastern stairway to the second floor. There were three offices at this end, the Chief of Staff's being the furthest at the northeast corner. Moore thought they should report their presence to the Brigade Adjutant, Major Dennis Angoy. He knocked twice at the first door.

"Yes!" came the answer from inside, and Moore led the way in. He and Beharry saluted.

"Morning, Major," Moore said. "We have an appointment with the Chief of Staff."

Major Angoy looked at his watch and raised his eyebrows. "I know," he acknowledged. "He's waiting for you." Angoy rose from his chair and moved around his desk towards the door. "Look, Alan, take it easy, eh? Don't provoke the man."

"Dennis, we shouldn't be here in the first place. The man made an unlawful request."

"Don't worry with that now. The man said you were disrespectful to him and you teaching younger officers like Beharry to do this same thing."

Moore was exasperated. He was about to explode when Angoy said, "Let's go."

They had just exited Angoy's office and walked a couple of paces when the Chief of Staff stepped out into the hallway and advanced towards them. They saluted, and the Chief of Staff acknowledged the salute.

"General, Captain Moore and Lieutenant Beharry to see you," Angoy said.

"These officers are late, and I don't have time to see them now. Have them report to Major Farley. He knows what to do." The Chief strode past.

"Yes, General," Angoy said.

"Come in here for a minute," Angoy said to the two officers.

"Is what going on here, Dennis?" Moore asked. "Why Farley? He's the Base Commander for Camp Ayanganna. What's he got to do with this?"

"He has trial authority," Angoy replied.

"We are going to be tried?"

"It's what the man wants."

"On what charge?" Lieutenant Beharry asked.

"If it's disobedience of an order, that's a court-martial offense," Moore said.

"I don't think he wants to go that far," Angoy replied. "Look, Alan, just bear your chafe."

"Is everybody telling me to bear me chafe and nobody saying what's right and what's wrong! What he did was damn wrong, and y'all know it."

Angoy shrugged his shoulders. "Y'all better go down and see Farley."

Moore felt frustrated. He had expected the Chief of Staff to shout at them in his office, but he did not anticipate being charged and tried. He figured there was no point in trying to press Angoy any more. He saluted, as did Beharry, and they left. They walked down the stairs and knocked at the door of Captain Ronald Stephenson, the Base Commander's Executive Officer.

"Let me do the talking," Moore said to Lieutenant Beharry.

Stephenson invited them in and offered them a seat.

"The Chief of Staff said Major Farley was expecting us," Moore said.

"Weh . . . Weh . . . well yes," said Stephenson, "bu . . . but the thing is that I have to ahm charge each of you sep . . . sep . . . separately and then ma . . . ma . . . march you in."

"What's the charge?" Moore asked.

"I ain't know. What you think the ah . . . ah charge should be?"

"You asking me? The man came in civvies on a Sunday and asked me to violate Standing Orders at Camp Stevenson by giving him an emergency vehicle to transport personal goods and y'all charging me! And then you asking me to tell you what the charge should be!"

"Ah..ah..Alan, is not we. Is the Chief say so."

"I see," Moore said. "Well, do what you have to do."

"Huh . . . huh . . . how about dis . . . disobedience of a verbal or . . . order?"

"What order did I disobey?"

"Is . . . Is the thing that," Stephenson said. Moore and Beharry exchanged glances. "Huh . . . huh . . . how about con . . . conduct unbecoming?"

"What conduct? How did I disgrace myself?"

"You..ah, you . . . ahm right. That not gon work. How about Article 17? Con . . . Con . . . Conduct to the pre . . . prejudice of good or . . . order and di . . . di . . . discipline?"

Moore looked over at Beharry and they both chuckled. Stephenson appeared a bit embarrassed but was laughing too.

"Look, Ronald, leh we get this thing over," Moore said.

"Aw . . . awright," Stephenson said. "Lemme ah . . . ah go in and tell the Base Commander the charge and I . . . ah gon come back and teh . . . teh . . . take you in, one . . . one at a time."

In a couple of minutes, Stephenson reentered the room and asked Moore to go with him. They marched into Major Farley's office. Moore saluted and Farley acknowledged. Stephenson read the charge falteringly, and Farley invited Moore to respond. Moore recounted the events of the previous day and ended by asking Major Farley why he was being charged when he was carrying out his orders.

Major Farley was fidgeting while Moore gave his account of his dealings with the Chief of Staff. Finally, Moore pressed him to explain why they were charged for carrying out their orders. Farley shifted his position a couple of times in his chair, cleared his throat, and then replied, "Alan, the Chief of Staff said you insulted him."

"How?" asked Moore.

"I don't know. I wasn't there."

"He requested a jeep to transport personal goods while off-duty. As Duty Officer, I was in charge of the security of the base at Camp Stevenson. I only had one jeep available and Standing Orders stipulate how that vehicle should be used. I told the Chief of Staff that. I was not insulting him."

"Well, he said you insulted him."

"What would you have done, Major? Would you have violated Standing Orders to provide him with the vehicle?"

"I am not saying that."

"What are you saying, Major?"

"Look, Alan. You know that I ain't got anything against you, but the Chief of Staff wants me to find you guilty."

"Well, Major. No point wasting any more time. What's the punishment?"

"Six months' loss of seniority."

"Six months?" Moore stared at Farley.

"Sorry, Alan," Farley said.

Moore said nothing else. They both knew that he was coming up for promotion to major in December. The calculated nature of the penalty was meant to hurt him, and it did. The silence was uncomfortable for both Farley and Stephenson. Finally, Farley turned to Stephenson.

"Ronald, I'll take Lieutenant Beharry now."

Moore knew he was being dismissed. He saluted and left the room. He went out in the hallway and simply stood there, teeth clenched, gazing at the flagpole.

Meanwhile, Lieutenant Beharry was marched into Major Farley's office to respond to a charge. After a couple of minutes, Captain Stephenson stepped out to get Moore. Lieutenant Beharry had described his role in the affair and had exercised his right to call a witness. Moore pointed out that the entire responsibility was his and that Lieutenant Beharry had simply followed the orders he had issued. He was then excused from further participation.

When Beharry emerged from Farley's office, Moore was waiting in the hall.

"Did he fine you?" Moore asked.

"No. He dismissed the charge."

"Good. The damn thing was trumped up to begin with."

"How about you, Alan?"

"Six months' loss of seniority."

"Six months?" Beharry said. "I'm so sorry, Alan."

"Well, Farley said he was told to find us guilty. At least he had the decency to let you go."

"This is so ridiculous though," Beharry observed.

"Is a new army from when we joined," Moore said.

"The People's Army!" Beharry's sarcastic tone brought out a smile on Moore's face.

"Which 'people'? They should rename it 'Some People's Army.'" They laughed.

"But six months' loss of seniority!" Beharry reflected aloud. "Boy, the man's vicious!"

Moore said nothing as he led the way down the steps onto the road. He looked at his watch—10:25. "Better let's go and see Colonel Cadogan. Look's like we in a parade before scoundrels this morning!"

2nd Battalion Headquarters was housed in a two-storied building across the street and up from the Guard Room. The two officers walked up the outside stairs to the landing and found the right half of the wooden door ajar. Moore entered first. Lance Corporal Patricia Seopaul, a dougla woman in her twenties, looked up from her typewriter and uttered a perfunctory "Good morning, Captain," followed by a "Good morning, Lieutenant."

"Exec in?" Moore asked.

"Yes, Captain," Seopaul replied, rising and walking over to the first office on the right where she stood in the doorway.

"Excuse me, Captain Isaacs. Captain Moore and Lieutenant Beharry to see you."

"Send them in," came the reply from inside.

"Leonard," said Moore as he entered Isaacs' office, "What's happening?"

"I should ask you that," Isaacs replied. "I hear you crossed the Chief of Staff."

"Word does get around," Moore said.

"What did they fine you?"

"Six months' loss of seniority."

"You joking?"

"Nah. Is true."

"How about young Beharry here?"

"He got spared."

"Good. You here to see the CO?"

"Yeh."

"Awright, leh we go in. Ramesh, take a seat."

Isaacs knocked on Colonel Cadogan's door.

"Come in, Leonard!"

Isaacs walked in ahead of Moore. Moore saluted and Cadogan acknowledged him. "Y'all sit down," Cadogan said. Moore looked at his new commanding officer and wondered if he had been cast out of the frying pan into the fire.

Colonel Hartley "Saddle" Cadogan sat forward in his chair, elbows resting on his desk. A light-brown man in his mid-forties, he had a thin moustache on a rectangular face, and his thinning hair exposed a receding, mound-shaped forehead, which dipped sharply before rising again to a normal roundness. The pronounced dip had earned him the nickname "Saddle" in primary school, so it was told. Cadogan looked over at Captain Moore as if expecting him to speak.

"Colonel," Moore began, "Colonel LaFleur suggested that I stop by and see you about the rotation."

"Ah yes," said Cadogan. "You coming with me, boy. F-Company is going to be deployed along the coast, in Berbice County."

"When do you want me to move out from Camp Stevenson?"

"Tomorrow morning. You can cross with the 05:00 ferry."

"What's the mission, sir?"

"To prevent sabotage. We have a political strike in the sugar industry. The government believes the Opposition agents will set fires to the sugar-cane fields. Try to stop them."

"So, will F-Company have to cut cane?"

"No, no, no. Look, you have to patrol the sugar estates to prevent sabotage. Also you got to provide security for the scabs they bringing in to do the work." Moore nodded to indicate he understood.

"Another thing," Cadogan added, leaning backward in his chair, "you got to search for arms. You know the drill. Go in there and terrorize their backsides!" Cadogan leaned back in his chair.

Moore stared intently at Cadogan.

"Look, Alan," Cadogan said, leaning forward again, "your politics might be different from the rest of we—"

"Colonel, I am army officer," Moore protested, "I am not a politician!"

"Maybe so," Cadogan responded, holding up what Moore recognized as a copy of the *Weekly Church Bulletin*, and letting it fall back on his desk. "We all know that your uncle is criticizing the government."

"Colonel, why is my uncle coming into this?"

"Well, people are wondering if you're reliable or not. Now I know you since you were a sub-lieutenant, since you came back from West Point. I know you awright. But some people think you've sold out."

Moore was exasperated at this back-handed compliment, but he knew that Cadogan was revealing the thinking of some senior officers. He had just fallen out with the Chief of Staff. He did not want to offend Cadogan, who was now going to be his commanding officer, so he remained silent.

"Look, I know you gon do a good job," Cadogan added.

"Thank you, Colonel," Moore said, recognizing that Cadogan was probably just trying to mollify him.

The feeling of loneliness that came over Moore was aggravated by the realization that he might not be able to see his family before the redeployment. He wanted to see Jeanene, especially after the phoney trial. Six months' loss of seniority. Now, it seems, he has to do everything they say or risk being called anti-government. He felt tired in spirit. He wished he could just leave. Once and for all, he thought. But it all depended on the papers coming through. Seven years already. His thoughts were interrupted by Colonel Cadogan.

"Have you decided where you gon put your command post?"

"New Amsterdam, Colonel."

"Just as I thought. Home turf, not so?"

"It is, but that's not the reason. It was either Rose Hall or Skeldon. I preferred Rose Hall but the Senior Staff Club there is under repairs, so we will set up camp outside of New Amsterdam."

"Just keep the soldiers away from the whorehouses," Colonel Cadogan said. They all laughed. "Is almost lunch time," Cadogan observed. "Why you don't get some lunch before you head back to Timehri? You'll probably see Captain Seepersaud. His company will be deployed on this side of the Berbice River. You might want to coordinate some things with him."

"Good idea, Colonel."

Moore saluted and left Cadogan's office, Captain Isaacs walking behind him. They paused briefly in front of Isaacs' office. Beharry was not there. They could hear him talking to Lance Corporal Seopaul in the reception area.

"Look like your boy Beharry trying to catch thing! Better tell him she is the Colonel's woman."

"I thought she was with his driver."

"That don't mean nothing," Isaacs replied. They both laughed.

"I gon see you, Leonard."

"Right."

Moore discussed the meeting with Beharry as they walked toward the Officers' Mess, the attention of both officers intermittently drawn to the gleeful squawking of the kingfishers and to the splashes from the incoming tide against the seawall protecting Georgetown from the Atlantic. The saltiness of the sea breeze in Moore's lungs felt purifying, and he could have walked on, inhaling more, but the road ended just past the Mess.

They entered through the main entrance fronting the road. The bar area was empty, except for the private behind the bar lazily rearranging glasses and bottles. He must have just come on duty, Moore thought, since it was a bit early for lunch. Moore ordered a Coke and was about to joke about Cadogan's head when Beharry interrupted him.

"How long has Saddle owned the chicken farm?"

"About six months. Why?"

"Nothing in particular. Is just that it's the first thing that comes to mind whenever his name is mentioned."

"I know. That's all he cares about too. The army just providing him with status and a labor force."

"What you mean?"

"Well, at the time he bought the land off the Linden Highway, about twenty-five acres or so, it was all bush. He got it really cheap from the government. And then clearing the land was easy."

"How so?"

"Be serious. The man had a battalion of over five hundred men. It was easy to get some of them on the property. Rank, and a few bottles of rum could go a long way, you know."

"How about equipment?"

"Hey, all he had to do was soft soap the CO of Engineer Squadron. They have chain saws, bulldozers, everything."

"And he got away with it?"

"Of course. Who gon stop he? Look, I wouldn't loan an operational jeep to the Chief of Staff, and you see where it got me?"

"Sorry, Alan. But why chickens?"

"What do you mean 'why chickens?'? Have you seen the price of a pound of frozen chicken?"

"No."

"Well, the army's got you spoiled. Jeanene has to go out and buy those things. It's about ten dollars a pound."

"What I meant was that Saddle didn't have any expertise on chickens."

"He didn't have to. All he had to do was go up the road to the Farm Corps at Garden of Eden. Who you think built his chicken pens? Who do you think takes care of the baby chicks for the first few weeks? Who do you think does the plucking for him?"

"I thought he did that himself!" Beharry responded quickly.

Moore laughed out loud. "You getting good, Beharry!"

Beharry was smiling too. "Anyway, I hear Saddle and the Farm Officer don't get along."

"Now maybe, because Saddle asking too much of the poor fella." Moore took a large swallow of the syrupy sweet drink and was waiting for the cold aftershock in his head to pass when he heard a familiar voice call out in his direction.

"Well, look who they let in here!"

Moore turned his head over his left shoulder just as Captain Seepersaud slapped his back and sat on the stool to the left.

"I heard about the 1/4-ton incident. Sorry, man. To tell the truth, I don't know what I woulda done if it was me."

"Well, it over now," Moore said.

"What did they fine you?"

"Six months' loss of seniority."

"Six months?"

"Yeh. Did you ever hear of officers being tried like this?"

"Different times, boy," Seepersaud said. "But six months, eh? That man really gunning for you. You and I were to come up for major in December."

"Well," said Moore, changing the subject, "did you hear F-Company coming down to the coast?"

"Yeh. Berbice County, right?"

"Yeh. How about B-Company?"

"East Coast Demerara and West Coast Berbice. I plan to set up my command post at the Enmore Sugar Estate."

"Boy, you're lucky. That's next door to the university. How come they letting you do this?"

"Well, I have one more year to finish up. I had requested disembodiment from the army, but they said they would consider it after the election."

Lieutenant Ingrid Peters entered the lounge and seated herself next to Lieutenant Beharry, who moved his stool closer to hers. Other officers were also entering the lounge. Moore continued his conversation with Captain Seepersaud but lowered his voice to a whisper.

"Ken, what's the position on your sponsorship?"

"I expect everything to be wrapped up by the end of the year."

"That's fast. You know I've been waiting for seven years."

"Is faster to Canada, but you should get through anytime now, from what I hear. Don't worry."

"Jeanene's worried they not going to let me go when the time comes."

"Don't ask them."

"How else you gon get out?"

"Abscond."

"You serious?"

"Of course. You got a valid passport, not so?"

"Yeh?"

"Well, the last time you went overseas on a course, did anyone stop you?"

"No."

"Well, just leave the same way, like you were going overseas on a course, except you don't come back."

"You would get arrested if you ever come back, though."

"You plan to come back here, Alan?"

Moore looked at Seepersaud. He had thought of leaving, but he always imagined he would return to visit. Most people did, but he understood from Seepersaud's question what the price might be for absconding. He did not answer. Seepersaud rose from his stool clearly intending to go upstairs to lunch. Moore looked around for Beharry, but Beharry was not there. He must have gone up with Ingrid Peters, Moore thought.

"That's Beharry's woman, you know," Seepersaud said, apparently referring to Lieutenant Peters.

"Where'd you get that from?" Moore asked.

"I'm telling you!" Seepersaud insisted. "Where you think Beharry stays when he in Georgetown?"

Moore looked intently at Seepersaud as he swung off the stool. He wanted Seepersaud to know that the information about Beharry had registered but that he remained skeptical.

The two officers went up the stairway to the dining room and made their way to the buffet table. Spooning rice and curried chicken onto his plate, Moore saw the Chief of Staff and Major Farley seated next to each other, engaged in quiet but intense conversation. The Chief seemed agitated. Farley seemed troubled and subdued. Moore guessed that they were probably talking about the trial. He led Seepersaud over to where Beharry was sitting with Ingrid Peters.

Moore was half finished with his lunch when Beharry and Peters rose to leave.

"Captain," Beharry said to Moore, "I think they need the seats." Moore looked over at the line at the buffet table and nodded. The dining area was full, and officers were filing out as they completed their meals. Moore saw Major Farley leave.

Moore was perplexed by the furtive look Farley had cast in his direction. The Chief of Staff's behavior was also interesting, Moore thought. Moore was directly in the Chief's line of sight as the Chief turned his head and spoke to staff officers on his left, but the Chief did not look directly at Moore or acknowledge his presence in any way. On other days, he would have, but, evidently, not today. Then the Chief got up and left. Moore felt a bit relieved.

His thoughts were interrupted by Captain Seepersaud. "When you moving out?"

"After lunch," Moore replied.

"No, no. I mean to Berbice County."

"Saddle wants me to leave in the morning. I was hoping to go home tonight, but I don't know."

"Where are you going to set up your command post?"

"New Amsterdam."

"Good. Saddle should leave you alone there."

"Why'd you say that?"

"He's too taken up with the chicken farm, and I hear he is going to plant peanuts on his other lands."

"Where'd you get that from?"

"OIC, Farm Corps."

"I hear he and Saddle not getting along," Moore said, fishing for information.

"Saddle asking too much of Farm Corps for his private farm. He would like to push out the Farm officer. That's the word 'round here, anyway."

"Christ, what's the place coming to?" Moore asked, not really expecting an answer. Seepersaud merely shook his head and smiled.

Finally through with his meal, Moore stood up. "Seeps, I gon square this joint. I got to go back to Timehri. Lo-lo LaFleur wants a meeting when I get back."

Seepersaud laughed out loud. "You gon get in trouble calling LaFleur that."

"He's a real lo-lo, if you ask me," Moore asserted defiantly under his breath. This set Seepersaud laughing again. Moore himself was smiling as he left.

Down the stairs and into the lounge, Moore noticed Beharry and Peters in a dart game by the bar. The Chief of Staff was at the window table at the north end with Colonel Cadogan and a couple of staff officers. Two officers were playing ping pong at the far left corner. Several officers crowded one table where the dominoes were being slapped down with great vigor. A few officers were sitting by themselves reading the newspapers, and several others were seated at the bar engaging in a jovial banter. The usual lunch activities, by the looks of it. Moore felt that Colonel Cadogan would probably keep tabs on his time, so he walked over to Lieutenant Beharry.

"Ramesh, time to square."

"Can I finish this game? Just two more throws."

"Awright. Lemme get McCurchin. You can meet me outside." Moore saw relief in Ingrid Peters' face and a smile that conveyed all the thanks in the world. Mind you, it was a minor concession, Moore thought. Maybe Seepersaud was telling the truth about these two. Is a shame though that they can't show their affections more publicly. But it's the society we living in. I wonder which family is the problem. Probably Beharry's. Brahmin family. Peters is mixed: Portuguese, Black, Indian or Amerindian.

Moore walked up the road toward the main gate and turned left into the Motor Transport compound. The jeep was parked by the gate, and McCurchin was having a gyaff with one of the soldiers. He walked over to the jeep when he saw Moore advancing.

"You all topped up, McCurchin?" Moore asked.

"Yes, Captain, but they need for you to sign for the gas. They getting strict."

Moore signed for the gas and turned over the paperwork to the MT clerk at the gate as they drove out. He would have headed over to the Officers' Mess, but he saw Lieutenant Beharry walking towards them. They waited for him to climb into the rear of the vehicle, and then drove out slowly.

At the main gate, the corporal stepped into the path of the vehicle and signaled McCurchin to stop.

"What's the problem, Corporal?" Moore asked.

"Captain Moore, the Base Commander called up a lil while ago. He wants Lieutenant Beharry to report to his office at 13:00 hours."

Moore looked at his watch. Five till. "Awright, McCurchin, turn around."

In front of the HQ building, the two officers got out.

"Stay here, McCurchin!" Moore ordered and led the way to Captain Stephenson's office.

"Ronald, is what going on?" Moore asked the Executive Officer angrily.

"Alan, the ah . . . ah Che . . . Che . . . Chief of Staff ahm wan . . . want Be . . . Beharry re . . . retried," Stephenson replied.

"What! Why?" Moore barked.

"For ah . . . ah being la . . . late."

"But I was late too!"

"He . . . he ain say not . . . nothing 'bout you."

"Who gon try he?" Moore asked.

"The Ba . . . Base Com . . . Commander." Captain Stephenson got up and began to walk towards the Base Commander's office. He looked up at Moore as though seeking forgiveness.

"Look, Al . . . Alan," he said, "is not we. Is the Chief . . . Chief of Staff. I . . . ah sorry man." Moore said nothing as Stephenson walked past him and headed in to tell Major Farley that Lieutenant Beharry was here. He reemerged shortly.

"Ra . . . Ramesh," Stephenson said to Lieutenant Beharry, "Major Fa . . . Farley ah re . . . ready."

Lieutenant Beharry marched into Major Farley's office, and Captain Stephenson closed the door behind them. A few minutes later, Captain Stephenson came out to get Moore.

"Al . . . Alan, Lieutenant Beharry wants you as a . . . a . . . witness."

Moore entered the Base Commander's office, and Major Farley addressed him.

"Alan, Lieutenant Beharry is charged with being late for his appointment with the Chief of Staff . . ."

"Major, so was I!" Moore protested. "How come Lieutenant Beharry alone is being charged?"

"Well, the Chief of Staff said he gave the instruction to Lieutenant Beharry."

"Awright," Moore said. "Here is why Lieutenant Beharry was late—"

"Alan," Major Farley interrupted, "it doesn't matter. The Chief of Staff wants me to find him guilty."

"I see," Moore said. "Well, get it over with. We got to go back to a meeting with Colonel LaFleur. And we don't want to be late for that!"

"I tell you what, Alan," Major Farley said, "Lieutenant Beharry is an officer under your command. You decide the punishment."

"How about a verbal reprimand?"

"Fair enough. Lieutenant Beharry, you are reprimanded for being late to your meeting with the Chief of Staff. And, gentlemen, this concludes this hearing."

Moore and Beharry saluted and left. Not far behind them was Captain Stephenson.

"Al . . . Alan, Ra . . . Ramesh," Stephenson called out. "I just . . . ah wa . . . want you to know is not we—"

"Is awright," Moore interrupted, "I getting to know how the place working."

NINE

THE CORPORAL AT THE main gate saluted as the jeep passed. Moore glanced over his right shoulder at Lieutenant Beharry, who sat with his elbows resting on his thighs, the back of his hands propping up his chin. Moore sensed anger and frustration and understood its source. The reprimand Beharry received was not especially significant. Junior officers get rebuked all the time. It was the fact of two trials in what was clearly a determined effort to punish him that got to Beharry. And Beharry probably felt as Moore did that the actual misdeed had been committed by their accuser and grand inquisitor. Talk about being "wrong and strong!"

Moore rested his head back and stared out the window. He had not given McCurchin any specific instructions and soon realized they were driving through the city. He wanted to close his eyes and go to sleep for a while, but they were approaching the center of the city, and the stops and starts at intersections compelled alertness, which he reluctantly conceded.

When the vehicle stopped at the roundabout in front of the Central Bank building, Moore looked over at the bundles of pavement dwellers in front of the stores. Observing the wretchedness of so many people condemned to penury by deteriorating economic conditions depressed him even more and added to an already urgent feeling that he had to get out of the city. Oh, he was accustomed to beggars. Back home in Rose Hall, there used to be house-to-house beggars, and there were beggars at the ferry stations and at the markets, but this spectacle of whole families, huddled together on the pavements with their hands outstretched, was new. Small wonder that Black people, who had looked the other way while the Party fixed elections and harassed the Opposition, were now taking to the streets in protest.

*   *   *

The sensation of sliding ended when Moore's head bumped McCurchin. There was also a thump in the rear of the jeep where Lieutenant Beharry was.

"Christ, McCurchin, is what going on?" Moore asked, waking up.

"Sorry, Captain," McCurchin replied. "Is the traffic from the airport. I just got tired waiting to make this left turn, so I took it before the next car got too close."

Moore didn't argue. They were back at Timehri. He was still irritable from the abruptness of his awakening, and his mouth tasted stale. The vehicle skirted the compound fence, entered the main gate with the usual protocol, and then came to a halt in front of the Admin building. Colonel LaFleur's office was upstairs, just above the Guard Room. Moore got out, straightened the beret on his head, and adjusted his glasses. Beharry came up and stood beside him.

"Ramesh, better go and check on your platoon. I got to go up and see what LaFleur wants."

The meeting with Colonel LaFleur was brief. Moore was sure LaFleur knew the outcome of their visit to Camp Ayanganna, but he no doubt wanted to hear Moore's version so he could report back to his friend, the Chief of Staff. Nevertheless, Moore obliged him with a brief recounting of the charge and the outcome, with very little commentary. There was an awkward moment; then LaFleur said, "Well, you boys try and behave yourselves," which Moore read as an endorsement of the Chief of Staff's position and of their chastisement. Well, what else would you expect? Moore asked himself. Birds of a feather!

"You have your deployment orders from Colonel Cadogan?" LaFleur asked.

"Yes, Colonel; F-Company will be deployed in Berbice County."

LaFleur nodded. "When are you moving out?"

"I want to make the 05:00 ferry crossing to New Amsterdam, so we will leave Timehri at 02:30 hours tomorrow."

"I know you gon do a good job out there, Alan."

"Thank you, Colonel."

"Just remember, though, that it is a political strike down there. Shake them up a little."

Moore did not respond. Instead he saluted and left.

Approaching the F-Company barracks, located behind the Admin Building, Moore could hear the loud voices of the NCOs and the cross chatter of the soldiers. He walked into the Company office where Lieutenant Mentore was speaking to the company Sergeant Major. Both of them greeted him, almost in unison.

"What's the situation here?" Moore asked.

"The men packing their kit, Captain," the Sergeant Major replied.

"Good," Moore said. "I want to see you and all of the officers in my office right away."

The Sergeant Major sent one of the company clerks to get Lieutenants Beharry and Persico, while Mentore followed Moore into his office.

"How did it go with the Chief, Alan?" Mentore asked.

"He didn't want to see me," Moore replied. "He had the Base commander put me on trial."

"For what?" Mentore asked.

"Conduct to the prejudice of good order and discipline!"

"You joking!"

"Six months' loss of seniority."

"What? Farley did that?"

"Well, everybody's saying is not them, is the Chief of Staff, so . . ."

"How about Ramesh?" Mentore asked.

"Verbal reprimand for arriving late at Camp Ayanganna."

"I just can't believe they're so barefaced."

"Well, no point crying over this. We got a big move ahead."

"I know, but is hard not to notice what the big boys getting away with. The Chief and his duty-free goods . . . You know what LaFleur did yesterday?"

Moore looked up from his desk. "What?"

"He flew in to Madhia to buy raw gold."

"How you know that?"

"I found out from Nizam Khan. He was flying in supplies to Madhia, Tumatumari, and Matthews Ridge."

"Did Nizam say that LaFleur was buying gold?"

"No, but you know that's what he was doing."

"Is just a rumor, Derryck. Anyway, don't worry, those fellas gon meet their end."

"Who say so? They're getting rich. LaFleur's buying raw gold cheap and sneaking it out of the country. And they had you all search those poor passengers on the Hudson flight yesterday."

"Better watch what you saying, Derryck," Moore cautioned.

"I ain't stupid, I only telling you. By the way, you know what Saddle Cadogan doing over at Farm Corps?"

"I have some idea."

"But do you know that Cadogan's trying to get rid of the Farm Officer?" Mentore asked again. Moore looked up intently at him. "Yes," Mentore continued, "he's shipping the poor fella out on a course in India."

"Where'd you get that from?" Moore asked.

"The Farm Officer himself. He came to the Mess for lunch today. He was mad like hell and complaining no ass."

The appearance of the company Sergeant Major with Lieutenants Persico and Beharry stopped the conversation. Moore invited them all to sit.

"Gentlemen," Moore began, "I'll be brief. As you all know, we've been posted to Berbice County. We are leaving Camp Stevenson at 02:30 hours tomorrow. Estimated time of arrival at the Rosignol ferry station 04:30 hours. We'll cross with the 05:00 ferry to New Amsterdam. Officers and senior NCOs are to report their presence on this base at 20:00 hours this evening. All other ranks are confined to base. Lieutenant Persico?"

"Captain, what is the deployment plan?" Persico asked, sitting on Moore's right with his beret in his lap.

"Lieutenant Mentore and 1st Platoon will be responsible for the security of the Skeldon Sugar Estate and its environs. That will include everything from Crabwood Creek all the way back to the sluice at Lesbeholden. They will be billeted at the Senior Staff Club in the Skeldon Sugar Estate compound."

"And 2nd Platoon?" Persico asked.

"Your platoon will be based at the Albion Sugar Estate and will be responsible for that estate and Port Mourant, but you will be expected to patrol from the Borlum Turn to Hogstye."

"Captain, that leaves the Rose Hall Sugar Estate to my platoon. Where will we be billeted?" Lieutenant Beharry asked.

"Ordinarily at the Senior Staff club. The problem is that they are doing some renovations, mostly roof work; so, your platoon will make camp at the Esplanade Park in New Amsterdam. That is also where I will set up the Company command post. Any other questions?"

"Yes, Captain," Lieutenant Beharry said. "Do you want us to sleep in the base compound tonight?"

"No, you can sleep in your own quarters. Just be sure you are with your platoons early o'clock. The trucks will roll out of here at 02:30."

"The men would like to know if they'll have to cut sugar cane," Lieutenant Mentore said.

"No," Moore replied, "they'll simply be patrolling. I understand that the government has hired scabs to replace the striking workers. Part of our job is to provide security for the scabs."

"Are we going to be conducting search-and-seizure operations?" Lieutenant Mentore asked.

"I have no specific orders on that," Moore responded, "but it might be a way of applying pressure on the strikers if the situation gets hot down there."

The officers sat quietly digesting the information. Then Moore added, "If there are no further questions, you can return to your platoons. Sergeant Major?"

"Yes, Captain?"

"Contact the Transport and Harbor Department at New Amsterdam and let them know we need to cross from Rosignol with the first ferry. Tell them we are operational. And tell McCurchin to stand by to take me home at 16:00 hours."

"Yes, Captain. How about the Police Headquarters in New Amsterdam?"

"Signal our time of arrival to all police stations in Berbice County, including Police HQ, New Amsterdam."

"Yes, Captain."

Shortly after the Sergeant Major left, Lieutenant Beharry reentered Moore's office.

"Alan, if you are going to town this afternoon, I would like a lift."

"As a matter of fact, I am leaving at 16:00 sharp. Your platoon ready?"

"Oh yes. The platoon sergeant took care of that."

"You know, Ramesh, I am not going into town. I am just heading home to Eccles."

"Well, do you think McCurchin could drive me into town; we could pick you up on the way back?"

"I want to leave home at 19:00 hours."

"That would work awright. I just want to go into town and have a meal. I spent the entire weekend on this base."

"I know, but you sure is a meal you going for?" Moore asked, smiling and recalling what Captain Seepersaud had said of Beharry and Lieutenant Ingrid Peters.

"Oh, yes, but anything else would be awright," Beharry smiled.

"Okay, we'll leave in forty-five minutes."

PART TWO

TEN

BY 02:25 HOURS, THE soldiers of F-Company were aboard the three trucks parked side by side in the Camp Stevenson drill square, drivers in the cabs and engines running. The 1/4-ton jeep idled in front of the trucks, close to the flag pole where Captain Moore was meeting with his platoon leaders and the company's Sergeant Major and Color Sergeant.

"You know the order of march," Moore said. "Lieutenant Mentore and first platoon, then Lieutenant Persico and second platoon, and Lieutenant Beharry and third platoon. The Color Sergeant will bring up the rear in the 3/4-ton. Any questions?" He waited a few moments. "Awright, mount up!"

Moore climbed in the front of the 1/4-ton and allowed the Sergeant Major, the signaler, and the two company clerks to settle in at the back before giving the okay to McCurchin. The jeep moved up to the main gate and stopped so that the Guard Room corporal could log in their departure—02:30 hours, Tuesday, January 18. Out of the gate, taking a sharp right turn and then hugging the security fence for another hundred feet or so, the 1/4-ton made its way past four rows of houses before it began to descend the hill for the junction with the East-bank road. In the left side mirror, Moore monitored the rest of the convoy snaking behind him.

McCurchin stopped at the intersection with the East-bank road, the brief stop bringing all of the other vehicles to an accordion cluster on the tail of the jeep. Moore could hear the loud hum of the truck engines as McCurchin turned the jeep toward Georgetown and pulled away from them. Within a few minutes, all of the vehicles were again in an orderly convoy formation, this time about fifty feet apart. At 50 miles per hour, Moore figured, the convoy should be pulling in to the Rosignol ferry station in a couple of hours. Satisfied, he settled back for the drive.

The convoy moved along like a humming spear, cutting through the silence of the night. For the first fifteen miles or so, the Demerara River on the left was their constant companion, and in between the bushes along the river's edge, Moore caught glints of light reflecting on the water. There were the occasional dog barkings and extended meows of cats in heat or in combat; otherwise, just stillness, and the alternation of bush and village. Traveling at this hour was wonderful, Moore thought, if you didn't have to shorten your sleep time to do it.

The cool night air, coming in at varying speeds through the open window, felt good against his face, and Moore thought of surrendering and closing his eyes except that he felt strangely awake. With nothing else to do and a long ride ahead, this seemed like a good time to think. So much had happened during the last forty-eight hours—the Chief, the bomb threat, the trial. Time to get out of this den of thieves, as Uncle Lenny calls all the place. And there was Jeanene and the children to think about. He readjusted his position and rested his head back as he reflected on the time he had spent at home only a few hours ago.

He had left Camp Stevenson for his home in Eccles promptly at 16:00 hours. Lieutenant Mentore had learned from Beharry that he was taking the jeep to town and had also asked for a ride. The jeep dropped him off at home in Eccles at about 16:30, and he had instructed both Beharry and Mentore to pick him up at 19:00 hours.

He had called Jeanene at work a couple of hours earlier and had filled her in on the day's developments in an effort to avert a tense dinner atmosphere. Jeanene had agreed to leave work early, but by the time she reached home with the children, it was about 17:30 hours. The children had run into the house ahead of their mother. Candy had her arms around his waist and her head buried against his stomach. He hugged her and bent over to kiss her forehead. Ian had caught up and wanted to be picked up, and so he was, Candy keeping one arm around his waist. This was how Jeanene met him. She kissed him on his cheek and went into the kitchen to prepare dinner. He moved over with the children to the sofa and sat down, Ian in his lap and Candy on his left side. The children talked almost simultaneously, sometimes about different things, one joining in developing the other's story if their father appeared to show interest by his questions. He learned from the children that they had gone to Christ Church Anglican the day before and that Uncle Lenny had preached. He was glad he had not known before and had not tried to stop Jeanene.

Moore could not help glancing at his watch as he listened to the children, and after a few minutes, when their excitement seemed to have subsided, he persuaded Candy to start her homework and Ian to play on the floor with his little cars. Temporarily relieved of the children, Moore went into the kitchen where Jeanene was cutting some small red peppers and tomatoes for a banga-mary stew. She was still in her bank uniform, a white blouse and a grayish, close-fitting skirt that came down to her knees. She had already slipped off her shoes and stockings. He stood behind her, hands lightly resting on her waist, and kissed the back of her neck.

"Tell me about the trial," she said.

"Oh, it was a farce. The Chief of Staff was angry I didn't give him a jeep to haul his stuff, so he used the Base Commander to punish me. It was spite, just spite."

"And you lost six months' of seniority, just like that?" Jeanene turned around and looked at him.

"Well, it doesn't matter. We gon be gone by then."

"I want us to leave this place," she said sternly and walked over to the sink. "I'll call the Embassy tomorrow. I want to know how long more we got to wait."

Moore did not say anything. He hoped she would let things rest there. Ian came into the kitchen and announced he was thirsty.

"Give him some ginger beer," Jeanene said.

"When did you make ginger beer?" Moore asked.

"I got it from Aunt Vickie when we went to see she and Uncle Lenny yesterday."

Moore reached in the refrigerator and poured some of the ginger beer into a glass for Ian, and then emptied the remainder into two glasses, one of which he carried out to Candy. He returned to the kitchen and offered the third glass to Jeanene, holding up the glass so she could sip, after which she said she didn't care for anymore.

"Why you don't go out and spend some time with the children?" she suggested. "They not going to see you again for a while. I should be done here in a few minutes."

With the cool night air still fanning his face, Moore wondered what he would do if the American Embassy indicated they still had a long wait. He thought he could resign his commission and become a teacher like his father, but they probably wouldn't let him. All schools were government-run, and the Party had long arms. Odd how things had changed so!

He remembered the years before independence, the disturbances of the 60's and people changing villages to feel safe. Uncle Lenny had just come back from his studies in England and was ordained in the Anglican church. The Opposition was then the government. Uncle Lenny opposed them then because he thought they would make the country a communist satellite, after securing independence from Britain. Moore remembered the visits from his uncle and his family to their home in Rose Hall. He enjoyed the company of his cousins. They went out to the sugar estate and brought back sugar cane, which they chewed for hours on end. They climbed the fruit trees in the yard, jamoon, one day, tamarind the next. In the afternoons, they swam naked in the canal, drying their hair before they got home so their mothers wouldn't know. The rest of the time, it was marbles or softball cricket, whichever they could get the neighbors' boys to play. The house too was alive with people, music, and the food, oh! Metagee, pepper pot, black cake, quinches, black pudding, sugar cakes, and cold ginger beer, mauby, or pine drink. No one ever talked of shortages in those days! But the country was a colony, and lawyers and doctors were holding meetings to tell people about independence. Alan's father was still the headmaster at Rose Hall Anglican School. Though not a politically active man himself, he was very approving of Uncle Lenny, who harangued the adults about the evils of communism and the subjugation of the Black race. He talked about the economic domination of the Indians over the Blacks, if that government continued in office. When the government changed in '65 and the Party took over, Uncle Lenny came back to celebrate. Those were happy days.

Independence had brought pledges of foreign aid from many countries. Sugar, bauxite, and rice, the three linch-pins of the economy, were filling the national coffers, and the future seemed secure. Seems like such a long time ago, Moore thought. Nevertheless, that was the situation when he accepted a scholarship from the United States government to attend West Point. After graduation, he returned promptly and was commissioned as a 2nd Lieutenant just after the first set of elections supervised by the Party. He remembered protests about the elections being rigged, but he was too engrossed in regimental duties and the excitement of officership to take much notice. The uniform attracted women, and he did not see Jeanene, his high school sweetheart, for several months. Then came the border assignment at Eteringbang. Bunker living and the uncertainty of supplies aggravated the loneliness he felt at that distant outpost. He thought frequently about Jeanene, and the first thing he did on his return to Georgetown was to contact her. He had been with her since, from virginity to two children.

Alan Moore had originally thought of the army as a career. His first promotion had been celebrated by his ailing father and his uncle, but both thought he should go on with his education, especially as they saw how things were going in the country. Not long after the elections, Uncle Lenny became very reticent about politics and very circumspect about the Party. He threw himself fully into family affairs after his older brother died, but when the Party declared itself the vanguard socialist party and began to harass its opponents, Uncle Lenny joined with other members of the clergy to speak up for civil and human rights. By the time Moore had made the rank of captain, Uncle Lenny had emerged as one of the leading members of the Council of Churches, and he and the government went to war. Uncle Lenny still thought that military service was honorable, but admonished his nephew about the misuse of the military to which authoritarian governments often resorted.

Moore had not thought much about it when his sister, Grace, filed sponsorship papers for his parents and him. Approval for his parents came very quickly, but his father did not want to travel. After his death, Alan's mother shuttled back and forth, finally settling in New York last year. Then conditions here began to deteriorate rapidly. The national coffers were empty—squandered, Uncle Lenny would say—and most would agree. Poverty had imposed an equality on all. People were starving. Disillusionment with the Party made Black people more receptive to new movements, yet it was far from clear that things were salvageable. Everyone who could, it seemed, was leaving, and Jeanene began to take a serious interest in the processing of the papers his sister had filed on their behalf.

Moore was sure from the conversations in the Mess that most officers understood the problems, though for a long time they found ways to avoid thinking about them. After all, their occupational and social world was insulated from everyone else. They had their camps, training sites, border locations, and, of course, their Mess. Sure they felt the shortages, but at least they were better taken care of than most people. Besides, who knew what would take the place of this government? Better to stay with the devil you know, they said, while they planned their own exit strategy. Wasn't that also true of him?

At 02:55 hours, the jeep was passing through the center of Eccles, and Moore thought of his wife and children at home in bed. He hoped he could make it back on Saturday. If not, Jeanene could come down to New Amsterdam with the children.

Now only a few miles outside of Georgetown, the convoy encountered occasional traffic, a car or a drygoods truck. It wouldn't be long before they were through the Independence Arch and on Carifesta Avenue, bypassing the city. Moore tried to suppress his yawns, fearing that he would induce yawning from McCurchin.

He thought of his friend, Captain Ken Seepersaud, and wondered when he would begin his deployment along the East Coast. With no ferry to catch, Ken was going to have a good night's rest and then move out after breakfast. Christ, his command post was going to be at Enmore Sugar Estate! He would be able to spend his nights at home with his family. Moore thought of Lakshmi, Ken's wife. He had introduced the two of them. Lakshmi and Jeanene had been classmates at St. Rose's. They used to be so close; now they hardly saw each other. He remembered that Lakshmi had wanted a job at the bank where Jeanene worked because it paid more than teaching. Jeanene had talked to an uncle who had party connections, but when Ken and Lakshmi found out, they decided that teaching was what Lakshmi really wanted to do. Moore was sure though that, with her qualifications, Lakshmi felt embarrassed that she needed to pull political strings to get the job.

Ken was not a political man, but Moore figured his sympathies were not with the Party. No one asked Ken, and he never declared. But just have a political discussion going, and Ken found a way to duck it. It had been the same with Nizam Khan at breakfast last Sunday, and it would be the same with Beharry, he knew. The Indian officers saw the Party and the government it ran as Black people's organizations. With recent strikes in the bauxite industry and one looming in the public service, the question these days was how did Black people see the Party and the government?

Moore realized he had dozed off for a while because he jerked awake when the jeep made the right turn onto the East-Coast highway.

"You awright, McCurchin?" he asked.

"I awright, Captain. You go back to sleep. I know the way, you know."

Moore looked back to check on the trucks and then tried to make himself comfortable again. They were driving along the seawall, and he could tell from the splashing of the waves that the tide was in. The breeze from the Atlantic was giving him a chill, so he rolled up the windows half way and rested his head in the corner formed by the backrest and the door. He woke up several times and saw lights approaching from the opposite direction, but he was too disoriented to tell what they were or to even care. He intermittently heard conversation between McCurchin and the Sergeant Major, who was no doubt trying to make sure McCurchin stayed awake. He even heard laughter from time to time. But mostly he slept, until the jeep pulled up behind a column of vehicles waiting to board the ferry. They had arrived at the Rosignol ferry station. He would have to get up now—there were decisions to be made. His mouth tasted stale and he needed to urinate.

The Rosignol wharf was configured like a huge open barn. A chain link fence running down the center of the wharf separated the vehicular traffic on the right from the pedestrian passenger traffic on the left. The ticket office was in the passenger section, as were the restrooms and some limited seating. A metal gate on the right half controlled vehicular traffic down the ramp to the ferry. Moore knew the routine. Once the gate was opened, the right half of the station would be filled with vehicles approximately the capacity of the ferry. It was therefore important to get into the enclosure to assure crossing. Right now, the gate was closed.

Moore walked up to the right side of the wharf and looked across the river to New Amsterdam. He could see the harbor lights and the lights on the moored ferry. Groups of soldiers were approaching the wharf and fanning out among the bushes along the river's edge. Moore smiled and then began walking in the direction of the toilets. He opened the door and stepped in, but the stench forced him to retreat and join the soldiers at the edge of the Berbice River. From there, he could see the ferry leaving the New Amsterdam pier and turning to head north to Rosignol.

When he returned to the wharf, the Color Sergeant notified him that they had been cleared by the ticket office for crossing, but that the travel warrant did not give them priority crossing. The gate to the holding area was now open and vehicles were being directed in, so Moore walked over to the harbor official admitting the vehicles and explained that the trucks needed to make the crossing. The harbor man and the police constable standing beside him seemed impressed by Moore's rank and tone. The harbor man explained that they were going to admit vehicles until the enclosure was filled except for a clear driveway from the ramp to the gate, so that vehicles on the ferry from New Amsterdam would be able to disembark without hindrance. The army vehicles would then be admitted down this driveway and be loaded onto the ferry first. Moore thanked him and walked off to join the other officers, who had left their trucks and were huddled around the Sergeant Major on the left side of the wharf.

The station seemed to bustle with activity now that the ferry was getting closer. The pedestrian passenger traffic had increased—students in uniform and commuting workers bound for New Amsterdam. Some of these came in walking. Others were being dropped off by hire cars, which then parked in a designated area on the right to await passengers disembarking from the incoming ferry. Fruit vendors and sellers of sweets were positioning themselves on the sides of the road to cater to outbound and incoming traffic. Then the loud hum from its engines announced the approach of the ferry. The large lettering on the bow read *Torani*. It was less than a hundred yards from the pier, but it was going past in order to execute a left turn that would point its bow back towards New Amsterdam after it was moored. Turn completed, the *Torani* drifted in slowly, its right side gently shouldering the pier, and its sailors tossing out thick ropes to moor the vessel.

The metal ramp that formed part of the side of the *Torani* was lowered onto the wooden ramp from the pier. Cars and trucks were slowly being driven off, passing between two long lines of disembarking pedestrians, though most of the passengers disembarked from the upper deck and descended down a set of winding stairs, supported by metal scaffolding that the Dutch called a stelling.

The scene was very familiar to Moore. He used to make this crossing at least once a month when he attended Queen's College in Georgetown and boarded with a distant relation. In those days, of course, there was a train from Rosignol to Georgetown. It was still a fascination to him to watch the commotion after the ferry docked and discharged its human and motor cargo. Taxi drivers, with a sixth sense no doubt nurtured by experience, sorted out the people heading to Georgetown from those making shorter stops. The bidding over passengers was intense. Then in a few minutes, it was all over. The vehicles were all moving off, and in their trail were the real short-stoppers on foot at some distance away from the ferry station.

The noise level had subsided, and people heading to New Amsterdam were beginning to board. The police constable approached Moore.

"Captain, we ready for the army vehicles."

Moore turned to the Sergeant Major. "Sergeant Major, let's get those soldiers back in the trucks."

The soldiers were in clusters in and around the station, but most seemed to be in the snackette outside the station, which had just opened. Moore looked over as the Sergeant Major called the soldiers and herded them back to the three trucks, many still chomping on their cassava pones or quinches. When the men were back in the trucks and the officers had boarded, Moore got into his jeep.

The jeep moved into the enclosure on the pier and down the ramp onto the ferry, where a sailor directed McCurchin to a corner parking space. Then came the trucks, followed by the 3/4-ton jeep. General loading followed the military vehicles. When the lower deck was full, the drawbridge action began. The *Torani's* ramp was raised to an upright position so that it closed off the open side of the vessel.

Captain Moore left the jeep and began the winding path between vehicles to get to the set of stairs to the upper deck, located at the bow end. He emerged at the unenclosed section of the upper deck, where people were standing by the rails looking over at the water or out toward New Amsterdam. Others were sitting on the wooden life rafts near the rails. People looked over at him somewhat in awe, not because he was a soldier, he surmised, but because the pips on his shoulder suggested that he might be an officer. There was an atmosphere of awkward friendliness: mutual, he realized. Most of these people had never been this close to an officer of the "People's Army." He stood against the front rail for a few minutes, enjoying the cool breeze fanning his face and staring out at New Amsterdam, the playground of his boyhood days, then turned around and walked through the door into the enclosed upper deck. The smell of stale urine from the toilet area to the right of the door overpowered the pungency of the Jeyes Fluid disinfectant and made him want to spit. The adjacent flooring was wet and badly discolored, a consequence no doubt of years of toilet overflow. Moving further inward, Moore noticed that many of the windows around the passenger deck were broken. The racks above, which used to store the orange life-vests, were empty. In frustration, he turned around and walked back to fresher air.

He remembered so well the day the *Torani* was commissioned. He was in the third form. This was before the Party came to power. His parents had brought him and his sister to the stelling to be among the crowd that had come out for the maiden crossing. He was barely five-feet tall, and the boat seemed so large and so beautiful. But that was a long time ago. Now, this boat, like so many things he knew, was decaying prematurely. The national feting was over, and there was now no money to give this once majestic boat the simple face-lift she deserved.

The New Amsterdam stelling was now only a hundred yards or so away. Moore descended the narrow stairs, holding on to the rails, and then wound his way around the parked vehicles to his jeep. Within a few minutes, the left side of the boat was rubbing against the pylons on the dock, and the thick moorings were secured. The ramp lowered, the jeep led the way out under fifty feet of covered enclosure and then onto the harbor road, leading out to New Amsterdam. About a hundred yards from the enclosure, it pulled off the road and parked on the unpaved area to the left and waited for the rest of the convoy.

One by one, the trucks lined up behind the company commander's jeep, and the officers dismounted and homed in on Moore, standing at the rear of his jeep. Each officer reported that his men were all accounted for. Moore directed the officers to re-board their trucks, and Lieutenants Mentore and Persico to proceed to their respective postings. He watched the two trucks pull out of the formation and move off before re-entering his jeep. Then the rump convoy made its way out on the harbor road that dead-ended on Strand, which was one-way from west to east. The convoy turned left on Strand and traveled for about a quarter of a mile until Esplanade Park came into view on the left side, just past the Police Headquarters on the right. The long side of the park fronting Strand was lined with flamboyant trees, and a narrow drainage ditch separated the trees from the street.

Moore's jeep entered the park through the wide grass-covered culvert that served as the entrance, and pulled up to the circular bandstand at the center of the park This would be the company HQ and the sleeping quarters for the officers. He climbed up the wide stairs onto the platform, which was about three-feet high and strewn with litter. It had a rail and an attached seat all the way around.

From the platform, he could see the entire park, which was the size of a football field, the perimeter away from Strand and closer to the Berbice River being defined by higher grass and weeds merging with shrubs. On that side, the land sloped gradually towards the river, only a couple of hundred yards away. From the New Amsterdam stelling, a line of courida trees ran eastward to the mouth of the river, but there were several clearings from which people were launching canoes and small fishing boats. The courida trees were more thickly clumped in the distant northeast, where the Canje Creek emptied into the mouth of the Berbice River.

A loud commotion drew Moore's attention away from the river to a solitary, untethered, dark gray donkey in the park. The motor engines and the voices of the disembarking soldiers had either scared the creature or encouraged him to show off. He began braying loudly and running in a semi-circular arc. Its brazen display of masculinity evoked unrestrained, raucous laughter. Perhaps anticipating Moore, and ignoring the remonstrations of the amused soldiers, Lieutenant Beharry ordered some of the men to chase the donkey out. The attempt proved fruitless—the donkey simply ran around the park, away from its half-hearted pursuers. Clearly the donkey regarded the park as its territory. The now incessant braying and the spectacle of the pursuing soldiers were attracting the attention of passersby. Captain Moore, himself amused by it all, and recognizing the need for some temporary coexistence, said loudly, "Awright, leave the damn thing alone."

Moore stepped into the park to observe the camp preparations, leaving the Sergeant Major to oversee the clearing of the litter from the bandstand and to organize it as the company HQ. The Color Sergeant was barking orders at the men erecting the mess tent and at the cooks preparing breakfast. Lieutenant Beharry had designated sites around the bandstand for the tents of the three rifle squads, each tent to accommodate two men. The noise from the entrenching tools driving metal stakes into the ground caused the donkey to bray and to trot around, displaying his manhood. This proved to be a ready source of entertainment for the soldiers, one of whom observed aloud that the donkey seemed to always ready. That declaration proved to be the donkey's baptism, and soon, they were all referring to the donkey as "Eveready."

By about 08:00 hours, the soldiers were invited into the mess tent to get their breakfast—two rice bakes prepared the day before, a hard-boiled egg, and a cup of very sweet, lukewarm coffee. Moore and Beharry retreated with their rations to the bandstand. They had hardly seated themselves when the noise at the park entrance made them rise up almost simultaneously. The sentry at the entrance was asking an insistent civilian why he wanted to enter the compound. Both officers walked over to the entrance, where the sentry told them that Mr. Sackiechand, standing there, was representing himself as Eveready's owner.

"That your donkey?" Moore asked pointing to the beast.

"Yes, officer," Mr. Sackiechand replied, "the fella always graze over here, you know."

"Well, go ahead and take him, but keep him away, awright? This is a military camp."

"I can't promise you, you know," Mr. Sackiechand said. "He too accustomed grazing here."

"Better try or he might end up in the pound," Moore warned. "Awright, come in and get him."

Mr. Sackiechand proved to be quite adept at lassoing Eveready, but he had to drag the donkey out of the compound, its resistance probably stiffened by the supporting cheers of its new-found friends. Moore walked back with Lieutenant Beharry to the bandstand and to breakfast, irritated by the prospect of having to deal with a regular presence of this donkey in or near his camp.

ELEVEN

GENERAL AGRIPPA SAT DOWN to breakfast in a crowded dining area abuzz with talk about the re-deployments. Several of the captains and lieutenants who greeted him had just come out to the coast from interior locations, and theirs appeared to be the loudest voices in the Mess. Having carefully avoided junior officers since he had Captain Moore disciplined the previous day, Agrippa affected deep interest in the state-owned *Cayman News,* his ears cocked to pick up any new bit of information.

The front-page article reported on the previous day's meeting of the Public Service Union in which rank-and-file members demanded action from the union leadership in response to the massive retrenchment of public service employees. Some called for strike action to stop further retrenchment. The article went on to say that the old leadership was being challenged by a younger cadre who felt like the government was taking the union for granted and that the leadership was simply standing by as public service employees got the axe on orders from the IMF. The meeting had ended without any decision, but the article mentioned elections for the union executive in two weeks and speculated on efforts to unseat the two-decade old executive that the paper described as stalwarts of the trade union movement.

A strike by this union would be one hell of a blow to the government, Agrippa thought. The union had not been on strike since the 1960s when the Opposition was in government. The union leaders were all card-carrying members of the Party, the rank-and-file were predominantly Black, and no one had done more than the Comrade President to build up the union by distributing government jobs. But now the IMF was saying that the public sector was too top-heavy, and the government's Standby Agreement with the IMF obliged it to take action. The axe was falling. Trouble ahead, Agrippa thought.

The short column at the right corner of the paper was captioned *"Pork-knockers Robbed on Trail."* It described the robbery of four miners coming out of the interior. Three of them were divers for a small mining company operating its dredge from a pontoon on the Potaro River. The fourth was a deck-hand on the pontoon. They had been robbed of about ten thousand dollars of accumulated pay.

By the time he was through reading about the robbery, Agrippa found himself flanked by the Quartermaster and the Paymaster, and for the duration of his breakfast of fried breadfruit and boiled eggs he chatted with them. The QM reminded him that the salespeople from the Nimble Earthmoving Equipment Company were due to see him next Monday, January 24th. Agrippa had not forgotten the appointment; after all, he had insisted on doing the negotiations himself. But he thanked the QM for the reminder, carefully appending an "I had forgotten about that, you know," which made the QM smile. Good, Agrippa thought, got to keep the QM happy because he would have to do the paperwork. Agrippa was not sure whether he should include the QM in the negotiations. Including him would cause less of a stir, especially since the Officer-in-Charge of Farm Corps had been sidelined in negotiations over equipment intended for the Farm Corps, and purchasing was a QM matter. OIC Farm Corps had argued that the existing equipment was still serviceable and the money could be used elsewhere. Agrippa had disagreed, ruling that new tractors, bulldozers, and harvesters would be bought and the existing equipment auctioned off.

Colonel LaFleur was waiting outside his office when Agrippa arrived. They exchanged salutes, and Agrippa invited him to enter and have a seat.

"How was your trip, Ovid?" Agrippa asked, leaning back in his chair.

"Good. I visited Madhia, Tumatumari, and Matthews Ridge. I came out yesterday." LaFleur's thick lips rippled, revealing sections of his gold teeth as if flashing Morse code.

"The new platoons all settled in?" Agrippa asked.

"Oh yeah."

"Did you get any other business done?"

"Some. I got an ounce for the diesel I took in. Of course, they paid separately for the diesel, and I bought four ounces of gold from the divers. A hundred and fifty an ounce."

"Not bad, but I was thinking . . . Did you see in the papers where some pork-knockers got robbed coming out from the interior by trail?" LaFleur shook his head; he hadn't. "Well," Agrippa continued, "the Islanders can take in eight passengers on their resupply runs, nine if there is no co-pilot.

Why don't we transport the pork-knockers out regularly and charge them a fee?"

"Who will collect it?"

"The pilots. We can give them a cut. We could make about two hundred U.S. a trip, and it would be steady money. We resupply those locations every two weeks."

"We could do that," LaFleur said nodding. "It would be steady. As a matter of fact, most of the pork-knockers—the divers, the deck-hands on the dredges, and the cooks—most of them would prefer to come to Georgetown to sport out their money, so we can bring them out and take them back in."

"Talk to the pilots doing the runs to Madhia, Tumatumari, Kamarang, Imbaimadai, and Matthews Ridge. Make sure they know to keep their mouths shut."

LaFleur nodded, but his eyebrows were furrowed. "Clive," he said, leaning forward and lowering his voice, "there is another way we can make some good money." Agrippa looked at him expectantly. "Here is how the mining business working. The owners of the dredges in the Mazaruni-Potaro river system don't stay in the interior. They live in Georgetown and only go in once a month to check the books and pick up the gold. They leave everything else to the foreman." Agrippa grimaced and shrugged his shoulders.

"Hold on," LaFleur said. "The foreman keeps two books, one which he shows to the ranger from the Ministry of Lands and Mines, and the other with the correct production figures."

"I see," Agrippa said.

"The world market price per ounce is three hundred and fifty American," LaFleur continued. "Lands and Mines pays two hundred and fifty, then charges fifty per ounce in royalty. So the company nets two hundred. The exchange rate is ten to one; so that works out to two thousand dollars our money, which Lands and Mines pays."

"How do we come in?" Agrippa asked.

"Well, the company sells the gold that it didn't declare to Lands and Mines on the open market. We could buy from them."

"At what price?"

"Look, the company nets two hundred American per ounce but gets it in local dollars. By the time they convert that to American dollars, if they can find somebody to do it for them, they will get somewhere around a hundred and eighty U.S. We can step in and buy for two hundred an ounce. We give them American dollars right away."

"And they gon take it?"

"Yes, man. And they gon cut back even more on what they declaring to the government. We get it to the U.S. and we make a killing! One hundred and fifty U.S. per ounce profit."

"We can still buy from the pork-knockers, right?"

"Oh yes. Look, out there, is everybody stealing. When the divers find a nugget at the bottom of the river, they would stick it in their briefs. Also, when they are washing the sand and gold, they add quicksilver for the gold to attach itself. Well, they would squeeze out a handful of the amalgam for themselves. These pork-knockers will sell what they steal even cheaper. You know? Fast sale."

"You could go in once or twice a month, depending . . ."

"Right. The army camps at Madhia and Tumatumari are just off the Potaro River, and Kamarang is just off the Mazaruni River. Routine inspections, that's all."

The possibilities excited Agrippa. He buzzed his PA for two cups of coffee. "Ovid," he asked, "you don't think the Foreign Affairs Ministry would get suspicious if we send large packages in the diplomatic pouch?"

"You're the Chief of Staff, man! They know that you and the Consul General in New York go way back. Besides, the people over at Foreign Affairs are always sending personal stuff in the diplomatic pouch."

"You're good, you know, Lo-lo," Agrippa said, smiling and nodding. LaFleur acknowledged the compliment with a wide gleam.

TWELVE

WHY DID COLONEL CADOGAN pick today to inspect the damn deployment, Moore wondered, finally allowing his eyes to open. And, Christ, on a Friday! He looked at his watch, but it was too dark for him to see the dial. He was sure it was not yet 06:00; a radio in the camp was still playing Indian film music from the half-hour curry powder show.

What a night! It wasn't simply that he had gotten to bed well past midnight, it was the creaking cot! If you turned to the right, it creaked; if you turned to the left, it creaked. Then came the bloody mosquitoes; they always seemed to find the spots on your body where there was no insect repellent. He wanted to sleep some more, but how could he? Horns from passing automobiles on Strand were sounding intermittently like crowing roosters, except without the comforting melody.

He looked over at Beharry's empty cot and figured Beharry must have gone over to the Police Divisional Mess to shower. He thought he'd do the same and probably get something to eat over there. Maybe the food would be better than the camp rations. He would need to take McCurchin with him since he had no assigned space over there and he didn't want his uniform just lying in a pile in some corner.

The ablution area on the third floor of the Police Divisional Mess was crowded, and by the time Moore had negotiated his way into the shower and gotten dressed, it was 06:30. He sent off McCurchin with his discarded clothing and went down to breakfast on the second floor.

The dining arrangement here was more scattered and louder than he was accustomed to at the army messes. There was no separate dining for officers here, though police constables tended to avoid the few senior ranks who were around. The constables clearly had a free run of the place, and they ran it very loudly.

Moore walked over to join Lieutenant Beharry and Inspector Frazier at the long table by the windows overlooking Strand. Frazier was laughing as he related some of the shenanigans from a previous army detachment billeted in New Amsterdam. Moore caught the last part before Frazier erupted in raucous laughter.

Frazier looked up at Moore. "You look bruk up, comrade? You've only been here three days."

"Is the damn cot y'all loaned me," Moore complained, taking the seat across from Frazier. "The blasted thing creaked all night."

"Was the same with Captain Felix when he was here," Frazier replied, "but at least he always had somebody with he." They all laughed. "Come to think of it," Frazier continued, "that's probably why the springs got stretched out."

"Well, how about a new cot?" Moore asked.

"Awright, comrade. Tell the Color Sergeant to come by and see me. I gon fix you up."

"Thank you."

"I understand Saddle Cadogan coming down today?" Frazier asked.

"Oh yes."

"How's his chicken farm going?"

"You'll get your chance to ask him."

"He staying over?"

"I don't think so," Moore replied, adding, "not unless he sees a chance to set up another chicken farm out here." They all laughed.

"But is not so the Americans do it?" Frazier asked. "Like McDonald's and what they call the other one?"

"Kentucky's?" Beharry offered.

"Yes. That's it!" Frazier laughed aloud, slapping Beharry on his back and shaking him fondly. Then, rising to leave, he said, "Bring Saddle by when he gets here."

Moore nodded. "You can give him my cot."

Frazier laughed out loudly as he walked away.

"Looks like Saddle got a reputation out here too," Beharry observed to Moore.

"Looks that way."

Breakfast came. Rather quickly, Moore thought. Three slices of fried breadfruit and a couple of hard-boiled eggs. The coffee was hot and tasted good. The service was not quite what he was accustomed to at the Officers' Mess at either Camp Ayanganna or Camp Stevenson, but he was a guest here. He liked the breadfruit, far better tasting than the rice bakes he would have had at his camp in Esplanade Park.

"What kind of a schedule do you have for Cadogan, Alan?" Beharry asked.

"It depends on what he wants to do. He was originally scheduled to come on Monday. What I plan to do is to take him to the sugar estates. We're going all the way to Skeldon."

"What you want me to do? The entire platoon's sleeping. They patrolled all last night."

"Just stick around. I'm sure Saddle will want to talk to you."

"If you think you'll get back by 20:00, I'd like to ride up with you."

"You know I'm going in Saddle's jeep?"

"You'll need someone to keep you company at the back."

"True, but leh we wait and see."

"When you expecting him?"

"I ain't sure. I estimate between 10:00 and 11:00 hours, if he leaves Camp Ayanganna by 08:00. It will take about 75 minutes to get to Rosignol, half an hour or so to cross? On the other hand, if he misses the ferry . . ."

Beharry did not say anything. Between bites, Moore spoke, "Of course, you know Saddle; the man does not like to be inconvenienced. I will bet money he don't leave Georgetown before 09:00. He's bound to go by the chicken farm."

"And check on his hire cars?" Beharry added, smiling.

"Oh yes," Moore said, nodding. "Anyway, as they say, 'when he come, he come.' I have some signals to respond to, and I want to check with the Color Sergeant about some supplies."

*   *   *

The bandstand that Moore was using as the Company HQ provided a good view of the mouth of the Berbice River. In between clearings of courida trees he could make out the Rosignol harbor in the distance. He could also see the New Amsterdam quayside and much of the quarter-mile access road from Strand. The access road's intersection with Strand was blocked by buildings, but close to the ferry's arrival and departure times, the intersection became alive with honking horns.

The ferry seemed to be off schedule today. It docked at the New Amsterdam station at 09:30. Moore did not expect Cadogan this early but looked out for a while after he heard the honking horns from the direction of the access road. Maybe the next ferry, he thought.

At about 10:35 hours, Beharry alerted Moore to Cadogan's presence in the park. Cadogan had stopped about forty feet from the bandstand and was observing some of the soldiers chasing after a braying Eveready. Moore noticed that the jeep had been pulled off onto the grass on the side of Strand and wondered why Cadogan had not driven in.

"What's with this donkey?" Cadogan asked as he mounted the bandstand steps.

"It grazes in the park and won't go away, so the soldiers adopted it as a mascot," Moore replied.

"I see," Cadogan scowled.

"Actually, Colonel, we've hired the donkey cart to transport supplies from the market because we've been using all of the vehicles for patrolling," Moore added.

"Well, it seems to be providing some entertainment," Cadogan said, looking over at Beharry as if inspecting his uniform. "The soldiers were calling it a name?"

The question was clearly directed at Beharry, but Beharry had his lips pressed together to restrain laughter. Moore quickly came to Beharry's rescue. "They call the donkey 'Eveready,'" he said.

Cadogan seated himself on a side bench and looked over at the prancing donkey. "I can see why," he declared and then asked Moore for an assessment of the situation.

Moore pointed out that there had been no incidents. The three sugar estates at Rose Hall, Albion, and Skeldon were patrolled intensively at night. During the daytime, the sugar estates' watchmen seemed to cope, with some help from the police. There had been no fires in the sugarcane fields. Security at the bauxite plant at Everton was good both during the day and during the night, and the fact that the mining operations were continuing decreased the likelihood of outsiders coming in. Nevertheless, he had sent out one squad from Lieutenant Beharry's platoon to patrol the area at night. In fact, he himself had led the patrol the previous evening.

"Have you conducted any searches and seizures?" Cadogan asked.

"No, Colonel. For one thing, we don't have the personnel. We patrol at night and sleep during the day. But it don't make sense to infuriate the strikers by searching their homes when no acts of violence have been committed."

Cadogan did not disagree. "What's the itinerary for today?" he asked.

"Well, Colonel. I thought we would just do a drive through at Rose Hall and then go up to Albion and have lunch with Lieutenant Persico. After that, we could go up to Skeldon and visit Lieutenant Mentore's platoon. Lieutenant Beharry is here, of course, but you could speak with the other officers about the situation at their respective locations."

Cadogan stood up. "Give me a few minutes to settle in, then we'll head out."

"Are you staying overnight, Colonel?" Moore asked.

"Yes . . ."

"Well, let me get the sergeant major to arrange sleeping quarters for you."

"Don't worry, Alan. I got a reservation at the *Rooster's Run.*"

"Oh!" Moore uttered, unable to hide his surprise and uncertain what to say. An uncomfortable silence followed before Moore resumed. "Well, Colonel, do you want me to ride over with you, or do you want to pick me up after you check in?"

"Actually, Alan, why you don't take your jeep? I think I might want to look 'round a little bit after the inspection, visit some people and so on, you know?"

"Yes, Colonel. Ahm, would you mind if Lieutenant Beharry accompanied me? His men are confined to camp, and his platoon sergeant can take care of them. I'd like Lieutenant Beharry to hear the other officers' briefings in case we have to reshuffle the platoons."

"Not at all. Bring him along. He can keep you company, and he can give me a run down on things at Rose Hall, so we don't have to go there this time."

Moore and Beharry exchanged glances, both surprised at how easily Cadogan had conceded.

"Awright," said Cadogan, straightening up to receive the salutes of his two subordinates, "I'll see you in a few minutes."

The two officers watched Cadogan walk out of the park to the jeep waiting for him on the grass, on the side of Strand. Beharry spoke first. "Looks like the man came down to play."

"Looks that way," Moore agreed, shaking his head.

* * *

Arms akimbo, Moore paced the bandstand. The jeep was parked by the steps, and McCurchin moved back and forth between the vehicle and a dominoes game under one of the flamboyant trees. An hour had elapsed, and Colonel Cadogan had not returned. Lieutenant Beharry, who had stopped by twice before, now reappeared at the foot of the stairs.

"Alan, why we don't go over to the *Rooster's Run* and get Saddle?"

"I don't know. I don't want to get involved in his private business."

"What private business, Alan? We are operational."

"You're right, Ramesh. Let's go. McCurchin!"

The jeep exited the park onto Strand, traveling east for one block before it turned down a side street connecting Strand to Princess Elizabeth Road. It made a right turn on Princess Elizabeth and went up four blocks before taking another side street onto the upper end of Strand, traveling east again, in the direction of the New Amsterdam market and the encampment further up. A hundred yards up the road and above the heads of the pedestrians, a vertical sign, "*ROOSTER'S RUN*," in faded red, green, and black colors, hung from one corner of a three-storied, cream-and-white building with a red, corrugated zinc roof. It could be read from both sides. Below this sign and forming an inverted T with it was another sign that read "*HOTEL*." The glass encasement was broken at several places, suggesting that some stone-thrower had used it for target practice.

Cadogan's jeep was parked at the front entrance, but the driver was not around. McCurchin pulled up behind the parked jeep, and Moore instructed Beharry to try to locate the colonel's driver. As Beharry approached the colonel's jeep, Lance Corporal Bascom came running from the cake shop across the street.

"Corporal Bascom, what's the situation with Colonel Cadogan?" Beharry asked.

"He checking in, Lieutenant."

"Well, he been checking in for over an hour!"

"Lieutenant, I am just the driver."

"Lieutenant Beharry!" Moore called out. Beharry turned around. "Don't say anything to him," Moore said quietly. "He'll just report you to Saddle and land you in trouble. Let's just wait here." Then looking over Beharry's shoulder at the hotel entrance, Moore exclaimed under his breath, "Talking 'bout the devil!"

Beharry turned around and saluted.

Colonel Cadogan stood at the entrance of the *Rooster's Run*, placing his beret on his head. Beads of sweat were running down the sides of his brown face. He reached into his hip pocket for his handkerchief and sopped up the perspiration from his cheeks and forehead and lightly touched up his moustache. Then he squinted and looked up in vain for the sun but phewed anyway in an apparent attempt to suggest difficulty coping with the outside heat.

Beharry whispered to Moore, "The man looks like he just did a six-mile run . . . or something."

"Or something is right!" Moore whispered. "Look again!"

Cadogan had stepped onto the pavement to allow a broad female frame to come through the entrance. She was a bulbous-bosomed, middle-aged woman with a reddish brown, pleasant but nondescript oval face. Her stiff hair was ironed back into a beehive and secured behind her head by clips. She seemed briefly disoriented by the presence of the other officers at the hotel entrance, but, in response to Cadogan's hand gesture, walked towards the rear of his jeep. Every part of her body seemed to be in motion, mostly up and down. She was rectangular from her shoulders to the bottom of her behind, except that the tightly drawn corded belt around the mid-section of her pink-flowered dress provided some small definition. Her wrists were adorned with gold bracelets, the accumulation no doubt from years of favors.

Cadogan did not introduce the woman to the officers. Instead, he stood at the rear of the jeep while Corporal Bascom lowered the tailgate for the woman to climb up. The exercise proved to be more of an athletic challenge than the woman in her narrow hemline could handle and, to the amazement and amusement of both Moore and Beharry, Corporal Bascom and Colonel Cadogan had to help her up, each holding one of her hands and Cadogan left-shouldering her rump. It was like pushing a reluctant mare into an oxcart. When Corporal Bascom closed the tailgate, Cadogan instructed Moore to lead the way.

Drifting back towards his jeep with Lieutenant Beharry, Moore said under his breath, "Imagine this man bringing his sweet-woman on a military inspection," and sucked his teeth.

"Easy, Alan," Beharry replied. "Is like Mentore said the other day, the big ones can do as they like. He gon leave tomorrow anyway." Then he added in a mischievous tone, "Just a little r and r at the R and R!"

Moore broke into a smirk. "Just get in the jeep."

THIRTEEN

*T*HE JEEPS MADE THEIR way eastward on Strand past the encampment at Esplanade Park to the outskirts of town and then joined the Berbice highway for the trek along the Atlantic coast. Cadogan knew the way and would normally have been in the lead vehicle. Not today; he probably did not want the sweet-woman to be in the constant view of the trailing jeep, Moore surmised. Cadogan's shenanigan had rekindled Moore's anger over his loss of seniority and the events that led up to it. There was no question, he thought, that Lieutenant Mentore was right about the way the big boys behaved. No question, too, that Uncle Lenny was right about the problems he was describing in his weekly columns. Yet, if you say anything, you'll get in trouble; and if you don't, it will eat your insides to admit that you're bowing to basic survival instincts.

McCurchin drew Moore out of his contemplations on the approach to the Canje Creek bridge.

"Captain, you remember the days when you had to line up and wait for the boats to pass through the bridge?" McCurchin asked, referring to the old, single-span, swing bridge which was dismantled after the Americans built this arched concrete bridge a few hundred yards closer to the Atlantic shoreline.

"Oh yes, but it's quicker now," Moore replied. The jeep was ascending the steep arch. "The view is a lot better now too," he added, looking over the side at the huge sugar boat heading into the Canje Creek to be loaded at the Rose Hall Sugar Estate. Still, he missed the old swing bridge. He remembered the years at Berbice High School when he rode his Raleigh bicycle over the bridge twice a day. If you were late to school, you could say the bridge was open. If you were late getting back home in the afternoon, the old bridge came to your rescue again. And what fun to ride up to the gate and watch the bridge opening! He remembered the grating sounds of the gears as the bridge swung each way and the giant clang when it closed. He remembered the large sugar boats, *Essex Queen*, *Lochaber*, and *Miss Phoebe*, pitch black a few feet above the water and white almost everywhere else, inching their way through. And the watchman, standing like Horatius at the bridge, yelling at the little boys who tried to go through the gate to have a closer look. But now the old bridge was gone. It's sad, when you think about it—old things and old values giving way to progress and God knows what else.

The jeeps descended the Canje Creek bridge into Sheet Anchor, a small village extending for half of a mile or so to No. 2 Village. It was one of the curiosities of life here that between the Berbice and Corentyne Rivers were clusters of villages with numbered names. Moore had always wondered why this was so, reasoning that the villages had perhaps all been numbered in the original layout. The British had renamed some, such as Albion and Skeldon, where they had sugar plantations, and freed slaves and Indian laborers released from their indenture had given names to others where they settled, like Eversham and Bengal. The rest, however, had retained their original numbers, and over time, strong affection and attachment developed around the numbered names. Today, you could cause a riot by attempting to change the name of No. 64 Village!

The Sheet Anchor village center provided the intersection for the road coming out from the Rose Hall Sugar Estate. The landmark at the head of the Rose Hall road was the Sheet Anchor rum stop, as familiar to Moore as the old Canje Creek bridge, except that the rum shop was still standing there, a lure to weary workers and a recurring source of torment to their wives. A ramp-like bridge from the side of Sheet Anchor road spanned the narrow drainage ditch and led up to a railed porch on the ground floor of that white two-storied building with a red corrugated zinc roof. Several barefooted men, probably sugar workers on strike, sat on the fixed seats along the rails, looking out to the road and talking. Barring the entrance of the rum shop were four wooden panels, the edges painted reddish brown, each bolted in through a metal brace that ran across them. It would be 15:00 hours before those bolts were withdrawn and the lively chatter moved inside so that the men could moisten their throats again and again. Moore noticed the brightness of the paint on the building—rare these days, but then rum was the country's first choice of celebration and final source of solace.

Only the residents knew with certainty the dividing line between Sheet Anchor and No. 2 Village, but everyone knew that No. 2 ended at the sharp, right-angled, Palmyra Turn, orienting the highway to the north. On the left, for about the next mile, was the village of Palmyra, its houses fronting the highway from lots of even width and depth and connected to the highway by culverts or footbridges, depending on family means. Across the canal on the right side of the highway, and as far as the eye could see, were sugarcane stalks in neat rows, the white plumage swaying with the breeze, a sight Moore had enjoyed since childhood. Today, he had to look at the fields through McCurchin's window since the jeep was a right-hand drive, and, following the rules of the road, they were driving on the left side. At the end of Palmyra came the Seawell Turn, sharply reorienting the road from north to east. For the next six miles up to the Borlum Turn, you could smell the salt air from the Atlantic Ocean, hardly a mile away to the left.

The left side of the highway, beyond the scattered housing close to the Seawell Turn, was a swampy area, where the salt water from the Atlantic had pushed past the line of courida trees, and, on the right hand side, the sugarcane fields soon gave way to rice fields on reclaimed lands, and then to swamp and scattered houses. The weather-worn primary school and the concrete health center announced arrival at the No. 19 Village. Footbridges of varying widths spanned the canal on the left side, and the unevenly spaced houses seem to have an easy coexistence with the creeping overflow from the Atlantic. No. 19 Village yielded abruptly to swamp on both sides of the highway all the way up to the Borlum Turn. As they made their way toward the Borlum Turn, Moore looked over at the kingfishers on their dives announcing that the tide was in.

This stretch of road past No. 19 Village always reminded Moore of his grandfather, who used to tell how before he went into the interior as a pork-knocker mining for gold, he rode shotgun on Mr. Banarsee's donkey cart on its weekly grocery run from Springlands on the Corentyne Coast, where he grew up, to New Amsterdam at the mouth of the Berbice River. Those were the days before independence, when the highway was just a graded, dirt road. Mr. Banarsee employed a regular cart driver to bring back bags of flour, cans of salted butter, and crates of salted codfish, split peas, potatoes, and onions, which he sold in his shop, but Mr. Banarsee paid Moore's grandfather two shillings to ride on the cart beside the driver, and at fifteen, he was happy to earn so much money.

For stretches of the road, the donkey could gallop and make good time, but the dirt road was badly pitted, and the rain made it water-logged and muddy. At times, Moore's grandfather had to walk behind the cart as the driver whipped the donkey to get the extra thrust out of deep pot holes. Night time always seemed to find them somewhere along the desolate, four-mile stretch between the Borlum Turn and No. 19 Village. Especially during the rainy season, the only light came from the kerosene lamp hanging below the cart from a nail at the front between Moore's grandfather and the driver. When the wind picked up late at night, Moore's grandfather said you could hear the voices of Dutchmen crying, "Neighbor, oi; Neighbor, oi." The driver would put his finger to his lips to caution him to keep still, lest they upset the dead. Moore's grandfather said that those were the spirits of Dutch slave owners condemned to roam the coast forever.

On those evenings when their grandfather re-told the story to them on the front landing, Alan and his sister, Grace, and their cousins would move in closer to the kerosene lamp and to their grandfather, making sure their bodies touched each other so that nothing else could get between them. Even now, late at night along this stretch of the coast, Alan would sometimes find himself listening out, as he knew others did, for the pleading wails of restless Dutchmen crying, "Neighbor, oi; Neighbor, oi."

In the jeep's left-side mirror, Moore caught a glimpse of Colonel Cadogan and rolled his eyes. It was a good thing they were in motion, he thought, but soon they would have to stop. He was not looking forward to that. He brightened when he thought of Jeanene's visit the next day. He planned to leave Beharry in charge of the camp for the weekend. This was one of the reasons he had brought Beharry on the trip to Skeldon—it would be the only recreation Beharry would have for a while.

Soon they had completed the open stretch, and village life began again when they entered No. 1 Village. Two miles up and the jeeps came to the Albion access road, laid out like the other sugar estate roads, perpendicular to the coastal highway. It was a narrow pitched road with a wide canal on each side to allow the sugar estate to flush their factory's foul-smelling effluent into the Atlantic. The jeeps pulled over to the side to accommodate a large bulk truck bringing sugar out from the Albion Sugar Estate. Rolling up his window to keep out the sour stench from the canal, Moore spotted a bloated fish caught in the reeds on the far side of the canal.

The Albion road separated the villages of Sand Reef and Guava Bush, the houses on each side randomly strewn along the road behind coconut palms, genip, and mango trees, their entrances announced by narrow foot bridges across the canals. Moore knew he had reached Albion when he saw the beginning of the fenced senior staff compound with large, white bungalows sitting on stilts and, just beyond them, the huge sugar factory and distillery, active monuments to two centuries of converting human toil into sweetness and intoxicants. The jeeps made a left turn just before the factory onto the road leading to the Presbyterian Mission school. On the right hand side, across the drainage moat, sat the Big House of the Administrative Manager, the modern-day, corporate descendant of the plantation owner. Like the Big Houses of the other plantations, this was a three-storied mansion, surrounded by flamboyant and palm trees on a multi-acre plot with hibiscus and croton hedges. Across from the Big House, on the other side of the road, was a larger compound where the lesser managers lived. This was where the jeeps turned.

The security guard at the gate waved them on, and they proceeded for a hundred yards or so down the main street before turning right, into compound of the Senior Staff Club. McCurchin brought the jeep to a stop by the external stairs. Moore and Beharry dismounted and waited for the Colonel and his sweet-woman.

Soldiers from Lieutenant Persico's platoon were relaxing in the breeze-way formed by the eight-foot columns supporting the building, the bottom-house, as it was called. One group sat around a small table slapping dominoes into position. The card table was quieter. A few soldiers were waiting to get into one or the other game, and a handful were just sitting flat on the concrete base of the bottom-house, backs against the columns, talking. The soldiers stopped their games and saluted the arriving group of officers, whereupon the Colonel told them to carry on.

Moore and Beharry led the way up the outside stairs into the Club house and veered to the left. The lounge and the game rooms had been converted to sleeping quarters for the soldiers, and their bedrolls on the floor clearly defined narrow territories for each soldier. Lieutenant Persico, who had taken one of the guest rooms on the next level came down and greeted the officers. He seemed momentarily confused by the presence of the woman and looked over at Moore as if he expected an explanation, but quickly sized up the situation and invited his guests for a drink at the bar, run by the regular Club attendant. The Colonel chose a Coke for the woman and himself, and Moore and Beharry followed suit.

"What's the situation here, George?" Colonel Cadogan asked Lieutenant Persico after they had seated themselves at the bar.

Persico looked over at the woman and then at Moore. Moore understood Persico's discomfort with discussing operational matters in front of non-military personnel but offered no help out of the dilemma. Persico faced the Colonel again. "Everything's going fine, Colonel. We had a few fires in the cane fields, but those have since been harvested."

"By whom?"

"Well, they using scabs from Fyrish and a few neighboring areas, but they're not sufficient to keep the factory grinding at full capacity."

"I see."

"As you know, Colonel, this is a very strong Opposition area, so the union meetings are like political meetings. They have large turnouts. I usually send a squad to support the police."

"How are the soldiers getting on here?"

"Well, there is not much to do around here. When they're downstairs relaxing, they sometimes whistle at the women passing by. I try to stop them, but I'm not always around."

"Any complaints?"

"Well, yes. The Admin Manager has talked to me about it. Also, the soldiers play their radios loud at night, after they get back from patrolling."

The platoon sergeant came up to tell Lieutenant Persico that lunch was ready. The officers and the sweet-woman followed Persico into the dining area, a small open space that had been converted to a dining area by the addition of an eight-foot table and ten chairs. Cadogan seated the woman and asked Moore to sit on her left side. He invited Lieutenant Persico to sit on his right. Lieutenant Beharry, who entered the room last, sat on Captain Moore's left.

Lunch consisted of curried fish and rice, with pickled cucumbers and lemonade. For Moore, this was a welcome change from the standard chicken fare. Throughout lunch, he felt an obligation to be attentive to the woman, and that proved to be a struggle. The woman was a chatter box. She spoke compulsively and incessantly. She spoke of her trip to Trinidad and how plentiful things were in comparison to here. She talked of the Colonel and what a great man he was. She spoke of her sister, of the Colonel, and again of Trinidad. Her stories were seamless and unending, punctuated only by the intermittent extension of her tongue in a flicking motion to clear the corners of her mouth. It was like having dinner with a large, bejewelled lizard. Beharry's amused face as he sat there without

117

speaking was, on the one hand, a source of reassurance and commiseration by someone else who saw through this, but, on the other hand, strained Moore's own ability to present a straight face.

What interested Moore, however, was the intensity of conversation Cadogan was carrying on with Lieutenant Persico. Indeed, lunch was not formally over until Cadogan had finished the conversation with Persico, and, as they filed out of the dining area, Cadogan called out to Moore.

"Alan, lemme have a word with you."

Moore stopped. "Colonel?"

"Alan, we are moving Lieutenant Persico out of F-Company. He will be the new Admin Officer for the Farm Corps."

Moore was silent for a moment, studying the Colonel's face and hoping for some amplification. The Colonel offered none. "When will this take effect, Colonel?" Moore asked.

"Monday. It will be published in the Brigade Orders coming out next week."

"We are going to be short-handed, Colonel."

"I know. Second Lieutenant Pilgrim will take over his platoon."

"Second Lieutenant? I thought he was an officer cadet."

"Well, yes, but he will be commissioned next month. He needs the experience."

Moore was not happy about the short notice or the replacement, but there wasn't anything he could say. They walked back to the group, and Cadogan sought out his woman. Moore sidled up to Persico. "George, is what going on?"

Persico shrugged. "I am not sure."

Moore believed part of this because of the surprise he had seen in Persico's face while Cadogan was speaking to him at lunch. But Moore also did not think Persico was telling all. Perhaps that wasn't fair to Persico, he thought. What could Persico tell him when they were standing so close to Cadogan? Maybe he would fill them in later, but then, how could he? He would be gone this weekend.

At about 13:30, Moore approached Cadogan about departing for Skeldon. Beharry hung back, Moore thought, to observe the loading of the sweet-woman into the back of Cadogan's jeep, then quickly jumped into the back of the lead vehicle. Out on the Albion road, and, in a few minutes, they turned right onto the Berbice highway. The highway stayed true to the Atlantic coastline meandering through small Indian villages and an occasional African village before entering the rice belt. With the Colonel's vehicle behind, McCurchin followed Moore's cue and stayed close to the 35 miles-per-hour speed limit in the built-up areas. That, and slowing down to a crawl for animals on the road and for roadside markets, made it 14:55 hours when they passed through the No. 62 toll gate.

By the time the jeeps reached No. 71 Village, school had been out for the elementary schoolchildren, and the road had become a sea of tiny, giggling faces in bright uniforms, crisscrossing the road. The jeeps slowed down and retained slow speed through No. 74, before accelerating through the desolate Long Road, separating sugarcane fields on the right and scattered housing on the left, into Springlands. Indian film music issuing from the *Arawak*—hotel, bar, and restaurant—welcomed the visitors to the Upper Corentyne's commercial center, which Springlands shared with No. 78 and No. 79 Villages. Moore decided to forego a courtesy stop at the Springlands Police Station on the right, postponing that consideration for the return trip. On the left side near the edge of the road, the Radio City Cinema's two large posters advertized its weekend double-feature—*Dragon Fist* and *Raiders of the Lost Ark*.

With very little vehicular traffic on the road, the jeeps made their way through the half-mile stretch of Springlands and No. 78 Village rather quickly. After they passed the Masjid on the left, Moore could see the seawall from various points on the No. 79 Village road. Toward the end of No. 79 Village, the vehicles slowed down for the pedestrian market traffic out of Skeldon, and just past the No. 79 koker, it was stop-and-go as they picked their way through the Skeldon market, with vendors on both sides of the road.

Moore's jeep emerged from the market to find soldiers from Lieutenant Mentore's platoon deployed along the road just outside the compound of the sugar factory. He directed McCurchin to pull up to where Lieutenant Mentore was speaking to the police inspector.

"Good afternoon, Captain," Mentore greeted Moore with a salute. The inspector saluted as well.

"What's going on?" Moore asked. Colonel Cadogan had now joined them.

"We had an incident out here," Mentore replied. "Some striking workers pelted the truck carrying the scabs. Some of the scabs jumped out and brandished their cutlasses."

"Anybody injured?" Cadogan asked.

"Not seriously. I think a couple of the scabs got cut from the stones. Fortunately, some policemen were in the market and they came over to prevent a fight. We came out to assist in dispersing the protesters."

"Well, I'm glad that's over," Cadogan said.

"It may not be, Colonel," Mentore said.

"Why not?"

"Well, Colonel, the police arrested three protesters. Just random arrests to intimidate the protesters and send them scurrying, so there could be some trouble."

"What kind of trouble?"

"The sugar union has a meeting at the market square this afternoon—17:00 hours, I think. It was scheduled before this incident. They could use the arrest to stir up the crowd."

"You don't expect them to charge the police station?" Cadogan asked.

"No, nothing like that. But we could have more fires in the sugar cane fields later on."

"I see."

"Also, Colonel, this is a mixed community and people get along very well. The problem is that the strikers are mostly Indian, and the scabs are Black. The police are worried about racial violence. By the way, Colonel, this is Inspector Pollard," Mentore said, introducing the police inspector.

"I know the Inspector," Cadogan said, "he used to be at the police station in Madhia."

"I was a sergeant then," Pollard said. "You got a good memory, Colonel."

"So, what y'all planning to do?" Cadogan asked Mentore.

"The police usually has a surveillance team at the meeting," Inspector Pollard said, preempting Mentore.

"I plan to deploy a squad to support the police and just as a show of force," Mentore said. "It might make them think twice about using inflammatory language at the meeting."

"How about the people you arrested?" Cadogan asked.

"Well, it looks like they served they purpose," Moore interjected. "The demonstrators were dispersed, and since no one is sure whether these fellas threw the stones, why not let them go?"

"We intend to do that," Pollard said. "In these cases, we would ask them to report to the police station once a day for about a week. That should keep them out of trouble and restrain others."

The market was now beginning to clear up on both sides of the road. The police unit withdrew, and Lieutenant Mentore ordered his men back into the truck. Colonel Cadogan suggested that Captain Moore and Lieutenant Beharry return with Lieutenant Mentore to the Skeldon Sugar Estate Senior Staff Club, where Mentore's platoon was billeted. He would join them after he had dropped off the sweet-woman at the stores they had passed in No. 78 Village.

FOURTEEN

A T THE SENIOR STAFF Club, Lieutenant Mentore instructed his platoon sergeant to let the men rest for about an hour, but to be sure they were loaded back on the trucks by 16:45. With that, he led the officers to the lounge upstairs, where every available space outside the slimmest perimeter around the bar was being used for sleeping or storage of soldiers' kit. Here, as at Albion, the soldiers tended to congregate under the Club in the open space framed by the concrete stilts supporting the bungalow. The officers seated themselves at the bar, and Lieutenant Mentore rehearsed with Moore the unremarkable report he intended to give Colonel Cadogan. He had just finished when they all heard the Colonel talking with the soldiers downstairs. Moore decided to use that moment to break the news of Persico's impending transfer to Lieutenants Beharry and Mentore.

"But why Farm Corps?" Moore asked. "Persico is a climber; Farm Corps looks to me like a dead end."

"But you don't know what they promised him," Mentore said.

"Did he have a choice?" Beharry asked.

"No," Moore replied, "but they generally don't send regular line officers to these types of service jobs unless they believe the officer might be willing. Besides, Persico doesn't know a thing about agriculture."

"The job is an admin job," Beharry said. "George doesn't have to be an agricultural expert. He gon have people on the farm who know what they doing."

"True, except that, so far, every commanding officer for Farm Corps has had agricultural credentials," Moore pointed out.

"But there weren't many of them," Beharry said. "Farm Corps is a recent thing."

"True, but still—"

"Why we beating 'round the bush?" Mentore asked. "Y'all know that Saddle don't like the CO for Farm Corps. The guy wasn't giving Saddle the help Saddle wanted on his private farm. I was in the Mess when the Farm Officer was complaining to us."

"But why George Persico?" Beharry asked.

"I gon tell you why," Mentore said.

Moore laughed. This was typical Mentore, he thought. "Awright, leh we hear the expert."

"George Persico is an ass kisser, and they know it. He gon go wherever they send he, and Saddle is sure George gon do whatever they ask he. That's the first thing."

"Awright, we agree with that," Moore said, smiling and looking over at Beharry.

"Secondly, y'all thinking like British officers about line officers and service officers. Them things don't work here no more. They can take an officer from Farm Corps and make he Chief of Staff, if they want. And talking about the Chief of Staff . . ."

They laughed aloud.

"I think there is a promotion in it for George," Mentore predicted.

"You might be right," Moore said.

"Not 'might', Captain. I am right!"

Moore looked at him and smiled, knowing that an elaboration was imminent.

"How many men in Farm Corps?" Mentore asked. "Counting all of the locations now, not just the farm at Garden of Eden."

"Straight head count? I'd say company strength," Moore said.

"Either he getting promoted on this job or he gon get a bigger command afterward," Mentore asserted, "but he ain't coming back here as a platoon leader."

"Sounds reasonable," Moore said. Beharry was nodding his agreement.

"But Saddle is going to use his ass in the meantime!" Mentore made a short, sharp stroke with his right hand.

Colonel Cadogan's entry into the lounge ended that conversation. He told the officers that he was pleased with the way the soldiers were working with the police and that he wanted to see the collaboration firsthand at the union meeting.

*   *   *

The union meeting did not begin until 17:30 hours, but people had moved into the area well before 17:00. They were standing or sitting on both sides of the highway used for the afternoon market. Many were sitting along the seawall. Still others stood or sat in their yards knowing that the loudspeakers would reach them. A handful of police officers were present, standing at some distance from the crowd. Moore counted five. The 3-ton army truck carrying Lieutenant Mentore and a squad of soldiers was parked about a hundred feet from the crowd's edge, behind Moore's jeep, which had also brought Cadogan and Beharry. Mentore left his soldiers on the truck and joined the other officers standing by the jeep.

The meeting was orderly, and there was no need to deploy the soldiers. The first speaker was more of a political agitator than a union man. He assailed the government for its "squanderamania" that had left the country prostrate. He called the President "the greatest ban-master in the world" for banning the importation of flour, dal, potatoes, cheese, and sardines. He lamented the low daily wage of the sugar worker and compared it to the rising prices of commodities. Their current daily wage, the agitator said, was lower than the price of a pint of cooking oil. Moore thought the analogy apt and the wage rates deplorable. He too would be on strike if he were in their situation.

The second speaker was the union's general secretary. This was the first of a series of whistlestop meetings for him. In combative tone, he outlined the correspondences the union leaders had sent to the Labor Minister, always beginning loudly and vehemently with "I wrote to the Minista," as though he were saying "I punched the Minista." He would then pause for effect. It was sheer flatulence, Moore thought, because by the speaker's own recounting, he achieved nothing out of the correspondences he had shot off to the Labor Minister, but the union man's hope was that the audience would be impressed, and, satiated by the aggressive tone of the reporting, would miss the lack of outcome. Then at the end, the union man seemed to be preparing the workers for a lower percentage increase than originally demanded when he reported that the Leader of the Opposition, and honorary head of the sugar union, was having talks with the President himself on a range of issues. The Opposition Leader would also raise these issues in Parliament. Moore smiled. Hadn't the Opposition boycotted Parliament for two years to protest the rigging of the elections? And hadn't Uncle Lenny described Parliament as a beautiful building but a barren institution crammed with people, none of whom knew exactly how they had gotten there? Still, the speaker clearly understood the mentality of the canecutters, isolated, as they were, in a world of No. 20

cutlasses and sugarcane stalks. The gladiatorial posturing and the rhetorical ranting about a distant world of Parliament, and Minister, and President were calculated to seduce the hapless souls into enduring the additional hardships necessary to prolong the strike.

The meeting ended at about 19:00 hours, and the crowd dispersed peacefully, leaving only some fishermen and traders tending their boats on the bank of the Corentyne River. Inspector Pollard came over to where the officers were standing.

"Colonel Cadogan," he said, "why don't you and these officers join me for a drink? The wife will prepare some dinner."

Cadogan looked at the other officers.

"Duck curry," Pollard added.

That did it. Cadogan accepted. He instructed Lieutenant Mentore to dispatch the truck back to the Senior Staff Club and to arrange for his driver to bring his traveling companion to the Springlands Police Station. Cadogan got into the front of the jeep with McCurchin, leaving Moore to join Lieutenant Beharry in the rear of the vehicle. After Mentore had sent off the truck, he also climbed into the back of the jeep, and Colonel Cadogan instructed McCurchin to follow Inspector Pollard's jeep to the Springlands Police Station.

Pollard's house was a two-storied bungalow behind the Police Station, and like the Police Station, it was painted yellow and had a red roof. The officers followed Pollard into the living room on the first floor. He retrieved his wife from the kitchen and introduced her to the guests, after which she promptly retreated into the kitchen. Moore, Mentore, and Beharry each settled for a Bass Ale. The Colonel joined Pollard in pouring from the rum bottle placed on the coffee table in front of them.

"Cheers," Pollard said, lifting his glass and taking a large swallow. He smacked his lips loudly before setting his glass down and leaving in the direction of the kitchen. He returned minutes later with two plates, one carrying the contents from a can of pilchard, and the other from a can of salmon. His wife followed him with a tray of sliced bread. Real bread.

Cadogan reached forward to help himself. "Where'd you get these?" he asked Pollard.

"We bought them. The wife baked the bread."

"But these are banned goods."

"Yes, but you know we live by the river, and people trading all the time with Suriname."

"Is not you who is supposed to stop them?"

"Stop them? How? We don't own the river. The international boundary line is the high water mark of the Corentyne River on our coast. We can only patrol that river with authorization from the Surinamese police."

Cadogan did not argue, nor did anyone else make an issue of the appearance of banned goods. The treats seemed most welcome, and everyone partook with great relish.

"Well, I envy you fellas out here," Cadogan said. Then turning to Lieutenant Mentore, he observed loudly, "Derryck, I notice you're very quiet. I bet you ain't starving down here." They all laughed.

A knock on the door, and the Colonel's sweet-woman joined them.

"Banned goods!" she said, helping herself. "Is everywhere you go 'round here, you finding banned goods."

Pollard's wife came in to let him know she was ready for the guests. On his invitation, the officers and the colonel's sweet-woman followed Pollard into the dining room, where he showed them to seats around a rectangular dining table. At the center was a large serving tray of duck curry and next to it a pile of dal puri. Mrs. Pollard stood back, waiting to see how else she could serve the guests. She was not joining them at the table.

"Where you get all the flour and the split peas?" the Colonel's sweet-woman asked, referring to the dal puri on the table.

"People smuggle those things in all the time," Mrs. Pollard answered. "The Inspector," she said, referring to her husband, "knows somebody who does get we what we want."

Pollard seemed embarrassed. "Well," he said, "There is this chap I know. I ask him and he says he gon ask around."

"Can you get me some flour?" the sweet-woman asked.

"Me too," Moore said, thinking of Jeanene's visit the next day. Lieutenant Mentore nudged him and, in a low whisper, told him he would get him some flour. Colonel Cadogan seemed to have a different interest.

"You said you got this from some chap? Is he a smuggler?"

"I know he got a boat that he uses to go up the river to Orealla and sell things to the Amerindians," Pollard replied. "I don't know if he is a smuggler. Of course, there are a lot of people with boats, and there is a lot of smuggling going on."

"What's his name, this fellow?"

"Deonarine, but we call him Pandit."

"Is he a priest?"

"No, I think the father was a pandit, so people started calling he Pandit, being that he was the eldest boy and all."

"Is he from Skeldon?" Cadogan asked.

"No, he from No. 79, not far from the koker. He got a shop there."

"What's he selling?"

"Well, like all the shops around, the shelves ain't got nothing much. Is mostly a cake shop, selling sweets, pine drink, mauby, and so on."

"Sound like a front for the smuggling business, if you ask me," Cadogan observed.

"I don't know 'bout that, Colonel. To tell the truth, they had that shop long before all these shortages. His wife running the shop. He himself is a teacher at Skeldon Lutheran School."

"So how does he do the business with the Amerindians?" Cadogan asked.

"He got people working for him."

"I see," Cadogan said, then after a few moments added, "I want to meet this fella. Can you send for he?"

"Well, Colonel Cadogan, Mr. Deonarine is a fairly prominent man. I just can't send for he."

"How does he get what you need?"

"I would send a list to he and he would say he gon ask around. Then he gets the stuff."

"How can I meet he then?" Cadogan asked.

"He does come to the seawall every evening, time like now," the Inspector's wife said. "He does give the boys a drink and check up on the boat."

Inspector Pollard appeared not too pleased with his wife's forthrightness. "But you don't know he gon be there now," he said, in a vain attempt to end this line of inquiry.

"Can you send someone to check?" Cadogan asked. "If he's out there, I want to walk over and meet he."

Inspector Pollard rose and went to the front door. He stuck his head out and called out to a policeman in the station.

"Look, run over to the seawall and see if Pandit by the boat."

They were finishing up the meal when the policeman knocked and confirmed to Inspector Pollard that Pandit was at the seawall. The officers thanked Mrs. Pollard for the delicious meal. The sweet-woman thanked her for the two two-pound bags of flour she'd given her, and they piled into the two jeeps. Cadogan stopped the jeeps just past the No. 79 Village koker and walked over to the seawall with the Inspector to meet Deonarine. Moore decided to join them. After all, he thought, this was an area his troops were patrolling, and he needed to learn as much as he could.

Deonarine was standing near the seawall giving instructions to the crew chief. He furrowed his eyebrows when he looked over at the group of uniformed officers approaching but seemed to relax when the Inspector waved to him.

"How you do, Pandit?"

"Half-and-half."

The voice had an effeminate shrill for such a large man, Moore thought. He was about five-foot eight, fair complexioned and stocky. He had a smooth, hairless, rectangular face, but appeared cylindrical from his shoulders down.

"Pandit," Inspector Pollard said, "I want you to meet these two officers from the army. This is Colonel Cadogan, and this is Captain Moore. I was just telling them how you's a very good friend and a very prominent member of the community. I want you to meet them in case they can ever help you." Then turning to Cadogan, he asked, "Not so?"

"Oh yes, yes," Cadogan said.

Deonarine was pleased but tried to be self-effacing. "Well, the Inspector and me, we like this," he said, bringing his index and center fingers together.

"Yes, the Inspector speaks very well of you. We just wanted to stop by and meet you, when he pointed you out on the seawall."

"Well, any friend of the Inspector . . ."

"Yes," said Cadogan. "You know, I come up here a lot. Next time, leh we have a drink."

"You must let the Inspector know. Then he can get hold of me."

The officers' visit had pulled Deonarine away from his men. The conversation now ended, Deonarine began walking back to his men. As the officers made their way to the jeep, Cadogan turned to take another look at him.

"He got a drop foot?" Cadogan asked Inspector Pollard.

"Why you ask?"

"Well, he walking like he about to go down on one side."

"Oh that," Pollard replied. "Nothing's wrong with the foot. The fella got a goadee!" Cadogan and Moore muted their snickering until they got to the jeep.

Moore had planned to take Lieutenant Mentore back to the Senior Staff Club, collect his flour, and head back to New Amsterdam with Lieutenant Beharry and Colonel Cadogan. This quickly changed.

"Alan, why don't you and Lieutenant Beharry go on? I'll be staying here for a few more hours."

"Yes, Colonel," Moore replied, wondering whether Cadogan's stay over might be connected to the smooth-faced smuggler. Birds of a feather?

FIFTEEN

*A*GRIPPA ROSE TO GREET the three salesmen from Nimble Earthmoving Equipment Company filing into his office. The fat one introduced himself as Harve, Harve Svensen. Agrippa could not catch the Swedish sounding last names of the other two, but Harve referred to them frequently as Bob and John. Harve, who did most of the talking, wore a long-sleeved, white, buttoned-down shirt, the left cuff only partially hiding his Rolex. His brown slacks rode so far below his protractedly convex stomach, they made him appear to have very short legs. His hair was wet, as were the upper part of his shirt and the lower parts of his pants. The other two, also with wet hair and clothing, seemed dressed for a golf course in their short-sleeved, polo shirts, straight-legged pants, and loafers. They had evidently not planned on the rainy season and had caught some rain along the way over to army HQ. While they waited on the coffee Agrippa had ordered, Harve explained that they had had to overnight in Port of Spain and had come in on the early Carib Air shuttle. They had just enough time to drop off their luggage at the Shady Tree Hotel by the seawall. Agrippa assured them they would enjoy Georgetown but cautioned them about the choke-and-rob gangs that preyed on pedestrians at night. The coffee now served, Agrippa moved quickly to business.

"As you know, I contacted your company before my last trip to the U.S., and one of your salespeople came from Minnesota to meet me in New York."

"That should have been me," Harve interjected. "I work in the international sales division. I was on vacation at the time."

Agrippa nodded. He noticed Harve's heavy breathing and how Harve's belly vibrated whenever he cleared his throat. "Anyway," Agrippa continued, "I gave him a list of the machines we wanted for our farming operations. The army is trying to do its part in the drive to feed, clothe, and house the nation."

"I have the list and our quote right here," Harve said, handing Agrippa a single sheet itemizing tractors, bulldozers, and a combine for a grand total of $119,000 U.S.

Agrippa looked over the list. "What will you actually sell these to us for?"

"That's it right there," Harve replied. "Our sales rep had shown you the suggested retail prices." Harve handed Agrippa several sheets with colored pictures of the various machines and the list price of each. "As you can see, we've come off those prices significantly. We want your business, General."

Agrippa compared the prices, nodding a few times to acknowledge the differences between the two sets of prices. "The way we would work this is that the Quartermaster will prepare the requisition request and attach these quotations. I will then present the request to the Defense Board for approval. I see no problem with approval. As a matter of fact, we will proceed with the order. They can approve afterwards."

"No disrespect, General, but you're sure about this?" Harve asked.

"Of course. Without the army, this government won't last too long. And I," Agrippa said, pointing to himself, "I am the Chief of Staff." The salesmen looked at one another and nodded.

"I have to approve all purchases for the army," Agrippa continued, studying the faces of his guests, "but what I would like is for you to give us quotations closer to the list price."

"I don't understand," Harve said. "You want us to bill you at a higher price?"

"Yes, but somewhere between the list price and this quote. We'll send you the payment and you can refund us the difference between that amount and this quote."

"What's the point—?"

"You can send the refund, say ten thousand U.S., into the account number I'll give you."

Harve glanced to his right and then to his left; the other two Americans were shaking their heads.

"General," Harve said, "we can't do that. We can't send a refund like this one to a private account. The auditors will question it, and the company will get into serious trouble."

"I see," Agrippa said. "You know my Farm Officer thinks we should stick with Massey Ferguson."

"Don't get me wrong, General," Harve interjected, "we very much want your business and we want to help you out, but there is this auditing problem."

"Look," Agrippa said, "I am giving you all over a hundred thousand dollars in business. Ten thousand is a small amount and it won't come out of your asking price. You get what you want out of the deal, and I get a little something."

The three salesmen looked at one another. One of them began whispering to Harve.

"Correct me if I am wrong," Agrippa said loudly, "but don't you all get commissions or bonuses on the sales that you do?"

"That's correct, General," Harve said.

"Then why can't you arrange to give out an additional ten thousand in commissions, with the understanding that it would be put by a private individual into my account."

Harve looked at each of the other two, and each nodded in turn. "We might could do that, General," Harve said.

"Well, good then. You will have to redo the quotations for the Quartermaster. Make sure you spread out the ten thousand so that your tractor doesn't appear to cost too much more than the Massey Ferguson."

"Very well, General."

"Awright," Agrippa said, rising and walking over to the hat rack to retrieve his beret. "Let's go over to the Mess and have a couple of drinks before lunch. I'll arrange for the QM to come over there. You can see him again today, or tomorrow if you prefer, after you've prepared the new quotations."

"General," Harve said, still seated, "we saw some heavy equipment by the seawall."

"Oh yes," Agrippa replied, "that belongs to the Ministry of Works. They are always doing something with the seawalls. You know, those walls were built by the Dutch in the 18th century."

"That's really something, General, we read about that before we came, but we were wondering whether you could introduce us to the procurement people over there. We have dozers and track hoes . . ."

"No problem. I'll call over there and arrange for you to meet the Permanent Secretary."

"General, anything you can do to get them to buy equipment from Nimble."

Agrippa looked expectantly at Harve. "We would, of course, make it worth your while," Harve added.

"Awright, awright," Agrippa said, seating his beret on his head.

* * *

General Agrippa decided to ride over to Parliament Building in the jeep—front seat and very much in charge. He felt giddy; he had just outdone the auditors at both ends of the Atlantic and parked over two and a half times his base pay into his New York account. When the jeep slowed down by the guard at the base entrance, Agrippa lingered to inquire how the corporal was doing, and the smiling corporal rendered a brisk salute when Agrippa motioned his driver on.

The meeting with the heads of security had been scheduled for 14:00 hours because the Comrade President was in Parliament's morning session for the Finance Minister's presentation of the IMF Standby Agreement. Although the Comrade President, as Defense Minister, was briefed daily on defense and police matters, Agrippa felt that he used these weekly meetings not only to give the security chiefs their marching orders but also to assess their own feelings for him and for his policies.

The Police Commissioner and the head of the National Service were already there, seated in the waiting room, but the Comrade President was finishing up another meeting in the conference room. Agrippa declined the secretary's offer of something to drink and sat down beside the others, after exchanging a brief greeting. You have to watch what you say to these fellas, he reminded himself; after all, they are the competition. Besides, like himself, the other chiefs were tense at these meetings, fearful the Comrade President would show his displeasure with them for one thing or another.

It was the graying Permanent Secretary who stepped out of the conference room to invite them in. At the head of the table sat the Comrade President, who as President, Commander-in-Chief, and Defense Minister, chaired the meeting. He was flanked by the Minister of Home Affairs on his left and his Permanent Secretary on his right. Agrippa's usual seat was next to the Permanent Secretary. However, this seat was today occupied by Lionel Cummings, Assistant Permanent Secretary of Home Affairs. It must be true then that Cummings was being groomed to move over to

Defense as Permanent Secretary, Agrippa thought. Cummings uttered a muted greeting to Agrippa, as Agrippa took the seat beside him.

The Comrade President wore a white shirtjac and darkly tinted glasses. Agrippa knew the dual purpose of the glasses—to conceal his eyes, red from bouts of drinking, and to hide the fact that he was looking intently at you. The Comrade President was a big man, at least a head taller than Agrippa in the sitting position. He seemed agitated today but chose his words carefully as though he were presenting a case at London's Old Bailey.

Agrippa feigned attention to the impassioned speech, elements of which he had heard repeatedly at public meetings, on radio addresses by the Comrade President, and in this very room. Like the other heads of the security forces, Agrippa understood what was being asked of them. Today, however, he was a bit more distracted. He looked intently at the Comrade President as he always had, but today it was a safe way of monitoring the clock on the far wall above the Comrade President's head. He was counting down the hours before his evening rendezvous with Brenda.

The Comrade President called for vigilance in monitoring the efforts by the foreign capitalists and their local quislings to destabilize the country. The Americans, he said, were using regional surrogates to produce tensions at the borders. This had started from the time the sugar industry was nationalized. "But the vanguard party would not be deterred from its historic mission of wresting control of the commanding heights of the economy." He paused and looked around expectantly. Cummings was the first to oblige with "Hear, hear," which then ricocheted from seat to seat.

Rotating his head from right to left and back to center, the Comrade President nodded, then cleared his throat loudly and resumed. "As you all know, we have been under pressure for some time, but we will overcome. Yes, we had to sign a Standby Agreement with the IMF, but as Comrade Lenin said, you sometimes have to take one step backward in order to take two steps forward." Again, a pause; more "hear-hears."

"It will cause some hardship, oh yes," the Comrade President declared, nodding his head. Agrippa found himself nodding with the others. "The retrenchment in the public sector has started and will continue. We have been holding meetings with the leadership of the Public Service Union, and they have accepted the grim necessity of these cuts." Again a pause; no "hear-hears;" instead, furrowed eyebrows around the room mirrored the Comrade President's own. "This does not mean that there will not be protests and that our leadership will not be questioned. But I know that I can count on you to support the Party leadership and to help us break the backs of those quislings, who see an opportunity to aid and abet the foreign destabilization effort."

He paused and looked around the table. One by one, the heads of security nodded their support. His gaze fell longest on Agrippa, who found himself nodding, not only to the Comrade President, but to everyone else in the room.

"The sugar strike," the Comrade President reminded them, "is now in its second week. It isn't about food as the union leaders and the placards say. It is a political strike, plain and simple, aimed at crippling the economy of this country, precisely at the time when we desperately need to keep our contractual agreements for sugar deliveries."

Agrippa was impressed by how emphatic the Comrade President was when he stretched out "pre-cisely." "What a talk-man!" Agrippa thought to himself.

The Comrade President then went after the sugar union, which was organizing demonstrations like the one outside of Parliament Building. "They are being joined by other groups of hooligans from the University and other unions, and priests who have grown fat from the offering plates of our people and now fear the forward motion of socialism. Comrades, the Party has so far been patient, treating them like misguided children who will soon tire of these antics. But it is clear that their motives are more sinister, and the time has come for them to taste the sharpness of our steel." The Comrade President paused, his jaws tightly locked, and looked around the table at each of them.

Agrippa knew whose steel the Comrade President was talking about. He nodded resolutely, his own jaws clenched, determined not to be outdone by the Police Commissioner and the head of the National Service.

The Comrade President continued in the same grave tone. "These recalcitrants and opportunists accuse the people's government of violating their human rights, their freedom of speech, and so on. They complain to foreign agencies that we restrict their purchase of newsprint. Well, Comrades, we have limited foreign currency reserves and we will use them to feed our people, with real food, and not with the printed words of disgruntled politicians and interfering priests."

As he said "priests," he stretched his neck forward and uttered an exaggerated hiss. Agrippa thought he did that very well.

"The Opposition complains it doesn't have access to newsprint. This has not hampered its efforts to promote havoc. The Opposition leaders want us to help them to promote more chaos. And why does the Council of Churches need newsprint? Look at this church rag published by the Right Reverend Lennox Moore." He pronounced each part of the title and name slowly and mockingly as he held up the *Weekly Church Bulletin* which had been put out the previous day. "This is the leader of the fifth column in this city, and he will be dealt with condignly."

If the Comrade President say is so, is so, Agrippa thought, but he himself did not see any reason to be afraid of the priest. Of course, he had not read the editorial to which the Comrade President was referring. Concerned that further discussion of the piece was at hand, he pulled out his copy from the folder in front of him and glanced down at it. It was the usual four-page newsletter on poor quality paper, folded at the center. Dated Sunday, January 23, the newsletter's front page had the title "*Weekly Church Bulletin*" and reported short news pieces about conferences and personalities in the Council of Churches. The second page, which required Agrippa's opening the bulletin, was the editorial that Reverend Moore contributed. This week's carried the title, "*Real Men Don't Eat.*" Agrippa read:

> The sugar workers' strike is now in its second week. Strikes by sugar workers, whether for union recognition or better wages, have become a recurring feature of life in this former sugar colony. This strike, however, is different. Like the mine workers' strike last month, the key demand of these workers is food. When the working class in a socialist system complains about its inability to feed itself, it is time to take stock of where we are in the development of this country.
>
> The "Food, Clothe, and House Ourselves" signs, firmly planted along the nation's highways, have faded, and the government would rather we forgot that the deadline for food self-sufficiency has long past. After all, it was just a slogan, and paint is far too expensive to be invested in reminding people of yet another promise not kept. Indeed, the signs of economic ruin are all around us.
>
> This has not stopped the Party and the government, which the Party has the audacity to call its executive arm, from continuing their push for socialism. The promise of socialism, they tell us, is "to make the small man

the real man." The slogan is painted on the seawalls and is posted in all government offices, government banks and cooperatives. It is splattered in Party and government publications, but most offending of all, it surfaces with great frequency in the speeches of those who eat well in this country. There is a certain cynicism to this top-down form of socialism. It seems to say: eat well and tell the small man what he cannot yet figure out, that he is the real man.

Sugar workers, like mine workers, will tell you that they are tired of hearing their bellies kalballai. They understand that in this socialist order, as in the previous colonial order, they really are the small men. They don't mind being the small men; they would just rather not be starving small men. It confuses them when the Party continues to assert that in this socialist system the small man is the real man. Come to think of it, it confuses us too. We have tried to reconcile these two contending propositions: From the crucible of practical experience, the workers seem to be asserting that the small man is a starving man. On the other hand, the Party says that the small man is the real man. The only way to reconcile these two is to assume that real men don't eat. Think about it.

Rev. Lennox Moore

Agrippa struggled not to smirk. He assumed an interested look as he lifted his eyes from the *Bulletin* and looked at the Comrade President. The meeting went on. Not because the Comrade President had anything more of substance to say, but because he repeated what he had said before, mixing in references to the heroic struggles of the peoples of China, North Korea, Cuba, Angola, and Nicaragua. Finally, at 15:40 hours, the meeting ended with the Comrade President stating his expectation that they would deal with the troublemakers.

Before leaving the room, Agrippa tapped Lionel Cummings and whispered an invitation to the Officers' Club. Cummings nodded acceptance but remained seated.

*   *   *

The Club was rather lively for a Monday afternoon, Agrippa thought as he entered. Several junior officers standing near the bar cleared a path for him, seemingly out of respect for his rank but probably to scamper away from him. He instructed Private Jarvis at the bar to show Comrade

Cummings to his table when he arrived, then he took the rum and Coke extended to him and looked around.

Most of the officers present were in uniform, though a few wore civilian clothes—dashikis or shirtjacs. This was the gathering place for officers before they went upstairs to the dining room, but there was an assortment of civilians also present, some of whom he could not recognize. The only females present were his Personal Assistant and Lieutenant Ingrid Peters.

Agrippa exchanged pleasantries with several small groups before merging with a seated cluster that included Colonels Cadogan and LaFleur. He had by now downed the first rum and Coke, and the ever vigilant bartender was standing next to him with another drink. He greeted the officers and sat down to the usual fare of war stories from the days when they served under the British, including at locations in the remotest parts of the country. He joined in but kept a watch for Comrade Cummings and for darkness. Soon Cummings emerged at the entrance, but no thanks to the national time change, it would be a couple of hours more before any hint of the cover of darkness he so eagerly awaited.

Agrippa signaled Cummings and the bartender over to his table. He introduced Cummings to the officers seated there and had the bartender get Cummings a rum and Coke.

"You know," said Agrippa to the colonels and the staff officers sitting there, "this is going to be the next Permanent Secretary of Defense."

"Oh no, no, no," Comrade Cummings remonstrated. "If you talking about the meeting today, I was there only because the Comrade President thought I should see how things operate there."

Agrippa felt that Cummings was just being coy. "Well, you're the man for the job," he said, and Cadogan and LaFleur added their "Oh yes! Oh yes!"

Cummings smiled and shook his head from side to side, suggesting plausibility, but continuing to dismiss the idea. After a few drinks, Agrippa invited Cummings to join him and the Colonels to dinner upstairs. They sat next to each other, but hardly exchanged words. Agrippa became involved in a lively banter with some of the junior officers, and Cummings merely observed, laughing often and occasionally asking questions of Colonel Cadogan, who sat on his other side. Agrippa expected Cummings to talk about the previous day's sporting at the Co-op College, but appreciated Cummings' discreetness in not raising the matter while they were in the presence of others. However, when Agrippa walked him out to his car, Cummings could restrain himself no longer.

"Man, you took off with Brenda the other day without a word," Cummings said, laughing and slapping Agrippa on his back. "We thought you kidnaped the woman!"

"Nah, nothing like that," Agrippa replied. "I just gave she a drop home."

"Well, you got the best of the crop. You see what that uniform can do for you!" Cummings was again laughing and slapping Agrippa's back, evidently to reassure him that this was being said in the friendliest of ways.

"You did well yuh-self," Agrippa said.

"It was awright for a Sunday afternoon," Cummings replied. "But that Brenda is something else. She can make a man feel young again. Not so?"

"You're right; she is something else," Agrippa acknowledged, aroused by the anticipation of disrobing her in just a few minutes.

"You gon keep she around?"

"No, no, no" Agrippa replied. "Is what wrong with you, man? I got a wife, you know."

"Yeh, but don't let that stop you." With that, Cummings was off.

Agrippa walked over to the staff car parked by the flagpole, Corporal Kyte at the wheel. Kyte got out and opened the rear door for Agrippa. It still wasn't very dark, but Agrippa estimated it would be dark enough by the time the car pulled into the alley to the rooming house where Brenda rented.

*   *   *

Agrippa knocked twice at the door. He could hear multiple voices of women and loud giggles. Brenda opened the door and led him down the passageway between the rooms. The other women renters were hovering about in the communal kitchen to the side. They wanted to be introduced, and it seemed that Brenda had promised to introduce them to this very important man. Brenda seemed to glow as she showed him off to each of the two Indian women, also in their twenties. After this brief ritual, he and Brenda walked into her room followed by loud whispers of what a nice man he was. Brenda's was a very modest room with a twin-sized cot butted against the wall, a wardrobe, and a small wall-mounted mirror.

Brenda was very pleased he had come and seemed willing to accommodate him. Agrippa maneuvered with an efficient single-mindedness that she seemed to interpret as an accompaniment of an important and busy man. A few kisses as they sat at the edge of the cot, an open blouse as he reclined her on the bed, and then a fully uplifted skirt gathered at her waist. The bed creaked violently. The giggles from the nearby rooms were audible and caused Brenda to smile up at him as Agrippa romped home with wild abandon.

Shortly after, he was on his way out to the car and on his way home before Vera returned from her two-to-ten shift. He took a quick shower and splashed on cologne to cover over any residual female scent, and then he assumed a semi-recumbent position on the sofa with a few LPs stacked on the phonograph.

Vera evidently noticed a change and commented on how relaxed and in good spirits he appeared. After she had showered, she sat up and talked with him before retiring to her room.

SIXTEEN

SADDLE CADOGAN HAD BECOME a frequent visitor to Berbice County, one visit a week in the first five weeks of F-Company's deployment there, but Moore rarely crossed paths with him. Of course, Cadogan came in his capacity as the Commander of 2nd Battalion, to which F-Company was attached, and he followed protocol by notifying Moore in advance. But his arrival schedule was never precisely known, and Moore was frequently out of camp when Saddle arrived for his perfunctory visits. On the few occasions when Moore was on hand, Cadogan would decline a guided inspection and head out alone. He checked quite frequently on Second Lieutenant Pilgrim, who had replaced Lieutenant Persico and who, Moore learned from Mentore, was a near relation of Cadogan. And there were sightings of Saddle's jeep, reported by Mentore's patrols, around the Springlands and No. 79 areas, frequently parked on the dam in front of Pandit Deonarine's shop.

The last week in February, and the sugar strike was now well over a month long. At several points, there were rumors of an agreement, but each time it fell through, and the sugar union leadership traded recriminations with the government. Moore read the accounts in the newspapers, but his Aunt Edmee, who lived in the family home in Rose Hall, knew more about the union side from her discussions with neighbors and former students, a few of whom were in the union.

Moore had by now developed a daily travel schedule that took him to Skeldon. He usually ate dinner with Lieutenant Mentore before returning. The food was better up there, and he often brought back a package for Lieutenant Beharry. Beharry traveled up to Skeldon with him on those Fridays, following a Thursday-night patrol, when his platoon would be confined to camp the next day. They had drinks and dinner with Mentore and returned to Esplanade Park later in the evening.

Moore had also worked out a weekend schedule with Lieutenant Beharry, which allowed him to be away on alternate weekends when Jeanene and the children came down to stay with him at their family home in Rose Hall. Beharry had the other weekends off, and Moore took charge of the camp. The soldiers were also now eligible for twelve-hour passes on Fridays, Saturdays, and Sundays, beginning at noon, with one squad receiving passes each of those days while the other two were confined to camp and to patrolling duties.

It was the sixth Friday since their deployment to Berbice County, and Moore was taking Lieutenant Beharry with him on his inspection trip to Skeldon. He had learned earlier in the week that Lieutenant Nizam Khan from the Air Wing was on leave and was visiting his parents in No. 79 Village. Lieutenant Mentore had suggested they all get together for a night on the town. Moore was looking forward to this, as was Beharry, but it was the anticipation of Jeanene's arrival the next day that really thrilled him.

They left camp at Esplanade Park at about 10:30 hours, after Moore had returned from using the telephone at Police headquarters, a frustrating experience of limited outside lines, poor connections, and busy signals. At least the Police allowed him the courtesy of telephone use, and he was able to complete all of his calls, including a brief one to his wife.

By 11:15, they had arrived at Albion. After lunch and a brief visit with Second Lieutenant Pilgrim, they were off to Skeldon. Pilgrim was inexperienced, and Moore had spent a great deal of time with him the previous day. This follow-up visit was partly routine and partly to shore up Pilgrim's authority with his platoon.

At about 14:15 hours, they entered No. 79, and Moore asked McCurchin to slow down. He looked down the dam leading to Pandit Deonarine's shop. Cadogan's jeep was not there. Moore looked over his shoulder and exchanged smiles with Beharry, an acknowledgment by both of their spying game. Moore instructed McCurchin to maintain the slower speed into Skeldon, and a few minutes later, they were negotiating their way through the crowded Skeldon market. Vendors of all types were set up on both sides of the road, and vehicular traffic was forced to inch its way through women with hand baskets wending their way from one side to the other to secure the best wares for the cheapest prices. It was curious to Moore how the layout of the market lured shoppers in. At the entrance were the vendors of cold drinks, flavored crushed ice, and pastries, followed by the vendors of fruit, fresh vegetables, and ground provisions, and at the other end, of fresh fish and shrimp, with that unmistakable smell.

Finally at the Senior Staff Club, the two officers sought out Lieutenant Mentore who, they were told, was in the platoon office on the second floor. It was for Moore and Mentore a daily encounter, without ceremony. Lieutenant Mentore went directly to business. He quickly described the previous night's patrolling activities and, since there had been no incidents to report, he brought up a disciplinary matter, involving three soldiers who had been AWOL for eight hours. Moore had them brought in and, after listening to their stories, fined them two-days' pay and suspended their pass privileges for a month.

*   *   *

At about 16:10 hours, Lieutenant Khan arrived on foot to get the three officers. They took Moore's jeep, and Khan directed McCurchin to a house in No. 78 Village. Moore sent McCurchin back to the Sugar Estate with instructions to pick them up in a couple of hours at the Khans' home, where the officers had been invited to dinner.

The wooden sign mounted on the right side of the weather worn, unpainted picket fence surrounding the house read *SAMAROO'S BEER GARDEN*. The two halves of the wide front gate had been pulled open to feed traffic directly into the bar entrance on the ground level. A phonograph inside was blaring out Indian film music for the patrons but no doubt also to lure in undecided pleasure seekers. The officers entered, and Mr. Samaroo, who tended the bar, showed them to a booth by a large window, the two hinged wooden covers for which had been flung open to let in light and air. Moore and Beharry sat beside each other across from the other two officers. The bar itself was configured as an L-shaped counter in the far right corner, with a refrigerator and a freezer behind it. The counter had a hinged section and a door below it to allow Mr. Samaroo to move between his customers and the bar. The frequent shuffling of feet above reminded the officers that the rest of the Samaroos lived upstairs.

Mr. Samaroo sold bottled beer, ale, and soft drinks. The licence mounted at the entrance read "Licensed to sell Beer and Malted Liquors," but Moore was told that Mr. Samaroo also sold rum to some of the regulars. He also prepared snacks on order, from a kitchen at the back, and Nizam Khan had made an advance request for pachownie and bhoonjal chicken. All of the officers had decided to have Bass Ales, which Mr. Samaroo served to them in open bottles. Derryck Mentore acted as the host and invited them to hoist their bottles. "Cheers" sounded almost like a battle cry, followed by what Moore considered a most welcome swig.

"Any recent sightings of Saddle?" Beharry asked Mentore, after all the bottles rested again on the table.

Mentore laughed. "Not in a while, but the man does lose his way whenever he comes on inspection tours. I just can't find him!" The others were now laughing with him.

"The intricate world of business," Moore tossed in.

"I think he in the wrong profession!" Mentore added.

"Wrong profession or wrong business?" Beharry asked.

"Why y'all don't leave the man alone?" Khan suggested, even as he laughed with the others. "The poor fella probably just getting a few banned items, same as everybody else."

"You don't know Saddle," Mentore said. "The man does do everything in a big way."

"By the way, Nizam, where do you get things like flour and so on from?" Moore asked directly.

"Look, Alan, is everywhere. A lot of people retailing this stuff. The border with Suriname is a river that we don't control. The border is porous, and we have shortages on this side. So what you expect?"

"We met a fella by the name of Deonarine. They call him 'Pandit'. You know him?" Moore asked.

"If is the fella from No. 79, yeh, I know him," Khan replied. "He taught me in school."

"You know he and Saddle really tight these days?" Moore asked.

"Business associates," Mentore added, grinning.

"I didn't know that," Khan said.

"Is Pandit in the contraband business?" Moore asked.

"Well, he got a shop and he will sell certain things to you if he knows you."

"But he got a boat too," Moore asserted.

"Yes, but you know how many people out here got boats? We living by a river you know."

"So, how long is your leave, Nizam?" Beharry asked, changing the subject.

"A week," Khan replied. "Turning out on Monday."

"You mean you been out here almost a week a'ready? Where you been hiding?" Moore asked.

"I had some family business in Georgetown, so I've been traveling back and forth. Is only since Wednesday night that I been staying in No. 79."

"These days, whenever anybody says they got family business in Georgetown, is with an embassy, and they planning to leave," Mentore observed.

"I want to," Khan admitted, "but not yet."

"You're right. Who gon fly Colonel LaFleur into the interior?" Moore asked in a jovial dig at Khan. They all laughed, but Khan became defensive.

"Well," he said, "LaFleur is the Commanding Officer for operations on the Venezuelan border."

"True," Moore conceded, "but you think his missions got anything to do with securing the border?"

"That's not for me to say," Khan replied. "Besides, I'm just a pilot in a resupply role."

Moore wondered whether there was any point in further probing Lieutenant Khan. Why not just relax and enjoy the company? Just then Mentore intervened.

"Nizam, is it true that a couple of weeks ago Clarence Austin had to remain overnight with his plane on the landing strip in Tumatumari?"

"Where you get that from?" Khan asked, adding, "I thought you fellas were out of touch down here!"

"I was at the Officers' Mess at Camp Ayanganna last weekend," Mentore replied.

"Yeh, is true. It was late, and Austin ain't got night flying experience."

"But that never happened before, Nizam," Mentore insisted. "None of the locations that Air Wing resupplies is more than an hour from Timehri. So is what kept Austin out so late he couldn't fly back?"

"Could be any number of things," Khan suggested, "mechanical for instance."

"Nothing mechanical was wrong with the plane; what you telling me?" Mentore insisted. "Austin was embarrassed by the incident. He said he got delayed waiting for somebody or other." He paused. "By the way, was Colonel LaFleur on that trip?"

"I don't think so," Khan replied.

"Nizam, you know if LaFleur got his own mining claim in the interior?" Moore asked.

"Not that I know of."

"Well, he got a fleet of hire cars, and people say he bought them with gold from the interior."

"He knows the pork-knockers well," Khan said, smiling.

"So what you saying? They just give him part of their gold?"

"No, I ain't saying that. Maybe he does help them out in some way."

"Oh, I thought it was the price of his friendship!" Moore said, and everyone, including Khan, laughed. Moore knew though that this conversation too would lead nowhere. Yet he suspected that Nizam Khan knew more about LaFleur's activities in the interior than he was saying.

The spiciness of the pachownie and bhoonjal chicken required several ales to wash them down. Mr. Samaroo was always on the lookout as to resupplying his customers but not as mindful about removing the empty bottles. By about 18:00 hours, a wall of empties divided the table, and Nizam Khan suggested that they walk over to his parents' home for dinner.

Khan's father greeted them in the front yard, explaining that he was on his way out on an errand, and apologizing for not being able to join them for the meal. The officers were welcomed by Khan's mother and invited to sit at a large dining table, the surface of which was covered by a plastic table cloth with a floral design. The officers were served by Mrs. Khan and her daughter, Nazeema, and their hospitality seemed boundless. Curried chicken and dal puri were followed by vermicelli cake and gul-gulah. At times, Mrs. Khan stood to the side of the table, like a coach at an eating contest, encouraging the officers to eat some more and sending Nazeema on numerous trips to the kitchen to get them more curry or dal puri or gul-gulah. When Nazeema was not flitting in and out of the kitchen, she hovered noticeably around Beharry, seemingly attentive to his needs in particular. During the entire meal, Mentore, who knew the Khans quite well, held court, and his compliments to Mrs. Khan set her aglow and prompted pleadings from her that they eat still more. Soon the officers were trying to convince Mrs. Khan that they really had had enough. The Khans' hospitality and Mentore's jokes and infectious laughter had made it a wonderful dinner, Moore thought.

At about 19:00 hours, Moore, Beharry, and Mentore thanked the Khans and walked out to the jeep parked at the side of the road. They were all invited back, especially Lieutenant Mentore, who, Mrs. Khan said, didn't have any excuse because he was based just next door, as she put it. In the jeep heading back to the sugar estate, Mentore said he thought Khan knew more of Colonel LaFleur's activities than he was saying, but hastened to defend Khan by pointing to probable fears of punishment for disclosure. Given his own recent experience, Moore was sympathetic to that possibility.

At the Club, Mentore jumped out of the back of the jeep, where he and Beharry were sitting. "By the way, Ramesh," he said addressing Beharry, "Mrs. Khan wanted to know if you were married."

Moore laughed out loud and turned around. Beharry, flushed and embarrassed, simply waved his right hand dismissively.

"Is true!" Mentore yelled out, as the jeep drove off to pick up the Berbice Highway back to New Amsterdam.

*   *   *

Moore knew that Jeanene was planning to cross with the 11:00 ferry, assuming it was on schedule. Throughout this sunny Saturday morning, he found himself looking out from the bandstand at Esplanade Park in the direction of the Rosignol stelling, which he could see faintly in the distance because of the elevation of the bandstand and clearings in the courida trees on this side of the river. Technically, he was on duty until noon, but he had notified Lieutenant Beharry he would leave the camp earlier to get his family.

At about 11:10, he noticed that the ferry was setting out from Rosignol. He took leave of Lieutenant Beharry with the understanding that there would be light patrolling that evening and on Sunday evening. A few minutes later, the jeep was approaching the wharf. McCurchin remained with the vehicle in the unpaved parking area on the right, and Moore walked up to the stelling.

Waiting for the *Torani* to dock, Moore thought of the conversation with Lieutenant Khan the previous evening and wondered whether Khan had not provided a clue about Colonel LaFleur's activities when he said that maybe the Colonel was helping the pork-knockers in some way. He tried to figure it out, but a headache from the previous night's drinking discouraged deeper exploration.

Soon the fluttering hum of the engines overpowered all other sounds at the wharf, and the sailors were casting out the thick ropes to be looped around the metal anvils on the wharf to moor the vessel. The *Torani* needed to reverse slightly to get the ramp on the passenger deck to line up with the platform at the top of the scaffolded metal stairs on the wharf. Then the passengers came briskly out, some running, presumably to make sure they would get a space on one of the hire cars. After the initial wave, the pace of exit became less frenetic, and Jeanene emerged with an overnight bag in her left hand and Ian's hand in her right, Candy holding Ian's other hand. When they cleared the last step, Candy galloped into her father's arms. Then came Ian. Moore relieved his wife of the bag, and they walked over to the jeep. Jeanene sat in the front, and Moore took the two children into the rear, Candy sitting closer to the front and Moore beside her, with Ian between his legs.

The jeep drove out on the harbor road and turned left onto Strand. In no time they were passing by the camp at Esplanade Park on their way out of New Amsterdam, with the Canje Creek bridge in sight. The kids were very excited by the view from the top of the Canje Creek bridge, where McCurchin indulged them by slowing down the vehicle to a crawl. At the Sheet Anchor rum ship, the jeep turned right onto the Rose Hall road. The Moore family residence was about two miles up, just past the Cumberland primary school.

In front of the house, the jeep slowly turned down the embankment on the left side of the road and onto the bridge over the drainage ditch, setting the loose wooden planks in harmonic motion as it went over them to stop at the gate. The front of the house was partially hidden on the left by a large, laden breadfruit tree and on the right by an even bigger mango tree. Sitting in a rocking chair on the landing at the top of the outside stairs was Aunt Edmee, in an upright Queen Victoria pose. She only rose when the children were up the stairs, embracing them, and allowing their parents to kiss her on her cheek.

The right half of the wooden front door was closed, the left half fully opened to the inside. The smell of freshly prepared cook-up rice greeted Moore as he entered, walking through the living room to the front bedroom where he set down his and Jeanene's overnight bags. The others had followed him in, and Aunt Edmee was leading them into the dining area to serve lunch.

Candy raced through lunch and announced she was going downstairs into the hammock, which led Ian to abandon the rest of his meal and dash out behind her. Aunt Edmee talked about the last letter she received from Alan's mother. It was very cold in New York, she reported, and her sister-in-law had to bundle up in a thick sweater, sitting all day by herself in a dreary basement apartment in New York. Aunt Edmee then talked about the letter she had received from Colin, Alan's cousin, who had gone to live in Brooklyn last month, recalling with patience Colin's struggle to find a job, and lamenting the fact that he was working as a security guard in that freezing cold weather, such as he had never experienced in his life. It wasn't, Moore thought, that Aunt Edmee had forgotten that she had already recounted all of this to Alan and Jeanene during an earlier visit and to Alan on some of his afternoon visits; it was what she talked about to everyone, every time she could. Many families did this, he knew; they talked about those who had left home and were living in America. It was a way of focusing attention away from the unpleasantness of life at home, and for many, it was a way of anticipating the new life ahead when their papers came through.

Aunt Edmee continued talking to Alan and Jeanene even as she readied herself to go to the Rose Hall market. Jeanene went with her, and Alan went downstairs to supervise the children. The house was on eight-foot stilts, anchored in small square concrete blocks resting on bare earth. The entire bottom house was open. This was where Alan, as a child, played marbles. It was also once the site for Sunday School, a long time ago. Now only the hammock hung there, fastened by rope to two of the posts supporting the house. It was a bag hammock, made of a ripped-open, hundred-pound jute bag that had once stored rice or sugar. The children seemed fine: they were both in the hammock, which Candy was keeping in motion by occasionally pushing on the bare earth with her feet. Moore walked past them to the backyard, taking the winding footpath which led to a dilapidated outhouse on the property just inside the back fence. He inspected the fruit trees before retracing his steps to the bottom house, where he stood by the hammock, pushing it in motion so that the children could keep their feet in it. His involvement added to their excitement. Candy pleaded with him to push the hammock harder, and Candy and Ian screamed each time the hammock reached its highest level.

When Jeanene and Aunt Edmee returned from the market, Moore retired into the bedroom for a nap and did not awake until after 16:00. The women were preparing dinner, so he thought he would take a shower. The water for the bathroom came from tanks supported just below roof-top level by a wooden platform. The tanks collected rain water channeled in from the gutters and passed through a strainer. Alan had arranged for the installation of the tanks during his father's illness, when the public water supply had become unreliable.

Dinner was a loaded plate of metagee and a cup of hot tea, followed by quinches Aunt Edmee had made prior to lunch. After dinner, they all retired to the front stairs, Aunt Edmee sitting in the rocker, Jeanene in a chair with Ian in her lap, both on the landing, and Alan on the top step with Candy resting her head against him. Aunt Edmee began reminiscing about the old days when Alan's father was the headmaster at Rose Hall's Anglican School, where she also taught. She recalled those days with the captivating tone of a Brer Anancy story, and Candy was especially interested in stories about her father as a young boy. Darkness, when it came, made Aunt Edmee's steady and untiring voice musical and soothing against the stillness that nightfall brought to the countryside. Aunt Edmee had lit two kerosene lamps in the house, explaining that one was never sure when the electricity would come on, if at all. The atmosphere around the house reminded Alan of the days before rural electrification, when a Coleman gas lamp hung from the ceiling above, and he did his homework by the light of a kerosene lamp on his desk. Isn't it natural, he thought to himself, to wonder at times like these whether we might not really be moving backward?

The story telling ended when Aunt Edmee began yawning and rose from the rocker. Ian first, and then Candy, had long since fallen asleep and had been taken in to bed. Now Alan and Jeanene followed Aunt Edmee in, and the late evening ritual of closing windows and bolting doors began. Alan and Jeanene retired to the front bedroom after Jeanene promised Aunt Edmee to get up early and help her prepare breakfast.

*   *   *

Moore was waking up, reluctantly. He thought he heard his name, then he felt the push.

"Alan!" Jeanene's voice was urgent. "Alan!"

"What is it?" he grunted.

"Somebody at the door!"

150

"You sure?"

"Yes. I heard the knocking. Several times."

Moore reached over to the bedside table for his glasses, then swung out from the bed and went over to the closet, groping in the dark for his revolver. He tip-toed over to the window nearest the front door to sneak a look at the knocker. There was no need—the creaking of the floor boards had alerted the knocker of his approach.

"Captain, is me, McCurchin."

"Christ, McCurchin, is what wrong with you?" Moore was furious. "You know what time it is?"

"Sorry, Captain."

"What time is it anyway?" Moore asked, looking at his watch though it was too dark to see the dial.

"I don't have a watch, Captain, but I left camp around 04:30."

"Christ!" Moore uttered. "Hold on." He went back into the bedroom and put on his pants and his shirt, which he left unbuttoned.

"Who is it?" Jeanene asked.

"McCurchin."

"What he want?"

"I don't know. I gon take care of it. Go back to sleep."

Moore came to the door and pulled down the vertical bolt at the top of the right half of the door and the horizontal bolt just above the door lock. He undid the latch on the lock and opened the right half of the door. He invited McCurchin in, but McCurchin indicated that he preferred to remain on the landing. Moore thought it better too; no point getting his aunt and the children up at this hour.

"Lieutenant Beharry sent me to get you, Captain," McCurchin said. "Inspector Frazier came to see the Lieutenant with some armed policemen."

"What for?"

"Is a long story, Captain. I can tell you on the way."

"Tell me now! Why?"

"Three soldiers broke into the New Amsterdam Police Station and released three other soldiers the police had arrested."

"Christ! Let me get dressed."

Back in the room, Jeanene wanted to know what was going on.

"We have a problem at the camp," he said to her, "some misunderstanding with the police. I'll be back as soon as I get it sorted out."

"Isn't Ramesh there?"

"Yes, but it's something I need to straighten out. Don't worry, I'll be right back."

Moore did not engage McCurchin in conversation as they sped back to New Amsterdam. They were back at Esplanade Park in no time. Three police constables, with what looked like .303 Enfield rifles, stood at the entrance where the sentry with his SLR barred their way. Just inside and around the bandstand, soldiers were talking among themselves in groups, presumably waiting for Moore's arrival.

The sentry and the police constables saluted as Moore made his way through. Some soldiers rushed up to him to tell him what happened, but he kept walking to the bandstand. The kerosene lamp was burning, and Beharry and Frazier were sitting across from each other. After a perfunctory greeting to Inspector Frazier, Moore asked Lieutenant Beharry to explain what was going on.

"Captain," Beharry began, "I was awakened at about 03:30 and told that Inspector Frazier was at the camp entrance with three constables. He informed me that three soldiers were involved in a jail break to free three others who had been arrested last night at a night club. The Inspector wanted me to turn over the six. I told him I couldn't do that until I had conducted an investigation."

"Captain Moore, the three soldiers—Burkett, Marks, and Wilson—were arrested while they were off duty, out of camp, and in civilian clothes. That was a police matter." Inspector Frazier sounded officious, Moore thought, but this was a tense situation.

"What was the nature of the charge?" Moore asked.

"Disorderly conduct," the Inspector replied, adding, "they were just mashing up the place from what I understand."

"Well, that's the problem, Alan," Beharry interjected. "The soldiers claim that the arrest was made by off-duty policemen at the same bar, who were jealous of the preference the women were showing the soldiers. The policemen left the bar and returned in uniform to make the arrest."

Several soldiers around the bandstand began airing their grievances against the police for harassment.

"One at a time!" Moore yelled. "Corporal Yussuf?"

"Captain, like I was telling the Lieutenant, the policeman had it in for the soldiers."

"Were you involved in any way, Corporal Yussuf?"

"No, Captain, but I was with the men at the bar earlier. The girls were favoring the soldiers, and the policemen didn't like that, so they were trying to pick a fight."

"I see. I notice that all of the soldiers are from your squad."

"That don't mean nothing, Captain. The fact is that the soldiers were wrongfully arrested."

"Where were you when it happened?" Moore asked the Corporal.

"Well, Captain, some of us had left the spot. That's when the police came back."

"Captain Moore," Inspector Frazier interjected, "I think we missing the more serious infraction here. Three armed soldiers—Lashley, Cummings, and Saroopchand—were involved in a jail-break, during which they held a policeman at gunpoint. That is a very serious offense."

"I am aware of that, Inspector, but surely you can understand the frustration that led them to it."

"Are you condoning their action?" Inspector Frazier asked.

"No, by no means," Moore replied, "but—"

"In that case," the Inspector interrupted, "I am asking that you turn them over."

Moore needed time to think and to consult with Lieutenant Beharry.

"Look, Inspector," he said in a conciliatory tone, "is almost 5 o'clock in the morning. Why not let tempers cool a lil bit and we can pick this up when we're fully awake and so on?"

"I am fully awake, Captain, and I want the original prisoners and the three assailants."

"Inspector, I would like to check out the details of what happened with Lieutenant Beharry. I don't think he has had time to do this. So, for the moment, I would want to keep the soldiers here."

"Well, Captain, the Senior Superintendent will be informed first thing this morning, and the Police Commissioner too," the Inspector warned.

Moore was now very worried. Once the police hierarchy became involved, he would have no choice but to notify Colonel Cadogan and the Chief of Staff. He tried another plea.

"How about a few hours to work this thing out, Inspector?"

"I don't see what there is to work out. If the soldiers had a complaint, they should have lodged it. They still could have lodged it after the arrest. But the arrest is now small potatoes. It's the breakout that is the big issue!"

"Inspector, I take this matter very seriously. I am prepared to bring charges against these soldiers, to try them, and to let you know the punishment, but I need some time to do this."

"For the record, Captain Moore, will you turn over the soldiers?"

"Not at this time, Inspector," Moore replied.

Inspector Frazier rose, tucked his swagger stick under his left arm, and strode off the compound, taking the three policemen with him. The soldiers around the bandstand began celebrating and making taunting remarks at the departing policemen. Moore decided to put a stop to that. "Awright, everyone get back to your tents and let's get some sleep. Sergeant Major?"

"Yes, Captain."

"Sergeant Major, the six soldiers—Burkett, Marks, Wilson, Lashley, Saroopchand, and Cummings—are, as of now, under camp arrest. They are to turn in their rifles, and under no circumstances are they to leave camp."

"Yes, Captain."

The crowd of soldiers dispersed. There was loud grumbling from a few, but slowly the voices died down. Moore took a seat across from Beharry in the bandstand.

"You know what this means?" Moore asked.

"I'm afraid so," Beharry replied.

"By 08:00, Colonel Cadogan and the Chief of Staff will be on our backs."

"Well, we'd better notify them before they hear it from the Police Commissioner."

"You're right. I'll send a signal to the Duty Officer at Camp Ayanganna."

"Didn't something like this happen before?" Beharry asked.

"Yes, a couple of times at interior locations. Last time, it was B-Company."

"Seepersaud's?"

"Yes," Moore said, smiling. "The Chief of Staff made the entire company march seventy-five miles from Rosignol to Camp Ayanganna."

"Just a little more than from here to Skeldon," Beharry observed despondently.

"Well, let's try to get a couple hours of sleep. I'll talk to the soldiers in the morning."

"How about the signal?"

"Yeh, I'd better send that off."

* * *

By 07:30, Moore was dressed in uniform and considering the approach to take with the Inspector. Beharry came back from the mess tent with two cups of hot water and made them some instant coffee. The camp was bustling with activity for a Sunday morning, and Moore sensed a tense, expectant air, which added to his own feeling of nervousness.

"I'm going over to see the Inspector in a little while," Moore said to Beharry, "why you don't get statements from the six soldiers? Then I want you to make out the appropriate charges."

Beharry nodded, "Right, Alan, but I don't think the Inspector gon give in."

"You're probably right, but I want to talk with him again. At least, I should find out how far the matter has gone."

"Good luck," Beharry said.

"I'll try the soldiers when I get back. It might help the situation if we punish them ourselves."

The Inspector was not at Police Headquarters. The policeman on duty—Moore wasn't sure whether he was the one held at gunpoint—gruffly pointed out to him that it was Sunday. Moore asked to use the telephone and called the Inspector at home. The conversation was brief and ended with the Inspector's declaration, "Comrade, the matter is out of my hands."

Moore returned to the bandstand where Beharry read him the signal from the Chief of Staff: "All officers and men are confined to camp, until further orders."

"Delay giving that to me, Ramesh," Moore said. "I need to swing by the house and let Jeanene know I would be tied up for the rest of the day."

"Okay," Beharry said. "By the way, I talked to the sentries. They claim they didn't see anything, but I think they knew what was going on."

"I am sure they did. How can six people sneak back into camp and them not know?"

*   *   *

At 09:15, Moore saw the green staff car pulling off to the side of Strand in front of the park entrance. A second car, Cadogan's, stopped behind it. From the bandstand, Moore saw a young woman in the Chief's car and the Colonel's sweet-woman in his. He ordered a soldier to ask Lieutenant Beharry to join him at the bandstand. The Chief of Staff and Colonel Cadogan, both wearing dashikis, walked into the park. They looked around the camp site and then walked up the bandstand. Moore and Beharry saluted, and, as Moore held his salute, he could see, from the frown on the Chief's face, that the General was in a foul mood. The Chief of Staff took his time acknowledging the salute.

"Captain Moore," the Chief began, "why is it you can't control your men?"

"Well, General—"

"Is Sunday morning and you got everybody upset. The Police Commissioner complaining to the Minister. The Minister complaining to the Comrade President."

"Well, General, as you know, there's always been friction between the police and the soldiers, and—"

"Don't tell me what I know or don't know, Moore! How come you and Lieutenant Beharry always in some kind of trouble?"

Colonel Cadogan stood there nodding every time the Chief of Staff spoke as if those were his exact thoughts, and the Chief looked at Cadogan, seemingly for confirmation that he was giving the upstarts their due.

"General, when soldiers at Camp Ayanganna break regulations, that's not the Base Commander's fault," Moore stated. The Chief of Staff looked at Moore suspiciously as if expecting Moore to say "nor is it the Chief of Staff's fault," which is what Moore was thinking. Instead, Moore added, "The important thing is that they are punished, and we intend to punish those involved with the incident."

"Oh yes, those involved with the incident will be punished," the Chief of Staff said, nodding. Cadogan nodded too, and Moore had a sinking feeling in his stomach.

"Captain Moore, this entire company needs some discipline. The Police Commissioner said the soldiers are lawless. You think I like it when he tells the Comrade President that?"

"No. General."

"No, it embarrasses me. This entire company embarrasses me!"

Moore said nothing.

"Lieutenant Beharry?" The Chief of Staff now stood directly in front of Beharry.

"Yes, General?"

"Lieutenant Beharry, I understand Captain Moore left you in charge of the camp."

"Yes, General."

"Where were you when the incident occurred?"

"I was in camp; asleep, General."

"Did you have sentries posted?"

"Yes, General."

"Did they see anything?"

"Well, General, they claimed they didn't."

"'They claimed they didn't,'" the Chief of Staff repeated. "Did you believe them?"

"No, General."

"So you believe that they were in on this too."

"I believe so; yes, Chief of Staff."

"Well, let me tell the two of you something. This entire unit was involved. You said so yourself!"

It was clear to Moore now: Agrippa and Cadogan had decided to punish the entire company.

"Captain Moore?" Here it comes, Moore thought. "Captain Moore, F-Company will assemble at Skeldon at 08:00 hours next Friday, March 4th, and will embark on a forced march to New Amsterdam. Do you understand?"

"Yes, General, but the other two platoons were not involved in the incident," Moore pointed out.

The Chief of Staff laughed out loud. "Captain Moore, you can tell that to them." The Chief of Staff looked over at Cadogan. Cadogan was nodding and laughing with the Chief of Staff. It was as if they had rehearsed the sequence.

The Chief of Staff seemed ready to leave. He had done what he came for. The bastard is gloating, Moore thought, observing the mocking grin on the Chief's face as the Chief of Staff walked past him and down the stairs.

"That, the donkey?" he asked Colonel Cadogan, looking out at the park. Cadogan nodded. "I see," the Chief said.

The Chief had already descended the stairs of the bandstand, when he turned and fired the final shot. "And Captain Moore," he said softly, but firmly for effect, "officers and men!"

"Yes, General," Moore responded. Looking over the heads of Agrippa and Cadogan at the two women peering curiously through the open windows of the two cars, he realized that an entire company and its officers had just been humiliated by the Chief of Staff and his battalion commander in the presence of their sweet-women and perhaps partly for their entertainment.

SEVENTEEN

F-COMPANY'S ROLE IN THE jail break made the rounds very quickly. Agrippa couldn't help picking up references to it in the cross-chatter at lunchtime on Monday. Officers were amused by the episode and impressed by the quick planning and execution of the raid on the New Amsterdam Police Headquarters. This was predictable, Agrippa thought, given the rivalry between the two forces. Even he had conceded to Colonel Cadogan that Captain Moore had trained his soldiers well, maybe too well. The question the Police Commissioner had raised with the Comrade President, and the Comrade President with Agrippa, was whether these men should be running around laying siege to police stations. Punishment of the entire company had received the grudging approval of the Police Commissioner.

In the Mess, F-Company's forthcoming march became the source of a betting pool, with officers speculating on how quickly F-Company would complete the sixty-mile stretch. Several officers said they were going to observe, and Agrippa felt sure that other ranks might also head down to Berbice County for the weekend. Clearly, Friday's forced march from Skeldon was going to be a big event, and it provided Agrippa an unanticipated opportunity. There was no need for him to be there to watch the soldiers walk sixty miles, but what an excuse to spend the weekend away from home with Brenda. He would have to prepare Vera. Their relationship had changed since December to a comfortable co-inhabiting of the house, and the distance between them had surprisingly narrowed since Brenda came on the scene. He and Vera still slept separately, but she cooked and cleaned on those days when the servant wasn't there, especially on Sundays. They shared news about the children and bits of gossip, shopped together, and attended a few dinners at friends'. Since he began his regular visits to Brenda's place, Agrippa had been home every day before Vera. He always appeared relaxed and sober, which pleased Vera. She stayed up later and talked with him when he wasn't on the phone with staff officers or with the Comrade President. She spent more time at home on weekends, but still kept him at arm's length. Sometimes he thought he was closing in on her, but she would slip out. Agrippa had the sense that he was on probation but that the period was ending.

Vera had been having coffee with him on Sunday morning when the Comrade President called about the incident in New Amsterdam. The Comrade President said he was very concerned, noting also that Commissioner Dalrymple was furious. Vera monitored the call and understood that he had to go down right away to New Amsterdam. Of course, after he left the house, he went by and picked up Brenda. He had returned Monday morning and had gone directly to Camp Ayanganna, changing into uniform at the office.

When Vera returned that evening, she wanted to talk about the incident.

"It was a mess," Agrippa told her, "it took a long time to get sorted out. I had to question the officers, go to Police Headquarters and call the Comrade President." He paused. "Then I had to talk with Commissioner Dalrymple, when he arrived." This was a lie, but how would she know?

"So what will happen to the soldiers?" Vera asked.

"The whole company will be punished," Agrippa replied.

"But Captain Moore didn't have anything to do with it," Vera observed.

"It's his company," Agrippa said. "His soldiers are attacking police stations, and he ain't got nothing to do with it?" Agrippa feigned annoyance. "There is no discipline in that unit."

"What was the punishment?" she asked.

"The company will do a forced march from Skeldon to New Amsterdam."

"When?"

"This Friday. I don't want to have to go down early Friday morning, so—"

"Why do you have to go?" Vera asked.

"I ordered the punishment, and this is a very high profile matter. The Police Commissioner is watching to see that we punish the culprits, and I would have to report back to the Comrade President."

"I see," Vera said. Agrippa sensed a note of frustration in her voice.

"I was thinking I should go up Thursday afternoon," Agrippa said, as if seeking her counsel.

"When are you coming back?" Vera asked.

160

"Well, the march won't end until Sunday," Agrppa said, appearing to be figuring. "I'll probably come back late Sunday or early Monday morning."

Vera was silent. She seemed to be studying him, so he maintained a resolute face, and to reassure her, he added, "I really don't want to go down there again, but I can't have soldiers executing my order and I not be there. Besides, the Comrade President would want a report so he can calm down Commissioner Dalrymple."

Vera didn't have an argument, but her long, searching look suggested suspicion. Agrippa noted it and decided he would keep bringing up the subject in the days before departure in a way to allay her concerns.

After their late afternoon romp on Tuesday, Agrippa told Brenda he was taking her back to New Amsterdam for the weekend. They would leave on Thursday afternoon and return Sunday afternoon or Monday morning. Brenda was ecstatic. Retrenched from government service two weeks earlier, she had complained to Agrippa about her longs days at home. She asked where they were going to stay and began to list what she was going to wear.

"You're sure you want me to go with you?" she asked, when Agrippa was ready to leave.

"Oh yes," Agrippa replied, though her emphasis on "me" struck him as implying "in preference to your wife?"

When Vera came home later that evening, she asked Agrippa what he had decided about New Amsterdam.

"I spoke to Colonel Cadogan," Agrippa replied, "and he thought I should go up with him on Thursday afternoon, seeing how the march will begin early Friday morning, but I haven't made up my mind. I mightn't even go. I could just have Cadogan report back to me."

"What about the Comrade President?" she asked. "It won't look bad to him? Your not going?"

"You're right," he replied, adding, "I will go down Thursday to be there for the beginning of the march and then come back. Not unless, I think it necessary for some reason to stay on." Vera seemed calm. Agrippa figured she had adjusted to the possibility of his weekend absence.

The next morning, Agrippa called the *Rooster's Run* on his direct line and made a reservation in Brenda's name for three nights, starting Thursday. That evening, Vera offered to help him pack, but Agrippa declined, saying he wasn't taking much: just a change of uniform and two pairs of civvies for the after hours. She asked if he had decided when he was coming back.

"Friday itself, after the march off," he said, "unless the situation requires me there longer."

At mid-morning on Thursday, Agrippa called Vera at home. Since he would not be seeing her before he left that afternoon, he wanted to let her know that the Comrade President himself had asked him to make sure that "Captain Moore and company," as the Comrade President put it, served out the full punishment. He lied about the Comrade President but was sure that she understood he would be away for the entire weekend on explicit orders from the Comrade President himself.

*   *   *

Returning from his weekend in Berbice County, Agrippa went directly to his office after he had dropped Brenda off at the rooming house. While he waited on a late breakfast his PA had ordered from the Mess, he went through the mail the brigade runner had brought back from the Comrade President's office last Friday. The bundle included one confidential memo about an official visit to India from April 9 through April 17. Dated Friday, March 4th, and copied to all government and Party personnel in the Comrade President's intended entourage, the memo spelled out amount of luggage and specific assignments of key personnel and groups, but what stuck most to Agrippa's mind was the implied expectation that wives be in attendance. The memo clearly stated that the Indian government would be catering to the professional interests of spouses and that a hospital visit was scheduled for his wife while he was inspecting military training facilities. He had known about the invitation from the Indian Government—it had been discussed at a Security Heads' meeting, but then April had seemed a far way off and he hadn't discussed it with Vera. What if she won't go? What would he tell the Comrade President, and how would he explain her absence to his Indian hosts? He decided he needed to soft-soap her before asking her to accompany him.

The next day, Agrippa stopped in at the maternity ward on the second floor of the Georgetown Public Hospital. He saw consternation in Vera's face as she looked at him from her desk: What could he want here? She asked to be excused from the huddle of nurses around her desk and walked downstairs with him.

"What's wrong?" Vera asked, when they were out in the courtyard.

"Nothing," he replied. "The Defense Board meeting at Parliament Building just ended and I was heading back to Camp Ayanganna. I was thinking about you, so I thought I'd stop by."

"God, I thought something was wrong with one of the children," she said.

"No, nothing like that. I hadn't come by in a long time, but you know . . ."

It was all a bit awkward. Vera tried to act indifferent, but from the way she would look up at the ward nurses peering through the windows on the second floor, then shake her head and smile, he knew she was pleased. He was aware, as was she, that the visit was clearly causing a stir. None of the other nurses received visitors of this stature. Oh, they knew her husband was head of the army, but here he was in person, in his olive green uniform with all kinds of adornments hanging from him. Yes, he thought, Vera was due for praise and admiration when she went back upstairs.

The frequency of his visits increased, and Vera softened to him. Their conversations at home became longer, and her bedroom door was reopened to him.

Agrippa's encounters with Brenda paralleled Vera's work schedule. He stayed at Camp Ayanganna until it was dark enough, then an hour with Brenda, and he would be home for at least an hour before Vera came in. Sometimes she seemed very tired when she got home, and being already sexually satiated once, he showed her every consideration. The rest of the time, the earlier kill served as an inspiration for him.

At mid-March, because of a nurse's illness, Vera's shift changed from the 2 p.m.—to—10 p.m. to the 6 a.m.—to—2 p.m. shift. Brenda, on the other hand, was still unemployed, so Agrippa could see her during the daytime, and he did: mid-mornings, mid-afternoons, and sometimes both. He thought of her like the cup of coffee he could have whenever he wanted a break from work or for any other reason. Of course, he stopped by the hospital sometimes en route to Brenda's and, sometimes, afterwards. The visits were not as frequent, but Vera didn't seem to mind.

For Agrippa, the arrangement was working out splendidly. Brenda's unemployment status and her availability made her his virtual slave. When he was in uniform, he made her understand that he had little time, and she performed on cue. When he was in civilian clothes, he led her to believe he was on his way to an important social engagement, and she accommodated him. There was an efficiency about the conduct of his relationship with Brenda that appealed to his military temperament, and the sense of being able to get away with all of this made him chuckle with self-satisfaction. At work sometimes, he hummed the refrain from the Penguin calypso:

> *A deputy essential*
> *To keep your living vital . . .*

A few weeks after their weekend at the *Rooster's Run,* Agrippa began to sense that Brenda was getting restless. She asked him several times about taking her out at least to the cinema. Agrippa told her how busy he was with all the security problems in the country and what not, but he did give her a little extra money, suggesting that she buy some nice clothes and go out with her flatmates to the cinema. She wasn't satisfied, he could tell, but she accepted the money, and the matter was shelved—temporarily.

Agrippa was drinking less, which pleased Vera. She swapped shifts sometimes to appear with him at functions held at the Officers' Mess. She went with him to receptions at the Comrade President's Residence and at foreign embassies, and when, in late March, he asked Vera to accompany him on the seven-day trip to India, she was overjoyed, rebuking him for not telling her about it earlier.

PART THREE

EIGHTEEN

CAPTAIN MOORE INFORMED HIS platoon commanders of the verbal orders from Colonel Cadogan that F-Company move out of Berbice County on Friday, April 15. Their final redeployment location would have to await the Chief of Staff's return from India, but the designated marshaling area was Camp Stevenson, Timehri. They would be crossing with the 04:30 ferry to Rosignol so they could be at Timehri by mid-morning. To accomplish this, Moore ordered Lieutenant Mentore and Second Lieutenant Pilgrim to move their platoons to Esplanade Park Thursday evening after dinner.

By 20:00 hours on Thursday, April 14, both platoons had arrived at Esplanade Park, and the company Sergeant Major and the Color Sergeant were directing the camp arrangements to accommodate the new arrivals. The entire park had come alive. Soldiers in groups were playing cards or dominoes by lamp light, or trading stories, but from the bandstand, where Moore and the other officers were sleeping, the loudness of chatter and the sporadic bursts of laughter seemed unending. The activities went on through the night until assembly time at 03:30 on Friday morning. Moore had only managed a couple hours of sleep but figured on resting his head in the jeep once the convoy departed Rosignol.

At 03:30, the Sergeant Major took the report from the platoon sergeants, and Captain Moore ordered his officers to get their men on the trucks. Moore's 1/4-ton jeep would be followed in order by the trucks carrying the platoons of Second Lieutenant Pilgrim, Lieutenant Beharry, and Lieutenant Mentore, with the Color Sergeant's 3/4-ton jeep bringing up the rear.

The crossing was very easy—the 04:30 was the first ferry of the day, and there was no chance of it being late. Very few pedestrian passengers and cars were aboard, but the army vehicles shared the lower deck with drygoods trucks bound for Georgetown. Identified on their sides by store names, such as, *Satish Maraj & Sons Ltd*, these vehicles went up empty and brought back goods for their New Amsterdam wholesale owners, though these days many came back half-empty.

The convoy left the Rosignol stelling at about 04:50 and settled into steady speed of 50 miles per hour. Moore reckoned on making Georgetown by 06:30 and stopping in at Camp Ayanganna so that the soldiers could relieve themselves and have breakfast. By 08:30, they should again be loaded up and ready for the last leg to Timehri. Moore rested his head back and closed his eyes, but it was difficult to get comfortable. Vehicular traffic into Rosignol for the New Amsterdam crossing was very heavy. The bright lights and the practice of tooting horns to greet opposing vehicles became a source of some torment. Further away from Rosignol, however, the traffic was more sparse, and Moore managed to doze off.

At first, he thought he was dreaming, but the loudness of the call jolted him awake.

"Captain Moore! Captain!"

"What?" Moore burst out, looking over first at McCurchin before turning around.

"Captain, the trucks are stopping," the Sergeant Major said from the back of the jeep.

"What the hell!" Moore looked into the left side mirror. "Stop, McCurchin! Stop!"

Moore stepped out of the jeep. They were just outside Onverwagt, about nine miles from Rosignol. Second Lieutenant Pilgrim's truck, which had been following him but had slowed, now pulled up behind the jeep and stopped. About half a mile back, Lieutenant Beharry's truck had pulled off to the side with its lights on, and behind it Lieutenant Mentore's truck and the 3/4-ton jeep. The soldiers from the trucks were out on the road and along the embankment on the left.

"What the hell!" Moore said, thinking there must be an accident but puzzled how that could be with hardly any other traffic on the road. Maybe one of the drivers fell asleep.

"McCurchin, turn around!"

Moore ordered Second Lieutenant Pilgrim to remain with his truck, and getting into his jeep, headed back to the other stopped vehicles. The noise reaching him from the soldiers on the road made Moore fear the worst, but closer to the scene, he discerned laughter, boisterous laughter.

The jeep stopped across the road from the trucks. Moore rushed to the back of Beharry's truck, which appeared to be the focus of attention of the soldiers forming a semi-circle several feet away from it. He was about to ask Beharry what the problem was when the stench hit his nostrils and he saw the outline of the donkey in Beharry's truck. Christ, they kidnapped the blasted donkey! Moore was irate. He covered his nose with his hand and walked up for a closer look. The donkey must have had diarrhea on the floor. Moore noticed that none of Beharry's soldiers were nearby; they were probably afraid to face him or Lieutenant Beharry. The platoon sergeant was vomiting near the bushes.

"Alan," Lieutenant Mentore said, "you should have seen it. Men jumping out the back of the truck!" Mentore laughed, and the soldiers around him joined in.

Moore turned to Beharry.

"Alan," Beharry said, "I didn't know anything about this. I didn't think to check the back of the truck before we left. I've never had to before."

"How did you find out?" Moore asked.

"Well, the truck started rocking, and the men were hollering and hitting the cab, so I stopped to see what was going on."

Some of the men from Beharry's platoon came closer, and Moore, looking for someone he thought might know a bit more about this, settled on Corporal Yussuf.

"Corporal Yussuf? What happened?" Moore asked.

"Is Eveready, Captain," Corporal Yussuf replied.

"I don't give a damn if is Princess Margaret! I want to know how it got there!"

"Well, Captain, I had nothing to do with this," Yussuf insisted.

"Awright, you had nothing to do with it. You're telling me you didn't see the donkey in the truck?"

"Well yes, Captain. I did see the donkey."

"Well, who put it there, Yussuf?" Moore noticed that the other soldiers from Beharry's platoon were coming in closer.

"Captain, you know how it is," Yussuf replied.

"Corporal Yussuf, we have a problem here, and you're not helping!"

"Captain, the soldiers got attached to the donkey," Yussuf said quietly. "They wanted to buy it."

"And do what with it?"

"Enter it in races," Corporal Yussuf replied. "They thought they could make a lot of money."

"Are you people crazy?" Moore was exasperated.

"It was just rum talk, Captain."

"Did they pay the owner?" Moore asked.

"No, Captain," Yussuf replied. "I think they were going to mail the money."

"This is stealing, Yussuf! What happens when Mr. Sackiechand reports to Inspector Frazier that the soldiers walked off with his donkey?"

"Captain, the soldiers were drunk. They weren't thinking straight."

"How did they get the alcohol in the camp?" Moore asked.

"Some of the soldiers brought it in with them from Skeldon."

"Awright, how did they get the donkey into the truck?"

"I didn't see that part, Captain," Corporal Yussuf replied.

"How did they get the donkey to stay so quiet?" Moore asked.

"They had a three-pound bag of sugar."

"Y'all been feeding the donkey sugar all the time?"

"Not me, Captain," Yussuf insisted.

"Awright, what happened here?" Moore asked.

"Well, Captain, Eveready went wild a mile or so back. Like it got belly ache. It started rolling around on the floor. Then it let out this big fart and started shitting all over the place. Talk about stink, Captain? The soldiers started jumping out the back of the truck even before it stop."

"Christ!" Moore looked over at Beharry, standing there, tense and subdued. Soldiers from Lieutenant Mentore's platoon were huddled in groups commenting and trying to mute their laughter.

"Where was the Platoon Sergeant during all of this?" Moore asked Corporal Yussuf.

"The soldiers got him tanked up last night," Yussuf replied.

"I see," Moore said. Beharry was shaking his head, jaws tight. Moore looked at his watch: 05:10. "Better start cleaning this truck," Moore shouted at the soldiers, "because you're getting back in! Lieutenant Beharry, lemme see you for a minute."

Moore and Beharry walked over to his jeep. "Ramesh, you got to return that donkey to Esplanade Park, and you got to do it before Mr. Sackiechand finds the donkey missing and reports to Inspector Frazier."

"Right, Alan."

"Can you imagine what will happen if the Chief of Staff finds out?" Moore asked.

"He's not in the country," Beharry noted.

"Oh skunt, Ramesh," Moore exclaimed, "he's only gone for a week. Cadogan said he's due back Sunday." Beharry was quiet, and Moore softened. "Look, if you hurry, you can catch the 06:00 ferry. Just come on up to Timehri when you're done. Okay?"

"Right, Alan," Beharry responded.

"Ordinarily I'd leave the punishment of the soldiers to you," Moore said, "but I was present in that camp when this happened. No weekend passes for the soldiers and NCOs in this platoon."

"Yes, Captain," Beharry replied with a deep sigh.

NINETEEN

A GRIPPA FOUND HIMSELF FLANKED at breakfast by Colonels Cadogan and LaFleur, the QM and the Padre. This was his first day at work since his return from India Sunday evening. He had taken Monday off to rest and readjust but still felt as if he were on Indian time—ten and a half hours difference, he reminded his audience. At 08:50, the junior officers had long cleared the dining room, but the coffee kept flowing, and Agrippa was still fielding questions from the senior officers. Yes, the Indian Army will be sending a team of engineers to advise on road construction in the interior, and they will reserve one space for us in their senior staff course. He talked about his visit to the Indian Military Academy at Dehra Dun and how much it reminded him of his visit to the Royal Military Academy at Sandhurst. Won't it be good if we could set up something like that here?

"General, telephone," Private Jarvis, the attendant announced. "It's your Personal Assistant."

Agrippa walked out into the hallway and picked up the phone resting on the table. The PA told him that there was a woman on the phone demanding to speak to him. Her name was Brenda, and she had called several times before, a few times when he was away in India and twice already this morning. The switchboard had her on hold. Agrippa was stunned. This was a violation of the understanding he had with Brenda: she was never to call him at work or at home. What could be so damn urgent? he wondered. I hope she is not—Oh shit.

"General?"

"Yes, Bernadette," Agrippa said. "Awright, put her on. Let me see who it is, eh."

"Hi." The voice sounded nervous but familiar, as if no introduction was necessary.

"I thought I told you not to call me at work," Agrippa said.

"I haven't seen you in a while," Brenda complained.

"I was out of the damn country," Agrippa said, making no effort to contain his irritation. "I just got back."

"You didn't tell me anything about it," Brenda complained. "I had to read about it after the delegation left the country."

"I can't tell you everything I am doing," Agrippa insisted.

"How about today?" Brenda asked. "Can I see you today?"

"Look, I am at work—"

"That didn't stop you before." The rebuke was whiney but quick.

"Where you calling from?" Agrippa asked.

"Upstairs, at the landlady."

"You gon be home?"

"Yes," Brenda replied.

"Let me see what I can do. This is my first day back at work."

"I gon look out for you," Brenda said.

"Awright, awright," Agrippa uttered with resignation and hung up as Brenda was saying goodbye.

What the hell is the matter with this woman? Agrippa asked himself as he walked back to join the officers in the dining area. He thought he detected something threatening about her tone. That and the fact of it being about 19:20 hours, Indian time, made him a little jumpy.

The officers were now standing in the dining area, and Agrippa was in no mood to detain them further. Promising to continue the conversation over drinks later on, he led the way out of the Mess. A quick stop by his office to tell his PA he was going to run an errand in town, then he left for Brenda's rooming house.

Brenda responded to the knock and welcomed Agrippa at the door. He strained a smile and followed her down the hallway to her room. He tried to stay calm, but, studying her to divine her purpose, made him acutely aware of a new fullness of her features. Brenda seemed to have done herself up in anticipation of his arrival. The scent of perfume was fresh. She wore a sleeveless floral dress with a hemline several inches above her knees so that it rode up as she sat down on the bed, revealing her smooth and somewhat thicker thighs. Her breasts and hips seemed fuller too. After an absence of nearly two weeks, the stirrings within him diluted the anger that had brought him there.

Still, he remained standing, torn between aggressively questioning her about her call or taking advantage of the moment and talking afterwards. When she stretched out her hands to him, inviting him to sit beside her, he moved up and stood directly in front of her. She wrapped her hands around him just below his waist and rested her head into his stomach. He stroked her hair and her shoulders, then reached forward for her breasts. Before too long, the entire dress had gathered at her midriff and the violently creaking bedsprings were registering the intensity of the encounter.

Lying beside her, he asked Brenda what was so urgent that she had to call him at work.

"I am pregnant," she said.

"Are you sure?" he asked.

"Yes," she replied. "When I missed my period at the end of February, I got really worried. But because of the union meetings and so on, I didn't go to the doctor. When I missed again in March, I went to the doctor."

"What did he say?" he asked, from his prone position.

"He said I am about two months pregnant."

"I see." Agrippa said, adding, "Christ!" under his breath. It was what he suspected but hoped wasn't true. Yet, lying beside her in this spent state, it seemed easier somehow to digest.

"Don't worry," he said, "I gon take care of things." Brenda looked over at him to discern his meaning, but he did not elaborate. "Don't worry," he repeated, and she did not press him.

Water was flowing through the taps today, so he showered quickly before heading back to Camp Ayanganna. He was followed in his office by a very anxious PA.

"General, the Permanent Secretary called. Also the Police Commissioner."

"Thank you, Bernadette. I'll use the direct line."

"Would you like some coffee?"

"Yes. Thank you."

His mind went back to Brenda as he waited for the coffee. This should be no big thing, he thought. It happens all the time, and people take care of it. I just need to ask around. The problem is who to call and what to tell them. I could always say I have this friend with this problem. Aah!

The PA knocked and brought in a tray with a cup of coffee, plus a kettle, some milk, and sugar, in case he wanted another cup.

He could give Brenda some money, he thought, sipping the coffee, and let her go someplace else like New Amsterdam and get a doctor to clean her out. His direct line rang. It was the Permanent Secretary.

"Clive, PS, here. The Comrade President wants a meeting with the security heads at eight tomorrow morning."

"Right," Agrippa responded.

"And look, Clive, we need to be able to reach you at all times." The PS hung up.

Agrippa wondered whether the tone was the old fella's or the Comrade President's. The protests around Parliament Building were getting everyone tense these days, he thought. Well, let's see what the Commissioner wants. He dialed.

"Commissioner Dalrymple."

"Clive here, Chief. Is what going on?"

"You know about the meeting in the morning?" the Commissioner asked.

"Yes, I just got off with the PS."

"The Comrade President wants us to set up a joint operational command."

"Why?" Agrippa asked.

"You don't see who is protesting? The sugar strike is over; is the civil servants this time. All of them are Georgetown people, supporters of the Party. Is like a damn revolt. I think it really shaking up the Party top brass."

"Where does he want the JOC set up?" Agrippa asked.

"Well, I think it should be over here. We are closer to the scene. And crowd control is a police function. So we will have to be close by."

"Is awright with me," Agrippa said.

"Another thing, Clive. The Comrade President wants a greater army presence around Parliament Building."

"Like what?" Agrippa asked.

"Vehicles with soldiers in them. Just driving around, you know? Help to intimidate the demonstrators."

"I see. Anything else?" Agrippa asked.

"Yeh. How about some army checkpoints at the entrances to the city?"

"Your idea?" Agrippa asked.

"No. I hear the Comrade President could not contact you for two whole hours this morning. The man really vex. Anyway, I just passing on what I heard."

"Thanks," Agrippa said. "Lemme talk to our people here about the JOC."

"Right, boss." Dalrymple laughed. At least he seems to be in a good mood, Agrippa thought as he placed the phone down.

*   *   *

When Agrippa's car pulled up at 07:55 the following morning, groups of demonstrators were already gathering around Parliament Building, but the entrances to the compound were free of obstacles. The meeting with the Comrade President was brief. The Comrade President confirmed what Dalrymple had said. Agrippa was able to get the Comrade President to nod his approval when he announced that the army had already set up road blocks at all major entrances to Georgetown and that he had assigned two field-grade officers and three junior officers to a joint operational command with the Police. He himself would be working very closely with Dalrymple.

For the next couple of days, Agrippa was very busy. And yes, he was in constant touch with the office of the Comrade President. He ate all of his meals at the Officers' Mess and only interacted briefly with Vera, who was now on the 10 p.m.—to—6 a.m. shift. Work also kept him away from Brenda, and while his mind visited the problem from time to time, it was already Friday and he had not progressed with his inquiries about ways of disposing of the pregnancy, except for Sergeant Maynard's castor oil solution.

Arriving home a little earlier than usual that Friday evening would, he thought, please Vera. But the look she gave him as he entered the house was a clear signal of trouble. It was one of those cut-eye looks, where she stared at him while her face was pointed in a direction slightly away from him, and her teeth were clenched.

"Some woman called," she said, looking at him for some reaction. He stood there trying to appear indifferent. "I think you carrying on again," she added, "and let me tell you right now, I ain't gon put up with this."

"Is probably just a woman who wants to join the army," Agrippa said, wanting to sound nonchalant and to throw Vera off scent.

"Since when do they have to call here? I ain't running no recruiting station here."

"You know how things getting in the country. A lot of people losing their jobs. People getting desperate. You should see how many of them hanging around outside the army compound."

"I thought y'all set up road blocks?"

"Before the roadblocks, I mean."

176

Vera stood there studying his face. "I still think you carrying on. Is the way the woman talked to me."

"What you mean?"

"She asked for the General, but she was sarcastic. She didn't sound like anybody who wants to join no army." Agrippa was feeling fatigued from the security efforts of the last two days. He could not think of a response quick enough. "And another thing," Vera resumed, "The woman sounded demanding. I telling you again: I ain't putting up with this." Vera picked up her handbag and headed for the stairs.

"Where you going?" Agrippa asked.

"I going to work."

"Is early yet," Agrippa observed, looking at his watch.

"You don't bother with that," Vera said, looking at him sternly, before walking down the stairs.

Agrippa heard the door shut behind Vera, a few moments later the car engine, then the familiar reversing out the gate, the pause, and then the forward motion. He fixed himself a rum and Coke and sat down on the sofa, rotating to prop his back against the armrest and his feet on the cushions. That was all he remembered when Corporal Kyte sounded the horn of his jeep the following morning.

TWENTY

*A*GRIPPA STAYED CLOSE TO Camp Ayanganna all day Saturday and Sunday, monitoring the patrolling reports and the planning of the Joint Operations Command. Officers at the Mess shared stories of their encounters at the roadblocks, but all reported calm on the streets of Georgetown. The protest, by newspaper accounts, had moved indoors. Young Turks within the Public Service Union were engaged in a bid to oust the leadership, which they reportedly described as lackeys of the Comrade President.

Agrippa did not see his wife at all over the weekend—she was asleep in the other room when he came home, and gone when he woke up. At the Sunday afternoon get together in the Mess, the Padre informed Agrippa that the Cuban doctor was back—he had returned to Cuba for two weeks, vacation time his government allowed annually for those serving overseas. Agrippa began to wonder whether Vera's friendliness towards him had signaled a genuine thaw in their relationship or whether it had been a way of killing time.

On Monday morning, April 25, Agrippa received an oral report from the Base Commander at Camp Ayanganna and read the signaled report from Camp Stevenson, neither containing anything unusual, but the piles of signals from the border locations worried him. Troop movements on the other side of the disputed western border were not uncommon, but weapon fire overnight, even if not directed across the border, was troubling. Test firing of weapons perhaps, but in this war of nerves at the border, even that was an escalation that he would have to report to the Comrade President.

The Sunday edition of the Opposition *Red Star* had predicted heavy demonstrations outside Parliament today, and reports from army patrols in the city confirmed that. The government-owned newspapers, Agrippa thought, painted such a rosy picture, you would think that the demonstrators were simply unruly ingrates who could not appreciate the beneficence of the Comrade President. Agrippa knew better, but he had already chosen a side. After all, the Comrade President picked him to be Chief of Staff over the candidate others thought more qualified. Nevertheless, as a security man, he learned a lot from the Opposition papers. The Comrade President paid close attention to them too. It's the first thing he brings up at meetings of the Security Heads.

At breakfast Tuesday morning, Agrippa read the *Red Star*'s report that the police had beaten a Roman Catholic priest demonstrating outside of Parliament Building the previous day. It also reported a successful insurgency within the Public Service Union, and pledges of support for public service workers from the sugar union, the bauxite union, and the University Association. It wouldn't be long now before there would be sympathy strikes along the sugar belt and in the mining areas. The paper was even alleging that the electrical blackouts and water interruptions were being orchestrated by the government to frustrate people. True, demonstrators had been assembling later than usual around Parliament Building. Nothing like stopped-up toilets to slow down a revolution! Agrippa smiled. Thanks to the standby generators and water cisterns on the Base, he was able to dress with relative ease after coming to base in his PT clothes.

After breakfast, Agrippa called Commissioner Dalrymple. "What's this I hear?" Agrippa asked, laughing. "Your people beating up a Catholic priest?"

"Well," said Dalrymple, laughing as well, "is not we really, you know. The Party gave orders for the Riot Police to rough up the demonstrators every once in a while. I believe the Riot Police mistook the priest for Reverend Moore. Many of the constables can't tell the difference between a Catholic priest and an Anglican priest. Come to think of it, I can't either."

"Was he out there—Reverend Moore, I mean?" Agrippa asked.

"He had been out there, but he wasn't when the incident occurred," Dalrymple replied. "The Comrade President vex bad."

"He called you?" Agrippa asked.

"Oh yes. You know, the man didn't so much mind that the priest got a licking. He just vex because it wasn't Moore." Dalrymple laughed out loud, and Agrippa joined him. "You know, Clive, I ain't see no end to this thing. They laying off more and more people, and prices skyrocketing. How people gon survive?"

"They better have relatives in America," Agrippa replied.

"Or visas to go there," Dalrymple added.

"I think I'll just drive around the city before that 10 o'clock meeting with the Comrade President," Agrippa said.

"Go 'long," Dalrymple said. "I just finished doing that."

Agrippa left Camp Ayanganna by jeep, armed with a service revolver and accompanied in the rear of the vehicle by two soldiers with rifles. He pulled up to the army road blocks and spoke each time to the corporal in charge. Then he drove by the Opposition headquarters, where there seemed to be a lot of activity, mostly people going in and out, and others simply milling about. From there he went to Parliament Building. At the entrances were uniformed policemen, but the crowd was thick, and the jeep had to stop several times and inch forward, as the riot police moved in to clear a path. Finally, the jeep pulled into the courtyard and deposited Agrippa near the stairway to the second floor.

The Comrade President seemed agitated, perhaps nervous. Agrippa couldn't quite discern which. He also appeared tired and not as confident. His language lacked the usual bombast. Instead he hissed, grasping for individuals and groups to strike at.

"Yes, I have read the newspapers!" he said. "Served the priest well. What the hell was he doing out there anyway? And those hooligans from the university! What are they doing out there? They should be back in those classrooms trying to earn their tenure instead of inciting riots in the streets of Georgetown." The Comrade President slapped the table with his right hand and looked around the table. Agrippa saw heads nodding and nodded his own.

"Then you have the sugar union pledging sympathy," the Comrade President continued. "Sympathy my eye! Everybody knows that the Opposition controls the sugar union. They just exploiting the misery of other people to try to bring down this government. But we shall overcome!"

The declaration was loud, but, to Agrippa, "we shall overcome" conveyed doubt. It seemed more of a question. Agrippa noticed the Comrade President scanning the room with a quizzical look on his face. He settled for a moment on Agrippa and then pulled away.

Agrippa knew that Dalrymple was right. The people out of work, demonstrating outside, were Black people, people the Party always thought they could count on. Of course, they had not been allowed to freely demonstrate their support through the ballot box, but the Comrade President provided them with jobs, and they accepted his rule. Now the security of a job had been taken away. The Comrade President had broken his pact—Black people were demonstrating their ire, and the Comrade President was not so confident anymore.

But the Comrade President's weakening confidence was not all Agrippa saw. It was the way the Comrade President looked at Agrippa when he said "we shall overcome." He wasn't sure. The Comrade President wasn't sure he could count on the army. That was how it struck Agrippa, and, like any shrewd businessman, he felt that this might be an angle to manipulate to his benefit.

Agrippa left the meeting feeling a little taller. It was only 11:30 in the morning, but he thought he would head over to the Officers' Mess and visit with some of the officers before lunch. The demonstration around Parliament Building had grown larger, and the chanting was louder. The demonstrators knew that government officials would soon be leaving for lunch and were waiting to heckle them as they left. The crowd, however, allowed his jeep to get through without incident. They were some familiar faces of Opposition Party leaders, and Agrippa raised his hand to acknowledge them.

* * *

Agrippa returned late to his office from lunch. He hadn't seen a need to hurry, and the discussions in the Mess were very intense. Officers were speculating on the ability of the police to handle the effervescing situation in Georgetown. They were betting that the government would eventually turn to the army. Dealing with their own supporters in the streets was, after all, a new situation for the Comrade President.

Agrippa was in very high spirits. Reviewing the signals that had come in from the border locations, he paused occasionally to figure out how to play his hand to advantage. The Defense Board would be considering promotions at the end of June. There was an opportunity.

The familiar knock on the door preceded his PA's face.

"There is that woman, Brenda, on the phone to you, General."

Agrippa sat there dazed. An ugly reality was refocusing his attention.

"She called twice already this morning," the PA was saying. "I told her you were busy, but she was very insistent."

Agrippa nodded and tossed his right hand in a motion to signal he would take the call.

"Hi," Brenda said.

"Yes? What is it?" Agrippa asked.

"I haven't seen you in a while."

Agrippa thought for a moment then said, "I will be right over." He picked up his beret and seated it on his head, then strolled purposefully down the hallway.

"I am going in town for a visual assessment," he said to the PA without stopping. "I will be right back," adding, "if the PS calls."

When he knocked at the rooming house, one of the Indian salesgirls answered the door.

"Where is Brenda?" he asked.

"She in her room," the girl replied. Agrippa walked down the short hallway, knocked at the door and, without waiting for an invitation, stepped in. Brenda rose from the edge of the bed, where she was sitting, and looked at him.

"Why do you keep calling me at the office?" he asked. She did not answer. "Why did you call my house?" he asked.

"Why you don't come and see me no more?" Brenda asked.

"Look, I am busy!" Agrippa almost screamed.

"You said you would take care of me. Now you don't even come to see me. You're worried about your wife? You used to tell me how bad she treating you; how you wanted to get rid of she. Now you worried about she?" Brenda paused. Agrippa said nothing. Then Brenda resumed in a more aggressive tone. "You can't take me out anywhere, but you take she with you to India." Agrippa ignored the barb. Brenda turned her back to him as if to figure out what to say or do next.

"Look," Agrippa said, "don't call me at work! You understand?" He was being loud and emphatic. "And don't call me at home again!" Anger and desperation were welling up in him.

"I gon call you whenever I like!" Brenda said defiantly. Then turning around to face him, she shouted as she also began crying, "You just can't leave me like this."

It happened so quickly Agrippa could not remember afterwards whether he had planned it this way, but pivoting on his left foot, he swung his right fist into Brenda's stomach. The softness of the resistance momentarily deluded him about the extent of the force he had applied until he saw her body tossed backward against the cardboard wall, which flung her back to the middle of the floor. She remained curled up there, her arms clutching her abdomen and her mouth open, gasping for breath. Heart thumping in his chest, Agrippa knelt down and brought her into a sitting position in front of him. She tried to push his arm away from her waist, but she did not have any strength, and her limp hand fell back beside her. The two Indian salesgirls called out almost in unison to Brenda to ask if she was all right.

"She awright," Agrippa said over his shoulder. "Don't worry."

Brenda started to breathe better, and Agrippa felt relieved. Brenda was pushing him away as she tried to stand, one arm still clutching her abdomen and sobs mixed in with her deep gasps for breath. Agrippa let her be and moved away from her. "Take a dose of castor oil," he said, "it will clean out everything." This utterance started Brenda shrieking and wailing, and Agrippa decided it was time to leave. He had composed his face into a strong grimace, lips lightly pressed together and jaws clenched. He could not avoid the look of fear and disgust from the two Indian salesgirls, but he turned away, confident that they would not dare tell about this, not if they knew what was good for them. He strode down the short hallway to the door, which opened just as he was reaching for the doorknob, and the landlady from upstairs, an old, frail Indian woman, stepped in front of him. She looked up at him and gasped as if expecting him to strangle her. Agrippa himself was momentarily confused about what to do, then the old woman slowly and awkwardly stepped aside to let him pass.

TWENTY-ONE

A GRIPPA HAD HARDLY SLEPT that evening, worried that Brenda might now become uncontrollable. More calls to the house, and God only knows what else. He had gotten up and sat in the living room a couple of times during the night, thinking of how to control the situation. He was sure Brenda would get to Vera somehow.

When Corporal Kyte came to get him at 05:45 for reveille, Agrippa told him to return at 07:00. Even then, he kept Kyte waiting for half of an hour, hoping that Vera would be back from work. At breakfast in the Officers' Mess, he ate the eggs but nothing else and had several cups of coffee. Officers greeted him as they came in but left him alone. It must have been obvious to even senior staff officers that he did not want to be bothered. This did not stop the officers from their usual banter, but none of it penetrated his mind as he pondered his predicament.

He walked back alone to his office and, in between official calls, he telephoned home but got no answer. The situation seemed strangely familiar, and he reminisced briefly on the last time Vera had left him, just to re-check the characteristics of the play. Of course, that was last December when Vera had tried to storm his room at Timehri. Then the evidence was more compelling. Now all she had was a phone call; the rest was just her instinct. At 10:00, he decided to return to the house.

The jeep pulled up to the open gate and stopped. The family car was parked under the house with the rear doors wide open. Vera's clothes were in the back seat. Yes, she was leaving him.

He was sure she heard his shoes on the hardwood floor when he emerged from the inside stairs into the living room, but she did not acknowledge his presence in the house. He went over and stood in the open bedroom door. Vera had her back to the door and did not turn around or stop packing her clothes.

"What are you doing?" he asked.

Hands holding a folded flowered dress, she looked over scornfully at him, then lowered the garment into the suitcase.

"Where are you going?" he asked, hoping by the slight variation of the question to elicit some response.

"That is none of your business! I'm leaving."

Not sure what she knew, Agrippa tested the water. "Did that woman call here again?"

This time, Vera stood erect and faced him, her lips quivering. "No, they brought she to the hospital bleeding to death!" The pronouncement was sharp, the stare cold and condemning.

The information, more than the stare, made Agrippa's heart race with anxiety. He had not imagined this possibility. He made no denials. His mind was focused on how to control the information from getting out of the hospital. He moved away from the door into the living room. She followed him.

"I don't know what you have become, but you are not people anymore," Vera resumed. "What kind of man would punch a pregnant woman in her belly? Tell me that! And for what? To hide your shame!" She began to cry. "To think, that girl is the same age as your own daughter!" Vera shouted. "And you told her to take a dose of castor oil? You blasted fool! You think she was constipated?" Vera walked off into the bedroom.

Agrippa knew the game was up. There was no way he could persuade Vera to stay. Now he had to protect himself, but he had to find out what happened and who knew. He felt sure Vera was going to let it all out, and as much as he wanted to escape the screaming he knew was sure to follow, he remained. The front windows off of the living room were all open, and Agrippa was worried that Vera's voice would be heard out on the street, so he moved out of the living room into the kitchen at the back of the house. Vera came back out of the room and followed him but stood several feet away.

"When they brought that woman into the Emergency Room, she was going into shock. God only knows how long she had been hemorrhaging! But, you know, as weak and disoriented as that girl was, she kept repeating one name—'Agrippa.' That's why they sent for me."

Arms on his hips, Agrippa breathed in deeply and blew it out lengthily and audibly.

"I told them in Emergency that I didn't know this girl. I tried to talk to she, but she couldn't understand what I was saying. Then I saw how the old Indian woman and the two Indian girls were looking at me, like they felt sorry for me. So I asked them why this girl was saying our name. 'Is not you,' the old lady said. 'Is who then?' I asked, but they wouldn't say."

Agrippa felt perspiration down his back and instinctively wiped his upper lip. He reached back to pull out his handkerchief and touched up his upper lip, then his forehead and both cheeks.

"The nurse in Emergency said the girl was having a spontaneous abortion. The minute I found out the girl was pregnant, I suspected you were involved. They wanted to do a DNC to remove the rest of the fetal tissue, but the girl needed a blood transfusion first. God, that girl had lost so much blood!" Vera broke into tears and went back into the bedroom. Agrippa took his glasses off and washed his face over the sink, drying it with the hand towel on the refrigerator. He was seating his glasses back on when Vera approached with a handkerchief that she was using to wipe her face. "After they carried the girl off, I talked to the old Indian woman again," she said calmly.

Agrippa felt he knew the rest. He attempted to walk out of the kitchen, but Vera was standing at the entrance. He turned around and went over to the sink and looked out through the window, bracing for the declaration that Vera was about to make.

"I asked the woman who had done this to this pregnant girl, but she wouldn't say. I knew she knew, but she was afraid. I tried to tell she that nothing would happen to she, but she didn't believe me. Finally, she felt sorry for me and said, 'Is General Agrippa.'"

For the first time, Agrippa felt afraid. His heart was thumping. He was sweating profusely and the leg, against which he was leaning, was trembling.

"'Is General Agrippa,'" Vera repeated. "'Is General Agrippa.' The doctors are mocking you." She advanced closer to Agrippa. "Do you know what they now calling your form of abortion? 'The Agrippa Solution!'" Vera made a big gasp for breath. "I feel so ashamed," she said quietly. "I just want 'Agrippa' removed from my name forever." Vera began sobbing. "The nurse told me that when the doctor heard what had happened to the girl, he called you 'evil and inhuman.' No wonder he avoided me all the time I was in Emergency." Vera began walking back to the bedroom. "God, I feel so ashamed. I can't show my face at that hospital again." Turning around sharply, she shouted, "You damn animal!"

Agrippa could hear Vera moving away, back to the bedroom. She seemed to be closing the large suitcase. Then he heard her taking it down the stairs to the car. She was closing the car doors. He thought she was going to start the car, but she came back up. Agrippa moved into the living room and sat down on the morris chair, staring in the direction of the stairway. Vera came out of the bedroom with her handbag and stood at the top of the stairs looking down on him. She seemed composed. When she spoke again, her voice was calm.

"When I found out that Brenda lives a block away from the hospital, I ran to the bathroom and screamed. I wanted to wash myself. To think you used to come and see me after you were done with that woman!" Vera wiped her eyes. "But as I thought about it all night, the scales began to fall away from my eyes. You think that having these outside women is one of the privileges of your position?"

Agrippa got up from the chair and moved back into the kitchen. He was not going to let her preach to him. She can leave if she wants.

Vera followed him. "I used to think of you as separate from the Party and the government, but you are all the same," she said in a mocking tone. "And Lord, look at what y'all doing to this country. People are starving. Children are dying by the hundreds of gastroenteritis. I see it every day. The conditions in the hospital are horrible. They have no linen, no vital signs chart paper. Needles have to be washed and reused. But the people at the top, you all! You can do whatever you please. Take whichever woman you want and do whatever you please with them."

Christ, Agrippa thought, just shut up and go. But Vera was not finished.

"Two days ago," she continued, "the police beat up an old Catholic priest. Yesterday, the army top man punched the belly of a young, pregnant woman. Who knows what you gon do tomorrow?"

With that, Vera descended the stairs, started the car, and reversed out.

Agrippa didn't see any point in staying at the house. He headed back to Camp Ayanganna, and, after an uncharacteristically brief lunch, was back in his office and on the phone to the Guard Hut at the base entrance. The corporal answered.

"General Agrippa here."

"Yes, General?"

"Stop the next patrol truck going into town and ask the NCO in charge to report to me."

"Yes, General."

It wasn't long before a sergeant reported to Agrippa. Agrippa gave him the address of the rooming house where Brenda lived and instructed the sergeant to pull up the truck to the gate at that house. The sergeant was to go upstairs and ask the landlady for directions to some person's house, any person. He was to make sure that some of the soldiers dismounted so they could be seen. Then he should thank the woman and proceed with his patrolling duties.

Agrippa was sure that the sergeant understood what he was trying to do. It was an old intimidation trick. Anyway, now he wouldn't have to worry about the rooming house people anymore.

He couldn't do much about the hospital. He felt sure that the nurses would be too frightened to speak openly about what had happened there. The doctors were more independent. But with all the problems in the country, who would care about a girl hemorrhaging. Besides, he could deny striking her. No one saw him do it.

He was sure Vera had already told her sister, but she was unlikely to tell anyone else. He couldn't do anything with Vera right now. With time, maybe. Her sister will try to get her to come back after a couple of weeks. But if she thinks she gon disgrace me with that damn Cuban doctor..

*   *   *

Army patrols had been reporting a worsening situation in Georgetown. The ranks of the demonstrators had swelled from each preceding day because of the continuing layoffs of public sector employees. Still, this was the most controllable element of the problem in Georgetown since they were all located in one place and the leaders were maintaining discipline. More troubling were the police reports of sporadic acts of violence throughout the city. Several Indian vendors at the market were beaten and their stalls looted. Women were having their handbags pulled away from them in the city streets in broad daylight. These were all police matters, but Agrippa knew that, sooner or later, the army would be called into a more active role.

He spent a lot of time on the phone with the Police Commissioner and also with his battalion commanders, Cadogan and LaFleur, reviewing army re-deployments. He knew too that the detachments in the interior were praying for relief.

It was almost 16:00 hours when the Comrade President called. "Clive, we need more troops in Georgetown."

"F-Company is at Timehri, awaiting redeployment to the interior," Agrippa replied. "We could bring it into the city."

"Isn't F-Company under Captain Moore, Rasputin's nephew?"

"Yes, Comrade President," Agrippa replied.

"I don't want him here. Send him to the border and bring out other troops."

"The three interior locations due for relief are Madhia, Matthews Ridge, and Tumatumari. They are not as close to the border as others."

"They far enough."

"The rotation will take about a week, Comrade President," Agrippa said. "You know the Islanders have limited airlift capacity."

"Well, proceed with that rotation. In the meantime, how about bringing in some of the other troops from the sugar belt?"

"Yes, Comrade President."

The Comrade President hung up, and Agrippa knew he needed to act quickly to get fresh troops into Georgetown. He called Vera's sister before he left the office, but no one picked up. He headed over to the Mess, but the shouting from the soccer field caused him to change direction. Officers had just started a soccer match, and he went over to the bleachers to observe. As usual, there was no referee. The few onlookers were calling out encouragement or jeers to the players, and he joined in, much to the amusement of the players, who seemed very animated by his presence. He remained and chatted with some of the officers after the game broke up.

The joking about the game continued over drinks in the Mess, and the immersion was refreshing for Agrippa. He felt a great urge to find out where Vera went, so he slipped out occasionally to telephone her sister. Nothing doing. After dinner, however, he did speak with Vera's sister, only to learn that Vera was adamant in her refusal to have any contact with him. Agrippa planned to call again and again over the next few days, calculating that Vera's sister and her husband, as in the past, would try to persuade Vera to return to him. For the moment, he took companionship with the officers in the Mess and in the uninterrupted flow of rum.

TWENTY-TWO

A T 16:25 HOURS, WEDNESDAY, April 27, Captain Moore received telephone orders from Colonel LaFleur that F-Company was to move out of Camp Stevenson the next day. The platoon assignments were specific—Lieutenant Beharry and Lieutenant Mentore, by trail to Madhia and Tumatumari respectively; Second Lieutenant Pilgrim by plane to Matthews Ridge. LaFleur was brief, and Moore did not remonstrate the infringement on his prerogative to make the platoon assignments in his company.

The following day, Moore saw Lieutenants Beharry and Mentore depart Camp Stevenson in their 3-ton trucks, following which he went over to the Air Wing to see Second Lieutenant Pilgrim and one squad of his platoon board the Islander for Matthews Ridge. The other two squads were scheduled to be flown on the Islander's supply runs later in the week. Moore stood beside the Islander talking with Pilgrim and Lieutenant Khan while soldiers from the Air Wing loaded supplies on the plane. The loading completed, Khan invited Pilgrim to board the plane with his soldiers. Lieutenant Khan was still checking the paperwork when an Air Wing guard told him he needed to report to the Admin Building. He returned a few minutes later and notified Captain Moore that Colonel LaFleur had decided to make the flight to Matthews Ridge. LaFleur had also asked that Captain Moore remain at Air Wing until he arrived.

Colonel LaFleur arrived at Air Wing at about 09:10 and took Moore aside. "Alan," he said, "I am supposed to speak to the cadets about the organization of the Brigade. I want you to fill in for me. You know all that stuff."

"When is your lecture, Colonel?" Moore asked.

"At 11:00. I know you gon do a good job." LaFleur did not wait for a response; he simply raised his hand in anticipation of Moore's salute and walked off to the plane.

Moore was irritated since he was already giving a lecture on being a platoon leader to the same cadets at 10:00. He told the soldier who had been bumped from the flight in favor of LaFleur to get into the jeep with his kit, and they left for the base compound. McCurchin stopped at the entrance of the single-level barrack building where the rump of the company was housed and where the company office was located. Moore instructed the soldier to report to his platoon sergeant and went into his office to jot down some talking points for his second-hour lecture.

At 09:55, Captain Moore walked over to the Training Corps building outside the base compound, to the right of the main gate. The parking lot in front was empty except for two 3-ton Training Corps trucks with their familiar cross-machetes emblems on the cab doors. Moore walked past them up a short flight of stairs and turned left into the classroom on the eastern side of the two-storied bungalow. The cadets stood up as he made his way to the lectern.

During the first hour, Moore talked to the cadets about leading by example. He spoke about bearing, personal appearance, concern for the welfare of the men, attention to detail, clarity of commands, and the importance of supervision. As an example of the need to supervise, Moore recalled an incident when a platoon leader had not checked on the loading of his soldiers into his truck and later discovered his men had stowed a donkey aboard. This brought on chuckles from the class.

The second hour went surprisingly well. Moore did not have the charts or diagrams, so he used the small portable chalkboard to sketch out the Brigade organization, erasing frequently to draw new diagrams. Nearing the end of the hour, he felt there was still a lot to cover but stopped and held a question-and-answer session, following which, he left. McCurchin was in the parking lot with the jeep, waiting to take him to the Mess.

The buffet line to the standard lunch and dinner fare of rice and curried chicken was crowded with lieutenants just out of hinterland locations. Moore had served at all of the hinterland locations and was amused by the attempts of returning officers to make their tour of duty appear tougher than anyone could remember. Then above the din, Moore heard the unmistakable voice of Lieutenant George Persico behind him.

"We've already taken care of the acoushi ants," Persico said.

Moore turned around. Persico stood beside Colonel Cadogan, halfway between the Mess entrance and the buffet table. Neither seemed to be in a hurry to get to the table.

"That's good, George," Cadogan said, pointing Persico in the direction of the buffet table.

"We should be finished with the extension of the piggery by half-June," Lieutenant Persico said.

"Very good, George," Cadogan said. "I told the Chief of Staff you were the man for the job." Cadogan placed his arm around Persico's shoulder and invited Persico to precede him. Their plates loaded, Cadogan insisted that Persico sit beside him at the head table. Once seated, Persico nodded once to Moore; otherwise he seemed attentive to every word or movement from Cadogan.

Moore saw Persico a few times that week in the Mess. He was usually in the company of Colonel Cadogan. On one occasion Persico came over to the bar to speak with Moore, inquiring about the new postings of the platoons and about his former platoon sergeant and some of the men, but the conversation quickly became a monologue in which hatcheries and poultry runs, foul pox, acoushi ants, and piggeries recurred with great frequency. Thereafter, Moore tried to avoid Persico but did observe with the benefit of distance that Persico comported himself with the hauteur of the top brass with whom he associated, nodding occasionally at officers of his own junior rank. And soon, word began to circulate in the Mess that Persico would be promoted to captain at the mid-June meeting of the Defense Board.

*   *   *

Two weeks after the deployment of his platoons, Captain Moore decided to visit the three interior locations. He had been advised by the Air Wing that he could be flown to Madhia and Tumatumari on the same day, provided his visit to the first site was brief. The plane would wait for him and take him on to Tumatumari, where he would need to overnight. The next day, he could be taken up to Matthews Ridge. Normally each location was resupplied once a week, but as a special favor the Air Wing had arranged to fly him back after a two-day stay at Matthews Ridge.

The flight from Timehri to Madhia was on an Islander piloted by Lieutenant Khan, who invited Moore to sit in the co-pilot's seat. The remaining eight seats were occupied by three soldiers and five pork-knockers, two of whom were holding Vicks inhalers even though they did not seem to have colds.

Moore enjoyed flying with Khan, who acted more as a tour guide than as a pilot. Khan explained that the trip from Timehri to either Madhia or

Tumatumari was an easy one—just a forty-minute flight over rain forest. However, the flight to any of the highland locations such as Matthews Ridge was much trickier, especially in rainstorms when visibility was very limited.

They had not been airborne long before one of the pork-knockers began complaining to another about not being taken all the way to Matthews Ridge. He said he had paid his money but would have to wait in Tumatumari for several days before a plane could take him up to Matthews Ridge. This struck Moore as curious indeed since this was a military resupply plane and he couldn't imagine who was accepting money from these civilians. He made a mental note to raise this issue with Lieutenant Beharry. However, operational matters dominated his brief visit to Madhia, and he was not able to get to this until Beharry took him back to the plane for the Tumatumari leg of the flight. Beharry laughed and told him to raise it with Lieutenant Mentore, since Moore would be overnighting with him at Tumatumari. However, Beharry did say that the passenger business was a racket that LaFleur was running.

At Tumatumari, Moore raised the matter with Lieutenant Mentore while they were relaxing before dinner.

"Derryck, on both trips out here I noticed a lot of pork-knockers on the plane. I thought somebody was doing them a favor, but then I heard one of them complaining that he had paid his money and would still have to wait here in Tumatumari. Beharry said it was a racket. Is what really going on?"

"You remember Nizam Khan told us LaFleur got money from the pork-knockers because he helped them?"

"Yes?"

"Well, that is how he helps them, by transporting them to where they want to go, except he using army planes and he pocketing the money."

"You saying he is like a bus conductor?"

"That's it! When the pork-knockers want to come out of the bush, the army planes fly them out. When they want to go back in, same thing. When they want to move from one area to another or when they want anything from Georgetown, LaFleur's their man."

"I see."

"They split the money in three—the pilot gets one share, LaFleur gets one, and the Chief gets one."

"Where'd you get that from?"

"Nizam Khan admitted he was getting a share. He said that the pilots are afraid to refuse."

"They thiefing?" Moore asked, laughing.

"They thiefing," Mentore agreed. "But you know I told y'all that a long time ago."

"What about these Vicks inhalers I see people walking around with?"

"They're hollow. The pork-knockers use it to keep some gold and diamonds. In fact, the pork-knockers say LaFleur prefers payment in Vicks!"

TWENTY-THREE

THE 08:00 MEETING ON Wednesday, June 1, began at 08:15, when Saddle Cadogan arrived. Agrippa was irritated. He expected Cadogan to blame the traffic or the rain, which had been drumming the rooftop for the past half hour. Cadogan blamed both. Agrippa suspected Cadogan was probably at his farm; after all, he was not even at reveille that morning. Agrippa had noticed that as he moved around talking to the officers at 05:55. He himself had made a special effort to come out to reveille and to be seen, as he had the previous evening, not leaving the Mess until late—21:15 hours, to be exact. He had checked his watch constantly that evening. He had circulated among the officers, trying to use his cheerfulness to hide his nervousness. Finally, he had settled down at a table but lightened on the drinking. He wanted to think straight.

It was raining when he left the Mess, but Corporal Kyte had pulled the jeep up close to the door. Once inside, he wrung both hands to shake off the rainwater and rolled his arms on his trousers to absorb the rest. It was a dark night, so the light beams from the jeep appeared much brighter, but once they turned on to Thomas Road, the rain on the canvas top sounded like buck shots, and the windshield wipers intermittently gave glimpses of sheets of water slicing the pitch road.

Agrippa used the beams from the jeep's headlights to help him unlock the door of his house and to guide him up the stairs. He located the kerosene lamp in the kitchen and attempted to light it. It took three tries. Twice the match stick broke when struck. He swore. He paused. He was too damn nervous, he thought. Why shouldn't everything go awright?

From the kitchen to the bedroom and out of uniform, Agrippa sat on the bed in his white singlet and boxer shorts. He knew he couldn't go to sleep. Back in the kitchen, he fixed a rum and Coke, adding some half-melted ice cubes from the trays in the refrigerator. He left the lamp in the kitchen and retired to the morris chair in the living room, glancing intermittently at the white envelope Vera's lawyer had sent two weeks ago. He tried to picture the scene but stopped himself. Still, his heart was thumping. This was going to be a long night, he knew. Padre had once said, "Why bark when you got dog," but what if something goes wrong? Don't worry, man, he kept telling himself, the boys are not going to let you down. He took off his glasses and wiped the perspiration from his forehead with the back of his hand.

Rising purposelessly, Agrippa decided to put out the lamp. Better try and get some sleep, he told himself. The raindrops on the rooftop would have been melodious on any other night. The later it got, the louder the thunder seemed. The neighbor's tethered dog was issuing long, plaintive wails and whimpers, its owners evidently not at home, and with each bout Agrippa wished the damn dog would shut up.

He gave up the bed and paced. First in the bedroom, then in the living room, and intermittently into the kitchen for another rum sedative. Frequently, but for brief moments, lightning illuminated the house and revealed its emptiness to him. He felt as anxious as Lady Macbeth for news that the evil deed had been done; only his wait would be longer.

When Corporal Kyte had come to get him at 05:45 in the morning, Agrippa had to wrench himself awake out of the morris chair. He was drained of energy. He had wanted to send Kyte away and go back to sleep, but that would have altered the plan. He went to reveille in gym clothes, although he was feeling cold and listless. To be seen at Camp Ayanganna performing any duty would further protect him, he thought. Now with Cadogan and LaFleur in his office, the endurance test of his day had begun. He knew he could bluff his way through the day. What worried him was the form the revelation would take.

The meeting today was one of several the Chief of Staff had with the two battalion commanders about company postings. The usual three-month rotation involved troops from the coast being moved to the interior locations and those in the interior moving to the coast—a straight swap. But the Georgetown situation had required some modifications, and now the senior officers met frequently to discuss the redeployment of each company. The problem today was what to do with Captain Seepersaud, commander of B-Company. Seepersaud needed a year more to finish up his university degree. The current deployment of B-Company along the east coast of the Demerara River had allowed Seepersaud to set up his command post at Enmore just outside Georgetown. Now his company was scheduled for redeployment to the hinterland. In anticipation of this, he had requested to be disembodied from the army for the year.

Agrippa held up the written request in mid-air as an invitation to Colonel Cadogan, Seepersaud's current battalion commander, to speak.

"I don't think we can afford to let Seepersaud leave the force at this time," Cadogan said. "We are short of company commanders. We have several overseas on courses: two in England and two in Cuba."

"I agree with that," Agrippa said, "but what do you recommend?"

"That his company be redeployed to border locations in the interior. Captain Seepersaud would set up his command post at Camp Stevenson. He could travel from there to the university as he did the last few years."

"Ovid?" Agrippa turned to Colonel LaFleur.

"Clive, I agree with Colonel Cadogan on this. If Seepersaud is allowed to go off for a year, it is my battalion that would be short-handed. Seepersaud is an experienced officer. I say we keep him."

"The problem," said Agrippa, "is that I had promised Seepersaud a long time ago that I would try to help him out during his final year. Besides, we have several officers trying to get their degrees, and we need to consider some form of assistance."

"The situation in Georgetown is tense," Cadogan said. "I don't know how Seepersaud will react if the government calls on us."

"I disagree," LaFleur said. "Seepersaud is a professional officer. He will carry out his orders."

"I don't know his politics either," Agrippa conceded, "but I think Seepersaud will carry out his orders. You know, it's our Black officers that the government is most worried about. Many of them, like yourselves, are from Georgetown. They know a lot of people here. Some of their relatives have lost their jobs. How will they react?"

"Let's say I agree with all this," Cadogan said, "what do you propose?"

"F-Company under Captain Moore has just relieved the three platoons of C-Company from Madhia, Tumatumari, and Matthews Ridge. Let's deploy C-Company along the east coast of the Demerara River and give operational control to Seepersaud. His command post would be here. But since he would be busy at university, Colonel Cadogan will exercise control over the company."

Cadogan shifted position in his chair. "What about the officer currently commanding C-Company ?" Cadogan asked. "Why can't he—"

"He was just acting. Isn't that right, Ovid?" Agrippa turned to LaFleur.

"Yes," LaFleur replied, "he's just a lieutenant. The regular CO is in Cuba, remember? He should be back in a couple of weeks. He can take over B-Company, when he gets back."

Cadogan looked skeptical. Agrippa suspected he wouldn't like the idea: it would cut into his business time.

"Look," Agrippa said, "we been supporting this government and we'll continue to, but the army has interests of its own. Having direct control of C-Company at this time can be very useful to us. What y'all think?"

The phone rang, the direct line. Agrippa picked up.

"Clive, Lionel Cummings, Home Affairs."

Agrippa froze. His heart raced. Cummings sounded aloof and officious. It was the way he said "Home Affairs" after his name, sounding almost menacing. Agrippa looked over at Cadogan and LaFleur to see if they recognized any panic in his face. He groped for a response.

"Lionel! What's happening, man? We hardly see you outside of work these days." Agrippa hoped the display of familiarity would throw LaFleur and Cadogan off scent and elevate the hurdle for Cummings, just in case.

"Well, you know the situation in Georgetown?" Cummings replied. Agrippa was about to speak, but Cummings cut him off. "Look, Clive, we got a problem. A serious problem."

"I am in a meeting with Colonel Cadogan and Colonel LaFleur right now."

"How long more the meeting gon last?" Cummings asked.

"Another half hour or so," Agrippa replied, trying to sound casual.

"Awright, why you don't call me back right after?"

Agrippa heard the click at the other end, then he put down the phone. Cadogan and LaFleur were staring intently at him. He felt he needed to say something to put them off. On the other hand, not saying anything would also put them off.

"Anyway," he said, as if there had been no interruption, "coming back to this Seepersaud business, what y'all think?"

"I don't see what controlling just one company gon do," Cadogan said. "I with you though about trying to protect the interests of the army."

"Look, we control all of the companies," Agrippa pointed out. "All I am saying is that direct control of C-Company gon give us greater flexibility. That's all. And we are in a situation where the government is going to ask us to do things. We support the government, okay? But we got to think about the army's interests too. What I am saying is we mustn't appear to be too willing."

"I agree with you," LaFleur said.

"Oh, I agree with that too," Cadogan joined in, "I just not so sure about this arrangement, but I gon go along."

LaFleur nodded his support.

"I gon write Captain Seepersaud. Saddle, you can talk to him in the meantime?" Cadogan sucked his teeth, and LaFleur laughed. Agrippa realized that he had slipped and called Cadogan by the nickname Cadogan resented. "Come, come, Hartley, is just a little joke," Agrippa added in a gentle tone, hoping to soft soap Cadogan. Cadogan relaxed a little.

"Ovid," Agrippa said to LaFleur, "I want to come up to Timehri to see how the redeployment going."

"Today?" LaFleur asked.

"Maybe. Let me see how things going here first."

"I leaving for Camp Stevenson just after this meeting," LaFleur pointed out.

"I gon try and let you know before you leave."

The two colonels rose, saluted, then left.

Agrippa sat alone for a few minutes. A feeling of malaise had settled on him. It had been a struggle to get through the meeting with Cadogan and LaFleur without showing signs of fatigue. Lack of sleep, combined with a feeling of chill and nervousness, made his body twitch involuntarily from time to time. He sank lower in the chair and closed his eyes, but reopened them when his body twitched sharply. He thought of what Cummings might be calling about and began to rehearse responses, but he couldn't get his mind to focus on anything too long. He was too sleepy and his head hurt, maybe from all the drinks he had had through the night. His stomach growled but he couldn't stand the sight of food. All he had had for breakfast was coffee. He could use a brandy, he thought, but that would mean walking over to the Mess and asking them to open the bar. What if Cummings called back while he was gone?

He pressed the buzzer at his desk and requested his Personal Assistant get him some coffee. He watched her leave, then he rose from the chair and walked over to the window on the eastern wall. He could see the Guard House directly across and then about a hundred feet up the drive to his right the entrance to the base compound. There was always activity at the Guard House. Intermingled with soldiers at the Guard House were civilian women, waiting no doubt to meet their husbands or child-fathers. He sometimes wondered whether the Guard House might not really be the nerve center of the base. If he walked out there now, he knew he would be saluted every step of the way, just like at reveille this morning. Every officer who crossed his path saluted, and every unit passing by him responded to an "Eyes Right!" command. The thought of all the power he had as army chief made him glow and strengthened his determination to hold on at all cost.

The door reopened, and his PA brought in the familiar tray. Agrippa walked back to his chair as she placed the tray on his desk. He sipped the coffee, holding the cup with both hands and staring intently through the north window. Yes, he was going to call Cummings, but he was going to stand firm. He placed the cup down and dialed the number.

"Home Affairs, Cummings."

"Lionel, Clive here," Agrippa said, assuming a familiar air. "What's going on, man?"

"Clive, I got a serious police matter to discuss with you," Cummings replied. "You better come over here."

"Come on, Lionel, what's going on?"

"Clive, where is your wife?" Cummings asked.

"She staying with she sister," Agrippa replied. "We had a bit of a problem. Domestic matters, you know?"

"I see," Cummings said. "You know that she was friendly with a Cuban doctor?"

"Well, yes. I talked to the woman about it, but she don't listen to me. I tell she the damn thing don't look good. I warn she that—"

"The doctor is dead, Clive."

"I sorry to hear that," Agrippa said, "but what that got to do with me?"

"He was killed last night. Murdered."

"You know that don't surprise me," Agrippa said. "These fellas come from Cuba or wherever and they start fooling around with other people's wives. Something ain't bound to happen to them?"

"He was with your wife when it happened," Cummings pointed out.

"So, is what you saying?" Agrippa asked. "You think it was me? You got to be joking. I was at the Officers' Mess all afternoon yesterday and into the night. I ain't see she nor she sweet-man."

"Well, Clive, she filed a report at CID accusing you," Cummings said. "She said it was army people who beat the man to death."

"How she know that?" Agrippa asked.

"She said they were wearing army boots."

"Look, Lionel, a lot of people wearing army boots these days," Agrippa asserted. "All the National Service people and the Party Youth Corps. Is a lot of people."

"She said that the faces were familiar," Cummings said. "One or two of them had come to your house in the past."

"I telling you, Lionel, the woman crazy! Is where this thing happen, anyway?"

"Happy Acre," Cummings replied.

"Happy Acre?" Agrippa asked. "That's a secluded area. Look, Lionel, this kind of thing happens all the time. People go to these secluded areas by the seawall or wherever and they get attacked."

"Clive, your wife was not attacked. They pulled the doctor out of the car but kept your wife in the car. They beat and kicked the doctor to death. Your wife said she tried to get out of the car, but they stopped she. She said she begged them to stop, but they kicked the man harder."

Agrippa remained silent this time.

"The police said that the man's head was busted up, his face disfigured from the blows."

"All I can say is that it was not me," Agrippa asserted. "I was not involved. I don't know anything about any of this."

"Your wife gave the police descriptions of the men. They looking for the attackers right now."

"Well, I hope they find them, but I telling you again, Lionel," Agrippa said, "I ain't got nothing to do with this."

"Clive, the Comrade President is very concerned," Cummings said in a somber tone. "He was up late last night talking to the CID people. He doesn't know what he gon say to the Cuban government. Then again, what gon happen when the Opposition finds out? And the newspapers?" Agrippa said nothing. "Clive, you can't use your position to bump off people because they fooling 'round with yuh wife."

"Look, Lionel, you talking like you think I behind this. That is nonsense. I told you where I was yesterday. A whole lot of officers can vouch for that."

"Awright, comrade," Cummings said. "We gon see when CID pick up the assailants. Better watch yourself though. This koker dam could break down anytime."

Agrippa heard the click but still held the phone for a few moments before hanging it up. His chest pounded. He tried to prop his chin up with his hands, but they were shaking, so he sat back in the chair holding both armrests. He felt the drops of perspiration in his left eye, took off his glasses and pressed his left shirt sleeve to his eye before reaching back for his handkerchief. He wiped his face once and put on his glasses but kept the damp handkerchief out, occasionally applying it to his cheeks and forehead.

Throughout the phone conversation, he felt like Cummings was stalking him. I wonder what they really know, he asked himself. And why did Cummings call? Why not the Police Commissioner? Cummings is a political appointee. I wonder what they really have and what they up to. Anyway, they can't prove anything against me. Why bark when you got dog? And even if the police find the boys, they gon deny they had anything to do with it. It was night time. It would be she word against they word. The bitch. Serve she right; she want to divorce me? She just lucky they didn't kill she too!

Agrippa stood up, without quite knowing why, and walked over to the east window. He looked out in the direction of the base entrance, then quickly walked back to the front of his desk and picked up the phone.

"Base entrance," the voice said.

"This is the Chief of Staff. Has Colonel LaFleur left the base?"

"Yes, Chief of Staff."

"You sure?"

"Yes, Chief of Staff. I been here all morning."

"Awright, thank you."

Agrippa pressed the buzzer. "Bernadette," he said, when his PA appeared at the door, "have the signaler contact Colonel LaFleur by radio and let him know that I coming up to Timehri. Also, have him send a signal to the Base Commander at Camp Stevenson."

"Yes, Chief of Staff. You want any of the staff officers to go up with you?"

"No, I going up alone. I want you to stay here as well."

"Yes, Chief of Staff."

Agrippa returned the salute of the sentry when the staff car exited Camp Ayanganna then rested his head back. He awoke to the voice of Corporal Kyte telling him they had arrived at Timehri. The car was parked in front of the Officers' Mess. He felt like he could have slept some more, but he straightened his beret and went upstairs to freshen up. Returning down to the car, he instructed Corporal Kyte to drive over to Camp Stevenson.

The hour-long nap from Georgetown had really picked up Agrippa's spirits. He spent the rest of the morning with Colonel LaFleur and the Base Commander, visiting the barracks of troops who had just returned from interior locations and those who were still awaiting transportation to interior locations. He joked with the soldiers and their officers and, just before noon, he returned to the Officers' Mess in the company of Colonel LaFleur and the Base Commander.

Agrippa was careful only to have one drink before lunch, and he nursed it as he moved from group to group in the lounge. The officers seemed to be enjoying the vivaciousness he exuded as he complimented each of them on some aspect of their work that he could recall. The loudness of voices and the laughter in the lounge continued in the dining room. He was very hungry, and the curried chicken and rice were most welcome, as was the custard which followed.

Agrippa noticed Captain Moore in the buffet line and decided that he could use Moore to portray himself as a relaxed man, certainly not one who had anything of which to be fearful. When Moore had taken his seat at the table, Agrippa called out to him.

"Alan, tell us how your men kidnapped that donkey, Eveready. How did they get it into the truck?" There was loud laughter around the room. Even Moore was laughing.

"Well, General, the men in Lieutenant Beharry's platoon backed the truck up to the bandstand where Eveready was standing. They coaxed the donkey into the truck with a paperbag of sugar."

The Chief chuckled and looked around the tables as if seeking encouragement to continue with this. "When did you discover the donkey? I heard the soldiers were jumping out of the truck."

"That's true, General. There was a lot of gas; the donkey was having diarrhea." The laughter was uproarious. The officers on both sides of Moore were slapping him on his back as they laughed.

"In the truck?" Agrippa asked, wanting to lead Moore to confirm this item of detail. There was a moment of silence around the room.

"In the truck," Moore confirmed, nodding his head. The laughter erupted again.

"Did you transfer the men out of that truck?" the Chief of Staff asked.

"Oh no, they had to ride with the donkey and all the stink," Moore replied, and the Chief laughed, slapping his hand on the table. Moore joined in, as did all of the others at the table, and looking around the room, Agrippa felt he had succeeded in showing himself to be free of worry.

After the meal, Agrippa visited with the senior officers in the lounge, and at about 15:00 hours, he began the return trip to Camp Ayanganna. He tried to sleep in the car but simply couldn't. Arriving back at his office just at 16:00 hours, he discovered that not much had transpired since he had left. None of his superiors had called; that was a relief. Cummings had not called back; that made him anxious. His PA did say that his wife had called.

Sitting in his office, Agrippa worried about what he would do to pass the time. He did not want to be alone—he wanted to keep up appearances and make his movements observable. He walked over to the Officers' Mess, had dinner and remained until about 21:00, when he felt he could no longer remain awake. He did not speak to Corporal Kyte on the way home, and once there, promptly prepared for bed. The phone rang; he picked it up.

"You murderer!" Vera screamed. "You arranged to have that poor man killed. You were the one. You think I ain't know?"

"You lucky they didn't kill you too," Agrippa said calmly.

"You still got time, and I believe you gon do it. You shameless murderer, you! That man was just a friend, but he was a better man than—"

Agrippa hung up.

TWENTY-FOUR

A GRIPPA SPENT THE REST of the week at Camp Ayanganna, busying himself with army matters. He wondered often what Cummings and the police might be up to, but took company with the officers—at reveille, at meals, and after work. On Sunday, he went up to Timehri for the Hudson Airways flight and spent the afternoon at the Mess at Camp Ayanganna, after he had off-loaded the bags at his house. As usual, the Padre was there with him at the far table looking out to the seawall, and they were joined by Saddle Cadogan and Lo-lo LaFleur. Agrippa sat quietly, holding his drink with both hands and sighing occasionally.

"Something worrying you, Clive?" the Padre asked.

"No," Agrippa said quickly. "Is what make you say that?"

"Nothing, except you looking in that glass a lot."

"Is the woman, you know. She wants a divorce."

"Sorry, Clive—"

"Nothing to be sorry about, Padre," Agrippa interjected. "I chased she out of the house. I just want this whole thing finished."

"Well, we with you," the Padre said, "you know that?" Agrippa shook his head. "But right now," the Padre continued, "some of the officers are looking over here."

"Is so?" Agrippa asked. The Padre was looking intently at him and nodding. "Well, Padre, leh we move around a little bit."

Agrippa rose and tried to sound convivial as he moved from group to group, but realizing that he couldn't keep up the act, he returned to the table by the north window and drank with the colonels. Throughout the afternoon and into the evening, he worried about the Security Heads' meeting the next day.

The meeting was scheduled for 14:00 hours. Agrippa came by jeep, two armed soldiers riding in the back. When he arrived at Parliament Building, the demonstrators outside were chanting loudly. The placards had become a familiar sight, and Agrippa knew most of them by heart. The most prominent had been "GIVE US THIS DAY OUR DAILY

BREAD." Today, however, there were two new placards. One said "FREE AND FAIR ELECTIONS" and the other "ALLOW INTERNATIONAL OBSERVERS." These had been the positions of the Opposition for a very long time. Now the calls seemed to have been taken up Black public service employees in the capital. Agrippa knew that this spelled trouble for the Comrade President because, until now, the Party counted these people as its supporters. He was aware that the pro-government leadership of the Public Service union had been ousted and that the attempt by the unions supporting the Opposition to wrest control of the Trades Union Council might now be successful. For the moment, though, he had his own problems to deal with.

Agrippa was not sure how the others would behave toward him in the meeting. By now, they would all have been aware of the circumstances surrounding the death of the Cuban doctor, the fact that it occurred while the Cuban was out with Vera, and Vera's charge that Agrippa had arranged the killing. The Comrade President had not called him since the incident, and he had not had any contact with the Police Commissioner. Only Cummings, the bureaucrat whose ministry oversaw the police, had contacted him. Agrippa decided to put on a defiant face; after all, they surely knew he was never at the scene of the crime.

The aging Permanent Secretary came out to get Agrippa, who was the only one sitting in the anteroom with the receptionist. The PS was polite and greeted Agrippa without any strain. Already seated in the conference room were Police Commissioner Dalrymple and Lionel Cummings. The Comrade President was due in at any moment, the PS told them as he showed Agrippa in. Commissioner Dalrymple's greeting was subdued and somewhat awkward. It sounded like a grunt. Agrippa felt Dalrymple's stare. Dalrymple seemed to be studying him most intensely. Cummings, on the other hand, seemed in good cheer; he nodded to Agrippa and smiled.

"You know, Clive," Cummings said, "you been inviting me for a drink? I free this afternoon."

"You want to come over to the Officers' Mess?"

"Yeh. That way I can meet some of the other officers."

"Five-ish?" Agrippa asked.

The door opened and the Comrade President entered, all eyes momentarily turning toward him. After the Comrade President sat down at the head of the table, Cummings turned back to Agrippa and nodded.

The meeting lasted an hour. The President castigated the same list of suspects—the Opposition party, the priests, the university lecturers, and the unions. Agrippa was struck, however, by how happy the Comrade President appeared. The Comrade President looked over at him several times and smiled. There seemed to be no expression whatsoever in his face that Agrippa could interpret as a condemnation. In fact, Agrippa felt very much at ease at the meeting. Only Commissioner Dalrymple seemed distant. The Comrade President's friendly disposition and Cummings' apparent about-face confused Agrippa, and he pondered it during the meeting and on his way back to Camp Ayanganna. He resolved to use the informality of the meeting with Cummings to milk him for information.

Cummings arrived a little early at the Officers' Mess. Agrippa and a staff officer had teamed up against two junior officers in a dart game. Agrippa offered his darts to Cummings, but Cummings declined, choosing instead to sit at the bar, sipping a Bass Ale and observing the game. By the time the game was over, Cummings was caught up in conversation with several officers, and Agrippa did not want to tip his own hand by tearing Cummings away. Instead, he invited Cummings to join the officers for dinner.

The seating arrangement at dinner allowed only for small talk. Agrippa ate mechanically and without relish, all the while studying Cummings and making faces that suggested he was following everything going on. After dinner, he led Cummings to the table by the window looking out to the seawall. Once they had been served drinks and Agrippa felt they would not be disturbed, he broached the issue with Cummings.

"Lionel, I don't understand you, you know," Agrippa complained. "One day, it looks like you after me and the next day, we friends again. What going on?"

"Clive, you are a very important man. You are the head of the army. You are also my friend. Naturally, when we heard about the killing and the accusation against you, we wanted to protect you. But we can only go so far."

"What you mean?"

"I mean that the matter is now in the hands of the police."

"Well, I told you I had nothing to do with it. The police will find out the same thing."

"I don't know, Clive. It don't look good."

"What you mean?"

"Here is what the police knows. Your wife went to the Starlite Drive-in with the doctor. After the first picture, they went over next door and parked in the open lot. There were other cars scattered around there. A jeep pulled up behind them. Four men dragged the doctor out and beat him while two others kept your wife locked up in the car."

"What kind of jeep?" Agrippa asked.

"A 3/4-ton army jeep."

"How she know it was an army jeep?"

"Come on, Clive. The wife of the Chief of Staff don't know an army jeep? Anyway, she also identified two of the assailants—Sergeant Maynard and Private Batson. The others wore army boots, but she didn't see them as clearly."

"I know Sergeant Maynard," Agrippa said. "He wouldn't do something like that."

"Your wife said Maynard was in charge. He didn't do the hitting. He directed it. Wasn't Maynard your orderly when you were a battalion commander?"

"Yes."

"That's what your wife said."

"Why would she pick on a good soldier like Maynard?"

"She said she saw him. He was closest to her. He wanted to make sure she was not hit." Cummings was emphatic. Agrippa remained silent.

"They didn't use names," Cummings continued, "except once. Maynard called out Batson's name. That's when she saw Batson's face."

"I still don't understand what any of this got to do with me."

"The police will question Maynard and Batson. They will probably be arrested."

"So?"

"Murder in this country is a hanging offense. Are you sure they will protect you all the way?"

"Well, they don't have to," Agrippa said. "I had nothing to do with it."

"So you say."

"Sound like you don't believe me, man."

"Your wife is a smart woman."

"What you mean?"

"She copied the license plate on the jeep." Agrippa was aware that Cummings was studying his reaction. "The police will check the log at the gate and at the Motor Pool to see who checked out the jeep."

Agrippa was having difficulty focusing. He didn't know how to compose his face.

"You know, Clive, I want to help you, and I think the Comrade President would like to help you. He likes you, you know?"

"Is where you get that from?" Agrippa asked.

"I know, man, I know," Cummings replied. "Is the way the man does talk about you."

Agrippa's mind was racing. Cummings' declaration was not much comfort to him right now. He thought of Vera—how he hated that woman. The only mistake I made . . .

"I can talk to the Comrade President for you, if you want me to," Cummings was saying. "He can understand how you must have felt, another man giving you blow and all."

Agrippa remained silent. To accept Cummings' offer was to acknowledge complicity in the murder, and he wasn't sure he was ready for that as yet.

Cummings pressed him further. "CID will stop by to question you. Better get yourself ready. Just tipping you off as a friend."

"Well, thank you." As soon as he said that, Agrippa wondered whether he had made a mistake.

"Well, I got to go now, Clive, but call me and let me know if you want me to talk to the Comrade President." Agrippa looked intently at him but still did not accept the offer. "By the way, Cummings continued, "your wife told the police about Brenda." He paused and looked at Agrippa then added, "and they are checking that out too."

Christ! Agrippa thought, his chest heaving and his breathing getting difficult. He wondered whether there was perspiration on his face and whether Cummings was seeing it. He felt very hot but he didn't dare reach for his handkerchief.

"If the police decide to arrest you or even if any of this gets out in the newspapers, you might have to go on administrative leave until it is all sorted out."

Christ! This fella knows how to turn the damn knife.

"Anyway, call me if you want me to try talking to the Comrade President. Mind you, I can't promise you anything, but once the police take over, is not much we can do. Think about it, eh."

With that and a pat on Agrippa's shoulder, Cummings rose. Agrippa was looking up at him but was at a complete loss for words. Then Cummings placed his hands on the edge of the table and leaned forward closer to Agrippa's face.

"You know, one thing really upset the Comrade President. He said that Maynard and those boys must really, really like you to do such a thing for you. And he is disappointed that you are going to let them go down and not help them." Cummings shook his head from side to side, then left.

Agrippa took a sip from his drink, scanning the room while the glass rested on his lip to see if anyone was looking over. Would they think he had a quarrel with Cummings? Could they read that something was wrong with him? Better smooth the waters before leaving, he thought.

Agrippa went over to the bar and set his glass down. "That was a good one you fixed, Jarvis," he said to the attendant. Agrippa knew there was nothing different about the drink; Jarvis probably knew that too. Nevertheless, Jarvis seemed very pleased, especially since the Chief's comment was loud and some of the officers looked over.

"Thank you, Chief of Staff. How about another one?"

"If you fix it like the other one."

"I gon do me best, General."

"And Jarvis, rev up the music a little, nuh. How about some Olatunji?"

"Now you talking, General!" Jarvis was being a bit too familiar, but Agrippa didn't mind. Besides the officers within hearing were amused by the exchange. They might just think the Chief was in a good mood. Agrippa tried to build this up by dipping a couple of times to the music as he moved about, and he heard several "Awright!" from different sides in the lounge. But the eddies in his stomach were compelling him to seek seclusion, and when he finished the drink, he signed his chit, waved to the officers, and left the Mess for his office.

True to habit, Agrippa took off his beret upon entering his office and hung it on the rack. He stepped into the lavatory and paused in front of the large mirror over the sink, staring at his rectangular face. Hardly a wrinkle. The hair was gray, but it had been graying since he turned forty.

210

He ran his right, open hand like a plumb bob from his chest down to his mid-section, flattening his shirt as he did so. The hand began to trace out a convex after he passed his diaphragm. He turned to look at himself in profile, sucking up his gut as if he were on parade. Then he faced forward again. Not bad for fifty-two.

Fifty-two. I would have served three more years as Chief of Staff if this damn thing hadn't happened. Possibly another five-year term. It don't matter what the rules say, this government can give you another term if it wants.

He stepped back from the mirror to get a fuller view of himself. He wore his uniform well, he thought. The bright red collar tabs, the crowns and pips on each shoulder, and the blue lanyard over the left. The power and the freedom this uniform gave him, not to talk about the wealth! Only a few years ago, he was just a civil servant with the rank of sergeant in the Volunteer Force. Give all of this up?

Agrippa sat down, resting his elbows on the desk, his open hands supporting his chin. He was sure from what Cummings said that they were on to him; they already knew about Maynard and Batson. God, I shoulda listen to Batson! He asked me if I gon take back the woman. I told him I didn't want no spoiled milk. He suggested we take care of the woman one time. He was worried she might recognize them. But I thought about the children. Now that bitch . . .

Agrippa rose and seated his beret on his head, adjusting the front band across his forehead to just slightly above his eyebrows and gently smoothing the felt back with both hands. He sighed deeply. He knew he had to help Maynard, Batson, and the others. For one thing, they might talk. But even if they didn't, he would lose the support of the officers when they find out what had happened. They wouldn't care about the Cuban man, but they would condemn him for cutting loose soldiers with such demonstrated loyalty.

Corporal Kyte was waiting by the jeep parked on the drill square in front of the Admin Building. He held open the door for Agrippa before returning to the driver's side. It would be dark in a hour or so, and Agrippa wished he could go over and see Brenda. Them were good days, he thought. I should have kept her and chased out the bitch.

Suppose I call Cummings and ask he to talk to the Comrade President, Agrippa wondered. Right away, that is an admission of complicity. I would be at their mercy. What if they offer to let the boys go and to call off the dogs in exchange for my resignation? I'll be out, just like that. Maybe that is what they hoping for. No wonder Cummings wanted to come to the Mess and meet the other officers. Maybe he's already feeling out Cadogan, the next ranking officer.

They probably want me to go quietly. They don't want a big scandal on their hands. They've just lost the Public Service Union. They about to lose control of Trades Union Council. The rank and file in the Party are revolting in Georgetown. Imagine putting the army chief on trial. The officers will never forgive the Comrade President for humiliating the army; that's why they want me to go to them.

They're bold face, though, Agrippa thought. They're beating up priests and university people and complain when some foreign doctor get he head busted up. I supported the Comrade President during the disturbances in the '60s. Mind you, he didn't call he-self "Comrade President" in them days. He was just the leader of the minority party. Then, he was telling people to burn and kill. That's why he wants to save Maynard and Batson. These boys used to be members of the Party Youth arm. But then was then, and now is now. Still, I bet the Comrade President's having second thoughts about putting me on trial. And Cummings coming in here and telling me to throw myself to the mercy of the Comrade President! They better remember what Stalin said 'bout the Pope. Is how many battalions the Comrade President have? Agrippa laughed but checked himself when Corporal Kyte looked over at him.

*　　*　　*

The next day, Agrippa gave instructions to the Base Commander that the sentries at the base entrance should refuse entry to police personnel who did not have clearance from the Chief of Staff. He also arranged through his driver for Sergeant Maynard to speak with him on his way over to the Mess for lunch, and he instructed Maynard to remain on the base. The same went for Batson. He wondered why he hadn't heard from Commissioner Dalrymple. Was the next move Cummings' or Dalrymple's? He thought he'd call Commissioner Dalrymple. What could he lose? Dalrymple knew everything Cummings knew, even more, probably. He dialed Dalrymple's direct line.

"Charlie, since when Cummings doing police work?"

"What you mean?"

"Well, he come in here with some cock-and-bull story about how the army bump off a Cuban doctor."

"Is not a cock-and-bull story," Dalrymple said. "Somebody bumped off a Cuban doctor, who, by the way was with your wife. And is your wife who reported it."

"Well, he naming some soldiers, and all I got to say is if y'all suspect some soldiers, let us know and we will take disciplinary action, like we always do."

"Not on this one, comrade. This is not a drunk and disorderly charge. This is murder."

"So what you saying? The police gon just walk into this base and start arresting people?"

"No," Dalrymple said. "We will get a warrant for the arrest of the suspects and we will expect you to cooperate."

"How come the police isn't handling it?" Agrippa asked.

"The police is handling it. Is just that the big ones on top are taking a strong interest for reasons you are aware of, and they want to handle that part."

"I see."

"Is a serious matter, Clive. Your wife has been in here several times. She said she hadn't seen any report in the newspaper. She thinks we covering it up. She talked to the Comrade President. I believe she might go over to the *Red Star* anytime now."

"Who dealing with us on this one, you or Cummings?"

"Well, the police investigation will continue, and we will make arrests at the appropriate time. But right now, the government calling the shots."

"What you saying, that Cummings is just a messenger?"

"You got to ask a question like that? You ain't know how this place working? Of course, he is a messenger."

"Awright, Charlie—"

"Look, Clive, I ain't excusing anything anybody do here, but I feel for you, you know. The wife carrying on like that with another man."

"That doesn't mean—"

"I ain't saying it does. I just saying I sorry about the situation."

"Thank you, Charlie."

*   *   *

Agrippa heard nothing more about the Happy Acre incident until Friday morning, June 10, and then, there it was on the front page of state-run *Cayman News*. The caption read "Cuban Doctor Killed in Mysterious Circumstances." The article stated that Dr. Carlos Rodriguez had apparently had a rendezvous in the secluded acre near to the Starlite Drive-in when he was attacked by several assailants. It said that the Police had leads that they were following. The rest of the article talked about the tremendous contributions the Cuban specialists were making in the spirit of proletarian solidarity. It ended by saying that the government and people of a grateful nation expressed their heartfelt sympathy to the family of Dr. Rodriguez.

Agrippa could not focus; he felt dizzy, hands trembling. He dropped the paper down on the desk and waited for his breathing to get back to normal. It was definitely over, he thought, that's why he had not heard from Cummings since Monday. And now, he did not want to hear from Cummings at all—it was between him and the Comrade President. He began to think of the terms he would ask for, should the Comrade President ask him to step down. Definitely, he would want an honorable discharge with his pension intact. However, until he heard from the Comrade President directly, he was going to do his job. Strange how much at peace he suddenly felt.

Aggripa did not return from lunch until 14:30. He had gone to the Mess at about 12:30, but with many officers arriving at Camp Ayanganna as part of the current redeployment, there were more officers than seats in the dining area, so they ate in shifts and drank in between. The crowd, and the fact of it being Friday, created a very convivial atmosphere in the Mess, providing Agrippa a most welcome immersion. He moved from group to group, getting informal reports from the officers returning from some of the interior locations. He also spent some time reconciling financial accounts with the pilots from the Air Wing, dealing with them one at a time.

His PA followed him back into his office to tell him that Cummings had called about 13:30 and had asked if the Chief of Staff would please return his call as soon as possible. Agrippa thanked her and settled down to reading signals, determined not to have any further exchanges with Cummings. He was through dealing with a messenger; besides, Cummings was not even his superior. As far as Agrippa was concerned, they had made a decision about him, and he wanted to hear it directly from the Comrade President.

About thirty minutes later, Cummings was on Agrippa's direct line.

"Look, Clive, I been thinking the situation's probably a bit awkward for you, so I talked to the Comrade President. I'm sure you saw the article about the doctor's death. We had to do something; your wife was threatening to go to the *Red Star*. Notice we didn't name anybody."

Nothing new so far, Agrippa thought. This fella taking his time. Anyway, leh we see what he got.

"We would like to protect you," Cummings continued. "In case you worried about the job, you shouldn't. We want you to continue as the Chief of Staff."

Safe! This was what Agrippa wanted to hear. He wanted to rush over to the Mess and celebrate, then he heard the rest.

"But, Clive, we need some guarantees from you."

"Like what?" Agrippa asked, though he knew he would agree to anything now, except an arrest of the soldiers and a trial.

"We on the phone, Clive. This is something we need to talk about in person. How about this afternoon?"

"You want to come over here? The lounge is now closed, but I can have the attendant open it."

"Can you think of a better place for a nice drink?" Cummings asked airily.

"I'll expect you at the Mess. Around 16:00?"

"Righto!"

Agrippa leaped from his chair, took in a deep breath, and grabbed his beret. He couldn't work anymore. He couldn't concentrate on anything. He felt intense relief bordering on joy. Still, 16:00 hours seemed so far away. He thought he'd pass the time by moving around the base and checking on some of the activities until Cummings arrived.

Agrippa was observing an intramural volleyball game in the court across from the Mess when Cummings arrived—on time. He stood with Agrippa by the sidelines for a few minutes, then they walked over to the Mess and sat at Agrippa's favorite table. No one was in the lounge except the private attending the bar, and he quickly brought them drinks.

"Thank you, Jarvis," the Chief said. "No music, awright?"

"Yes, Chief of Staff."

Agrippa and Cummings clanked glasses and took a swig. Then Agrippa leaned forward, both arms resting on the table, and looked directly at Cummings.

"Like I told you the other day," Cummings began, "the Comrade President likes you and he wants to protect you. And he hopes the feeling is mutual?"

"Oh it is, Lionel, it is," Agrippa said, adding, by way of a mild remonstration, "you got to ask a thing like that, man?"

"Good. He wants you to continue as Chief of Staff, but I have to tell you, is not going to be easy for him to cover up the mess y'all getting him into. First, he got to talk to the Cuban government and explain how one of the people they sent to help we out died like this."

Agrippa wasn't sure whether he should try to assert his innocence again. He decided against it. He knew it would be a waste of time. Better to focus on the terms.

"Then," Cummings continued, "there is your wife who can cause a lot of trouble. Anyway, we will deal with all of that. But the Comrade President feels that if he can protect you against your enemies, you should protect him against his enemies. That ain't fair?" He looked at Agrippa for confirmation.

"Oh yes, that's fair." Agrippa sounded almost enthusiastic.

"He doing you a big favor and is only fair that he should expect you to return the favor, not so?"

"Yes, yes. That is fair."

"Right. As we say in this country 'hand wash hand make hand come clean.'"

Agrippa nodded.

"In the next election," Cummings said, "we want the army to escort the ballet boxes from all over the country to a central counting area, and we would like you to work closely with us on that. You know elections coming up in December?" He looked to Agrippa for agreement. Agrippa nodded.

"You know we trying to build socialism in this country and, in every socialist country, the party is paramount. We want you at the next Party Congress in September to take a pledge of allegiance to the Party as the paramount institution in the country. We believe that if you do that, Commissioner Dalrymple will also take the pledge."

Agrippa nodded.

"The Comrade President thinks that all soldiers should understand the policies of the Party. So periodically, each army unit could spend a couple of days a year at the Co-op College where they would receive political instruction."

"Some officers might not like this," Agrippa asserted. "They believe the army should support the government of the day."

"Well, we would like your help to weed them out, starting with Captain Moore."

"Most will come 'round, but we'll see what to do about the others." Agrippa looked at Cummings and hoped that he would interpret this as agreement. Cummings did not press him.

"I glad we can get all this unpleasantness behind us," Cummings said. "I will have a document for you to sign at the meeting on Monday." Cummings raised his glass. Agrippa did not.

"How about Maynard and Batson?" Agrippa asked.

"They will not be charged but, to pacify the police, we will have to let the police talk to them. But you got my word, they will not be charged or detained." Cummings raised his glass again.

"We will be considering promotions at the Defense Board meeting later this month," Agrippa said.

"Yes?"

"I want to be promoted."

Cummings stared at Agrippa as if to say "You joking!" Only he didn't speak.

"Y'all asking a lot from me," Agrippa asserted. "And as you have been telling me, word will get out that the doctor was with my wife when he died. A promotion would show people the government didn't believe I had anything to do with his death."

Cummings shifted positions in his chair and looked away from Agrippa once or twice. "I gon talk to the Comrade President, but I can't promise you that."

It was worth a try, Agrippa thought, but he was still very pleased by how differently things were turning out from what he had imagined earlier in the day.

Raising his glass, Agrippa said, "Awright, leh we fire one!"

* * *

As requested, Agrippa arrived early for the Security Heads meeting, Monday, June 13. In the presence of the Comrade President and Cummings, he signed duplicate copies of a document in which he acknowledged complicity in the death of the Cuban doctor and appealed to the Comrade President for clemency. A second document, also signed in duplicate, outlined the terms Cummings had offered Agrippa. Cummings collected all copies, and Agrippa and the Comrade President shook hands.

The meeting began after Commissioner Dalrymple arrived. The Comrade President announced that Lionel Cummings had been appointed Permanent Secretary of the Ministry of Defense. Agrippa had no doubt that now, as his immediate civilian superior, Cummings would monitor his compliance with the terms.

TWENTY-FIVE

COLONEL LAFLEUR'S CALL WAS very brief. Captain Moore was to assemble F-Company at Timehri for redeployment to Berbice County. Lieutenants Beharry and Mentore were to return to Timehri by trail after the relief platoons arrived at their respective locations. The third platoon at Matthews Ridge would be flown out over a few days. LaFleur estimated that F-Company should be fully reconstituted at Timehri by August 19, at the latest. The soldiers would then be eligible for two-day passes before the move to Berbice County. Since the election date had been set for the first day in December, F-Company would not be redeployed in mid-November but would remain in Berbice County until mid-January. LaFleur also informed Moore that the army and the police would be working closely together during the election season. Hence, it was desirable that the three platoons set up camp at police stations in Berbice County.

Moore assigned Lieutenant Mentore's platoon to the police station at Springlands. Because of the bad relations between Lieutenant Beharry's platoon and the police in New Amsterdam, Moore decided to post Second Lieutenant Pilgrim and his platoon at the New Amsterdam Police Headquarters. Lieutenant Beharry would take his platoon to the Albion Police Station further down the Berbice Highway, where the company command post would also be located. By the end of the fourth week of August, all of the three platoons of F-Company had settled into their positions and had begun light patrolling.

The seasonal rains had not come in July, and now at the end of August, drought conditions were apparent everywhere—dried-up streams on both sides of the six-mile stretch from the Seawell Turn to the Borlum Turn and carrion crows along the road, taking respite from feeding on the carcasses of dead animals in the patches of pasture on both sides of the road. There were also severe water shortages throughout the country, and the water needed to be boiled because of an outbreak of cholera in the interior. On account of the heat and the water conditions, Moore had prohibited patrolling from mid-day to mid-afternoon. In any case, he didn't think there was much need for patrolling—it was still some time until the election, and conditions in Berbice County were quite calm.

Although the date of the election had been set, only the Opposition seemed to be holding public meetings, and these were generally orderly. The Party was conducting its campaign mostly from the government-owned Radio Demerara and the government-owned *Cayman News*. The police were always present at the public meetings, but Moore kept the soldiers away. Still, from the Albion Police Station, the soldiers could hear the Opposition candidates through loudspeakers at the regular meeting site only a few hundred yards away. The Opposition speakers typically went through the litany of abuses by a government they said had rigged the election each time and had plundered the treasury, leaving the small man to face scarcities, high prices, unreliable water supply, blackouts from electrical load-shedding, disease—the list went on. Now with the election date set, the government would not let in international observers, a clear sign that they planned to rig yet another election. The speakers exhorted the crowds to oppose any attempts at rigging the election. It was the same message in Georgetown, where the Opposition, from bitter experience, was calling national and international attention to the way the government might conduct the election.

Moore had asked his platoon leaders to follow garrison routine—physical training in the morning, drilling in the police compounds, and squad tactics, including dry-fire exercises, on selected days. How they shuffled those around he left to the platoon leaders, except for the physical training, which he insisted on daily to get the company ready for the annual fitness run. He himself participated with Beharry's platoon, often leading the exercises. He visited Second Lieutenant Pilgrim in New Amsterdam on Tuesdays and Thursdays, stopping by for lunch with Aunt Edmee in Rose Hall on some of these trips. On Mondays and Wednesdays, and on those Fridays when he did not go home to his family, Moore went up to Springlands to visit Lieutenant Mentore's platoon.

On Tuesday, August 29, Moore drove up to New Amsterdam to check on Pilgrim's platoon, arriving at about 10:00 hours. He was barely inside Pilgrim's make-shift office at Police Headquarters, when Pilgrim waved a memo at him.

"Captain, you not going to believe this. I just got a signal from the Brigade Adjutant. They want me on a Board of Inquiry into the Farms Corps."

"Farm Corps?" Moore was astounded. It had hardly been six months since George Persico had taken over as the commanding officer, and he had been promoted to captain in June.

"What happened at Farm Corps?" Moore asked.

"I don't know, Captain," Pilgrim replied. "The signal doesn't say. It just says that I have to be at Camp Ayanganna at 08:00 on Monday, September 5."

"Who is chairing the inquiry?"

"Major Farley."

"I see," Moore said, recalling his last encounter with Farley. "Well, better start setting things up here for the platoon sergeant to take over while you're gone."

"Yes, Captain."

Moore visited with the soldiers of Pilgrim's platoon, who seemed to be in very good spirits, complaining jokingly of how hard Pilgrim was pushing them in the morning exercises. Moore was pleased by how briskly the soldiers moved about. The platoon should do well in the annual fitness run, he thought. He also felt that Pilgrim might be settling in quite well after all. Still, as he moved about, he could not stop thinking of what could possibly have happened at Farm Corps to warrant a board of inquiry.

After he left Pilgrim, Moore had McCurchin drive over to the New Amsterdam market where he bought some bananas and some mangoes for himself and Beharry. Then they headed out of town, passing by the *Rooster's Run* on the left side of Strand, the Police Headquarters on the right, and Esplanade Park at the edge of town. He looked over at the Park, as did McCurchin.

"Captain, I can't help it, you know. Every time I pass by here now, I have to look for Eveready," McCurchin said.

Moore smiled. "He probably at work, pulling Mr. Sackiechand's cart."

*   *   *

Moore returned to the Albion police station at about noon. Beharry had been out with his platoon in the field behind the police station, but the exercise had concluded, and the platoon sergeant was marching the platoon back to the compound. Beharry walked over to where Moore was standing in the compound and saluted.

"Ready for lunch, Captain?"

"Yeh, leh we go," Moore replied.

They sat at a small table in the police recreation room, and the Indian woman assisting the cook served them a plate of rice and sijan curry, with a couple of fried banga-mary draping the rice. She also brought them two large tumblers of lime-wash, and at Moore's request, a jar of pickled wiri-wiri peppers.

Once he was sure they would not be interrupted, Moore spoke quietly to Beharry.

"Have you heard about any problems at Farm Corps?" he asked.

"No. Why?"

"Well, Pilgrim just received orders to sit on a board of inquiry into Farm Corps."

"What?" Beharry was incredulous. "They just promoted Persico!"

"I know. So what did he wrong?"

"I don't know. Maybe is not he who did wrong."

"True," Moore agreed.

"That is big news though. They can't hide it."

After lunch, Moore tried calling Captain Seepersaud three times, but then not wanting to tie up the limited outside lines the police had, he gave up for the day. He thought he would stop by Camp Ayanganna some time during his visit home that weekend, if he had not learned anything by then.

The next day, he went up as scheduled to visit Lieutenant Mentore's platoon at the Skeldon police station. He arrived there at about 10:30 and waited on Lieutenant Mentore, who was in his office with the assistant paymaster. Soldiers from Mentore's platoon were coming into the office one at a time to collect their pay. After about half an hour, they were through, and the paymaster left for the other locations. Moore entered and closed the door.

"Have you heard of an inquiry into the operations at Farm Corps?" Moore asked.

"You joking!"

"No. Pilgrim is on the Board."

"Pilgrim? He just got in the army!"

"Maybe that's why," Moore suggested.

"They just promoted Persico, ahead of me and Beharry, and now they investigating him? Must be serious."

"I thought he and Cadogan were really tight," Moore said. "Why didn't Cadogan protect him?"

"Maybe that's the problem—Cadogan was taking too much from Farm Corps. It got to be that. You know I don't like Persico, but the man is a good administrator. You talked to anybody at Camp Ayanganna?"

"I tried to reach Ken Seepersaud, but I haven't been able to get through."

"How about Ramesh? He got contacts at Ayanganna."

"I didn't know that."

"Ah come on, Alan! You don't know 'bout him and Ingrid Peters?" Moore smiled but did not reply. "The thing I don't get," Mentore continued, "is why they put Pilgrim on the Board, but I gon bet money that is Cadogan's doing. Pilgrim is junior and he gon bend to pressure. With him on too, Cadogan will have a direct line into the Board and at least one vote to protect himself, just in case."

*   *   *

Back at Albion that afternoon, Moore learned from Lieutenant Beharry that the inquiry was into Captain George Persico's management of the Farm Corps' operations at Garden of Eden.

"How did you find out?" Moore asked.

"I talked to Ingrid Peters."

Moore nodded and smiled. "Did she say what precipitated the inquiry?"

"Yes. They had to slaughter three thousand chickens at the farm Monday of last week."

"Christ!"

"That's not all. The Chief of Staff ordered the annual audit of Farm Corps, due next month, to be moved up. They did the audit last week Thursday and Friday. The word is that Persico could not account for some of the equipment that he signed for when he took over Farm Corps."

"He is finished," Moore said, shaking his head. "He gon be court-martialed for negligence and incompetence."

"Poor George. Mentore said that Saddle was going to use his ass."

"Saddle's protecting himself though," Moore said. "That's why he got Pilgrim on that three-man Board."

"Looks like George could be cashiered."

"At least," Moore said. "I'll do a bit of checking when I go home this weekend."

*   *   *

Jeanene had just put the children to bed and joined Moore on the sofa when she alerted him to the sound of a car idling in front of the house. Moore got up to check and saw George Persico paying the hire car driver. He told Jeanene and then went down the stairs to meet Persico.

"How you doing, Alan?" Persico asked as he approached the door.

"I should ask you that, George."

"Well, not good. I need some advice, Alan."

Moore invited Persico up. Jeanene greeted Persico and offered to get him a drink before retiring to let them talk, but Persico declined.

"Is what going on, George?" Moore asked after they had sat down across from each other.

"You heard about the Board of Inquiry?"

"Yeh, I heard something about a lot of dead chickens," Moore replied.

"That's part of it, but right now they want me to resign so that they wouldn't have to do the inquiry."

"I see. Who's they, George?"

"I don't know exactly, but Saddle Cadogan, for one. He's afraid things might come out about him. He must have talked to the Chief of Staff. Anyway, a fella from the Party told me that if I resign, they won't press forward with an inquiry or a court-martial, and they will let me go with an honorable discharge."

"You know this fella well?"

"I know he well enough. He acting as an intermediary for them right now."

"Well, George, it don't seem like I can do anything."

"I know. I just wanted to talk to somebody I could trust, and I know how these people treated you back in January. Anyway, we worked together a long time, Alan."

"Yes, we did, George, and I am sorry this thing happened. Beharry and even Mentore feel that way too. Mentore said you were a very good administrator."

"Well, that's the thing, Alan. You know I ain't no slacker, but Cadogan would never let me do the job."

"Like how?"

"He always finding ways to get me away from the Farm, then he would give orders directly to the soldiers. He would take large amounts of foul pox vaccines from the Farm without signing for them. He would tell the corporal he was busy, that Captain Persico would sign. Then he would call me and ask me to do him the favor of signing. I did it a couple of times. We had to raise his chicks through the critical stages, then transfer them to his farm."

"How about the chicken slaughter, George?"

"That should never have happened. Saddle asked me to borrow the three water tenders over the weekend, because of the drought. The understanding was that he would take water to his farm once a day and bring the water tenders back for use at Garden of Eden. Alan, the man kept the water tenders for the entire weekend. The senior NCOs were away, and the soldiers on duty, being new recruits, didn't know anything about chickens. Anyway, they waited till late for the water tenders, then they gave the chickens water from the drainage ditches. The chickens started acting sick on Sunday. When Farm operations resumed Monday, thousands of chickens were sick from coliform infestation and had to be destroyed. This is why Saddle doesn't want an inquiry—because he gon have some explaining to do."

"What about the audit? The equipment they say you can't account for?"

"Alan, I've only been there about six months. I didn't lose any equipment. True I don't know where all of the equipment were because I never did see them. When they appointed me, Saddle made me sign for equipment that were part of the Farm Corps inventory, but they were scattered at different locations. I didn't physically see them. I asked to see them, and Saddle asked me if I was doubting his word."

"But, George, you ought to know better," Moore said.

"I know, Alan, but Saddle arranged for me to get promoted. I didn't want to appear ungrateful."

"Well, it look like he got more than his money's worth. I still don't understand what happened to the equipment."

"Saddle and the Chief of Staff would lease the equipment out at cheap rates to friends. I ain't got no way of proving it, but I believe they received expressions of appreciation. These people did not take care of the equipment; so, after a while, a lot of it was laid up. We found a couple of tractors abandoned at Butcnabu."

"If these things are true, George, I don't think these people want you to appear at an inquiry."

"The Party man told me that if there is a court-martial, I will be found guilty of negligence. I would receive a dishonorable discharge. He said that Cadogan will survive one way or another. The Board will think I was just trying to blame other people for my own mismanagement."

Moore remained silent for a while, then asked, "What you gon do about the offer?"

"I gon give them what they want."

"I really sorry, George."

"Thank you, Alan. You were always fair to me. I can never forget that. You know the day Saddle offered me command of Farm Corps, you remember the day he brought the sweet-woman?"

"Yes?"

"I told him I wanted to talk it over with you. That's when he promised me the promotion, and you know what they say—'the thing full me eye.' I thought I was on my way up. Now, look at me. I can't sleep. I don't eat. I feel so ashamed. I avoiding everybody. I didn't want you to get mixed up: that's why I came nighttime." Persico was taking quick breaths and trying to clear the mucous in his nostrils. He leaned forward and rested his chin on his clasped hands.

Moore remained quiet; he could think of no way to console Persico. "What are you going to do now, George?" he asked. "Did anyone offer you another job?"

"No. I on me own. I been thinking of going to America somehow."

Moore thought of the way Persico used to defend the system, whenever anyone else was being critical, but felt badly for even remembering that at a time when Persico was virtually on his knees. "I hope it work out for you, George."

"Thank you, Alan, and thank you for listening. Is strange, eh? The people I used to hang around with want me to disappear, and the people who didn't like me would never believe that I didn't do wrong. But is true, Alan, I didn't deliberately do wrong."

"I believe you didn't do wrong things, George."

The conversation ended awkwardly. Persico rose and Moore accompanied him down the stairs, where they shook hands. When he returned upstairs, Jeanene was sitting on the sofa, wiping tears from her eyes. Moore sat quietly beside her, leaning forward with his chin propped on his hands and staring ahead. After a few moments, she wrapped her arms around him.

PART FOUR

TWENTY-SIX

RAIN FINALLY CAME TOWARD the end of October, riveting the rooftops at night and into mid-morning. The rest of the day tended to be sunny, but sprinkles in the late afternoon were the prelude to heavier rains at night and a repeat of the cycle. The nights were cooler and the daytime milder. But just as the weather cooled, the political temperatures began to rise.

In their newspaper and in their public meetings, the Opposition demanded that international observers be allowed to monitor the December 1st election. They were supported by the Bar Association, the Council of Churches, and human rights groups, all of whom joined Opposition members in their picketing exercises outside of Parliament Building. Even the *Cayman News* reported on the protests, though it represented these activities as disruptive and in bad faith. Moore read the *Cayman News* at the Albion police station and the Opposition's *Sunday Red Star* when he visited Aunt Edmee. Government restrictions on newsprint had forced the Opposition to limit its publishing to the Sunday edition. Aunt Edmee also had the most recent issue of the *Weekly Church Bulletin*.

On Tuesday, November 3, after his visit with Second Lieutenant Pilgrim in New Amsterdam, Moore went to have lunch with Aunt Edmee. McCurchin declined an invitation in, opting instead to visit a lady friend for half an hour. Aunt Edmee greeted Moore at the door and then returned to the kitchen to finish cooking. He sat in the rocking chair on the landing with a copy of the *Weekly Church Bulletin*, which he opened to the editorial. It was titled, "*Why No International Observers?*" Moore read:

> It is now election season, and we have a case of dueling socialisms. The Party in power claims to be the vanguard socialist party with paramountcy over all institutions in the country. The Opposition criticizes the ruling party for its lack of socialist orthodoxy, as if there were an orthodox way of bringing a country to its knees, but their general point is well taken, namely that the ruling party holds true to no principle.

Food shortages continue unabated. Unemployment is increasing, each day reaching a new historical high. Who dares count the number of beggars on the pavements? National infrastructure is crumbling. By the planeload, people are fleeing north, as if our manifest destiny is to re-colonize America. This is the legacy of this self-proclaimed vanguard party after two decades of rule under his benign-ness, the Comrade President. One is inclined to ask, humbly, of course, on what basis is the Comrade President seeking to continue in office? That is a more difficult question to answer than the question of how he plans to continue in office, and the signs are clear that he does not intend to play fair. He is trying to muzzle the press by restrictions on the importation of newsprint and by using the Party-controlled courts to levy heavy financial penalties in libel suits brought by Party officials against publications, including this one. Now the Comrade President has refused to allow international monitoring of the elections, fearing the world will find out what we have already experienced in these five-year rituals.

The Comrade President's orchestration of the election is reminiscent of the shell game that a swift-handed, smalltime, swindler offers daily in front of the Globe cinema. He has three thimbles and a button that he shuffles from one thimble to the next. He invites onlookers to find the thimble hiding the button, insuring that the free trial is always successful. People waiting to buy their movie tickets usually gather round to be entertained by the swiftness of the showman's hands and by the jingle he repeats. The first line brags of the swiftness of his hands; the rest cautions the unwary.

> *The more you watch, the less you see.*
> *The less you watch, the better for me.*
> *And if you don't watch, you'll never see.*

Listen carefully to the Comrade President's utterances on international observers and the defenses provided by his radio station and newspaper and you will hear echoes of the shell master's jingle, only rhythmless and drab, and dire in their consequences.

Rev. Lennox Moore

Folding the bulletin, Moore walked into the kitchen and stood behind Aunt Edmee, who was straining the rice into the sink. "Aunt Edmee, did you read this editorial that Uncle Lenny wrote?"

"Yes."

"Why's he trying to antagonize those people?"

"He not trying to antagonize anyone. He just saying what he thinks is true."

"But they can do bad things to him."

Aunt Edmee did not respond right away. She turned around and set the rice pot back on the stove, then reached for two plates, which she placed on the kitchen counter. "Alan, your uncle is sixty-six, going on sixty-seven. I ain't going to tell him what he to do. Besides, he believes every Christian is obliged to speak up for the poor and the oppressed. To tell the truth, I have never seen such suffering here in all me life."

Moore said nothing. He knew, though, that Aunt Edmee was not quite finished. He went into the bathroom and washed his hands, then sat at the dining table. Aunt Edmee brought a heaping plate of rice and a bowl with two large hoori in a tomato-and-shallot sauce and set them down in front of him. The aroma made his mouth water, and he could not wait for her to sit down. She duplicated a setting for herself, except that the servings were much smaller.

"That all you going to eat?" Moore asked.

"Yeh. That's plenty. I ain't young no more, you know."

"Who say?"

She smiled. "Don't worry with you." She went back into the kitchen for two glasses of lime wash and set one in front of him, before sitting down. It wasn't soon enough for Moore. He ploughed into the meal, spooning the sauce into his plate and mixing it with the rice, then adding a piece of hoori before bringing the mixture to his mouth. He looked up at Aunt Edmee, who was looking at him, smiling. Then she began to eat. Between bites and sometimes while she chewed, she spoke.

"Your Uncle Lenny is a follower of one man, Jesus."

"I know that, Aunt Edmee, but still . . ."

"He is an admirer of Mahatma Gandhi and Martin Luther King, Jr. Both of them lost their lives fighting wrong. I know how your uncle feels. We all wanted we independence, but who woulda thought that we own people woulda treat we so bad. Do you want some more stew?"

"Just a little more of the sauce." Aunt Edmee went into the kitchen and brought some sauce, which she added to the bowl in front of him, then she sat back down.

"Your uncle is a simple man. He don't eat no meat and no fish. He don't wear no fancy clothes. Sometimes, I think he does look like a scarecrow, he so meager." She laughed, and Moore smiled. "But this small man ain't afraid of no Comrade President, I gon tell you that."

"Still, I don't think he should provoke them."

"Don't worry about your uncle. You are a good boy; you married a good girl. Take her and your children and go somewhere you can be happy." Moore was getting uncomfortable. He avoided looking directly at Aunt Edmee, looking around to distract himself, but Aunt Edmee wanted a response. "You hearing me?"

"Yes, Aunt Edmee."

"And another thing, Alan. Being in the army or the police and so is not a bad thing, but you mustn't raise your hand against people wrongfully. You had a good upbringing. You must be true to what you know."

"That does sometimes get you in trouble too."

"I know. Jeanene told me how they treated you. But you must forget that. Put your trust in God. He not gon let you down." Moore nodded and rose. He had heard the jeep pull up in front of the house.

*   *   *

When Moore returned to the Albion police station, the constable on desk duty told him his wife had called and asked that he call her back. He went up to his assigned office on the second floor, sat down, and dropped his beret on the desk. It was 13:45. The rain which had started when the jeep had entered Albion, was now pounding the corrugated zinc sheets above him. He dialed his wife's number at the bank.

"Co-op Bank, Mrs. Moore."

"Mr. Moore here," Alan said, hoping to hear her laugh.

"Oh, Alan, the letter came!"

"From the Embassy?"

"Yes!"

"When did it come?"

"Today. I called the Embassy this morning and they said the letter was mailed two days ago, so I went home for lunch to check. And there it was."

"You have it there?"

"You crazy? I'm at work."

"Well, what did it say?"

"We have an appointment date, Thursday, December 15. We have to take in our papers like police clearance, birth certificates, affidavits of support, and passports."

"Well, we better talk to the travel agency."

"I already did that. We can travel anytime after we get our visas. I was thinking we could spend New Year's with Uncle Lenny and Aunt Vickie, like last year, then we could go some time after."

"Don't forget we have to give notice to the landlord and get our things out of the house by then. But leh we talk more about this at home."

"Can you come home this weekend?"

"I gon try. I gon try to leave here early on Saturday morning and head up to Camp Ayanganna. I can transact some business there until midday. You know I'm technically on duty till then?"

"I know."

"Awright then." Moore rested the phone on the receiver and leaned back, feeling flush with excitement.

TWENTY-SEVEN

MOORE RETURNED TO ALBION after his weekend at home with a sense of foreboding. The election campaign had begun to take a nasty turn in Georgetown. The Opposition *Red Star* and the *Weekly Church Bulletin* complained about thugs breaking up political meetings. Both publications alleged that the thugs were doing the bidding of the Party. Uncle Lenny said he was present at one of those meetings when the thugs swooped down on the crowd, wielding sticks. The police did not intervene. Uncle Lenny had spoken about this in his Sunday morning sermon. He said that what is wrong is wrong, and Christians must speak out against it, because silence meant complicity.

The pace of the election campaign had picked up tremendously. In New Amsterdam, the Party followed the Opposition, holding meetings frequently—in Esplanade Park, outside the New Amsterdam public market, and in several of the suburbs. In Skeldon, the preferred meeting place for both groups was the market square. The Party expended little effort in some traditional Opposition areas like Albion, Port Mourant, and No. 64 Village. Otherwise, they shadow boxed all along the coast. Cars with loudspeakers mounted on the top advertised the meetings, posters appeared everywhere, and partisan slogans were painted on almost every roadside structure that was not a home or business.

Each day, Moore drove west to New Amsterdam and then back east to Skeldon by way of Albion. Saddle Cadogan suggested he move the company command post to New Amsterdam, but Moore was adamant, and Cadogan had yielded with a frown. Moore recognized that such a move would make his inspections easier, but he did not want to have Second Lieutenant Pilgrim observing his activities too closely, since he suspected that Cadogan regularly debriefed Pilgrim.

On Friday, November 11, the Party rushed through legislation in Parliament, expanding the detention powers of the police. That Sunday, *the Red Star* and the *Weekly Church Bulletin* questioned the need for the legislation, suggesting that the Party was positioning itself to suppress any form of protest because it did not intend an honest vote.

Late Tuesday night, Moore was awakened by the constable on duty, who said his wife was on the phone. He took the call in the Police Annex, where he and Beharry were bunking.

"Jeanene?"

"Yes?"

"What's wrong? The children awright?"

"Nothing's wrong with the children. Is Uncle Lenny."

"What's wrong with him?"

"They searched his home for arms."

"Who did?"

"The police and the army."

"What! Are you sure?"

"Yes, he said so."

"God, I don't know what to say. Is he awright?"

"Yes, he is awright, but he very upset. They pushed Aunt Vickie out of the way. And you know she got a bad heart."

"Is she awright?"

"Well, it depends on what you call awright. Police and army people walking into your house in the middle of the night and pushing you around? I don't think that is right at all!"

"You know I don't think is right either, but don't let me and you quarrel over this. It's not my fault, and worse of all, I can't do anything about it."

"Why would they search the home of an Anglican priest for guns? Uncle Lenny look like he can hold any gun?"

"The government don't like Uncle Lenny and they just trying to intimidate him, that's all. They know he ain't got no guns."

"And what kind of hooligans would push a seventy-year old woman with a bad heart?"

"Well, you just said it—they are hooligans."

"Do me a favor, Alan. Whenever you visit Uncle Lenny and Aunt Vickie, please take off that uniform. You gon take it off soon, anyway."

Moore changed the conversation. "I gon try and come home this weekend, but that will be the last time until this election is over."

"I gon be glad to see you, Uncle Lenny and Aunt Vickie too."

"I gon call them tomorrow," Moore said.

"Good."

"Awright, you better go back to sleep now."

"You too."

When Moore returned to the Annex, Beharry was still awake in his bunk, so Moore related the exchange with Jeanene to him.

"Sorry, Alan. I don't know what this place coming to."

"I don't know either." Then Moore laughed. "Jeanene said that I should take off the uniform when I go and see Uncle Lenny."

"I can understand why."

"Is not like it used to be, eh?"

"Nah," Beharry replied, suppressing a yawn.

"You ever heard the old Chinese proverb—'Never make a nail out of good iron or a soldier out of a good man?'"

"You think we getting to that point here?" Beharry asked.

"I wonder."

*　　*　　*

A week before election day, the government decided that the ballot boxes would be transported to a central location to be counted, after the polls closed. Sensing a new rigging effort afoot, the Opposition demanded the ballots be counted in the districts where they were cast. In their public meetings, they called on supporters to form human chains to prevent the ballot boxes being taken away from the polling stations.

Within the army, new orders came down the chain of command. The army was to join with the police to circumvent body blocks or other forms of obstruction from Opposition supporters and to ensure that the ballot boxes were transported in army trucks to Georgetown. Captain Moore was notified that the ferry across the Berbice River would make two late runs to transport all of the Berbice County ballot boxes from New Amsterdam to Rosignol. Moore's responsibility was to see that the boxes were loaded on army trucks, convoyed to New Amsterdam, and transferred onto the ferry.

Election day came, and voting along the Berbice Highway was generally orderly. Moore spent the morning in New Amsterdam, where he had overnighted. He observed the polling in several precincts before heading out to Rose Hall, then back on the Berbice Highway through No. 2 Village, Palmyra, Fyrish, and Albion. At No. 2 Village, Palmyra, and Albion, all Opposition areas, individuals complained that they were not allowed to vote because the presiding officer said his roll showed them as deceased or having already voted by proxy. People gathered in groups to hear the complaints, but there was no organized protest.

By noon, Moore was at the police station in Springlands. Saddle Cadogan's jeep was parked in the compound, but the colonel was nowhere in sight. Moore walked up to Lieutenant Mentore, who was in the compound watching the soldiers from his platoon line up for lunch. They had just exchanged a quick greeting when Colonel Cadogan emerged from the police station and advanced toward them.

"Lieutenant Mentore," Cadogan called out, "load your men onto the trucks and send them over to vote at the primary school in No. 79 Village. They expecting them there."

"Colonel," Mentore replied, "the platoon already voted here in Springlands."

"Lieutenant Mentore, are you disobeying a verbal order?" Cadogan asked.

Mentore looked at Moore, but Moore bent his head.

"No, Colonel," Mentore replied. "Sergeant Blackett?" Mentore called out to his platoon sergeant, who was with the soldiers at the lunch line.

"Lieutenant?" the sergeant replied.

"Get them men on the trucks and take them to vote again in No. 79 Village."

"Yes, Lieutenant."

Moore felt badly, but if they were bent on rigging the damn election, there wasn't much he could do. Besides, every time he interfered, he got into trouble. At this point, he didn't want anyone or anything to affect his departure from the country. In any case, Colonel Cadogan was issuing the orders, and Cadogan had seniority. Moore knew that Lieutenant Mentore didn't see things this way, and he noticed that Mentore made a point of avoiding him for the rest of the time he spent at Springlands. Moore also noticed that Mentore did not accompany his men to No. 79 Village, and Cadogan did not order him to. Largely to avoid Cadogan, Moore decided to forego the situational report from Lieutenant Mentore and to check out some of the neighboring precincts for himself.

Polling ended at 18:00 hours, and the army and police took over the ballot boxes. Moore had returned to Springlands to await the arrival of the 3-ton truck from Lieutenant Beharry's platoon. The plan was to load this truck with ballot boxes from Crabwood Creek, east of Skeldon and head west, picking up the ballot boxes from all the villages along the

Berbice Highway up to the Borlum Turn. Second Lieutenant Pilgrim was to duplicate the collection effort from New Amsterdam up to the Borlum Turn.

At Springlands, Moore observed the ballot boxes being sealed with the appropriate stickers and the signatures of the presiding officer and party representatives placed on the boxes.

Originally, representatives from all political parties were to be allowed to accompany the boxes, but, at the last minute, the police, acting on government orders, barred the Opposition representatives from the truck at each stop. When it first occurred at Springlands, Moore shook his head, remembering the jingle Uncle Lenny had quoted in his editorial:

The more you watch, the less you see;
The less you watch, the better for me;
And if you don't watch, you will never see.

The ballot convoy moving west toward New Amsterdam consisted of Captain Moore's jeep, followed by Lieutenant Beharry's truck, carrying a squad of soldiers and Beharry riding in the cab. A police jeep with an inspector and two armed police constables brought up the rear. Colonel Cadogan had driven ahead of the convoy, and was missing for about an hour, before resurfacing in Albion.

As the convoy moved westward collecting the ballot boxes, the Opposition seemed to have regrouped, and resistance to the removal of the ballot boxes stiffened. At Albion, Colonel Cadogan ordered Lieutenant Beharry to use live fire to disperse the crowd blocking the truck from taking the ballot boxes. Protesters were demanding that the ballots be counted where they were cast. Beharry ordered a squad to fire a volley over the heads of the protesters. That was sufficient to clear a path.

Reports reaching Moore and Cadogan from the Police Headquarters, New Amsterdam, indicated that Second Lieutenant Pilgrim had ordered his soldiers to fire into a group of protesters at Rose Hall Sugar Estate. There were two fatalities. Moore was stunned, as was Beharry. Cadogan muttered something about the protesters bringing this on themselves. Additional reports indicated that, in reaction to the shootings at Rose Hall, the Opposition had organized massive demonstrations at the stellings at New Amsterdam and at Rosignol. Moore knew that these reports were being studied in Georgetown, and by about 20:00 hours, he received new instructions from Colonel Cadogan. The ballot boxes would be flown out to Georgetown by the Air Wing. The four-mile stretch of road between

No. 19 Village and the Borlum Turn would be used as a landing strip. The trucks with the ballot boxes were to converge on this stretch of road. Cadogan estimated that they needed four trips by an Islander to complete the airlift. They would normally have had an hour more of daylight, but the clouds were gathering, and before the first plane arrived, it started to rain.

Moore used a squad each from the platoons of Second Lieutenant Pilgrim and Lieutenant Beharry to set up road blocks at each end of the proposed landing strip, about a mile long. One truck with ballot boxes came in from New Amsterdam and the other from the direction of Springlands. One truck and one jeep, headlights on, were parked on the inside of each road block, facing the landing strip and providing illumination for the pilots. Two Islanders, one flown by Lieutenant Nizam Khan, landed within twenty minutes of each other and were loaded. All of the boxes from Pilgrim's truck were transferred, and the truck was sent back to the road block to illuminate the landing strip for the take-off. Most of the boxes from Beharry's truck had been transferred to the planes, so Cadogan radioed to Georgetown that he would only need one more trip by an Islander to pick up the rest of the ballot boxes.

About an hour later, Lieutenant Khan landed again for the last load of boxes. Moore and Cadogan were driven up in their separate jeeps to about a hundred feet of the plane and the drivers pulled off the side of the road. Lieutenant Beharry was behind them with the 3-ton truck carrying the boxes. The truck came up to the plane and stopped. A squad of soldiers did the loading. It was a quick transfer, after which Lieutenant Beharry ordered the squad leader to take the truck and the men back to the road block and to turn the truck around so that its lights could be used to illuminate the landing strip. Beharry then went over and joined Moore, standing by the plane waiting on Colonel Cadogan. Cadogan had pulled Lieutenant Khan away and was talking to him several feet in front of the plane, his arm over Khan's shoulder.

When Cadogan came back to the two officers, Moore noticed Lieutenant Khan had remained at the front of the plane and was looking away from them.

"Alan," Cadogan said, "I have to get back to Georgetown tonight, so I gon fly back with Lieutenant Khan."

Moore didn't see a problem. The Colonel signaled to his jeep, and Corporal Bascom drove up and then backed up to the plane. The Colonel then ordered Bascom to load his things into the plane. Moore and Beharry noticed Bascom taking out boxes from the Colonel's jeep and putting them on the road in preparation for loading them on to the plane, but the plane was already fully loaded, he remembered, so he went to the other side to observe. Corporal Bascom began unloading ballot boxes to make room for the Colonel's personal effects, which Moore presumed to be contraband goods.

"Corporal Bascom!" Moore called out. "Leave those ballot boxes on that plane!"

Cadogan walked up close to Moore and spoke almost in a whisper. "Look, Alan, I got some stuff here I want to take back with me. Do me a favor, for once."

"Colonel, we could hold your stuff until tomorrow. Corporal Bascom would bring them to you. I gon see to it, but you can't take out those ballot boxes."

"What's the problem, Alan? You think these ballot boxes will decide who gon rule this country?"

Moore remembered the analyses of the last election. What Cadogan was saying was precisely what the Opposition had been saying and what Uncle Lenny had been writing about, except Moore himself had not witnessed any of the mischief, before today. Moore glanced over at Beharry and sensed the same type of alarm he was feeling.

"Colonel Cadogan, this is illegal," Moore pointed out.

"Alan, is what wrong with you? You born at night or something? You ain't know this election is just for show? And is only seven ballot boxes we talking about; what you think that gon decide?"

"I don't know Colonel, but my orders—"

"Your orders were to bring the ballot boxes to the landing zone. You done do that. From here on I take over. Right?"

"Yes, Colonel."

"Look, Alan, don't let me and you get wrong over a few stupid ballot boxes that ain't going to decide nothing."

"What am I supposed do with these ballot boxes, Colonel Cadogan?"

"Same as they gon do with the rest eventually. Burn them!"

"Colonel, I can't do this!" Moore protested.

"Look, Alan, all of these boxes are for the Opposition anyway. You want to help the Party stay in power?" Moore was unsure what to say. Cadogan pressed home, "Burn the boxes!"

Moore stood there, feeling Beharry's eyes riveted on him. He didn't know what to do. Seething with anger and frustration, he walked towards his jeep, Beharry a few paces behind him but turned around mid-way. "Colonel Cadogan, I can't do this. These ballot boxes have to go in."

"Awright, Captain Moore, you take them in first thing in the morning. Do you understand?"

"Yes, Colonel." Moore saluted and watched the plane take off with Cadogan, leaving a disheveled pile of ballot boxes on the side of the road.

"I think we should report this," Beharry said.

"To who?" Moore asked in a quiet defeated tone. "You realize what would happen in this country, at this time, if we say anything?"

"I don't want to have anything to do with those boxes," Beharry asserted.

"You think I want anything to do with them?" Moore asked, then sucked his teeth loudly. "Corporal Bascom," he called out. "Give McCurchin a hand loading those boxes in my jeep."

"Yes, Captain."

Moore stood in the drizzle observing the two soldiers, aware of the tension between him and Beharry and being careful to avoid eye contact with him. In a few minutes, the exercise was over. "Awright, McCurchin, lower the back flap and tie it down." Then, turning to Beharry, he said, "You better ride in Saddle's jeep."

"I was planning to." As Moore turned to go, Beharry spoke again. "Saddle said these ballot boxes were not going to decide anything, but he made my platoon vote twice."

Moore looked at Beharry and then walked away, ashamed to admit that the same thing had occurred at Springlands, in his presence.

TWENTY-EIGHT

From their cots in the Police Annex, Moore and Beharry listened to the election coverage on the government's Radio Demerara.

"Where are the ballot boxes, Mr. Jhattoo?" the Opposition member of Parliament asked.

"Mrs. Sahoye, they are being transported to Queen's College," replied Mr. Jhattoo, the criminal lawyer, representing the Party.

Beharry looked over at Moore. "Alan, the boxes from Berbice County were flown directly to Georgetown. They should have been at the counting center hours ago."

"I don't know what's going on," Moore replied, "but judging from what went on here . . ."

"Why were our representatives not allowed to accompany the ballot boxes when the Party's representatives were?" the woman asked the Party man on the radio.

"Do you know," Beharry said to Moore, "when we went to collect the boxes in the 3-ton, the police blocked Opposition reps from following us? The police were taking orders from Party officials!"

Moore looked at Beharry but said nothing.

"The government was afraid of sabotage from Opposition supporters," the criminal lawyer on the radio replied. "Didn't the Opposition leader call for supporters to block the trucks from leaving the precincts?"

"Yes, because the ballots were always counted in the precincts. And right now, no one but the government knows where the boxes are. Why don't you tell the people where the boxes are?"

"I already told you: the boxes are on their way to the counting center," the Party man replied.

"It is now 10 o'clock at night and none of the ballot boxes have arrived at Queen's College," the Opposition woman said. "The polling booths closed at 6 p.m. Why would it take more than four hours to transport ballot boxes from precincts in Georgetown to Queen's College in the center of the city?"

"Look, these are all election details the Election Commission will explain eventually," the criminal lawyer replied, "but they don't detract from the fact that the vast majority of the people support the strides the Party has been making. The question tonight is not whether we will win a majority but how big a majority."

"What strides has the Party been making?" the woman asked. "Look at the retrenchment in the Public Service. Look at the shortages. People are starving! Haven't you noticed?"

"You all are singing the same tune over and over," the criminal lawyer replied. "Wait until the ballots are counted, and you will hear what the people have to say. I will predict that the people will give the Comrade President an overwhelming vote of confidence."

"The only votes the Comrade President will get are the ones he steals as he did in the last election and the one before! I ask you again, as the Party's representative and the government's representative, tell the people where the ballot boxes are."

"We know where seven of them are," Beharry said.

Moore looked over at Beharry. "Look, Ramesh, you know I didn't have much choice. Cadogan was going to dump the damn boxes. At least, I am taking them in."

"Where?" Beharry asked. "No one seems to know where the others are."

"Well," said Moore, "we know they're supposed to go to Queen's College so that's where—"

"Wait, wait," Beharry interrupted. "Listen to this."

"I would like everyone to know what we have just found out," the Opposition woman said on the radio. "Army trucks have been taking the ballot boxes to Camp Ayanganna. I ask you, Mr. Jhattoo, why are the ballot boxes at army headquarters?"

"Army headquarters?" Beharry exclaimed, looking over intently at Moore.

"Don't look at me," Moore said, "I don't know anything about this."

"It is just a rest stop before the trucks go on to the counting center," the criminal lawyer on the radio was saying.

"The army headquarters and Queen's College are two miles apart on Thomas Road," the woman on the radio pointed out. "Why do the trucks need a rest stop?"

"I am not a dispatcher, Madam," the criminal lawyer on the radio replied. "I am here to talk about serious issues, not about every stop the trucks make."

"Oh my God," Beharry said, "they are going to cook up the books! But why is the army involved?"

"You have to ask that?" Moore replied. "We have a Chief of Staff who is a hustler. Last September, he went to the Party's Biennial Congress and pledged the allegiance of the army to the Party. Did he consult any of the other officers?" Beharry did not reply. "Captain Felix was so angry, he thought we should do something about it. He also talked with Captain Seepersaud."

"Alan, the three of you command the only companies on the coast," Beharry said.

"Well, I had to tell Felix I am planning to leave," Moore declared. "He wasn't too pleased."

"How about Seepersaud?" Beharry asked. "How did he react?"

"He was waiting to hear what I had to say," Moore replied. "After I spoke, Felix let it drop. But I have a feeling he and Seepersaud have been talking."

At midnight, the situation at the radio station had not changed. Her voice hoarse and raspy, the Opposition representative kept asking why the ballots boxes were being interned at the army headquarters. It was as if she were calling in vain for help for a victim being raped in public view. Moore got up from his cot and turned the radio off, shaking his head in anger as he thought of Colonel Cadogan's words: "You think this election will decide who gon rule?"

The next morning, Moore set out with McCurchun for Georgetown, departing the police station at 03:30. They arrived at the New Amsterdam stelling at 04:00 to find it deserted but for the ticket clerk, two policemen, and a few stelling workers. The drygoods trucks, which on Fridays arrived early to ensure crossing, were not running today. From a radio in the ticket booth, Moore heard the coverage on Radio Demerara—different representatives from the parties, but the struggle remained the same. Why were the ballot boxes still at the army headquarters? This time, however, the Party's representative had a new explanation: they were awaiting the ballot boxes from the hinterland before they would all be taken to Queen's College for counting.

At 04:50, the jeep drove off the ferry ramp at Rosignol. With hardly any traffic on the road, the jeep moved at a steady clip of 50 miles per hour, slowing only to avoid cattle on the road from time to time and at police roadblocks set up outside every police station. Outside of Georgetown, the traffic was heavier, and the jeep drifted in behind an accordion-like chain of vehicles waiting to negotiate the army roadblock ahead. Clearing the roadblock at 06:40, the jeep turned off the highway onto Vlissingen Road and quickly came up to the junction with Thomas Road. The roadblock here allowed only military vehicles in, and Moore logged in the jeep's entry at Camp Ayanganna at 06:45, Friday, December 2nd.

One company was conducting physical training on the drill square in front of the Headquarters building, another unit in the soccer field. The second barrack building up from Headquarters was cordoned off by soldiers with submachine guns. Four 3-ton trucks were backed up to the building, and men in white shirtjacs flitted past the plain glass windows. The jeep pulled up to the roadblock, where Sergeant Maynard stood with two soldiers, their submachine guns at the ready.

"No one is allowed in here, Captain Moore," Sergeant Maynard said, saluting. "Chief of Staff's orders."

"Is Colonel Cadogan on the base?" Moore asked.

"I don't think so. He was here late but left early this morning."

The jeep backed out and continued along the main road, then turned into the compound of 2nd Battalion Headquarters. Moore sent off McCurchin to breakfast but remained with the jeep, resting his head back and closing his eyes. When McCurchin returned, Moore walked over to the Officers' Mess. It was 07:30.

At the entrance to the dining hall, the concierge informed Moore that the dining area was reserved for the day and that officers would be eating on the first floor. The brief interaction at the entrance allowed Moore to see the Chief of Staff and several government or Party people at breakfast. He descended the outside stairs and re-entered the Mess through the main entrance, taking a seat beside Lieutenant Ingrid Peters.

"Is what going on, Ingrid?" Moore asked. "The place so tense."

"Haven't you been listening to the radio? The base is under occupation."

"The ballot boxes still here?"

"Yes, they have them next door. Only Party people and the Chief allowed. Sad day. But what brought you here?"

"I need to see Colonel Cadogan."

Lieutenant Peters studied his face but did not follow up. Instead, she wanted to know if Ramesh Beharry had received notice of his interview for entry into the January Junior Staff course. Moore confirmed that he had been informed to report on December 15 for the interview. Peters asked about Derryck Mentore and Moore let her know that he was due to go on leave the sixteenth; his fiancé was coming in the next day. Peters said that Mentore was lucky his leave was approved, but it seemed the further away from Georgetown your posting, the better your chances. Of course, Mentore had applied a long time ago, Moore pointed out.

Moore left the mess with Lieutenant Peters at 08:05, just as the trucks at the cordoned-off building were lined up in convoy formation with escort vehicles at the front and aft. An MP in the middle of the road signaled the officers to wait until the vehicles had begun moving through the main gate. Moore parted company with Lieutenant Peters in front of 2nd Battalion Headquarters and ran up the stairs. Lance Corporal Seopaul greeted him as he entered.

"Can you say what time Colonel Cadogan will be in?" Moore asked.

"No, Captain," Lance Corporal Seopaul replied. "Colonel Cadogan is operational. He is in the city, but I can't say where."

Moore was desperate. He instructed McCurchin to drive to Queen's College. The entire compound there was guarded by soldiers and the main entrance on Camp Street by soldiers and police, with three government men in white shirtjacs deciding who would be permitted to enter. In front of the side entrance on Thomas Road and the main entrance, picketers, with signs alleging army tampering and calling for free and fair elections, were keeping watch on the compound. Among the pickers was the familiar scarecrow of a man with a white collar around his neck, whom Moore wanted to avoid at all cost. Inside the compound, near the stairway of the College, soldiers were unloading ballot boxes from the trucks in the presence of people Moore surmised to be representatives of the Party and of the Opposition.

Moore realized that with this type of scrutiny, he could not now deliver the boxes without setting off a firestorm. What to do with them? That was the question that required an immediate answer. "Burn them," Cadogan had said, and now Moore decided he had no other choice. He instructed McCurchin to drive to his home in Eccles, arriving there at about 08:45. He opened the gate to allow McCurchin to back the jeep up to the small store room under the kitchen, and unlocked the door, pulling it half-open to block the view of the neighbors on the left and using his body to block the view from the other side while McCurchin unloaded the boxes and stacked them on their sides. He decided not to leave a note to Jeanene that he had been home—she would want to know why. When McCurchin was finished, Moore locked the door, and they left for Berbice County.

The distress he felt about his role in the conspiracy to destroy ballot boxes kept Moore awake in the jeep. He knew that he could not dispose of the ballot boxes for at least a couple of weeks, and he worried about the peril and shame he could bring to his family by their possession. He wanted to strike back at Colonel Cadogan in some way, but none came to mind, and he eventually succumbed to fatigue.

*   *   *

By early afternoon, they were back at the Albion Police Station, where Moore went through the handful of signals that had arrived. One from the Chief of Staff ordered all coastal detachments to intensify their patrolling, and Moore decided to focus on the New Amsterdam-Rose Hall Sugar Estate area, where two Opposition supporters had been shot the previous day. He ordered Lieutenant Beharry to conduct daytime patrols there so that Second Lieutenant Pilgrim could concentrate on evening patrols.

The Saturday newspapers reported vigils outside the central counting center at Queen's College by Opposition and civic groups as the counting proceeded by hand. The ballots from the hinterland did not arrive until Saturday evening, so Radio Demerara reported, and at 18:00 hours on Sunday, three days after the polls had closed, the Chief Election Officer announced the election results on Radio Demerara. The Party had won thirty-seven of the fifty-three seats in Parliament.

The election results were celebrated more in the Party newspaper than in the streets. The Monday, December 5 edition of the *Cayman News* announced—"*The Comrade President Has Done It Again!*" The Opposition's *Red Star* carried the headline, "*Fraudulent Elections!*" and the article stated that the Opposition planned to boycott Parliament and to mount a campaign of civil resistance against the government. That evening at 20:00 hours, the Comrade President addressed the country on Radio Demerara. He thanked the people for their strong expression of faith in him and in his government, and pledged to use the mandate he had received to complete the socialist transformation of the country. "The small man will be the real man!" he asserted. He ended with a note to those who would use civil resistance to cause havoc and mayhem—"they will feel the sharpness of our steel!"

On Sunday evening when Moore returned from Springlands, he found a copy of the *Weekly Church Bulletin* Beharry had brought back from New Amsterdam and left on his cot. The title of his uncle's editorial inside was "*Let My People Go!*" Moore sat down on his cot and read.

> The results of the election have now been declared and the Party has done it again! Of the fifty-three seats in contention, it has emerged with thirty-seven, putting it in a position, with an extraordinary majority, to amend the constitution at will. A few reflections on what we have just witnessed merit comment even in these perilous times when house searches, beatings, and libel suits are the order of the day.

> Citizens will recall that, in the previous election, the Party invented the idea of overseas voting which, according to later British investigative reporting, allowed horses and the dead to cast ballots in favor of the Party. The bagfuls of ballots were transported into the country by trusted ambassadors. The Party's generosity to the Opposition was stretched thinly when it conceded them one percent of the overseas vote, even though it was well known that Opposition supporters had been fleeing the country by the planeload.

> In the most recent election, the Party dispensed with the overseas ballot but probity in the pursuit of power seemingly has limits. With the collusion of the so-called People's Army, the Party quarantined the ballot boxes at Camp Ayanganna, allowing no Opposition representatives visitation rights. After twelve hours, the ballot boxes, seals broken and districts mislabeled, were brought to the central counting center. The results we now know. The Party made massive inroads into Opposition strongholds at a time when unemployment stands at over 30 percent and food shortages spawn industrial strikes and protests. A nation, whose rallying cry has been captured by the placard, "Give Us This Day Our Daily Bread," voted overwhelmingly for its tormentors, so we are asked to believe.

> Pressed to explain the quarantine, Party spokespeople have argued that the safety of the ballot boxes warranted it. Safety from whom? From Opposition supporters told by their leadership to block their transportation to the central counting center. Yes, the Opposition wanted the ballot

*counted at the voting centers where representatives from all parties would
be present, because they feared precisely this type of finagling.*

*So where does this all leave us? What values will be nurtured by a
state whose very existence is based on fraud and corruption, and whose
defense is one lie spun into another and another? Shakespeare's Henry
V provides us no comfort. "What rein," he asks, "can hold licentious
wickedness when down the hill he holds his fierce career?" And yet we have
an obligation to our young, indeed to all of our people, to create a moral
society, and critical to this enterprise is the obligation to say that what is
wrong is wrong. Mahatma Gandhi taught us that non-cooperation with
evil is a sacred duty, and we regard this regime as evil. That this accords
with the Opposition's call for civil resistance might be used to label us as
agents of the Opposition. No matter. No one in this country can have
any illusion about the magnitude of the theft and disenfranchisement
that has just occurred.*

*In the Christian calendar, this is the season of Advent, and the sadness
of the unfolding drama is magnified in its temporal juxtaposition to our
celebration of truth and good and liberation from death in the birth of
Christ. But the God whose love delivers us from death also demands our
liberation from tyrants here on earth. For God said to Pharaoh, "Let my
people go."*

Rev. Lennox Moore

Moore sat still for a few moments pondering the article. He felt sure
the Comrade President would see it as a declaration of war and let loose
the mongoose squads, no matter the truth in the article, evidence of which
he had in his own storeroom in Eccles. "Wrong and strong" was the core
belief and practice of the Party. The pledge to make the small man the
real man was just a sop to socialists outside the country to prop up the
Comrade President or at a minimum to prevent them from criticizing
him.

Moore went over to the small table with the company clerk's typewriter,
and typed a letter, resigning his commission, effective December 31.
He dated the letter December 15, since he intended to drop it off by
Colonel Cadogan's office on Thursday, after his visa interview at the U.S.
Embassy.

TWENTY-NINE

"**W**HEN YOU HOT, YOU hot!" Lieutenant Mentore's unmistakable voice and the crisp slap of a domino against wood greeted Captain Moore when he entered the Springlands Police Mess on Wednesday, December 14. The card table where Mentore was playing was surrounded by soldiers, but two of them moved aside to allow Moore access. He waited for Mentore to look up, then flipped his wrist and indicated his watch. Mentore nodded and refocused on the two ends of the domino chain on the table. Placing one of his two remaining dominoes down, Mentore said to the other players, "Rap your hands." Both players rapped the table. "Yes!" Mentore exclaimed, slapping the final ticket down and standing up. "I told y'all before—you playing with the master! I invented this game."

Picking up his knapsack and a small suitcase, Mentore walked out with Moore to the jeep, where McCurchin had the engine running. Mentore placed his luggage in the rear before he climbed in, and Moore joined McCurchin in the front.

"What time you make it, Captain?" McCurchin asked.

"Ah, make it 14:35," Moore replied looking at his watch, and McCurchin logged their departure time before driving off. The ride to Albion was slow. The rain, which had been falling continually since morning, held up for ten minutes through Long Road before it began drizzling again, and just as the vehicle was picking its way through the cows on the No. 73 Village road, the downpours started. For stretches on the road, the rain hit the cab like buck shot and the canvas like a loud sewing machine. At times, visibility was poor, and Moore instructed McCurchin to slow down.

It wasn't until 15:45 that the jeep pulled up at the front entrance of the Albion Police Station. Moore sent McCurchin to get Lieutenant Beharry, and a few minutes later, they were rushing back to the jeep, Beharry carrying an overnight bag. Looking over his shoulder, Moore waited until Beharry had climbed into the back and taken a seat across from Mentore.

"Awright, McCurchin," Moore said, "leh we go, but drive slowly. I think we can make the 16:30 ferry easily. We have priority crosssing."

"Don't take on worries, Captain," McCurchin said, "I gon get you there safe."

"Don't tell me 'bout taking on worries! Just drive slowly. I don't like the way this rain coming down."

"Awright, Captain."

By the time the jeep passed the Borlum Turn and started down the desolate, six-mile stretch to Palmyra, the rain was coming down in sheets, and with the dark clouds above, Moore could hardly see more than twenty or so feet ahead. He was winding up his window further when he saw the two 3-ton trucks parked on the left side of the road. "What the hell! Slow down, McCurchin."

No one was in the cab of the first truck, but the hood was up on the truck ahead, and two soldiers, their uniforms drenched, were looking at the engine. Moore instructed McCurchin to pull over close to the front of the lead truck. The soldiers stopped what they were doing and saluted Moore.

"What's the problem, soldier?" Moore asked through the window of the jeep. He did not know the soldiers, and his question was directed at either of the two who cared to answer.

"I think is the fuel pump," one soldier replied, squinting at the rain drops. He appeared to be the driver of the truck.

"How do you know?" Moore asked.

"Well, Captain, from the way it stopped. It stop and go, stop and go, and then it just stopped."

"So why you think is the fuel pump?" Moore asked.

"Captain, this is one of the trucks they converted from gasoline to diesel. They told us that if air gets in the line, the truck will behave this way. I see it happen like this before."

"I see," Moore said. "Can you fix it?"

"No, Captain," the soldier said. "They got two nipples on the fuel pump and you have to bleed them. I know that but I don't know how to do it."

"How about your partner there?" Moore asked.

"He like me, Captain," the soldier replied, "he just a driver."

"Huh," Moore uttered, looking over the soldiers, both drenched. Moore then noticed the crossed machetes on the door of the truck. "These

Training Corps trucks?" he asked, tensing up as he pondered why Training Corps trucks would be out there.

"Yes, Captain," the soldier replied.

"Well, what are you all doing here?"

"Captain, Colonel LaFleur sent us to drive these trucks back."

"From where, soldier? I haven't seen these trucks out here before." Then, turning over his right shoulder to the back of his jeep, Moore spoke to Lieutenants Mentore and Beharry. "Have either of you seen these vehicles out here before?"

"No," the officers responded almost simultaneously.

"Captain," the soldier said, "we were told the trucks were on some kind of mission and they got left behind. We're supposed to take them back."

Moore was puzzled. He turned back to his officers.

"Do either of you know of any Training Corps exercises out here?"

"No, Alan," Lieutenant Mentore replied, "but we can't leave them here."

Moore felt frustrated. He knew he couldn't leave two soldiers stranded like this. Colonel LaFleur would be furious if he found out that Moore had not helped two soldiers he had sent on this mission. But he was still puzzled. What could these Training Corps trucks be doing here? Why hadn't LaFleur informed him that Training Corps would be conducting an exercise in an area that was under his surveillance? He determined that he would raise this with Colonel Cadogan at Camp Ayanganna the next day. In the meantime, he was unsure what to do.

"Alan," Lieutenant Beharry called out from the back of the jeep, "we still have some time, why don't we get a mechanic from Albion?"

"Awright," Moore conceded; then, turning to the soldiers, "you all stay here until I return. And get out of the rain!"

McCurchin turned the jeep around, on Moore's instruction, and headed back to the Albion Police Station. Once there, Lieutenant Beharry went in and spoke to the police constable on duty. There was no mechanic at the station. The police used local mechanics, and the constable recommended Busjit's Repair Shop a mile up the road, a place Lieutenant Beharry said he knew.

They drove up to the repair shop, which was on the left side of the road, adjoining a two-storied house, the home of the proprietor. The yard was littered with rusty, cannibalized vehicles, hub caps, car parts of no use to anyone, and scrap metal of all shapes. Moore picked his way through and asked one of the young Indian mechanics for Mr. Busjit. The boy, who seemed hardly seventeen and was evidently an apprentice with the shop, pointed to a dark-complexioned, Indian man with graying hair, standing in his short pants and rubber sandals, shirt fully open in the front to reveal a convex stomach pressing against a discolored singlet. He was issuing instructions to several of his apprentices with an urgency and irritation that came with the ending of the workday.

Mr. Busjit looked over at Moore but did not move. Even when Moore walked up to him, Mr. Busjit continued belting out instructions to his young charges. Then he stopped abruptly and acknowledged Moore.

"Yes, chief?" Mr. Busjit asked.

"Mr. Busjit, we have a diesel truck on the side of the road. We think the problem might be the fuel pump. Can you check it for us?" Moore asked.

"Look, you see all this work around you?" Mr. Busjit asked. "I can't finish them. I ain't got no mechanics. These lil boys don't know what they doing. You got to keep behind them all the time."

"How about you, Mr. Busjit? Can you spare a few minutes just to bleed the nipples on the fuel pump? We'll drive you out and bring you back," Moore offered.

"I don't want to drive in no army jeep," Mr. Busjit stated firmly. "You fellas come here election time and push people around and carry off the ballot boxes. You all shouldn't show your faces 'round here."

"Mr. Busjit—"

"Even if I could help, and I not saying I can, what you think people gon say 'bout me 'round here?"

The apprentices were all looking over, and Moore wasn't sure what to say. This was an Opposition stronghold, and sentiments ran high that the election was rigged against their party and that the army had helped the government. Beharry came out of the jeep and stood beside Moore. That seemed to help because Mr. Busjit's composure softened.

"Mr. Busjit, can you help us?" Beharry asked.

"Where the truck at?" Mr. Busjit asked.

"Just past the Borlum Turn," Beharry replied.

"Awright, give me a few minutes," Mr. Busjit said.

Moore was relieved. Mr. Busjit was not happy about helping them, but he would. Moore and Beharry hung around the shop for about ten minutes before Mr. Busjit was ready.

"Look," warned Mr. Busjit, "if is anything too complicated, I coming back."

Moore and Beharry looked at each other and nodded agreement. With that, Mr. Busjit started an old Morris Oxford and followed the jeep to where the trucks were.

The rain had abated, and Mr. Busjit was able to work without the inconvenience of getting wet. Moore, Beharry, and Mentore stood at the side of the road and waited. About fifteen minutes later, Mr. Busjit called out to the soldier to start the truck. The vehicle started right away. Mr. Busjit lowered the hood and stepped away from the truck, indicating by a wave of his hand to the soldier that he could drive the truck away whenever he was ready.

Moore and Beharry walked up to Mr. Busjit.

"We're going to be back tomorrow," Moore said. "Can we pay you then?"

"No, is awright," Mr. Busjit said, "don't bother."

"Thank you, Mr. Busjit," Beharry said.

"Is awright," Mr. Busjit said and walked off to his car.

Moore looked at his watch. It was 16:40. "If we hurry we can make the 17:30 ferry," he said aloud, then turned to Mentore and Beharry. "Derryck, why don't you get in the first truck, and Ramesh the second. I'll lead off. Keep those soldiers in line."

Thus the mini-convoy of right-hand drives was formed. The jeep was leading at a 50-miles-per-hour clip on the left side of the road, and the trucks followed with a fifty-feet spread between vehicles. A couple miles on the stretch and the rain came down in earnest again, but traffic was light, and Moore did not see a need to slow down the convoy, except for potholes in the road. He expected they would be pulling into the New Amsterdam stelling around 17:10 or 17:15, depending on how the traffic was on the outskirts of New Amsterdam.

Even at this speed, it seemed to take longer than usual to clear this six-mile stretch to Palmyra. Finally, Moore could see the Seawell Turn about a hundred yards ahead. He checked his watch: 16:55. He began to relax. There was no question they would be at the stelling in time for the ferry. Getting all the vehicles across on the 17:30 ferry might be difficult but certainly the jeep shouldn't have a problem. The trucks could cross with the later ferry; he had, after all, done what he could to get them to this point.

Without slowing down, McCurchin entered the Seawell Turn, executing a sharp left that made Moore slide along the seat. When the jeep straightened out again, Moore looked over sternly at McCurchin but didn't say anything. They had gone another hundred feet or so when McCurchin gasped, "Oh God!" and then Moore heard the loud slam of metal against metal and a shrill, scraping sound that put Moore's teeth on edge. He did not have to ask McCurchin to stop. In no time the jeep was on the grass on the left side of the road, and Moore and McCurchin were out.

Moore stood speechless and trembling as he looked in the direction of the Seawell Turn. A huge white cloud hung over the road, and some of it was drifting over to the houses on the right. At the base of the cloud, Moore could see the outline of a truck lying on its side across the road, the canvas top and the cab dome facing him. The canvas was ripped open at several places, and busted white bags were strewn along the village side of the road. People in the houses nearby had run out of their yards onto the bridges over the drainage ditch on their side of the road. Moore thought he heard one woman holler, "Oh God, is gunpowder!" Another corrected her, "No, is flour. Look at the bags. Is flour they smuggling!"

Moore felt the blood drain from his face. He heard McCurchin say "Oh God, Captain!" as he started running toward the trucks. Moore stood there fearing the worst of all possibilities; he was having difficulty concentrating. It took McCurchin yelling out "Captain!" to get Moore finally moving forward into a fast run. Vehicles from both directions had stopped, and a crowd was beginning to gather around the scene of the accident.

Partially trapped under the cab of the truck lying on its side was the driver, whom Moore surmised to be dead. Heart racing, he checked for a pulse; there wasn't any. He moved quickly around the cab to the right edge of the road. That's when he saw Lieutenant Beharry on his knees on the grassy embankment, his olive green uniform spotted in red and white and his arms cradling the bare head of Lieutenant Mentore, the rest of Mentore's body lying on the grass. Beharry's face was tucked into his chest, and from the rocking movement of his body, Moore knew Beharry was crying. Moore rushed over to Beharry and knelt down. He could now see cuts on Beharry's head and Mentore's still body.

"Ramesh," Moore called out. Beharry looked up. His face was bleeding from several cuts and from his nose. Tears were streaming down, and he tried to speak. Mouth wide open, he struggled to say something, but nothing issued out. His head dropped back to his chest, and he sobbed. Moore knelt down and checked Mentore's wrist for a pulse. There wasn't any. Oh God, why him? Moore asked silently, tears welling up in his own eyes. He patted Beharry on his shoulder and encouraged him to let go of Mentore's body. "Come on, Ramesh," he said to Beharry, standing up.

Moore watched as Beharry set Mentore's head down on the grass, then pick up Mentore's beret from the embankment and place it on Mentore's head.

"Is the other driver awright?" Moore asked. Beharry shook his head.

"Christ!" Moore said and walked up to the second truck, which was standing diagonally across the road, its front end extending onto the embankment on the right side. The driver's side was smashed in, and the driver was slumped back with a wide gash on his forehead. Moore climbed in and checked for a pulse, but again found none. He felt panicky. He dismounted quickly and moved around this truck to the village side of the road, where Beharry now stood by himself sopping blood from his forehead with his shirt sleeve.

"What happened, Ramesh?" Moore asked.

"It happened so fast, Alan. I was looking over at the sugarcane fields when my driver hit the brakes. That's when I saw the truck in front, perpendicular to the road and sliding along the road, except that the main body of the truck was sliding faster, turning the cab in our direction. I knew we were going to hit it on the passenger side. I could see Mentore—Oh Christ!" Beharry paused and looked away. Moore remained silent.

"The driver of my truck applied the brakes and tried to avoid hitting the truck by angling to the left onto the embankment. Maybe, he thought he could swerve around the cab of Mentore's truck. The next thing I knew we had slammed into the side, close to the cab. That door flew open and Mentore just—Oh Christ!"

McCurchin came up to the two officers, and Moore decided not to press Beharry any further. Instead, he instructed McCurchin to rush to the New Amsterdam Police Headquarters and report the accident. He wanted to send Lieutenant Beharry with the jeep for medical treatment, but Beharry refused to go. Some Indian women from the nearby houses came over to where the officers stood and guided Beharry to the house directly across from the accident. With three dead bodies at the scene, Moore was not sure what to do. He walked around for a few minutes, then sat on the opposite side of the road, looking blankly across the canal in the direction of the sugarcane fields.

Moore was not sure how long he sat there, nor was he aware yet of how soaked his uniform was. His world had begun collapsing around him when he saw the huge white cloud and heard the woman's voice saying "Is flour they smuggling!" Now there were three dead bodies, among them his friend, Mentore. When he thought of his own predicament, he felt guilty that he wasn't mourning Mentore's death. When he thought of Mentore, his grief became unbearable, and all thinking ceased. He felt irretrievably lost. He buried his head between his knees and wrapped his arms around it. The first words of comfort followed the feel of two arms reaching around his chest and lifting him.

"Come brother, you mustn't stay here."

Moore raised his head and, over his shoulder, saw an older Indian man behind him. He responded to the voice and rose. The man guided him as he wobbled across the road, down the embankment on the other side, and over the bridge into the yard. People had gathered at the bottom of the stilted house. Beharry was sitting with a bandage around his head and holding a piece of cloth against his nose. He did not have his shirt on, but his upper body was draped in a bed sheet.

The Indian man unbuttoned Moore's shirt and dried his upper body with a towel. Moore felt incapable of doing this himself. In any case, the man had not asked him. Then the man draped a bed sheet over him to keep him warm and made him sit down in a chair. An Indian woman brought him some hot tea in a large enamel cup. Moore steadied the cup with both hands and with quivering lips began to sip the tea. He was sure they were looking at him, but he hoped they wouldn't see the tears dropping into the cup.

THIRTY

*I*NSPECTOR FRAZIER ARRIVED WITH two police constables, who spent an inordinate amount of time measuring on the road. Frazier took statements from Moore and Beharry. He had already taken a statement from McCurchin. Beharry reconfirmed what he had told Moore about the acccident, but Beharry also described how he had tried to brace for the impact, but was still flung forward against the corner of the dashboard and the left side door. Further explanation of the cause of the accident was provided by one of the police constables doing the measurements on the road. He reported to Inspector Frazier in Moore's presence that the tires of both trucks were completely bald and in violation of the traffic codes. Both Moore and Beharry protested their innocence about the flour cargo to Inspector Frazier, but they could tell that Frazier did not believe them. Beharry took out the letter he was carrying from the Brigade Adjutant, summoning him to Camp Ayanganna the next day. Frazier read the letter and kept it.

A hearse from the New Amsterdam Public Hospital came and took away the dead bodies. At Moore's pleading, Inspector Frazier sent Beharry to the hospital in Moore's jeep and in the company of a police constable. A newspaper reporter had arrived from New Amsterdam and was taking pictures and talking to people. Moore was grateful to Inspector Frazier for keeping the reporter away from him and Beharry. Finally, Inspector Frazier asked Moore to get into the back of the police jeep, and they drove off to the New Amsterdam Police Headquarters.

At Police Headquarters, Inspector Frazier notified Moore that, while he had not caused the accident, he was transporting contraband goods. For this, he would be charged. Since the accident occurred while Moore was in command of a convoy transporting contraband, he had a residual responsibility for that as well, and the appropriate charges would be drawn up. Frazier informed him that he would be kept in a holding cell that night. Moore asked Frazier if he could notify his wife by phone. Frazier said he would see and left as two detectives came in to interrogate Moore. The interrogation lasted about an hour, but it seemed longer to Moore, and it went over the same areas Frazier had covered with him. At the end of the interrogation, Moore was served a cup of coffee.

At about 21:30, the police constable on duty gave Moore a blanket and took him to an eight by four cell with a cot braced against the long side. The constable offered Moore a final opportunity to relieve himself at a toilet down the hall, which Moore grasped after he noticed a discolored posey in the corner of the cell. Moore divested himself of his uniform and gave it to the constable with a plea that it be hung up to dry, then reclined in the cot. He awoke when they called him the following morning.

Moore was allowed to brush his teeth and to shower, and his uniform was returned to him. Breakfast consisted of coffee, two boiled eggs, and fried breadfruit, which Moore considered very generous treatment of a prisoner by the police. After breakfast, he was returned to the cell until Jeanene arrived at about 07:45.

Normal visiting time with prisoners was in the afternoon and limited to ten minutes, but Inspector Frazier allowed Jeanene to visit with him in the presence of a police constable for over an hour. Moore retraced everything that had happened, and Jeanene cried intermittently. Finally, Inspector Frazier came in to let them know that Police Commissioner Dalrymple had come down from Georgetown to question Moore; Jeanene had to leave. Moore asked her to go over to the hospital and check on Beharry's condition before returning to Georgetown.

Moore was taken down the hall to the interrogation room used earlier by the detectives and seated at the table. In a few minutes, Commissioner Dalrymple came in with the Assistant Commissioner, resident at New Amsterdam. Moore rose when they entered. Dalrymple smiled in appreciation of the respect shown him and introduced himself and the Assistant Commissioner. Dalrymple conveyed an affability which made Moore almost forget that he was a prisoner. Moore was sure both of these officers had read the reports of Inspector Frazier and the detectives, and by now, he had told the story so many times, it had become a mechanical exercise, which he was ready to repeat. Dalrymple, however, was interested in the contraband flour.

"You know, Captain Moore, is not a pleasant thing when another uniformed officer is placed in the lockup," Dalrymple began. "We feel sorry, but as you know, we got our duty to do."

"I understand that, Commissioner," Moore responded.

"Good. Mind you, if we can help you, we will, but that depends on the circumstances and how you cooperate with us."

Moore nodded.

"Awright, Captain, tell us how you got involved with these trucks carrying contraband."

"Well, Commissioner, my family had an appointment at the American Embassy this morning at ten o'clock. Yesterday, after making my inspections in Berbice County, I was heading home to Eccles to overnight before the interview. Lieutenant Mentore had asked for a ride to Georgetown. He was due to go on leave on the 16th, but I had assigned company duries at Camp Ayanganna for the 15th. To help him out, you know—closer to home?"

Commissioner Dalrymple nodded. "And Lieutenant Beharry?" he asked.

Lieutenant Beharry had been summoned for an interview at Camp Ayanganna today, as a matter of fact, and he was traveling up with me to overnight in Georgetown."

"Awright," Dalrymple said, "proceed."

"We had just passed the Borlum Turn and were on the stretch to Palmyra, when we saw the two trucks."

"And you had not seen these trucks in Berbice County before?" Dalrymple interrupted.

"No, Commissioner. Those were trucks from Training Corps, which is based at Camp Stevenson in Timehri. For those trucks to be operating away from base, the drivers had to have authorization from a senior officer, and they had to have logged out."

"Huh," Dalrymple said, eyebrows furrowed, and exchanging glances with the Assistant Commisioner.

"Also, Commissioner, for those vehicles to cross on the New Amsterdam ferry, which they obviously did, they had to have a travel warrant, signed by a senior officer. Those are usually kept in the vehicles."

"And you have said that the drivers told you that they were on orders from Colonel LaFleur to drive the trucks back?"

"Yes, Commissioner. That was what they said when I asked them what the Training Corps trucks were doing in an area under my control."

"Now, Captain, your Lieutenant Beharry said something about Colonel Cadogan being involved with contraband, along with some fellow by the name of Deonarine."

"Well, Commissioner, the truth is we don't know how the contraband got where it got. Lieutenant Beharry was speculating because we all saw a very close relationship between Colonel Cadogan and Pandit Deonarine, who operates a boat on the Corentyne River."

"My point to you, Captain Moore, is that if these senior officers are as involved as you all are suggesting, it might be difficult to find the very information you are telling us to look for. You get what I'm saying?" Commissioner Dalrymple looked over at the Assistant Commissioner, who was nodding his agreement.

"I see what you saying, Commissioner, but the army has procedures for dispatching vehicles—"

"Don't worry. We gon check." Commissioner Dalrymple rose, as did the Assistant Commissioner.

Believing the interview to be over, Moore got up and moved closer to the officers.

"Commissioner, I am really counting on you to check the logs." It was an awkward statement, almost desperate in tone, and Moore did not expect a reply, but the Commissioner did pause to listen. "Commissioner, I also want you to know that neither Lieutenant Mentore nor Lieutenant Beharry bears any responsibility for what happened. When I placed my jeep at the head of that convoy yesterday, I took command. Those officers were under my orders, and I accept full responsibility. I am sorry about what happened to Lieutenant Mentore. He was a very close friend, and I would like to attend his funeral. I would request that Lieutenant Beharry be released. He was simply on orders from the Brigade Adjutant to report to Camp Ayanganna the next day."

"We have no intention of holding Lieutenant Beharry, especially based on what you have said to us today and to Inspector Frazier yesterday."

"Thank you, Commissioner."

Commissioner Dalrymple extended his right hand to Moore, and as Moore shook it, Dalrymple reached across with his left hand and patted Moore's forearm.

THIRTY-ONE

*A*GRIPPA SENSED SOMETHING WAS wrong but couldn't quite figure it out. From outside, the dining area had sounded louder than he could remember but it fell to a hush when he entered. Everyone seemed to be looking directly at him.

"Carry on, carry on," he said with a perfunctory wave of his hand before taking his seat and reaching for the newspaper. He froze when he unfolded it and saw the headline—"*Army Captain Arrested for Smuggling.*"

"General, have you heard anything?" a staff officer was asking.

"No," he replied, lips dry and his heart racing.

"Do you know where they are keeping him?"

"No," he replied, trying to read the article.

Army Captain Alan Moore was arrested and charged with smuggling flour into the country, following a collision between two army trucks that resulted in the death of two soldiers and Lieutenant Derryck Mentore, he read. The accident involving both trucks, which were transporting the contraband goods, occurred at Palmyra, just as the trucks had cleared the Seawell Turn. The Police report on the incident states that the two 3-ton army trucks, whose tires were almost completely bald, were in a three-vehicle convoy led by Captain Moore. Eye-witnesses said they heard the sound of the collision and saw a huge white cloud . . .

Agrippa's hand was shaking. He looked up at the other officers. "Colonel Cadogan will be going down to New Amsterdam to check this thing out," he announced.

"What about Captain Moore, General?" Captain Felix asked.

"What about him, Captain Felix?" Agrippa asked.

"I think he should be turned over to the army."

"Well, leh we see what the police got first," Agrippa said. He fixed himself a cup of coffee, pouring hot water from the kettle into a cup with instant coffee, sugar, and some evaporated milk. He drank quickly and set about fixing another. They brought him boiled eggs and rice bakes. He ate the eggs, hardly tasting anything and feeling almost a choking sensation each time he swallowed, necessitating a flush down with coffee. His nerves were on edge. He felt jumpy; he could hardly think. He picked up the papers and left the Mess.

Colonel Cadogan was waiting for him at his office. Cadogan seemed nervous and frightened. Agrippa signaled for Cadogan to follow him in. When Agrippa heard the door close behind Cadogan, he turned sharply around.

"Is what the skunt going on, Saddle?" Agrippa asked. Without waiting for a reply, Agrippa shouted, "You didn't tell me you were going to use the officers deployed in Berbice County!"

"I didn't use them, Clive."

"Well, how did Moore get involved?"

"I don't know, Clive. I don't know how Moore and the other officers got mixed up in any of this. They must have passed the trucks somewhere and decided to escort them back."

"And what kind of kiss-me-ass trucks LaFleur sent down there? The tires all bald!"

Cadogan was silent. "What we gon do now, Saddle? Tell me!"

"Nothing, Clive, until we find out what really going on."

"You know that this thing happened yesterday and is only now I finding out? The police never contacted me! I think they getting back at me for the jail break the soldiers did last March."

Agrippa nearly mentioned how the police were sidelined in the case of the Cuban doctor but stopped himself. He was sure though that this was paramount in Commissioner Dalrymple's decision not to notify him.

"Did you talk to Commissioner Dalrymple?" Cadogan asked.

"No, I just found out about the blasted thing! Anyway, let me try now." Agrippa dialed the Commissioner's number.

"General Agrippa here. Let me speak to the Commissioner, please."

"Sorry, General Agrippa," the woman said, "but the Commissioner is in Berbice County. He should be back before lunch. I will let him know you called."

"Thank you." Agrippa hung up the phone. "Christ! Something's going on. We have to get Moore out of there before Dalrymple figures out our involvement."

"How?" Cadogan asked.

"I don't know. Look, you are his commanding officer. Go down to New Amsterdam and check on him and on Lieutenant Beharry. And find out what the police know."

"Awright, Clive. I gon leave right away."

"Remember, Saddle, our position is that Captain Moore should be turned over to the army."

Colonel Cadogan saluted and left. Agrippa noted that Cadogan had not fussed about being called "Saddle." Anyway, this was his blasted plan, he thought. He was the one who said we should do it—how the payoff was going to be so big!

Agrippa remembered the meeting at the Officers' Mess at Timehri in September. The smuggler, Pandit Deonarine, was seeing someone off at the airport, and Saddle had invited him and some of his relatives for a drink at the Mess. Saddle eventually pulled the smuggler off into the game room to talk over matters; he had already done some exploratory work with Deonarine. Saddle had assured Agrippa and LaFleur that he had the market ready. "Flour in time for Christmas and New Year? It would be gone in no time." That was what Saddle said, and LaFleur had agreed. The market price was ten dollars a pound, but it would be easier to sell each hundred-pound bag at eight dollars a pound. Since it would cost four dollars a pound to buy it in Suriname, the profit per pound would be an even four dollars. Each truck would carry one hundred bags, and if LaFleur could arrange for two trucks . . .

"The problem," the smuggler said, "is transporting so much flour across the river and storing it."

"Well, September just start," Cadogan said, "we got the rest of the month, then October, November, and half December."

"How about storing the flour? I can't hide two hundred bags of flour at my house. And my shop not big enough either."

"How about the rice mill along the dam?" Cadogan asked.

"It got the space," the smuggler said, "but who gon ask the owner?"

"I gon arrange that," Cadogan said. "What you say now?"

"It gon work but, you know, it gon take a lot of gas to go back and forth across the river."

Agrippa smiled, thinking, "This is a smart-man."

"I gon see that you get it," Cadogan said about the gas.

"Another thing," the smuggler said, "the Police Inspector is my friend, but is a lot of flour we talking 'bout. He bound to notice."

"I gon talk to he," Cadogan said.

The smuggler smiled. Cadogan raised his glass, "Well, leh we fire one." They drank, then Cadogan encouraged the smuggler to rejoin his relatives in the lounge.

"Can we trust that chap?" Agrippa asked after the smuggler had rejoined his relatives.

"Oh yes," Cadogan said. "He wants to keep good with the police and the army."

Then there was the problem of transportation. Agrippa had pointed out the shortage of serviceable vehicles, but the solution that Lo-lo LaFleur proposed appeared very clever at the time. He suggested that they use two trucks that came into Motor Transport for servicing or repairs—simply wait until they were fixed up, then use them to pick up the flour before sending them back to their unit. LaFleur had also suggested that trucks from Timehri would draw less attention than if they came out of Camp Ayanganna right in the middle of Georgetown.

The trucks were supposed to have left Timehri at 05:00 on December 12 and head out to No. 79 Village. Three days ago. They should have been back yesterday evening. The drivers had been instructed to say that their assignment was to drive the trucks back to Timehri, since it was anticipated that they might cross paths with elements of F-Company deployed in that area. Any additional questions, they were told, should be referred to Colonel LaFleur. Something went terribly wrong.

Agrippa's direct line rang.

"Clive, Lionel Cummings here."

"What's up, P.S.?" Agrippa asked, trying to sound nonchalant.

"Is your boy, Alan Moore. You must know by now, we got him in a holding cell in New Amsterdam. The Comrade President wants him brought to the maximum security prison in Georgetown and—"

"I think he should be turned over to the army to be court-martialed," Agrippa said.

"You want to tell that to the Comrade President?" Cummings asked.

"No, but you are the Permanent Secretary to the Defense Ministry," Agrippa insisted. "The officers would expect you to see that one of their brothers is properly treated."

"Brothers? You said 'brothers?'" Cummings sounded sarcastic. "Don't play the ass with me, man. Captain Moore is a thief-man! He was caught smuggling contraband. Three people, one of them an army officer like himself, died. The Comrade President wants to make an example of him. Nail his ass to the cross so that his uncle, the preacher-man, can see."

"You do what you want, but all of these officers will be looking up at that cross too," Agrippa admonished.

"You threatening this government?" Cummings asked.

"I ain't threatening nobody," Agrippa replied. "You say you want to nail his ass to the cross. I just telling you who all gon be looking. You mightn't like his uncle, and I mightn't like him, but Captain Moore is a popular officer."

"Popular or not, he going on trial. By the way, smuggling is a civil offense, so don't bother with that thing about turning him over to the army. The Comrade President says he got to wear jail clothes, and when the Comrade President say is so, is so. Forget all this officer business!"

"I see," Agrippa said. "Why was I not notified of his arrest?" Cummings did not respond, so Agrippa continued. "When the officers asked me about it at breakfast, I told them I didn't know anything about it. They weren't happy. And you know how much they like policemen?" Agrippa wanted his sarcasm to register hostility, which he was sure Cummings, who came over from the Ministry of Home Affairs, understood only too well.

Cummings was quiet for a few moments, then in a more gentle tone said, "Well, you know now, and it is a police matter."

"Right," Agrippa said, and Cummings hung up.

Agrippa could not work. Cummings said it was "a police matter." Now Agrippa wondered what Commissioner Dalrymple was up to. Was there a way to derail Dalrymple's investigation, whether Moore got cleared or not?

*   *   *

Just before lunch, Commissioner Dalrymple called. "I just returned from visiting your boy, Captain Moore." Dalrymple seemed to be in great spirits, almost triumphant and satisfied with himself.

"I see," Agrippa said. "How is he?"

"He's doing awright, you know? He's doing awright. A bit stunned."

"How about Lieutenant Beharry?"

"He's awright. They re-set his nose and treated his bruises and cuts and so on, but they discharged him from the hospital. He said he had an interview at Camp Ayanganna, so I brought him back with me."

Agrippa was surprised. "He wasn't charged?"

"For what?" Dalrymple responded.

"Well, you arrested Captain Moore for smuggling; Lieutenant Beharry was with the flour convoy?"

"Not so fast, Comrade," Dalrymple said. "I did not arrest Captain Moore; Inspector Frazier did, on suspicion of smuggling. That is important, on suspicion of smuggling."

"I see," Agrippa said, wondering why Dalrymple was being so precise.

"Now Lieutenant Beharry had a memo in his possession from the Brigade Adjutant instructing him to report for an interview at 14:00 at Camp Ayanganna the following day. Furthermore, Captain Moore said, while protesting his own innocence, that whatever might be the outcome of the investigation on him, Lieutenant Beharry had simply asked for a lift to Georgetown so that he could be ready for the interview the next day. So Inspector Frazier did not detain Lieutenant Beharry after his discharge from the hospital."

"I see," Agrippa said, not quite knowing now what else to say or do.

"I gon tell you something, Clive. That boy, Captain Moore, is innocent. I know that and I think you know that too. Something else. I feel sorry for him because the Comrade President is not going to let him go. The Comrade President's got him and he gon keep him locked up. He's got a grudge against the entire Moore family."

"Anything I can do?" Agrippa asked.

"No," Dalrymple replied, "but I gon tell you if I think of anything."

Agrippa thought Dalrymple was enjoying this. "Look, Charlie, you think you could let Captain Moore remain in uniform?"

Dalrymple laughed. "You know, is everybody interested all of a sudden in Captain Moore's dress."

"Who else interested?" Agrippa asked.

"Well, my officers want him to stay in uniform, but the Comrade President and the Party want him stripped of his uniform and put into jail-men's clothes."

"So what you gon do?" Agrippa asked.

"Well, they're not running the jail, so I gon keep him in uniform as long as possible, probably till he sees a magistrate. By the way, Moore asked for permission to attend Lieutenant Mentore's funeral."

"You gon let him?"

"I can't. Prisoners don't have that kind of privilege. Besides, the Comrade President is going to the funeral. But I feel sorry for Moore. I understand he and Mentore were very close."

"Yes, they were," Agrippa said mechanically, his mind racing ahead to consider how best to protect himself since the police seemed to have figured out what happened.

"One thing I don't understand," Commissioner Dalrymple continued as though he were talking to himself, "how could Captain Moore get two Training Corps trucks all the way from Timehri without authorization? How come the trucks were not logged out at the Motor Transport section where they went in for repairs?"

"I didn't know that," Agrippa said. "You sure 'bout that?"

"Yes, I'm sure about that."

"I just don't know what happened," Agrippa said, trying to show surprise but remembering that Dalrymple had asked the same question about the jeep at the time of the incident with the Cuban doctor. "I'll have to look into it," he added.

"Well, let me know what you find out because we're looking into it too." With that, Dalrymple hung up.

Agrippa knew that Dalrymple did not expect him to provide any information nor would he likely trust any information that Agrippa provided. Dalrymple was merely hinting that his investigation had moved forward. Clearly, Dalrymple had used time to his advantage. Now it was up to Agrippa to cover himself, and he decided that he would do precisely that, no matter the cost.

Agrippa's thoughts were interrupted by a knock on the door. His PA didn't need to announce Colonel LaFleur, standing behind her. Agrippa rose up as his PA stepped back to let LaFleur enter. He waited until she closed the door behind her, then exploded on LaFleur.

"You see the shit you get we into? Lieutenant Mentore and two soldiers dead; Captain Moore in jail; Lieutenant Beharry got his head all busted up. Is you and Saddle talk me into this thing, you know. He said it gon be so easy. Big payoff, Saddle said! You said you gon provide the trucks. The kiss-me-ass trucks had bald tires. What the rass wrong with you head, Lo-lo?"

"Chief, look, I'm sorry," LaFleur said, his gold teeth flickering as he spoke.

"You're sorry? You rass up the work and now you telling me you're sorry?"

"Clive, we didn't have no other vehicles."

"You telling me that all you had were these bald-headed trucks?"

"We have other trucks, but we agreed to use two trucks that came into MT for servicing."

"You were supposed to take them after they were serviced, Lo-lo. Is what really wrong with you?"

"Clive, the trucks came in to MT to have the tires replaced two weeks ago. I checked and the NCO told me that he expected the trucks to be ready in three or four days, but there is a shortage of tires. You know the country ain't got foreign currency to import the damn things. So December 12 come, and I had to do something."

Agrippa never liked LaFleur's gold teeth. He was especially irritated today by the way they were flashing bad news.

"So you send down trucks with bald-headed tires? Is sense you ain't got, Lo-lo? The people who sent the trucks for servicing knew they were unsafe. You took those trucks and sent them to haul hundreds of bags of flour in rainy weather."

"Clive, I didn't know it was going to rain."

"You didn't know? Lo-lo, every second-standard schoolboy in this country know that December is rainy season! How come you ain't know? Look, go 'long you way. I done with you. Go look for four bald-headed tires and put them on your jeep."

"I thought the whole idea was to keep back as far as possible, so nobody could trace the operation back to we?"

"Oh, is so? You think the officers won't figure out that is you who authorized those trucks to leave the MT compound at Timehri? You think Dalrymple stupid? He done figure out the whole thing. The only thing that gon save we is that the Comrade President is more interested in keeping Moore in jail than in finding out the truth. But the officers, Comrade, that is a different matter."

"Well, I'm sorry, Clive."

"Go hide you-self someplace. As far as I'm concerned, you're a real lo-lo."

Colonel LaFleur saluted and left with a noticeable pout on his face.

*　　*　　*

Agrippa went directly home after work. He didn't see any point going to the Mess; all the officers talked about was Moore's incarceration. Corporal Kyte had picked up some fried chicken and plantain chips for him. He downed a couple of rum and Cokes before he started on the chicken and chips. He was about halfway through the meal when the phone rang. He got up, licking his fingers, and picked up the phone. It was Colonel Cadogan.

"Clive, I'm up here in Springlands. Is too late to get the last ferry from New Amsterdam, so I'll stay on and travel back in the morning."

"What did you find out?"

"Well, I didn't speak to Lieutenant Beharry. Commisioner Dalrymple gave him a lift to Georgetown."

"Who'd you talk with, Saddle?" Agrippa could not hide his irritation.

"I talked to Captain Moore. He was reluctant, but he related his encounter with the trucks and what happened at the Seawell Turn. I have a feeling he told Dalrymple more than that."

"Like what?"

"Like about Pandit Deonarine."

"What makes you think that?"

"He seemed a little hostile and suspicious."

"You can't blame the man. Anyway, what else you know?"

"The police can vouch for the whereabouts of Derryck Mentore and Ramesh Beharry because they were billeted in police compounds. Moore moved around a lot, inspecting and so on."

"I see. Anything else?"

"Yes. Detectives from New Amsterdam questioned Deonarine, but he is a real smart-man."

"How so?"

"The man had his boat out of water for the past two weeks. The boat was getting fixed up, close to the seawall, where everybody could see it."

"So he's in the clear?"

"Yes, but we too."

"How?"

"Well, if Deonarine, who really smuggled over the flour, didn't smuggle it, according to the police, then who did? And if they don't know that, how they can come after we?"

Agrippa felt relieved. With no boatman to apprehend and no logs to track, the investigation might run aground. "What about Moore?" he asked.

"I don't think we should do anything," Cadogan replied. "Moore is the only suspect. The police caught him with the flour. I'm sorry it happened that way, but he's helping to keep the police from we."

"No, he's not. Commissioner Dalrymple believes Moore is innocent. The Police are holding him until they finish their investigation. Then they will come after us. We can't wait for that to happen. We have to get Moore into army custody and move ahead with a court-martial." Cadogan was silent. "One other thing," Agrippa added, "I can bet money the other officers will be checking to see how those trucks got out of Timehri. If they find out, there's no telling what they might do. Right now, they seem awright with us trying Moore, so you find a way to get him to us."

THIRTY-TWO

"**A**WRIGHT, ALAN," INSPECTOR FRAZIER said, signaling with his head for Moore to get out.

Moore had driven by the Camp Street prison before but never looked at it closely. Today, he had no choice. He estimated the brick walls around the prison to be about twenty feet high. Above the brick ran three rows of barbed wire, one on top of the other, with spacing of about eight inches between the rows. At the entrance were two tall, solid metal gates, bolted shut. Moore's attention was diverted to an observation hut directly across the street from the prison gates, when Inspector Frazier returned the salute of the guard manning the hut.

"Why here, Inspector?" Moore asked. "I haven't been convicted of anything."

"Orders," Frazier said; then, facing Moore directly, he added, "Look, Alan, the people at the top are calling the shots. Besides, this prison is not just for convicts. Most of the people held here are remand prisoners."

Inspector Frazier led Moore down the embankment to the metal gates and pressed the buzzer on the left side. A small rectangular shutter slid open, and a pair of eyes peered out. The shutter was closed back. Moore heard the sound of bolts being undone and a small door, inset in the left half of the metal gate, opened to allow Inspector Frazier and Moore to enter.

Immediately in front of them was a two-storied, yellowish-cream building with a red roof, which Moore figured to be the administrative building. The first level had a wide, open walkway at the center, dividing it into two separate wings. Through the open door on the left side, Moore saw the Armory, and, across from it, a sleeping area with beds. Inspector Frazier led him up to the Admissions Office on the second floor. On the left side of the office was a large holding area for prisoners awaiting processing; on the right were the offices of the senior prison officers, including the OIC, as the sign indicated.

"Inspector Sugrim," Frazier said to the Indian prison officer on the other side of the counter separating Admissions from the hallway, "this is Captain Moore. I believe you expecting him. Here's the file."

"Why he wearing that uniform?" Inspector Sugrim asked.

"We had him in temporary custody. There wasn't any reason to put him in other clothes."

"Well, he has been interdicted from duty, so he either wears civilian clothes or we'll put him in prison clothes."

"He hasn't been convicted of anything, so why don't we try and keep him out of prison clothes. What you say?"

"Is awright with me, but he can't go to a cell in that uniform."

"Well, go ahead and process him. Let me see what I can do."

"I can't process him."

"Why not?"

"Because you don't have a magistrate's warrant to hold him in remand."

"Look, Inspector Sugrim, don't worry 'bout no magistrate's warrant. The order came from the highest level, awright?"

Inspector Sugrim needed no further persuasion. "Awright, how about the uniform?" he asked.

"You mean to tell me you ain't got nobody his size can lend him some clothes till tomorrow?"

"Awright, awright," Sugrim conceded. "He about my size."

"Thank you." Turning to Moore, Frazier said, "Alan, believe me, I am very sorry, but I wish you the best."

"Thank you," Moore said, and watched as Inspector Frazier disappeared down the stairs.

"Name?" Inspector Sugrim began, looking down at the form he was filling out.

"Alan Conrad Moore."

When he had completed the paperwork, Inspector Sugrim handed Moore a faded blanket, a mess pan, and a toothbrush, and mechanically recited the prison rules. Moore would share a cell with two other prisoners in the remand section of the prison. He could have two visitors a week for ten minutes at a time, except for his lawyer, who could visit for an unlimited amount of time. Visiting hours were from 14:00 to 16:00 daily. Food could be brought in by relatives and friends.

Inspector Sugrim left for a few minutes and reemerged with a shirt and a pair of pants. "Step into the holding area and put these on," he said to Moore. "You can keep your boots." Then he yelled out, "One for the Brick Prison!"

A prison officer came up and instructed Moore to follow him. They went down the stairs into the open walkway and turned right to face the interior of the prison compound, surrounded by a chain-link fence, which Moore estimated to be about twelve feet high. Entry was through a gate, manned by a prison guard. Once they were through the gate, Moore saw the rest of the layout of the prison. He had known that the prison occupied an entire city block; now he could see how. In reality, the Camp Street Prison, or Lot 22 as it was more commonly known, consisted of several prisons, and the officer gave Moore a descriptive tour. On the immediate left and closest to the administration building was the two-storied Juvenile Prison. Directly behind it were two three-storied buildings, which housed remands, but also provided space for a workshop, a library, a kitchen, and an infirmary. Each of the two remand buildings had a chain-link side, against which Moore could see faces pressed.

On Moore's right was a three-storied brick building, whose long side was perpendicular to Camp Street. The prison officer told him that it was known as the Brick Prison and that it housed convicted prisoners and some remand prisoners, especially high profile ones and potential escapees. Next to the Brick Prison, and along the same axis, was the Wood Prison, a three-storied building, housing remand prisoners on the first two floors and condemned prisoners on the third. At the very center of the prison complex and surrounded by a twelve-foot fence was the exercise area. The prison complex was crisscrossed by concrete drains, the odor from which suggested they had been used as urinals.

The officer led Moore into the first floor of the Brick Prison and showed him to the cell he would be sharing with two others. He pointed to the mattress without a blanket on the concrete floor. Moore walked over and dropped his blanket on the mattress, then followed the officer to an adjoining open space where Black and Indian prisoners were sitting at two long tables, playing dominoes and draughts. A couple of crumpled newspapers lay on one of the tables. The officer explained to Moore that this was where he would remain until the time for lock-up.

Very aware of the stares of the other remand prisoners, Moore took a seat at the table with the newspapers. A large Black fellow in a dominoes game at the other table kept referring to Moore as "the big one" in the discussions they seemed to be having about him. They obviously knew the story because he heard the words "smuggler" and "flour." News traveled fast, Moore thought, but there it was looking at him from the table top, the headline on the *Cayman News*, "*Army Captain Charged With Smuggling Flour*." Reading the account in the government's newspaper, Moore became even more despondent about his ability to establish his innocence in the whole affair.

Moore's attention was drawn back to the dominoes table when the large Black fellow called out loudly to a certain Winslowe sitting at the Moore's table and asked him to tell them again about the box. The prison officers nearby were laughing, and Moore got the impression that this exercise had been going on for some time. Winslowe seemed a bit slow witted, and his stuttering speech made his story funnier to the audience. Yet he seemed not the least bit bothered to relate the story of his incarceration over and over.

Winslowe claimed that he found the box on the side of the road after the drygoods truck had driven off. The police, on the other hand, had charged him with theft, based on the complaint from the truck driver that Winslowe had swiped the box off of the truck when it had stopped in Sparendam. Winslowe related his version slowly, and with great sincerity, undeterred by the intermittent eruptions of laughter. Occasionally, the big Black fellow asked for amplification. "So Winslowe, the box just fall off the truck?"

"Yes. I standing right there. The truck move off, and the box just sitting there."

"So how did the police find you?" the big Black fellow asked.

"I standing by the culvert with the box, nuh. They come and say how I thief the thing. I say the box fall off the truck when it speed off."

Everyone laughed, then it began all over and continued until the prison officers announced dinner. It came on a cart and was spooned out into the mess pans—rice and traces of salt beef in a stew. The prisoners also got a cup of coffee, weak, lukewarm, and very sweet, but Moore welcomed it. After dinner, they were marched back to their respective cells.

Moore discovered that his two cellmates were Winslowe and Balgobin, an Indian cane cutter, who had been charged with beating his mother-in-law. The space in the cell was so small that when the cell door was slammed shut, there was nothing else to do but to lie down on the mattress. There were also no light fixtures in the cell, but just as the door closed, Moore noticed the posey in the corner.

Moore had difficulty settling in on the mattress—there was no pillow and the thought of his face making contact with the dingy mattress bothered him. He lay on his back and looked up at the ceiling—not that he could see it. Then the silence broke, and Balgobin began egging Winslowe to tell the story.

"Winslowe, I lying here thinking you's an innocent man," Balgobin said.

Oh shit, not again, Moore thought. But there went Winslowe.

"Is a true, true thing I telling you, Bal. The box fall off the truck; it just fall off . . ."

The story was funny, and the game was funny. Moore could see why it went on and on, and it also helped pass the time. No one but Winslowe believed the story. Winslowe was so transparent and the story so unconvincing to listeners, but every time Winslowe told it, he spoke with sincerity and emphasized a different line as though the new emphasis would help to convince everyone.

And then it hit Moore—the utter hopelessness of his own case. No one believed Winslowe no matter how many times he told the story and no matter where he placed the emphasis to elicit sympathy. Why would they believe Moore? Who would believe him when he told them that he was driving along and he came upon these two trucks which he decided to lead back to base? He didn't know they were carrying flour until he saw the white cloud. They would laugh at him. The self-appointed cell boss, that oversized Black fellow, would ask him to tell it over and over, and every night, Balgobin would encourage him to start all over.

But surely his situation was different? He replayed all of the events leading up to the accident, trying to find the key to his exculpation. He tried not to think of Derryck Mentore's death. The loss of his friend was bad enough; the accusation that he had caused it through a smuggling scheme was too much to bear. Why did he order Mentore and Beharry on those trucks? If only he could do it all over again . . .

Moore tried to imagine himself in a bunker at one of the interior locations. He closed his eyes and hoped that fatigue would work its magic. Twice he awoke as his body jerked involuntarily. The third time, there was a pounding on the door before it was unlocked and opened.

"Last chance to empty you po for the night," the shadow at the door said. It took Moore a few moments to figure out that the prison officer was referring to the posey in the corner. Fortunately, no one had used it as yet, but that would change before morning.

At 06:00 the next day, the cell doors were opened, and prison officers, almost in unison, were shouting, "Time to empty the po!" Winslowe and Balgobin looked at Moore, and Moore decided they needed a system, which he quickly spelled out to his cellmates. He would volunteer to do it today, Balgobin the next day, and Winslowe the day after.

The prisoners were instructed to brush their teeth and to shower. Moore dreaded putting the same singlet and briefs he had worn the past two days and nights, but the feeling was transitory. They were then herded off to the dining area for a breakfast of one rice-flour bake and a lukewarm cup of weak, over-sweet coffee.

After breakfast, Moore and his cellmates were taken into the prison compound for half an hour of exercise under the watch of a prison officer. Moore took off his shirt and lay it on the grass, stretched for a couple of minutes, then ran to-and-fro laps to the far fence while Winslowe and Balgobin watched in amusement.

Back inside the Brick Prison, they were taken to the crowded recreation room. The same groups from the previous day were re-forming, and the board games began. Moore remained by himself and read the newspaper. Thankfully, there was nothing about the accident in the paper today. Across the room, the cell boss was holding court, and Moore overheard several references to himself as "the big one." He realized that this was unavoidable—he stood out from them because of his reputation and bearing.

Today the cell boss began with Balgobin, a relief to Moore who dreaded hearing Winslowe again.

"So, Balgobin," the cell boss began, "is what they say you did?"

"Well, is not what they say, is what me mud-in-law say," Balgobin said.

"Well, is what you mud-in-law say you did?" the cell boss asked, laughing in apparent appreciation of the distinction Balgobin had made.

"She complained 'bout how I beat she," Balgobin said.

"But you didn't beat she?" the cell boss suggested.

"No, man. I didn't catch up with she or I woulda give she a good cut-ass." The men laughed.

"So, is what really happen, Bal?" the cell boss asked.

"She always interfering, you know. So, this day, I had a couple of rum in me head. She come over to the house and start she interfering. I grabbed the cutlass. Look, talk about run. She jump over the fence." There were roars of laughter; the big Black fellow and others were slapping their hands on the tables. Even the prison officers were laughing. Moore kept his eyes on the newspaper, but he was smiling and shaking his head.

"Is what kind of cutlass you use, Bal?"

"I got a No. 20. Is the one I use to cut cane."

"So you used the No. 20 on she?"

"No, I didn't catch she. I fell down and cut me-self on my neck. Look here. You see?"

They went over the story a few more times, then they switched to Winslowe.

"So Winslowe, you didn't thief the box from the truck?"

"No, man. The box fall off the truck. Is true, true thing I telling you."

Along with the slapping of dominoes on the wooden table, this was how the banter went until lunch time. After a lunch of rice and boiled pumpkin, Moore rested his head on his arms, folded flat on the table. He managed to get some sleep, jerking awake several times owing to eruptions of laughter. At 14:00 hours, the prison officer called out to Moore and informed him that he had a visitor. The prison officer had called him by his rank. Thereafter, the other prisoners began calling him "Captain," and it made him feel a little better.

Moore was brought to a room in the administrative building and left alone with Mr. Latchmansingh, the lawyer Jeanene and Uncle Lenny had retained. Mr. Latchmansingh explained that Moore would have to appear at a preliminary hearing in the magistrate's court on Monday, December 19. At that time, Mr. Latchmansingh intended to get the magistrate to let Moore out on bail on the argument that he was an army officer with no prior conviction. The lawyer asked Moore for his version of the story, having explained that he had already talked to Lieutenant Beharry and Private McCurchin, as well as to Mr. Busjit, the mechanic. The lawyer explained to Moore that, with the truck drivers dead, the difficulty of exculpation had increased enormously. It would be helpful to their investigation to have Moore out and interacting with some of his former colleagues. The lawyer suggested that some of the questions raised in an article that appeared in the Opposition's *Red Star* were helpful to Moore's cause because they provided a more sympathetic explanation of Moore's movements than the account in the *Cayman News*.

The hearing in the magistrate's court was very brief. A Police Inspector argued against the granting of bail, telling the magistrate that the police were still conducting their investigations which would determine the full complement of charges. He reminded the court that this was a special case; the defendant was involved in a smuggling operation that resulted in three fatalities. Further, there was a great likelihood that he could leave the country by the same route he was transporting contraband.

Moore sat in court silently until the magistrate rendered his ruling—bail denied. A scream came from the back, and soon Jeanene was sobbing loudly and protesting her husband's innocence. Uncle Lenny and Aunt Vickie tried to console her. Moore saw them taking Jeanene out of the courtroom as he himself was being escorted through the side door by the bailiff.

Moore saw his wife that afternoon during visiting hours. The meeting was awkward. He sat in a three by three cubicle with wooden panels on three sides and a thick meshed front; she sat on a chair on the other side of the mesh. A prison guard stood a few feet away. Jeanene sobbed; Moore tried to console her.

When Jeanene was calmer, she told him she had decided to move in with Uncle Lenny and Aunt Vickie right away and gradually move their belongings so that she could turn over the house to the landlord at the end of the year. Moore agreed that was the best course. He wanted to tell Jeanene about the ballot boxes he had placed in the storeroom, but the guard was either in front of him or to one side where Moore could not see him. Then Moore heard a prison officer shout, "Time!"

*   *   *

Jeanene came to see him again on Christmas Eve. They had agreed she would come on Christmas day, so he was surprised she had decided to use up the visit on Christmas Eve. She seemed very frightened and kept looking over her shoulder at the prison officer. Fortunately, several visitors were talking to the prisoners, and only one prison officer was on duty, plus Moore was in the furthest cage. With simultaneous conversations taking place, Jeanene pulled up to the meshed partition.

"What's wrong?" Moore asked.

"Alan, the storeroom," she whispered.

"Oh God! Jeanene, I meant to tell you."

"What are those boxes doing there?" Jeanene asked.

Moore looked intently at his wife for a sign that the prison officer was not focusing on them. When she so indicated, he said, "Jeanene, give them to Beharry. Beg him to burn them, please."

"How did you get them?" For the first time, Jeanene's voice conveyed doubts about him.

"Beharry will explain," he whispered. "But, please, get Beharry to take care of them right away."

THIRTY-THREE

FIRST DAY BACK IN the new year, and Agrippa sat in his office with a splitting headache. New Year's day had fallen on Sunday, so the drinking and celebrating went on all weekend through Monday, the official holiday. He was meeting Captain Moore's wife at 10:00 hours and figured that the meeting would last until lunch time, even though there wasn't anything he was prepared to do for her. Her husband's entanglement with the flour trucks worried him, especially since the other officers were likely to figure out that Moore was innocent, but Agrippa could not think of a way of extricating Moore without admitting complicity in the ill-fated scheme. After lunch, he was going up to Timehri to give a lecture at the Junior Staff Course that had begun that morning. He knew that Lieutenant Beharry was in that course, and he was dreading that encounter but felt sure his presence would intimidate Beharry into silence.

The only person who could help Moore, Agrippa thought, was Commissioner Dalrymple, very unlikely because the Comrade President had made it clear to Dalrymple and Agrippa that he wanted Moore kept in jail and convicted. The Comrade President now had a way of striking back at Rev. Lennox Moore, and he was not about to give it up. Dalrymple would probably cooperate in order to get reappointed for another five-year term. Agrippa observed that the Comrade President took time at his Old Year's Night party to treat Dalrymple like a hero, walking around with his arm around Dalrymple and touching glasses with him. Agrippa felt ignored and angry—he had received no recognition whatsoever for his role in handing the Comrade President the entire election.

At 10:05, the PA showed Jeanene into Agrippa's office and left. Agrippa rose to greet Jeanene, whom he had known for about ten years. Her face seemed tense, her eyes blood shot, and he could well imagine what she must be going through.

"Jeanene," Agrippa began, "I am very sorry about Alan."

"Have you visited him?" she asked.

283

"No, but Colonel Cadogan and the Padre did. You know, is a criminal charge he's facing. Is between him and the police. There is not much the army can do."

"But there is," Jeanene insisted.

"Tell me," Agrippa said, trying to sound accommodative.

"How can two trucks leave the Motor Transport compound at Timehri without anyone knowing?"

"We would like to find out too, but the drivers are dead."

"But there are standard procedures for these things," Jeanene insisted. "No truck can leave the compound without logging out. Who signed the log?"

"No one did, that's the problem. We looking into that."

"Isn't there always a guard at the gate?"

Agrippa nodded.

"Have you checked the guard roster?" Jeanene asked.

"We looking into that too. As a matter of fact, the police want the same information."

"You're looking into that? I have that information. All the officers know that! How come you're just looking into it?" Jeanene was looking straight at Agrippa. "My husband is in jail," she added and wiped below her eyes with her handkerchief.

Agrippa did not say anything. He knew she was right: by now, all the officers probably knew how the trucks got out of the Motor Transport compound at Timehri. This was not good. The officers were not happy when he pledged the allegiance of the army to the Party at its September Congress, and they had not had any salary increase in three years. Padre thought some of the officers were meeting in secret. What if the company commanders staged a coup against the government? What would they do to him? Would a public trial of Captain Moore trigger a coup?

"The trucks hauling the flour belong to Training Corps, not so?" Jeanene asked, and Agrippa nodded. "Well, have you checked with Colonel LaFleur? That's his command."

"I can't divulge the content of my conversations with senior officers," Agrippa replied.

"Have you checked when those trucks came into MT for repair?" Jeanene asked.

"We know that information."

"Tell me, General, how would my husband, who was in Berbice County at the time, know about two particular trucks that would be brought in for repairs way out there in Timehri?"

"I don't know, Jeanene, and I am not saying he knew. There are many things about this case that puzzle me." Agrippa knew he was telling the truth about the last part.

"No, Alan didn't know. But Colonel LaFleur knew about those trucks, and the officers are saying that only someone of that rank can authorize the departure of a truck without logging it out."

Agrippa did not say anything.

"Why would Alan want two trucks with bald tires when he has three serviceable trucks under his command?" Jeanene asked.

Agrippa shook his head and shrugged his shoulders.

"Alan and I had an appointment at the American Embassy the next morning," Jeanene said. "Why would he be smuggling two trucks of flour the day before?"

"That's another thing that puzzles me," Agrippa replied.

There was an uncomfortable silence. Then Agrippa said, partly as a reassurance—an empty one, he knew that—and partly as a way of bringing the meeting to an end, "Look, Jeanene, we monitoring this thing closely, and if we can do anything, anything at all, to get Alan out, we gon do it."

"I am going to be frank with you," Jeanene said, standing up, "I don't think you've done anything for my husband, and none of the officers I've talked to believe you are doing anything for Alan." Jeanene was staring intently at Agrippa.

Agrippa rolled his eyes and shook his head.

Jeanene walked towards the door, then turned around. "Let me tell you something—you are not going to treat my husband like George Persico. This is a small country, and this is a small army; people know a lot about what's going on here and it will all come out if Alan is put on trial. Colonel LaFleur or someone else caused my husband to go to jail, and I want you to get him out."

Agrippa was relieved when Jeanene walked out of his office but worried about the contacts she was having with other officers and about how those officers would react if Moore were convicted as the Comrade President wanted. Still, he could think of nothing he could use to get Moore out. He looked down at his watch; a bit early for lunch, he thought, so he called the number the young woman had given him at the Old Year's Night party.

After lunch, Agrippa headed out to Timehri in the staff car. He had Corporal Kyte drive through Georgetown so that he could observe the protest outside Parliament Building. The Opposition boycott of Parliament was continuing, and the heavy picketing exercises of December were expected to continue, especially after the Comrade President's New Year's message acknowledging worsening conditions in the country. The Opposition wanted to know how come he was winning elections by landslides, when a desperate situation was getting worse. Of course, the question was rhetorical, since the Opposition knew about the rigging. Agrippa was aware that the Opposition hated the army for its role in the rigging and for its harassment of the Opposition supporters. He had seen Opposition pamphlets with photographs of soldiers loading the ballot boxes onto army trucks. Other photographs were of the army searching people's homes in Opposition areas.

The sun was out, but there were still puddles of water on the road from the morning rains. The picketers were bunched up on the street in front of Parliament and were walking from one entrance to the next and back. The relief column was on the side of the street under the shade trees. Some of the placards read: "DOWN WITH FRAUD AND CORRUPTION," "WANTED: FREE AND FAIR ELECTIONS," "NON-COOPERATION WITH EVIL," and "GIVE US THIS DAY OUR DAILY BREAD." In another few minutes, the staff car passed under the Independence Arch, and they were on the East-bank road to Timehri.

Agrippa knew that his appearance on the first day of the Junior Staff Course was mostly ceremonial. His talk was titled, "The Role of the Army in National Development." He had presented it over and over, and many of these officers were already aware of what he was going to say, but he was going to say it, and they were going to listen. He went over the key points he was going to make. He would tell them how critical the army was to the preservation of national sovereignty. The western neighbor was claiming as much as five-eighths of our national territory. The presence of the army in the disputed area was to alert the government of any incursions so that diplomatic efforts could be mobilized against the aggression. The army was also the spearhead of the effort of a coastal people to develop the virgin hinterland. These two functions, in essence, were the role of the Border Battalion.

The other key functions were internal—to support the Party in its efforts to effect the socialist transformation of the society and to protect this government against the machinations of the Opposition party. This one, he took straight from the Comrade President. He smiled. It's called the People's Army, and it should really be protecting the people from the machinations of the Comrade President, but then I wouldn't be the Chief of Staff, he thought. The idea of the army supporting the constitutionally elected government of the day ended last September when he pledged the army's allegiance to the Party and the Comrade President.

Agrippa arrived at the Training Corps building, located outside the fence surrounding the base at Camp Stevenson, just as the previous lecture was ending. The officers were given a five-minute break and then reconvened for his presentation. Training Corps had been the subject of much discussion of late, and now in the building where it was headquartered, he could not help thinking about the trucks involved in the accident. Worse still, he felt these officers might be thinking the same thing, and that made him uncomfortable. He hardly made eye contact with them but looked above their heads to the wall clock at the back and the picture of the Comrade President hanging just below it.

Once or twice, he looked at Lieutenant Beharry when his head was down. Agrippa could see the shaved patches on Beharry's head from the stitches. The abrasions on Beharry's face seemed healed up but reflected more light because of what appeared to be some type of poultice. Agrippa was disturbed; he wondered what the other officers must have said after seeing Beharry's appearance. He looked away every time Beharry raised his head and was relieved when he was through with the presentation. In the past, he could stretch the speech to an hour, while he joked with his junior officers. Today, there was no such interaction, just a mechanical regurgitation of things they must have heard him say before. No one asked questions afterwards.

Following the lecture, Agrippa visited with the Base Commander of Camp Stevenson and with Colonel LaFleur, who hung back as though he was afraid Agrippa might scream at him. Agrippa was amused by LaFleur's discomfort and was determined to provide no relief to LaFleur during this visit. Agrippa and the other senior officers retired early to the Officers' Mess for drinks. He excused himself and made one phone call to confirm that his lady friend would come up, then notified the Base Commander that he was staying up at Timehri for the evening. With that decision, the Officers' Mess became transformed into a festive site. The attendant at the bar played Agrippa's favorites—"*Soul Makossa,*" "*How You Could Knock So?,*" and "*A Deputy Essential.*" At about 16:45, the young woman arrived. Even with a few rums already under his belt, Agrippa recognized that the young woman was not as attractive as Brenda or Vera, but she was free, he reminded himself. They ate supper promptly at 18:00 hours, and when it had darkened outside, Agrippa retired with the woman to his room in the Officers' Quarters.

*   *   *

Agrippa was up early, determined to leave Timehri before reveille. He left the Officers' Quarters with the woman through the side stairway outside his room. The staff car was parked below as he had instructed Corporal Kyte, but Kyte was not there. He looked at his watch—05:25.

"I don't know where this shagging driver is," Agrippa said.

"Looks like he left you a note on the windshield," the woman said.

Agrippa lifted the windshield wiper and retrieved the piece of scrap paper that it had pinned down. He walked over to the light at the back of the building and read.

"Thief-of-Staff!" headed the scrap paper. "Slip and slide, but fall on your own backside."

Shaken, Agrippa stood there for a minute trying to figure whether this was the first or the final warning from the other officers. He had to find a way to get Moore out of jail—he was sure this would appease them. He tried to compose himself on the way back to the car, where Corporal Kyte was standing beside the woman.

"What did the note say?" the woman asked.

"Stupidness, just stupidness," Agrippa replied and stuffed the paper in his pocket.

Agrippa dropped the woman off at her flat in Georgetown and proceeded to breakfast at Camp Ayanganna. What immediately caught his attention as he stepped out of the car were pieces of paper on the side of the road in front of the Officers' Mess. He picked up one of them. It was a ballot paper with an X marked for the Opposition party. What the hell? He picked up another; same thing. He decided he would have a word with the Base Commander. When he entered the dining area, he found the floor littered with cast ballots. The kitchen attendants had started to pick them up but decided that the Base Commander needed to see them.

"What's going on?" Agrippa asked, to no one in particular.

"Is some kind of prank," the Base Commander said.

"What's funny about this?" Agrippa asked.

"I don't know," the Base Commander replied, adding, "They found the ballot box at the camp entrance on Thomas Road. They have it in the Guard Room."

"Have them bring the box to my office," Agrippa said.

"Yes, Chief of Staff," the Base Commander said.

"And tell them back there to clean up the place," Agrippa ordered, pointing to the kitchen.

"Yes, Chief of Staff," the Base Commander said and went off in the direction of the kitchen.

Agrippa sat down and looked at the front page of the *Cayman News*, but officers were speculating loudly about the ballots. Agrippa remembered the trucks on election night bringing the ballot boxes into Camp Ayanganna. The only people who had access to those boxes were Lionel Cummings and some of his Party associates. Officers had nothing to do with the boxes, he felt sure. When Cummings said they were ready, the boxes were transported to the central counting place. So where are these ballot papers coming from? Agrippa was stumped. Cummings had some explaining to do.

After breakfast, Agrippa went directly to his office. The Base Commander was waiting for him with the ballot box. He had had the kitchen staff collect all of the ballot papers and place them back into the box.

Agrippa instructed his PA to call the Elections Commission and to check out the code on the box against their master list.

"It has to be an officer or a member of the kitchen staff," the Base Commander said, "and I can't see the kitchen staff doing that."

"No question it's an officer or officers," Agrippa agreed, "but why would they do that? Where did they get the ballot box from?"

"Maybe the Party people got careless with the boxes and left one somewhere," the Base Commander said. "Some officer might have picked it up."

"Maybe, but why did they spread it out like this?" Agrippa asked.

"Probably just a joke," the Base Commander replied. "You know we have some officers like that. Remember the one who streaked naked past the Mess?"

"Why did they put the ballot box on Thomas Road, a public road?" Agrippa asked, determined not to be distracted by the streaking incident.

"I don't know, Chief of Staff."

The PA knocked and came in. "Chief of Staff, the number on the ballot box is the identification number of Albion."

"That's a major Opposition area," the Base Commander observed.

"Yes, I know," Agrippa said. "Awright, Bernadette, thanks." The PA left.

"Well, keep your eyes open," Agrippa said to the Base Commander, "and see what the kitchen staff knows."

"Yes, General," the Base Commander said, then saluted and left.

Agrippa wondered whether he ought to contact Lionel Cummings but decided against it. If it was a prank, it would just draw negative attention from the Comrade President. There was a knock on the door, and without waiting to be invited in, the PA opened the door and stuck her head in.

"General, is the Base Commander from Camp Stevenson. He said it's very, very urgent."

"Awright, put him on."

When his extension rang, Agrippa picked it up. "General Agrippa," he said.

"General, Major MacAndrew, Camp Stevenson," the voice said with haste.

"Yes, David, what's going on?" Agrippa asked.

"General, we have a peculiar situation out here."

"Yes?" Agrippa cringed his forehead and sat up.

"General, we found ballot papers all over the Officers' Mess at breakfast today. An open ballot box was lying in full view on the side of the Airport road in front of the Mess."

Agrippa listened silently, trying now to make sense of the second occurrence.

"Any idea who's behind this?" Agrippa asked.

"No, General," the Base Commander replied, "but I don't think is just one person."

"Why not?" Agrippa asked, without telling the Base Commander about the incident at Camp Ayanganna.

"Well, General, it just seems to me to be more than one person. There was another ballot box found at the airport by a police constable. That box was unopened. It has the seal and signatures of the polling officer and the party officials."

"I see," Agrippa said. "You'd better bring down those boxes to me."

By noon, all three ballot boxes were in Agrippa's possession, and he had confirmed their origin in the Albion precincts. He telephoned Lionel Cummings.

"Permanent Secretary Cummings," the voice said, terminating a laugh.

"Lionel, Chief of Staff here," Agrippa said.

"Clive!" Cummings almost shouted. He seemed to be in a gay mood. "You just catch me. I was about to go off for lunch at the Police Officers' Mess."

"Sound like you celebrating, Lionel," Agrippa observed.

"Well, yes. We just finished a meeting with the Comrade President. We gon appoint Commissioner Dalrymple to another term. As a matter of fact, we already give he the letter at the meeting. It gon be published in the next Official Gazette," Cummings said.

"I see," Agrippa said, jealous and angry that he himself had been passed over for promotion. "This ain't got anything to do with Captain Moore, eh?" he asked Cummings.

"As a matter of fact." Cummings paused, then exclaimed, "We got the chappie!"

"How you so sure?" Agrippa asked. "They ain't try him yet."

"Don't worry 'bout that; we got that taken care of."

"Commissioner Dalrymple thinks the man is innocent," Agrippa pointed out.

"I don't know 'bout that. I know he's done investigating."

"You mean he stopped?" Agrippa suggested.

"'Done,' 'stop,' what difference it make? They caught Moore with the flour and the trucks. Leh we see which lawyer gon get he out of that."

"Well, I feel sorry for him because I think he's innocent too."

"Is what wrong with you, all of a sudden?" Cummings asked. "We catch him red-handed—trucks, flour, everything."

"The trucks were not logged out," Agrippa pointed out, hoping to see more of Cummings' hand.

"Moore could have arranged that with somebody inside. He is a captain, you know!"

"But he was on his way to the American Embassy for a visa to leave," Agrippa pointed out.

"All the more why he did it. He wanted some spare change."

"I hear he's got a good lawyer," Agrippa said, hoping to see even more of what Cummings was holding.

"We got a good judge," Cummings said with such finality Agrippa understood exactly where Moore stood. "Anyway," Cummings continued, "I just telling you all this as a friend. Call me back after lunch and we gon talk 'bout what you calling for."

"It can't wait," Agrippa said firmly.

"Awright, what's so important?" Cummings sounded irritated.

"We have a situation at the two army bases. There are ballot papers flying all over the place."

"What kind of ballot papers?" Cummings asked.

"From the last election, Comrade." Aggripa did not feel like being at all respectful, especially after the news about Dalrymple's reward.

"Impossible!" Cummings declared. "All those things were destroyed after the election."

"So, where they coming from?" Agrippa asked. "We recovered three ballot boxes, one intact with all the seals and signatures."

Cummings was silent for a few moments, then in a subdued tone he asked, "Where'd you find them?"

"The ballots were scattered in the Officers' Messes at Camp Ayanganna and at Timehri. The boxes were on the public road. The one sealed box was at the Timehri airport."

"Who you think put them there?"

"Officers—who else?"

"How did they get them?" Cummings asked.

"You asking me? You were in charge of the ballot boxes when they came into Camp Ayanganna election night!" Agrippa was loud and accusatory. "You were so damn busy cooking up the books, you lost track of the real ballot boxes. Now, we have officers running around with them. Who is to say the next time they won't turn over a few to the Opposition or scatter them at the airport just before a flight? You know what gon happen then? You gon have so much rioting in this country!" Agrippa sucked his teeth loudly into the phone.

292

"Why do you think the officers are doing this?" Cummings asked.

"You have one of their brothers in jail," Agrippa said calmly.

"So what you saying, they want we to release Moore?"

"Something like that."

"They crazy!" Cummings almost shouted. "I done tell you that. Captain Moore is a thief-man. He was caught smuggling two truckloads of contraband! The Comrade President not going to put up with no thief-man, and I with he on that!"

Agrippa did not answer right away. When he did, he spoke slowly and deliberately. "I see. Well, look, leh me tell you something, Comrade. Many of these officers know how the Comrade President won the election. They know that you and the other Party boys were in the Officers' Mess switching the ballot boxes, election night. Or you forget? As far as they are concerned, the Comrade President is a bigger thief-man than Moore! Y'all hijacked an entire election. You smuggled truckloads of ballot boxes! So don't talk to me about 'thief-man,' you and the Comrade President are the biggest thief-men around!"

Cummings did not answer. Agrippa could sense that Cummings was feeling cornered, even desperate. Agrippa became sarcastic.

"Look, Cummings, if you afraid to go to the Comrade President and admit you rass up the work, I can do it for you."

"Clive, leh we try and work this thing out nuh, man," Cummings pleaded. "The Comrade President not going to like this, you know. I gon try and find a good time to raise it with he. What you say?"

"Better don't take too long," Agrippa cautioned, "I think these officers mean business."

"I gon call you back later this afternoon," Cummings said.

Agrippa hung up. He was feeling exultant.

*　　*　　*

Agrippa met Cummings in the Officers' Mess at 15:00 hours. Cummings had called shortly after lunch and chosen this venue, and Agrippa had arranged for the lounge to be open. They sat at Agrippa's favorite table at the north end of the lounge looking out to the seawall. Private Jarvis served them a rum and Coke each and retreated behind the counter. Agrippa asked Jarvis to put on some music; he thought that would provide some noise cover for the conversation he and Cummings were about to have.

Cummings was very nervous. He took a deep swallow from his glass and looked at Agrippa as though he was trying to read something in his composure. Then he took another drink before he began.

"Clive, I spoke to the Comrade President about the Moore business. You know he ain't got nothing against the boy, is the uncle he don't like."

Agrippa was amused by the declaration and sensed a softening of position. He waited for Cummings to resume.

"The Comrade President is prepared to ask Commissioner Dalrymple to turn Captain Moore over to the army to be court-martialed for smuggling, if you can guarantee that Moore would be cashiered out of the army."

Agrippa was ready for this and responded promptly.

"Too late for that, Comrade," he warned, "I don't think the officers would accept that. As a matter of fact, that would really make them mad."

"Huh," Cummings uttered. "What do you propose?"

"At this point, I would say the officers want Captain Moore released from jail, all charges dropped, and that he be free to leave the country as he was planning to. When he resigns his commission, it would be voluntary and with an honorable discharge."

"I see," Cummings said. "I would have to talk to the Comrade President 'bout that."

"Don't take too long," Agrippa warned. "You shoulda seen the looks the officers were giving me at lunch." Agrippa smiled to himself. He knew this was an outright fabrication, but he was going to put some fire under Cummings' backside.

Cummings was beginning to sweat. Agrippa guessed that Cummings feared he might lose favor with the Comrade President over the missing ballot boxes.

"Cummings, don't worry so much, man. I am sure the Comrade President know the old saying, 'hand wash hand make hand come clean.'" Agrippa smiled at the scowl that came over Cummings' face. Comrade Cummings didn't seem to appreciate the old saying, when someone else was using it.

"One other thing," Agrippa said.

Cummings looked at Agrippa suspiciously. "What's that?" he asked.

"When we met here in June, you agreed to add another pip to my shoulder in December. Well, December come and gone, no pip, but I see you doing something for Commissioner Dalrymple."

"Look, Clive, you raised the matter then, and I said I would see. We got you out from criminal prosecution, and we let you keep your job," Cummings pointed out. "The police got a whole file on that investigation, you know."

"I helped you to win the election," Agrippa responded.

"Well, you not getting promoted," Cummings declared.

"I see," said Agrippa. "Well, I hope you know exactly how many ballot boxes missing because I plan to carry on with my work. The ballot boxes are your business."

Cummings steadied the drink with both hands and looked at Agrippa. Agrippa could see fear in his eyes. "And you know, Cummings, I glad you tell me about the police file you got on me. I glad." Agrippa was nodding his head, his lips curled up; Cummings was looking straight at him. "You know, one of these days when I get a couple of rum in me head, I might slip up and talk about what go on here election night. You know what they say? 'Mouth open, story jump out.' Leh we see what that file gon do for you then. People bound to say y'all trying to spite me for telling the truth."

Cummings was sweating more profusely. He kept raising the glass to his lips, and Agrippa could hear the pieces of ice roll around the otherwise empty glass.

"You want another drink?" Agrippa offered.

"No, thank you," Cummings replied. "I better get back and talk to the Comrade President. One pip, right?"

"Yes, just one," Agrippa answered. "The one I shoulda gotten in December."

"Awright," Cummings conceded.

THIRTY-FOUR

*T*HE MOORES ARRIVED AT the Timehri airport at about 08:00. Alan Moore felt strange being there—a passenger, in civilian clothes, in the line to the counter of Hudson Airways. Ticketing was slow, and Alan was amazed at the patience he could muster as he moved his baggage forward a few inches at a time for about forty minutes. Their baggage finally checked in, Alan and Uncle Lenny shook hands and embraced while Jeanene and Candy hugged Aunt Edmee and Aunt Vickie in turn and cried, and Ian seemed unsure of what to do as his older aunts kissed him. Then it was time for the family to meet the immigration officer.

Although his papers were in order, Alan was nervous. By now, the airport officials surely knew who he was, and he remained fearful of a final humiliation, orchestrated by the all-knowing, ever-present Comrade President, whose picture hung prominently in the airport's main lobby. Alan presented the passports, tax clearances, and tickets to the officer at one of the two tables set up for this screening. The officer took the passports into a room, then returned and handed them back to Alan along with the tickets. Alan was surprised the officer did not ask for his discharge papers. Uncle Lenny, who had remained close by with his wife and his sister, now signaled that they would go up to the viewing deck.

Cleared to proceed to the waiting room, the Moores walked through the arched metal detector, Jeanene first and Alan last. The flight was not scheduled to leave for another hour and a half—too much time, Alan thought, for something to go wrong. Lack of sleep last night and a virtually empty stomach aggravated his sense of nervousness. He wondered if everyone who was leaving felt as he did. Probably not, he thought, looking at the many happy faces around him. Still, he felt as if he were tiptoeing out of the country, and this was not the way he had imagined his departure.

Reflecting on the events of the last couple of months made him sad and angry. Fortunately, these reflections were rendered short-lived by his son climbing into his lap. Alan was holding Ian in his lap and talking softly but firmly in his ear when he became aware of the green pair of trousers in front of him. His heart skipped a beat. He looked up. Standing there were Captain Seepersaud and Captain Felix, who must have used their rank to get past immigration. It was good to see them. Though Alan had wanted to avoid drawing attention to himself, their presence, in defiance of the official portrayal of him as a smuggler, lifted his spirits and made him feel a little more whole. They brought best wishes from many others and planned to go up to the viewing deck and remain until the plane departed.

The plane arrived shortly after the officers left and, half an hour later, passengers were invited to board. They were told to stop on the tarmac and identify their luggage before climbing up the stairs to the plane. A line had formed and extended back from the exit into the waiting room, and Alan stood behind Jeanene and the children. The firm tap on his right shoulder startled him and made him glance quickly around. Standing beside him were Ramesh Beharry and Ingrid Peters, and calling out to him from the immigration barricades were several officers from the Junior Staff course. Alan embraced Beharry and wept. Hardly any words were exchanged, or any he would remember, but between them, there was no need for words. Ingrid Peters and Jeanene had tears in their eyes as they looked on. Then the Moores left the waiting area for the tarmac, and Beharry and Peters went up to the viewing deck to join the other officers.

Alan and Jeanene identified their luggage on the tarmac to the Hudson Airways' officials, who marked the bags with chalk, a sign to the baggage handlers that the bags were ready for loading. Up the stairs to the entrance of the plane, Alan and Jeanene turned and waved in the direction of the viewing deck where they last saw Uncle Lenny and the others. Jeanene showed her seat assignment to the hostess who pointed her in the direction down the aisle on the right. Alan said hello to the Captain, whom he recognized from the bomb scare last January.

Alan had arranged to have Jeanene take care of Ian, at least until they were airborne. He just wanted to be alone, but as soon as they had buckled their seat belts, Ian began to fuss. He wanted to exchange seats with Candy, and Alan finally gave in. Looking out of the airplane window at the viewing deck, Alan thought he saw Ramesh Beharry and Uncle Lenny, and his mind began to replay the events that led to his incarceration. He struggled to shut it out and to focus instead on the prospect of seeing his mother and his sister, Grace, in New York. He wondered how the children would cope, arriving in the heart of winter. There was the issue of school for both Candy and Ian. With the school term already underway, they would be completely new and so foreign. He remembered when he went to West Point for cadet training—the American cadets wanted to know where he was from. Did they live in mud huts back home and was hide-the-coconut the national sport? Will it be like that for Candy and Ian? he wondered.

And what would he tell when they were older and asked about where they were from and why they had to leave home? He would tell them that where they lived had become inhospitable, and that they left because parents need to make a better life for themselves and their children. He would let them know that he once wore the uniform of the old country and served honorably. It would not sound heroic, but in time he hoped they would understand what that meant and be guided by it. He would tell the stories his grandfather had told him and his sister, how he rode on the donkey cart from Springlands to New Amsterdam and heard the night cough up the ghosts of old Dutch slave masters crying, "Neighbor, oi! Neighbor oi!" He would tell them about all the struggles of their people, slaves and indentured laborers, and about the value of freedom. And he would tell them how an old scarecrow of a man, with a white collar and thick glasses, challenged a tyrant on scraps of newsprint.

The plane started moving, and the Moores encouraged the children to wave goodbye through the window. Candy and Ian obliged. They seemed excited to do that. For his part, Alan said a silent final farewell to Uncle Lenny, Aunt Vickie, Aunt Edmee, and his friend, Beharry. Soon the plane was airborne and shortly afterwards, it banked. Alan looked down at the Demerara River winding its way backward to its source. A fleeting glimpse, then came the dense forest, and the Atlantic coastline. This was it. No turning back. But what about the pledge?

And though I rove o'er hill and dale, and brave old Neptune's foam,
O'er crags and rocks and mossy dells, I still will turn me home;
For when at length I come to die, I want no gilded tomb,
Just let me rest within thy breast, where thy sweet flowers bloom.

His eyes teared up. He knew it was not true for him anymore. He would never come back and certainly not ever be buried here. It had not been a fascination with New York that had stolen his love of home and made him outbound. It was betrayal by local leaders, self-indulgent and corrupt, that forced him and so many others to look for hope elsewhere. It was their drive for power and privilege at any cost, presented in the dazzle of imported ideologies, that led them to poison the spring of democracy in that fair land. Not foreign markets but elite greed had kept their people destitute. And it was not a foreign enemy but the knock on the door by local goons that made people fearful. Now he, like so many other fractured and brutalized souls, was seeking rehabilitation elsewhere.

The flight of this plane meant immediate freedom for him from his tormentors. Looking back, he felt proud of his service, except at the end. He had looked the other way when they cheated. How differently things might have turned out if he had taken a more forceful stand then! He would always regret the decision to put Mentore and Beharry on those trucks that fateful day. Why hadn't he raised the canvas flap and looked into the trucks? So focused was he about being safe he had not realized that safety came from a willingness to risk in the first instance. He would never forget the image of Ramesh Beharry on his knees, on the side of the road, cradling Derryck Mentore's head, his own face buried in his chest and sobbing. Why did Mentore have to die? He was such a joy to the people around him—honest, sincere, a bit loud, but amusing. Was there a game he hadn't invented? Thinking about this made Alan smile, and then he started to laugh. He didn't realize how loudly until he heard Jeanene calling him.

"Alan! Alan! People looking," she whispered sharply. He turned towards her. Her face softened. "What's wrong?" she asked.

"Nothing," he replied, smiling. "I just remembered something Beharry said to me after Mentore's funeral."

Jeanene studied his face for a moment, then resumed facing forward.

What was it Beharry said again? Oh yes, he said that they shouldn't worry about Mentore—Derryck was going to be awright. He was going to have God laughing the minute he got up there. Yes, Beharry said, he could just picture it: Mentore walking in there with that impish grin and loud voice, "How about a game of dominoes? This is your chance to take on the master! I invented the game, you know."